DEEP HURT

AN INGRID SKYBERG THRILLER

EVA HUDSON

VENATRIX

First published 2014.
This version published by Venatrix 2020.

978-1-9160195-3-9

DEEP HURT

1

Ingrid Skyberg reached the stairway in her apartment building and stupidly looked up at the dozen or so flights ahead of her. The action meant she lost momentum completely. It was a bad habit she'd gotten into after her daily five-mile run, and that brief pause made the final climb seem ten times harder. Nevertheless, ignoring the burn in her thighs and calves, she pushed on up, two steps with each stride, her breath labored, but her mind gloriously clear.

Triumphantly, she reached the top floor and punched the air. Just as she was putting her key in the lock, her cell phone buzzed. She answered the call without looking at the screen to see who was calling. Big mistake.

"Ingrid? Is that you?" Svetlana Skyberg's Russian accent was still unmistakable even after nearly forty years in the US.

"Who else would it be? You're calling me on my cell." Ingrid turned the key and kicked open the apartment door. Speaking to her mother instantly made her feel like a petulant teenager. She tried to subdue the irritation the sound of her mother's voice always provoked. "Everything all right? You OK?" Ingrid hadn't spoken to her in months.

"Me? Of course I am OK. Why wouldn't I be?"

The indestructible Svetlana Skyberg: two packs of specially imported unfiltered cigarettes a day for the last forty years and still going strong. Ingrid shut the apartment door with her behind and wandered into the kitchen. She pulled a fresh bottle of water from the fridge. "Then why are you calling?" A split second later, she remembered. How could she have forgotten? Svetlana only contacted her when… Ingrid got a sinking feeling in her stomach.

Oh no, not again.

"Have you seen TV? It is on the news in England?"

"I don't own a TV."

"Why not? Is FBI not paying you enough to buy a TV now?"

"Mom… tell me why you're calling."

"They found another house."

Ingrid closed her eyes and made a low moaning sound.

"What? You're complaining? You don't even know what I am going to tell you. You need to know. You must listen to me."

"Please, Mom. I don't have time for this. I have to get ready for work."

"So now you can't spare five minutes for something so important?"

Ingrid knew the amount of time she spent speaking with Svetlana was irrelevant—as soon as she put the phone down she'd replay the events of eighteen years ago over and over. It was the anger and resentment, swiftly followed by guilt and remorse, that would go on for hours afterwards.

"Three girls, they found this time. Alive. You hear me? *Alive.*" She took a deep breath. Ingrid pictured her sucking on one of her long cigarettes. "What am I saying? They are not girls. Not now. They are full grown women. One of them is thirty-two. For God's sake, Ingrid—don't you see what I'm saying? She is Megan's age."

A chill ran across Ingrid's shoulders and down her arms. Her hands started trembling. She was still sticky with sweat from her run, but suddenly so cold. "Have they identified them?"

"Not yet. Already they have given the police their ages. But not names. Or maybe the police are not telling the news people."

Ingrid wandered into the living room and rested one hand on the back of the beaten up old leather couch to steady herself. Was it possible? Could Megan Avery still be alive? Her mouth had gone dry. "What else do the news reports say? Have they apprehended the perpetrator?"

"You mean have they arrested the stinking bastard who did this? What's the matter with you, sounding so much like a cop? You're speaking to your mother. We are talking about your friend."

"I'm an FBI agent, how do you want me to sound?"

"Like a goddamn human being for once."

Ingrid pulled the phone from her ear and considered hanging up. She could hear her mother still speaking at the other end, the words indistinct, the sound just an annoying buzz in the distance, but the tone of her voice was unmistakably angry. Like a wasp trapped inside a jar. They always had this effect on one another, Svetlana had an uncanny knack of pressing all of Ingrid's buttons. It wasn't even the words themselves, her accusatory tone was enough to make Ingrid want to scream at her. And yet her mother was the picture of charm itself with her friends back home. She saved her criticism for her only child. Ingrid had never been able to do anything right in Svetlana's eyes.

"Did they say if the women are unharmed?" Ingrid asked, cutting across whatever venomous statement her mother was in the middle of.

"How can they be unharmed? They have been held against their will for years and years. God knows what tortures they have suffered."

"Are they in the hospital?"

"The police sent them all straight to the nuthouse for assessment. It's not *their* brains that need testing. It's that goddamn evil bastard's."

Ingrid walked shakily to the door leading out onto the roof terrace of her apartment. After struggling for a moment with the stiff key, she stumbled outside and drew in a deep breath. "You still haven't answered my questions: have the police arrested him?" She paced to the end of the roof, the wooden deck creaking beneath her feet. "Are they looking for anyone else?"

"The police have not arrested anyone. They are searching the house. Like they're going to find him hiding in a closet somewhere. They did find some vicious dogs tied up in the yard." She mumbled something in Russian Ingrid couldn't make out.

Then she fell silent.

Ingrid didn't want to ask any more questions. She didn't want to know anything else about the case. They'd been through this too many times already in the last three or four years. Svetlana would call her about the latest case of recovered abductees. The rescued women would then be identified, and once it was clear Megan Avery wasn't one of them, the phone calls from Svetlana would cease. Until the next time.

Ingrid braced herself for what was inevitably coming next.

"I'm at Kathleen's house now," Svetlana said. "All night we have watched the news together." She took another long pull on her cigarette.

Here we go.

"I told her she should not get her hopes up. Like she has every other time this has happened."

Ingrid gripped the metal rail at the edge of the roof.

"Kathleen wants to speak to you."

Ingrid closed her eyes and said nothing. Her mother never gave up. Even though Ingrid had made it perfectly clear she couldn't speak to Megan's mom.

"Ingrid? You still there? Ingrid?"

"I'm here." The tremor in her voice took her by surprise.

"Tell me this time you will talk to her. Like a grown up. Like…" She paused. "Like a goddamn human being."

Ingrid wanted to hurl the phone over the side of the building.

"Well?"

"You know I can't. Nothing's changed. I just can't do it."

Svetlana said something in Russian again. This time she didn't mumble. But Ingrid had heard all the Russian curse words her mother could throw at her. They were accompanied by, 'coward', 'no child of mine' and 'your papa would be ashamed'. Bringing Ingrid's dead father into the conversation? That was a low blow. Something Svetlana reserved for special occasions. It had the desired effect: Ingrid's eyes started to sting. "There's nothing I can say to Kathleen that will make things better."

"How can you say that? When have you even tried?"

"No matter what I say I can't justify why I'm alive and Megan is dead."

"We don't know she is dead. Not for sure. Besides, Kathleen has never asked you to justify anything."

"But that's what's in my head. I can't face her. Don't you get that?"

"For once, why not stop thinking about what is in your head and think about what is in hers?"

Ingrid squeezed her eyes shut, forcing out the tears. How could Svetlana be so cruel? Hardly a day went by that Ingrid didn't think of Megan and the loss Kathleen had to endure. But she made no comment. She didn't have the energy to fight.

"Megan's vigil is coming soon. Why not come home for once and light a candle for her?"

Ingrid wiped her damp cheeks with the back of her hand. "I can't." The words came out in a sob.

"Stop feeling so sorry for yourself, like always. I should have known already what your answer would be."

If you knew then why put us both through this?

"If you won't speak to Kathleen, at least promise you will do one thing for her."

"What?" This was new. Normally Svetlana would hang up about now.

"Ask your FBI friends for any information they have about this house and these women. It's no good just watching news on TV. They tell the TV people only what they want them to know."

"You've never asked me for my professional help before."

"I've got more reason to this time."

"I don't understand."

"The house where they found these women is only thirty miles away."

2

After Ingrid had promised her mother she would ask one of her contacts in the Bureau for more information, Svetlana hung up without bothering to say goodbye. Ingrid marched back into the apartment, threw her cell phone on the couch and headed for the bathroom. She hoped the sensation of hot water pummeling her skin and flattening her short hair against her scalp might banish the distressing conversation with Svetlana from her mind.

But instead it gave her time to think. And all she could think about was Megan Avery.

Megan at fourteen, the way she'd looked when Ingrid last saw her: flushed cheeks, sparkling eyes, a little breathless maybe, as she and Ingrid hurried from the carnival to return home before their curfew at ten. Ingrid walked as fast as she could, Megan struggled to keep up. Like Ingrid, she had carried quite a few extra pounds right through her baby fat years and into her teens. Megan's mom liked to cook and enjoyed spoiling them. Ingrid never complained. She took after her father when it came to her appetite. Svetlana had always eaten like a bird. Another memory popped into her mind: Svetlana poking a talon-like finger into the soft flesh of her upper thigh, a disgusted look on her face, her voice shrill and harsh as she told her just how lazy she was.

Ingrid scrubbed shampoo into her scalp with both hands, her eyes squeezed shut, and started humming some dumb pop song she'd heard on the radio the day before. Anything to shut out the other sounds that had begun playing in her head: the high-pitched and slightly out of tune carnival steam organ melody, the distant screams of the people on the roller coaster. She hummed a little louder. Then the shampoo reminded her of the sickly sweet smell of the cotton candy they had eaten. It was an aroma she'd tried to avoid ever since. It brought on the rush of memories faster than anything else.

She quickly rinsed out the suds and turned off the shower. She stepped out of the bathtub and stood dripping on the floor. Disoriented for a moment, she'd forgotten where she'd left her bath towel. In that instant she was back in the bathroom of her childhood home.

The house that was only thirty miles from where those women were found. So close to where Megan had been taken. Was it possible she could still be alive? For years Ingrid had held on to that hope. It was the reason she'd been so determined to join the FBI. After Megan disappeared, everything Ingrid had done had been carefully planned to get her another step closer to her goal. She worked hard in high school and college, got herself fit, made endless sacrifices in her personal life, until finally she was accepted into the Academy at Quantico. She had dreamed of heading up her own team and one day tracking down the man who'd snatched away her best friend. A tiny part of her also harbored the fantasy that somehow Megan was still alive and Ingrid would be the one to liberate her from her prison.

But over the years she'd slowly begun to realize what a forlorn hope it was, that in all likelihood Megan had been abused and murdered within hours of being abducted. And in time Ingrid had learned how to live with that realization.

After her conversation with Svetlana, a glimmer of that same hope had come back to torment her. She was compelled to find out anything she could about this latest case for her own peace of mind: not just because her mother had asked her to.

Just forty minutes after stepping out of the shower, Ingrid was making her way from the basement parking lot of the ugly six-story concrete building situated on the western side of

Grosvenor Square in Mayfair to the FBI's Criminal Division office on the third floor. She had extra purpose to her step as she hurried along the rosewood-paneled corridor. When she reached the twenty by thirty foot, low-ceilinged room, she was surprised to discover it was empty. Jennifer Rocharde, the administrative clerk and currently the only other member of the Criminal Division team, wasn't sitting at her desk.

With Jennifer out of the way, Ingrid considered calling Mike Stiller, her most reliable contact within the Bureau. But it was still only four-thirty a.m. on the East Coast. Mike was keen, but even he wouldn't be working that early in the morning. She didn't want to leave him a voicemail message—her request for information would need careful handling.

For the next three hours she struggled to complete a report for her most recent case. The Metropolitan Police investigation into the armed mugging of an American tourist had been relatively straightforward, but writing up her assessment of their work had proved more difficult than she'd expected. She found it almost impossible to concentrate on anything other than what might be happening with another investigation that was being played out over four thousand miles away. A cursory check of the major news sites online hadn't revealed much more than Svetlana had told her. Without hard facts, all the reporters and so-called experts could do was speculate. It was worse than no news at all.

At a quarter before twelve she reached for her cell phone and out of the corner of her eye noticed that Jennifer had risen to her feet.

"Hey," the clerk said, scooting around her desk on the other side of the office and hurrying toward Ingrid's, "I'm going for coffee. Can I get you anything?"

"That'd be great." Ingrid was relieved Jennifer was going out, which meant she didn't have to. There was no way she wanted an audience for her potentially awkward phone conversation with Mike Stiller.

"Let me guess," the clerk said, studying Ingrid's face carefully, "double espresso."

"It's that obvious I need caffeine, huh?"

Mildly embarrassed, the young clerk pushed her long, strawberry-blond hair behind her ears and nodded. "If I'm not out of line mentioning it, you've seemed awfully quiet this morning. Is everything OK?"

"Nothing a few early nights wouldn't fix," Ingrid lied. She forced a cheerful smile and watched Jennifer turn on her sensible heels and leave the office. She waited another couple of minutes before picking up the phone. Jennifer wouldn't be gone long. Ingrid hoped she'd have enough time to persuade Mike Stiller to agree to help her. Given what had happened three months ago, he might take a lot of persuading.

3

Since Ingrid had first started working at the embassy, back in December, she'd relied on intel from Mike Stiller more times than she cared to admit. As the weeks turned into months, she had discovered that when it came to the collation of information, working around the system—circumventing the strictest of Bureau protocols—was sometimes the only way to get things done. That wasn't something she would even have considered doing before her move overseas. But so far, her new pragmatic approach seemed to be working out just fine: Mike felt indispensable and Ingrid got to see higher classified intel that her level two security clearance would normally have given her access to.

She scrolled through her contacts list for his number and hesitated when she found it. After what had happened a couple of months ago, Mike might decide he never wanted to help her again.

Ingrid's break-up with her fiancé might make the conversation very uncomfortable. Mike was probably closer to Marshall than he was to her. Marshall may have asked him to choose sides. This was the first time she'd needed a favor from her old D.C. field office colleague since she'd ended her engagement, so there was no way of knowing if he'd agree to help her or not.

There was only one way to find out. She hit the call button and hoped for the best. Mike answered right away, no doubt eager to feel both busy and indispensable even before seven a.m. Eastern Standard Time.

"Agent Stiller—how are you this fine and pleasant August morning?" Ingrid was struggling to inject an upbeat tone into her voice.

"It's seventy-five in the shade and humidity's set to reach eighty-five percent by two p.m. The office air conditioning has stopped working, my iced tea has no sugar in it and I've got an appointment with the dental hygienist at lunchtime. So I'm just peachy." He let out a weary sigh to emphasize the tragic nature of his situation. "Thank you for having the courtesy to inquire about my well-being, but I'm sure that's not why you're calling."

"You know me so well."

"Listen, I don't have a lot of time."

"I'll be real quick."

"I don't just mean now. I've got a lot on my plate at the moment. If you need a favor, you might have to ask some other pliable schmuck."

Mike had to have been talking to Marshall.

"You know I wouldn't be asking if the circumstances didn't call for your skills and expertise." She continued to keep her tone as light as she could.

"I have a new boss. The regime here isn't as… relaxed as it used to be."

It seemed to Ingrid a pretty lame excuse. Why didn't he just come right out and admit his loyalties lay with his old friend, Marshall Claybourne?

"Hey, I'm not asking you for classified information, just a little heads up on a current case. It's really important."

Mike didn't say anything. Normally his curiosity would have gotten the better of him.

"Just a couple phone calls to your contacts in the Minneapolis field office," she said.

"All our calls are monitored now."

"You're kidding me."

"The new boss is pretty tough. Takes no prisoners, you know what I mean?"

"Come on, Mike, it can't be—"

"It's Marshall, OK?"

"What?"

"The new boss—it's Marshall. Started last month. He's busy trying to prove himself right now. I'm sure he'll mellow with time."

"But I thought he was your friend."

"I guess only when I was useful to him."

Ingrid wondered if maybe he was getting at her, but quickly dismissed the notion. Marshall's demands would be in a whole different league to hers. Obviously the breaking off of their engagement had done nothing to diminish his determination to haul himself up the greasy pole. She didn't know if she felt relieved or disappointed that the end of their relationship had affected him so little.

"Listen, I'm sorry it didn't work out for you guys," Mike said after a long pause.

"It was in the cards. You and me can still be friends, right?"

"Sure we can. But getting you intel? It's just not possible. Right now I gotta keep my nose clean. Marshall already got two agents transferred. And I like working here."

Ingrid wasn't sure what to say. Mike was still her best hope of getting all the information she needed, as fast as she needed it.

"Hey, are you OK?" he asked her.

"Fine." She could already hear Svetlana's mocking tone when she told her that the one time she'd asked for Ingrid's help, she'd failed to deliver. "If you can't help me, then I guess I do have to find somebody else who… I mean I need to…

"You sure you're OK? You don't sound fine. What's going on?"

"I should let you get back to work. I don't want you getting crap from Marshall on my account." Her voice wavered and she let out an involuntary sob.

"I'm so sorry—I didn't realize you were so cut up about Marshall."

"God, I'm not! No way!"

"It's OK—I understand. You guys were together for a long time."

"It's not Marshall, I swear."

"Then what the hell...?"

Ingrid took a moment to compose herself. "I guess you must know about the case in Blue Earth County? The rescued abductees?"

"It's impossible to avoid it." She could hear him breathing noisily at the other end of the line. "Wait a minute, don't you come from around there?"

This was the part she'd been dreading. In the two years she'd worked with Mike out of the D.C. office, she'd managed to avoid the subject of Megan Avery entirely, even when she'd surprised him by putting in a transfer request to the Violent Crimes Against Children Unit. "The house where they found the girls is thirty miles from my home town." She could feel her throat tightening. "Megan, my best friend, was abducted eighteen years ago. I need to know if she's one of the women they found." She stalled and took a breath.

"Jesus Christ. I had no idea. Tell me what you need."

Ingrid swallowed, grateful Mike hadn't asked her for any more details about Megan's disappearance. "All the information the local feds gather in as close to real time as you can get it. Including any audio or video interviews the witnesses, victims, or suspects participate in. I don't want to get information from FBI reports, I want the facts straight from the source."

"That's gonna be tough."

"I wouldn't ask if it didn't mean so much to me."

"Sure. I understand."

"Can you do it?"

Mike didn't answer right away. Ingrid wondered if maybe Marshall had just stepped into the office.

"Mike?"

"I'll make some calls. I can't promise anything—it might take a little while to set up. You want me to send files to your private email account?"

"Please. This is strictly between you and me." Ingrid swallowed again. Just mentioning Megan's name to Mike had been tougher than she'd imagined. "As soon as you get positive IDs for any of the three women, you will let me know?"

"You didn't even need to ask."

"Thanks, Mike." She hung up and leaned back in her seat. She'd been squeezing her cell phone so tightly it had left deep indentations in her right hand. She concentrated hard on forcing the muscles in her neck and shoulders to relax.

Mike Stiller had never let her down before. She prayed this time would be no exception. She planted a hand across her forehead and leaned her elbow on the desk. All she could do now was wait.

"Jeez—I guess you really need this, huh?" Jennifer said as she appeared at the door. "Sorry I was so long. The line at the cafeteria took forever. I think the espresso machine isn't working properly." She carefully placed the small cardboard cup on Ingrid's desk.

Before Ingrid had a chance to drink any coffee her landline started to ring. She stared at the phone for a moment, trying to get her head together.

"Want me to get that?" Jennifer asked.

"It's OK." The words came out louder and harder than she'd meant. "Hey—thanks for the coffee."

The clerk smiled back at her and returned to her desk. Ingrid answered the call.

"Agent Skyberg, US embassy."

"Hello, this is the duty sergeant, calling from Holborn Police Station, I've been asked to inform you about an incident that happened earlier today at a hotel in Bloomsbury."

Ingrid grabbed pen and paper from her desk. "Give me the details, sergeant."

"I don't have them all, this is a courtesy call, more than anything."

"Give me what you got."

"American family, husband went on the rampage, attacked his baby daughter and left her for dead."

"Left her? Has he been apprehended?"

"No. He snatched his eight-year-old son and took the boy with him. He's still on the loose."

Ingrid's pen remained poised over the notebook. "When did this happen? How long has he been out there?" She heard the rustling of paper.

"Haven't been given an exact time—earlier this morning."

"And what about the wife? Where is she?"

"At the hospital."

"He attacked her too?"

More rustling.

"No, that doesn't appear to be the case."

"Is there someone else I can speak to who has more information?"

"Sorry, no, not at the moment. The bulk of the team are at the hotel. The rest are at the hospital."

"Which hospital?"

The sergeant gave her the address and hung up.

Ingrid grabbed her jacket from the back of the chair and her purse from the drawer beneath the desk. Over the last eight months she'd gotten used to being the last to find out about incidents when they occurred, but had never received such limited information about a case before. She tried not to read too much into it, and headed for the door.

4

Ingrid parked her motorcycle on Chenies Street and walked three blocks north to the rear entrance of University College Hospital. Although she'd never before set foot inside the building during her eight months in London, she had often been struck by its appearance. It looked more like a skyscraper office block than a hospital: seventeen stories of tinted green windows and pearly white cladding towering over the intersection between Euston and Tottenham Court Roads. She supposed from the top few floors the patients must get a pretty impressive view of the whole of London.

A plain clothes detective was waiting for her just inside the entrance when she arrived.

"Agent Skyberg?" the muscular man in the cheap gray suit asked Ingrid as she glanced around the expansive reception area.

She nodded back at him. Unruly tufts of shortish dark blond hair stuck out from his scalp at different angles. His face was covered in stubble and the shirt beneath his jacket was a little crumpled. Ingrid suspected he'd had an unplanned early start.

"I'm Detective Sergeant Brad Tyson, I believe our duty sergeant has passed on the details of the case to you." He guided her toward a wide corridor to the right of the entrance, three elevators on each side.

"Actually, the details were a little sketchy." Ingrid saw no point in criticizing the duty sergeant's reticence. She didn't want her relationship with the investigating team to start off on the wrong foot.

"Let me bring you right up to speed, then." After pressing the 'up' button of the express elevator he stood back and studied her face for a moment. "If you think that's strictly necessary, in the circumstances."

"Why wouldn't it be?"

"I've had the embassy's role explained to me. I know when an American citizen is involved in a crime—victim or perpetrator—you like to keep an eye on the investigation, offer assistance, write your report, etcetera, etcetera."

He had just made her job sound almost an irrelevance, but Ingrid did her best to ignore his dismissive tone. She said nothing, just nodded at him encouragingly so that he might actually get to the point.

"But with the Air Force so closely involved in this case, I suppose the US government is pretty well represented already."

"Air Force? What do you mean?"

Before Tyson could answer, the elevator doors opened to reveal a crush of bodies crammed inside. Ingrid and the detective stepped to one side as the occupants started to pile out. Two or three were on crutches, a couple more, hooked up to IV machines, clutched packs of cigarettes in their spare hands. A man in a wheelchair rolled out without looking where he was going. Ingrid wondered how they'd all managed to breathe in such a confined space.

"It's a very busy hospital," Tyson said by way of explanation.

Ingrid and Tyson eventually managed to make it into the elevator, followed by another twenty or so people. Most of them were carrying bags of apples and grapes and a variety of less healthy snacks, with magazines and newspapers tucked under their arms. All of them had weary expressions on their faces.

During the ascent, Tyson made banal small talk and Ingrid played along, just as keen to be discreet. But once the elevator stopped at the eleventh floor and Tyson pushed a path to the front, Ingrid following in his wake, the doors had barely closed before she repeated her earlier question. Her tone more urgent this time.

"Tell me exactly who is involved in this investigation."

"I assumed you knew."

Ingrid now suspected the details she'd been given earlier weren't so much sketchy as deliberately vague. "Let's assume I know nothing at all and start over, shall we?"

"The US Air Force have sent one of their Security Forces officers." Tyson headed down the stark white, brightly-lit corridor and Ingrid followed. The further they walked from the elevator lobby, the more she could detect the familiar aroma of every hospital she'd ever visited. It was a mix of sterilizing alcohol, disinfectant and something non-specific—a smell Ingrid always associated with illness and disease.

"You're telling me the man we're looking for is a serving officer?" she asked as they pushed through a set of double doors.

"First Lieutenant Kyle Foster, stationed at RAF Freckenham in Suffolk."

"And exactly what authority does this Security Forces officer have?"

"I'll introduce you to the Major shortly. He can tell you himself."

"He's already here?" Ingrid stopped walking, forcing Tyson to do the same. "You informed the Air Force before you contacted the embassy?"

Tyson looked at her indignantly, as if she were questioning his competence personally, rather than the protocol of the Metropolitan Police in general.

"We needed good quality photographs of Foster and his son. We had to contact the base first."

"And you couldn't inform the embassy at the same time?"

"You'll have to bring up any complaints with DCI Radcliffe. He's the senior investigating officer." He started walking again.

"Wait a minute." Ingrid wanted more information before she walked all over whatever relationship the military policeman had managed to establish with the investigating team. "How long has the 'Major' been here?"

Detective Sergeant Tyson slowly came to halt and turned to face her, an irritated expression on his face. "An hour or so, why?"

"You've given him all the facts of the case?"

"Only as far as we know them. We're still waiting to speak to Mrs Foster to find out exactly what happened this morning."

"You haven't spoken to her yet?"

He took a step backwards and looked up at the ceiling, his irritation clearly mounting. "She's been too distraught. Wanted to be at Molly's side. In case she came round."

"Her daughter's still alive?"

Tyson narrowed his eyes. "You didn't even know that?"

"I told you—the details I've been given are sketchy at best."

"Molly's sustained head injuries. She's unconscious. Hooked up to so many machines you can barely see her for all the leads and wires."

"Is she going to be all right?"

Tyson shrugged. "Doctors can't tell us that. Not yet."

"I'd like to speak to Mrs Foster. She's an American citizen. She needs to know the embassy will help any way we can."

"You'll have to go to the back of the queue. DCI Radcliffe's going to interview her soon. With Major Gurley."

"The MP?"

"I think he prefers to be called a Security Forces officer."

Ingrid didn't give a damn what he preferred. As far as she was concerned all armed services cops were cut from the same cloth. "I want to be part of that interview."

Tyson shook his head. "Not my decision to make—you'll have to speak to the DCI about it." He continued down the corridor, marching toward another set of double doors.

As Ingrid hurried to catch up she wondered just how much access DCI Radcliffe was planning on giving her. It seemed the Air Force MP had everything sewn up. She needed to make him understand just what the pecking order should be here.

Tyson pushed through the doors and pointed to a couple of chairs lined up against the corridor wall. "Make yourself as comfortable as you can. There's a vending machine just through those doors. The coffee's drinkable, but the tea is disgusting. And however desperate you get, don't be tempted by the soup—croutons or not, it tastes like dishwater."

"You really just expect me to sit and wait?"

The detective shrugged. "Sit down, stand up. It's up to you."

"Take me to the SIO—I need to speak to him."

"He'll speak to you when he can. He's tied up right now." He tried to move past Ingrid, but she blocked his path.

"Tied up doing what?"

"I'm not sure that's any of your business."

"OK—where's the Security Forces guy?"

"Major Gurley's with the DCI."

"Great—I can meet them both at the same time." Ingrid hurried to the first door along the corridor and tried the handle: it was locked. She moved on to the second. "You could just tell me where they are. Save me interrupting someone else's meeting." Before she reached the second door, another, diagonally opposite, opened abruptly and a very tall man dressed in gray and white camouflage battledress stood in the doorway, his head turned towards the room. Ingrid rushed over to him. "Major Gurley?"

He spun around to face her. He was late thirties, with a tanned complexion and blond buzz cut. His features were chiseled, his jawline lean, his eyes pale blue. He wore a puzzled expression, but the quizzical smile faded once he glanced towards Tyson.

Ingrid stuck out a hand. "I'm Agent Ingrid Skyberg, from the FBI's Legal Attaché program at the embassy. I've been assigned to this case."

Bemused, his gaze switching quickly from Ingrid to Tyson and back again, Gurley shook her hand. "Pleasure to meet you, agent."

He was joined in the doorway by an ashen-faced man in his early fifties dressed in a suit that looked far too expensive to afford on a cop's salary.

Ingrid introduced herself again.

"DCI Paul Radcliffe." His mouth twitched upwards at the corners. "I think you may have had a wasted journey."

"This is a matter for the US Air Force Security Forces, agent. No need for the FBI to get involved," Gurley said. "I've got it covered." He gave her a warm smile. If it hadn't been for the content of what he'd just said, Ingrid might almost have believed it was genuine.

She didn't smile back.

"Now, I can provide you with an update each day, or a digest every forty-eight hours, if you'd prefer. Though I'd hope we can have First Lieutenant Foster safely in custody by the end of today."

"Police custody," Radcliffe added, either for Gurley's benefit or hers.

"Of course," Gurley turned his smile on Radcliffe. This time there was no mistaking its insincerity. Ingrid supposed the DCI wasn't fooled by it for a moment.

"If you could excuse us, detectives." Ingrid turned first to Radcliffe, then quickly to Tyson. She could be as polite as Gurley if that was the game he had chosen to play. She started to walk away. When the tall military policeman didn't follow she said, "Major Gurley? If you have a moment?"

"Please—call me Jack," he said and with two long strides was standing beside her.

"I don't know whose orders you're following, but after the Metropolitan Police Force, the FBI has jurisdiction. If anyone has had a wasted journey, it's you. I'm sorry you've traveled all the way from Suffolk unnecessarily." She forced a smile. "Naturally, I can give you regular updates."

"There seems to be a misunderstanding here. I'm sure a short phone call to the Special Agent in Charge at the embassy can clear everything up for you. My orders come direct from the Pentagon," Gurley said.

"I believe the misunderstanding is yours, Major." Ingrid was doing her best to tamp down her rising anger. How dare he patronize her like this? Who the hell did he think he was? As she reached into her purse for her cell phone—she was more than willing to 'clear things up' at the embassy—a woman in a dark blue pant suit pushed through a set of swing doors into the corridor. She rushed over to the two detectives.

Ingrid edged a little closer to them.

"The ICU team have taken Molly down for another scan, sir," the woman said. "Mrs Foster can give you twenty minutes."

5

Ingrid hurried to the detectives, eager to make her case before Gurley did. "I'm sure you won't have a problem if I sit in on the interview, chief inspector," she said. "In a purely observational capacity, of course."

Radcliffe looked at the MP who was standing with his feet wide apart, his long arms folded across his chest.

"Major Gurley and I have a few wrinkles to iron out in terms of exactly who has authority here, but I wouldn't want you to delay your interview on our account," Ingrid quickly said before Gurley had a chance to respond.

"Just as long as you do. I don't really care which one of you represents the US government, but keep your personal quarrels out of my investigation."

"Absolutely." Ingrid nodded toward Gurley, who managed to dip his head in agreement.

"I don't want a peep out of either of you, clear?"

"Crystal," Gurley said.

Radcliffe led them down another corridor, stopping when he reached a uniformed officer standing beside a closed door with a notice above it that read, 'ICU Room 4'.

"Everything all right, constable?" the DCI asked the squat man wearing a dark blue stab-proof vest over his uniform.

"Nothing to report, sir. The team got Molly out and away

without incident. PC Lewis has accompanied her to the MRI room on the first floor."

Ingrid noticed the officer had a night stick, pair of cuffs and Taser attached to his belt. "You're guarding the little girl?" she asked Radcliffe. "You think Foster is likely to come back and try to attack her?"

"I'm not taking any chances." He opened the door and let the female detective enter the room first.

Ingrid followed close behind them. The room was bright—sun streamed in from a large window to the right of the door. Opposite the door, next to a collection of monitors, was a vacant space where Molly's bed must have stood just a few minutes earlier. Somehow the emptiness felt more distressing to Ingrid than the sight of a small child lying unconscious in a hospital bed. She looked away toward the window and focused on the woman standing to one side of it. She was wearing a light blue and yellow summer dress, a bright orange sweater wrapped across her shoulders. She gave the impression of someone who had dressed in a hurry, which was hardly surprising, Ingrid thought, given the circumstances. The woman turned slowly away from the window and seemed to recoil as she took in the scene at the door. Seeing a group of people standing there, including one in military uniform, must have been a little overwhelming for her.

The female detective, who Ingrid supposed was the Fosters' family liaison officer, hurried to Mrs Foster's side and held her arm as she led her to a large recliner armchair in the corner of the room. Ingrid saw Foster's face for the first time and noticed her eyes were bloodshot, her cheeks blotchy. She couldn't have been older than thirty-five. The woman slowly eased herself into the chair and continued to stare at the group standing awkwardly just inside the room.

"You'd better get on and ask your questions," she said, her voice shaky. "As soon as they bring Molly back from her scan I want you all out of here."

DS Tyson ducked out of the room. He returned moments later carrying a chair in each hand. He set them down opposite the armchair, as the family liaison officer introduced both detectives to Mrs Foster. She glanced toward the door, at Ingrid and Gurley, a deep frown etched into her forehead. DCI Radcliffe introduced Ingrid. Then Gurley.

"And Major Gurley you already know, I presume," he said.

Carrie Foster nodded at them both but wouldn't make eye contact. "Can we please get this over with?"

Radcliffe and Tyson sat down, leaving the FLO to crouch beside Mrs Foster's chair. Gurley leaned against the wall next to the window, Ingrid stood behind the two detectives.

"We'll be as swift as we can," Radcliffe told Mrs Foster. "Our main priority is getting Tommy back. We need to locate your husband as soon as possible. But we really need to know exactly what happened this morning, to get some idea what we're dealing with."

Carrie Foster opened her eyes wide, her gaze fixed on the ragged Kleenex she was holding.

"First off, do you mind telling me why you're here in London?" Radcliffe asked.

The woman looked up at him, a puzzled expression on her face. "It was a mini-vacation. Sightseeing, you know? Apart from our trips home, it was the first time we'd left the base." She shook her head. "I should never have agreed to it. It was way too stressful to take on something like that."

"For you?"

"No! For Kyle. All of us crammed into that small hotel room." She wiped her nose with the disintegrating Kleenex. "The kids were overexcited. Really noisy, you know?"

"And that was a problem?"

"Noise is one of the triggers for Kyle."

"Triggers?"

"You know he's being treated for PTSD?"

Ingrid sensed Radcliffe stiffen slightly. He threw a glance toward Gurley, who remained expressionless.

"Let's assume we know nothing at all. We'd much rather hear the facts from you," Radcliffe said.

Carrie Foster continued. "Kyle was diagnosed around eighteen months ago. But he's not been right for a lot longer than that."

"He's still been on active duty during that time?"

"He's been going to counseling sessions at the base. His doctor says it's under control."

Ingrid made a mental note to speak to the Air Force doctor about Kyle Foster's condition.

"OK. Let's go back to the events of this morning. I realize how difficult it is for you to go over things again. But I really need you to tell us everything you remember."

Carrie Foster sniffed. "It's all right—I understand." She snatched a breath.

"Can we start right at the beginning?" Radcliffe said. "Who woke up first?"

"Kyle showered and dressed before the kids woke up. He seemed fine. A little tired maybe—he didn't sleep that well. You see, he has these nightmares. Has done ever since he came back from Afghanistan. Once a bad dream wakes him, he finds it really hard to get back to sleep."

"So everything was all right before your children woke up?"

"Yes. Peaceful. Happy, even. Kyle was singing in the shower."

"What happened after that?"

"Molly woke up. It was time for a feed. She started to cry just as soon as her eyes were open. Her crying woke Tommy. Right away he sprang out of bed—a little A-frame bed the hotel had fixed up alongside ours. Then he started to jump up and down on it. Like I say, he was excited. Kyle told him to stop, but he just bounced even harder. Jumping higher and higher. Until the bed collapsed underneath him."

"Was he hurt?"

"No—Tommy thought the whole thing was hilarious. Then he climbed on our bed and bounced on that instead. Kyle shouted at me to do something. He swore at me. But Tommy doesn't listen to a thing I tell him. I was holding Molly by then, trying to pacify her. Trying to stop her crying." She blinked slowly. "That's when it happened." A sob escaped from her mouth.

"Take your time, Mrs Foster."

The FLO took her hand and squeezed it tight.

"Kyle started yelling at Molly to shut up. When she didn't he snatched her from my arms and started shaking her. So hard. I tried to grab her back. But he shoved me away and I hit something. I have a big bruise halfway up my thigh." She rubbed her leg with a fist, staring blankly into space. She was clearly back in that hotel room. Reliving the events of the morning.

"Can you tell us what happened next?" Radcliffe said gently.

"Kyle carried on shaking her. Until the crying stopped." She swallowed. "Then he threw her on the bed. I mean *threw* her." Her eyes were moist.

The FLO grabbed a pack of Kleenex from a pocket and handed it to Mrs Foster.

"Thank you." Carrie Foster pulled out a tissue and dabbed her eyes. "Then Kyle ran out. Said he couldn't breathe and needed to get air. As soon as I could, I locked the door behind him, and I called for the ambulance."

Jack Gurley shifted his position, straightening his back then crossing one ankle over the other before leaning back against the wall.

"He came back just before the EMTs arrived."

"How long before, would you say?"

She shrugged. "Seconds maybe. I don't know. Not long."

"He managed to get back into the room, even though you'd locked the door."

"I opened it when the manager came. The other guests had complained to him about the noise. Kyle had been shouting. I might have been screaming. I don't remember. I guess they were worried what was going on."

Radcliffe leaned closer to Mrs Foster. He lowered his voice. "Where was Molly when the ambulance crew arrived?"

"In my arms. She wasn't moving. Or making a sound. I thought she was… I mean I thought…" She sobbed again. "One of the EMTs asked me what happened. I hesitated. I didn't want to believe what Kyle had done. I just looked at him."

"What did you tell the paramedic?"

"I said Kyle had shaken Molly and she'd gone quiet. The

other EMT started to move toward Kyle, his hands up, telling him to take it easy. I guess Kyle panicked." Her eyes widened even more as she stared at the floor. "He had the EMT moving closer on one side and the hotel manager stepping into the room from the hallway." Another sob escaped her throat. "That's when he grabbed Tommy. Picked him up and ran right out the door. Barging into the manager as he went." She shook her head. Then looked up at Radcliffe, staring into his face. "Why didn't anyone try to stop him?"

Radcliffe gave her a half-shrug. "No one really knows how they're going to react in a situation like that," he said soothingly. "It all happened so fast, they probably didn't even work out what was going on until it was too late."

"Someone should have stopped him." She turned her stare toward the window and Major Gurley. "You've got to find them. I want my little boy back."

Gurley tensed but said nothing. Mrs Foster turned back to the DCI.

"Is there anywhere your husband might have taken Tommy?" Radcliffe asked her.

She shook her head numbly. "He doesn't know London. Where would he go? Do you think he's hurt Tommy? Why did he take him? If he wanted to run away, why take my boy with him?"

6

The door into Molly Foster's hospital room opened and her mother jumped to her feet. She ran to Molly's bed as it was wheeled back in. Molly looked smaller than Ingrid had expected. She seemed tiny lying in the adult-sized bed. Her short curly hair spread across the pillow each side of her pale face. Her lips were almost colorless.

"Is she OK? What did the scan show?" Carrie Foster asked the ICU nurse dressed in a crisp white short-sleeved tunic and dark pants.

The nurse gave her a warm smile and laid a reassuring hand on her arm. "The swelling in her skull hasn't got any worse. We'll know more when the radiologist has studied the scans. He'll speak to the consultant and then the consultant will come and explain everything to you."

"How long before that happens?"

"Hopefully before the end of the day."

"What? That's hours away."

The nurse helped the porters position the bed into place and reattached the monitors. She switched the tube feeding oxygen into the little girl's nostrils from a portable cylinder tucked beneath the bed to a supply coming out of the wall above it. Ingrid was relieved to discover the child was breathing without the aid of a respirator.

"I'm sorry, Carrie," the nurse said when she'd finished her tasks. "We have one radiologist covering for two of his colleagues at the moment. It won't affect Molly's care in any way. You don't need to worry about that."

Carrie Foster stroked her daughter's forehead. She seemed to have forgotten the detectives were even in the room. Major Gurley stood in silence at the foot of the bed with Radcliffe. After a moment DS Tyson cleared his throat.

"We'll leave it for now, Mrs Foster," Radcliffe said. "But we will need to speak to you again later."

The female FLO ushered them all towards the door and closed it behind them.

Once outside, Ingrid took DCI Radcliffe to one side asked him for an update on what was being done to locate First Lieutenant Foster and his son.

"I've already updated Major Gurley." He glanced back towards the room. Gurley was peering through the round window set into the upper third of the hospital room door. "Perhaps you could liaise with him?" He turned to walk away. Ingrid scooted in front of him.

"I'd rather hear it from you."

"Look, I told you before, whatever's going on with the embassy and the US Air Force is no concern of mine. You get things sorted out between yourselves."

"I'm about to call my boss to resolve the situation. I'd like to be able to give him a progress report at the same time."

Radcliffe puffed out an impatient sigh. "I've posted officers at the major train terminals and Victoria Coach Station. We're going through CCTV footage from the streets surrounding the hotel. We've questioned all the guests present at the hotel when the initial response officers arrived. And we have statements from the hotel manager and receptionist."

"Do their accounts match up with what Carrie Foster just told us?"

"Of course. Why wouldn't they?"

"Just being thorough." Ingrid looked back towards Gurley. He was speaking with DS Tyson. Tyson was nodding gravely.

She wanted to know what they were talking about. "And what about the EMTs... the ahh... paramedics? You've spoken to them?"

"They were just finishing their shift when they picked Molly up. We've managed to interview one of them, and before you ask, yes, his account matches Mrs Foster's."

"Do you have CCTV footage from inside the hotel?"

"It's a small, family-run establishment. Three star. They don't have cameras recording their guests' every move." He beckoned to his detective sergeant and tapped a finger against his wrist-watch. "I suggest you resolve your issues sooner rather than later with Major Gurley. I see no point in you replicating each other's duties."

Ingrid watched as Tyson shook Gurley's hand, then hurried toward his senior officer. Gurley disappeared into the mens' restroom.

Radcliffe handed her a scrap of paper. "The hotel is only about five minutes away on foot," he told her. "Ask for Brian, he's the Crime Scene Manager. He'll walk you through events, as we understand them, in situ. Help you to picture what happened." He glanced down at the note. "Pass that on to Gurley if he's got the gig, would you? I don't want to be endlessly repeating myself." He gave what seemed to Ingrid a reluctant smile and briskly walked away.

Ingrid seized her moment. She snatched her cell phone from her purse and called her immediate boss at the embassy, Assistant Special Agent in Charge Sol Franklin.

"Hey, Sol. Do you have a couple minutes?" she asked as soon as he picked up.

"For you...?"

"What do you know about this case in Bloomsbury?"

"The Air Force guy who ran amok?"

"I feel like I've walked into it completely blind. The intel I got from the Met was severely lacking, to say the least. I get the feeling they were surprised I even showed up."

"Have you met Major Gurley yet?"

"You know about him?"

There was an extended pause. "I didn't know in time to warn you, if that's what you mean. I only just got off the phone from the Legal Attaché himself."

"You did?" Sol hardly ever spoke to the head of the FBI program at the embassy. He normally received his instructions from his next in command, Deputy Special Agent in Charge, Amy Louden.

What the hell was going on?

"You're telling me the Legat is involved with this investigation personally?"

"He just got off the phone from the Pentagon. I gather there was a rather fraught—my word, not the Legat's—discussion with the Chief of Staff of the Air Force."

The Legal Attaché and the Chief of Staff? With such big hitters taking a personal interest in the case, Ingrid was surprised Sol hadn't taken it on himself. "Listen, I realize you can't give me all the details of your conversation, so I'm not even going to ask, but can you at least tell me who should be liaising with the cops here?"

Another pause.

"Sol—just spit it out. If I'm off the case, I'm off the case. I can live with that."

"That would be far too straighforward."

"I don't understand." Ingrid kept her eyes peeled on the door to the men's restroom. She wanted to get this resolved before Gurley reappeared.

"A US pilot on the run in a host nation doesn't look that good… politically."

"Politically? Maybe I would give a crap if a fourteen-month-old girl wasn't in a coma and an eight-year-old boy hadn't been abducted." She turned around and started walking, concerned if she stayed still a moment longer she might feel the need to punch somebody.

"You don't need to get involved with all the political BS," Sol said. "That's my job."

"So why are you even telling me about it?"

"Because I need to explain the strategy the Legal Attaché and the Air Force big cheese cooked up between them."

Ingrid didn't like where she thought this might be heading. She pulled up abruptly.

"You and Major Gurley better start to play nice with one another. You've got to work together on this. Show a US government united front."

Ingrid let out a groan. "I'm not taking orders from that arrogant son of a—"

"You don't have to."

"As much pleasure as it might give me telling him what to do, I don't think he'd agree to follow my orders either."

"Working *together,* didn't I say? You're going to cooperate with one another. Gurley has his chain of command, you have yours. But on the ground you two liaise with the local cops as a *team.*"

"I like to work alone."

"I don't care. My hands are tied on this one."

"For God's sake, Sol."

"No point in arguing. Just don't let me down."

It wasn't that long ago Ingrid had saved Sol Franklin's life. She wasn't about to disappoint him now. She never could. But the thought of working with an opinionated military cop? She felt a wave of heat pass from her chest up into her throat.

A moment later Sol said a brusque goodbye and hung up.

"I'm guessing you just had the exact same conversation as me." A Texan accent. A voice so close to her ear she felt Gurley's warm breath against her skin.

She pulled away and wheeled around to face him. "Jesus! What are you doing creeping up on me like that?"

"Don't tell me, your boss at the embassy, huh?" he said, undeterred. "Major General Walker called me himself. Might have considered it an honor." He raised a sandy-blond eyebrow at her. "Under different circumstances." He ran a hand over his buzz cut and put a hat on his head. "Looks like we're stuck with one another. I suggest we make the best of it. Sooner we track Foster down, faster we can get back to normal." He held out his hand. Reluctantly, Ingrid shook it.

He smiled a wily smile at her, moving just one corner of his mouth. "As long as we're clear on one thing."

"And that is?"

"We both agree that for practical purposes, on the ground… I'm in charge."

7

Ingrid practically had to break into a jog to keep up with her companion's lengthy strides. When they'd made it out of the hospital and onto the noisy, bustling Euston Road, she'd made it quite clear there was no way she'd be taking orders from Gurley. He'd merely laughed in her face. After that they continued the journey to the Fosters' hotel in a hostile silence. Gurley was at least right about one thing, Ingrid thought: a swift resolution to the situation would be best for all parties concerned.

The hotel was situated in a side street just off Russell Square —a favorite location for American tourists on a budget. The slightly down-at-heel, three-star establishment took up four row houses in the middle of a Georgian terrace. Three of the front doors were sealed shut. The shabby exterior looked in need of urgent redecoration.

Ingrid led the way and quickly found a uniformed police constable chatting to a woman behind the reception desk. "We're looking for Brian, the Crime Scene Manager," Ingrid said and flashed her badge at him. He pointed her toward the stairs.

"Second floor. You can't miss it."

They tramped up four shallow flights of stairs, still not speaking to one another, and discovered another uniformed policeman on the second floor landing. He directed them to the other end of a dimly-lit corridor. Ingrid peered into the gloom, only just managing to make out two Tyvek-suited crime scene examiners standing outside an open door, talking to a woman dressed in a dark suit and vivid pink shirt. On her feet the woman was wearing overshoe bootees.

Ingrid hurried towards them. She waved her badge in the air by way of introduction and asked for Brian, the CSM. The woman, who was a detective constable, handed Ingrid and Gurley a pair of bootees each.

"I'm not sure they're big enough," the detective said, her gaze working its way slowly from Gurley's feet to his face. "You are rather a tall specimen."

Gurley glanced down at the small blue bootees and quickly rejected them. "It's OK, I can see all I need from out here," he said.

Ingrid couldn't help but feel a little irritated at Gurley's attitude. It seemed as if he'd decided this exercise was a waste of his time and wasn't prepared to participate. She peered into the room.

"That's Brian's arse, right there," the detective told her and pointed to a man crawling on his hands and knees beneath a low couch.

Ingrid slipped the bootees over her shoes and entered the room, taking care to step on the plastic platforms laid out twelve inches apart to get to the other side. "Brian? I'm Agent Skyberg… from the embassy."

The CSM made a little groan then carefully backed out of the confined space without hitting his head. He wriggled backwards like a man who had learned the hard way not to move too quickly in tight spaces. With some effort, he heaved himself vertical and looked Ingrid up and down. "I was expecting a bloke," he said, unapologetically.

"Sorry to disappoint."

"Oh no, not at all. You'll do nicely." He smiled a lascivious smile at her and Ingrid prepared herself for a barrage of double entendres and inappropriate remarks about her appearance. "What do you need to know, my lovely?"

She was still tuning her ear to the various regional accents in the UK, trying to get a grip on most of them. She quickly decided "Brian the CSM" was Welsh. Most probably south Wales, if she had to choose. She rapidly outlined everything Carrie Foster had told her about what happened that morning. "Is this scene consistent with her statement?"

Brian stuck out his bottom lip and surveyed the room, nodding as he turned his head left then right. "That could work." Then he started to shake his head. "Bloody domestics. I've seen the aftermath of too many of them over the years. They never get any easier to deal with, especially when there's kiddies involved. Bloody tragedy." He stared into Ingrid's face. "You got kids have you?" His gaze dropped to the small triangle of bare flesh that was visible above her shirt.

"I don't."

"Then you wouldn't understand."

"Oh I think I can empathize just fine."

"No—that's what I thought until I had one of my own. Turns your world upside down. Got five of the little buggers now. Love them all more than life itself. How could he do something like that to his own baby girl?"

Ingrid glanced around the room, taking in the built-in closet, the couch, the broken A-frame bed, and finally the kingsize. The room was in need of urgent redecoration, even more so than the exterior of the hotel. She wondered what the room rate was for a run-down place like this. Maybe First Lieutenants in the US Air Force got paid a lot less than she imagined. She completed another 360 degree turn and tried to work out if anything seemed out of place. From Carrie Foster's description of what happened, Ingrid felt sure something was missing. Then she worked out what it was. "Has your team removed any large items of furniture?"

"No. Only small ones. Why do you ask?"

She turned back toward the door. "Hey, Major Gurley." Gurley was busy talking to the detective in the bright pink blouse. He looked up, a slightly guilty expression on his face. "How tall would you say Carrie Foster was?"

He shrugged back at her. "Bit shorter than you, maybe."

"That's what I thought." Ingrid scanned the room again. But there was no solid piece of furniture at the right height that would cause a bruise on her mid-thigh. She'd been expecting a table, a desk or a low bureau. But nothing fitted the bill. "Detective, have you seen a list of the injuries sustained to Mrs Foster and her daughter?" she asked the pink-shirted woman.

"A list was emailed to my phone a little while ago," she said. "I haven't had chance to look at it properly yet."

"Do you think you could look at it now?" *And stop flirting with my colleague.*

The detective quickly located the file on her smart phone. "What am I looking for exactly?"

"Did the doctors confirm a large bruise on Mrs Foster's thigh?"

The cop scanned the email. "Yes—here it is. Large hematoma. Left thigh, eight inches below pelvis."

Ingrid made a note of the details and studied the room more closely. There really was very little floor space, no wonder tempers had been fraying. Four human beings in such a cramped environment would have tested the most patient of souls. She tried to put herself in Kyle Foster's place, bringing to mind the mild, self-diagnosed version of Post-Traumatic Stress Disorder she'd been suffering from on and off since Megan was taken. She closed her eyes and could immediately recall the sickly sweet caramel aroma of cotton candy. The distant sound of carnival organ music grew louder the harder she concentrated. Her breathing became shallower as her heart started to pound. Then her temperature increased as if someone had turned on a heater. She could absolutely understand Foster's need to flee. It felt claustrophobic in there. But to hurt his daughter? If it had all been getting too much for him, why not just run? But then Ingrid supposed in his head he wasn't so much hurting his daughter as making the noise go away.

"You OK?"

Ingrid felt the CSM's elbow nudge her arm. She snapped open her eyes. Sweat had begun trickling down her back, and was prickling at the nape of her neck. She had to get out of that room. "I'm fine," she told the CSM, even though it was obvious she was anything but.

"Are we done here?" Gurley called from the doorway.

Ingrid needed to speak to Carrie Foster again. If the facts surrounding her injury were already being called into doubt, what else about her statement might prove unreliable?

8

A black embassy sedan was waiting for them when Ingrid and Gurley emerged from the hotel. Ingrid asked the driver to drop her on Gower Street so she could pick up her motorcycle: she didn't want to add to the embassy's growing pile of unpaid parking tickets. As she stood on the sidewalk and watched the limousine merge into the long line of traffic, the relief of getting away from Gurley for a while was greater than she'd expected.

Although the traffic from Bloomsbury to Mayfair was heavy all the way, on the bike Ingrid managed to arrive at the embassy parking lot ahead of Major Gurley. She took the opportunity to visit Sol's office on the fifth floor, but when she got there his desk was empty. She called him and discovered he was heading up the welcoming committee in the Criminal Division office two floors below.

"An update, if you wouldn't mind, agent?" he said when she got there.

Ingrid started to lay out everything she'd learned in detail, interrupted occasionally by the beep of Sol's cell phone. When she stopped abruptly halfway through her account, Sol turned around to see what had caused the sudden halt.

"Major Gurley, you made it," he said and extended a hand. "I'm Sol Franklin. Ingrid you've met, of course." He put his arm around Gurley's wide back and guided the MP to Jennifer's desk. "And this is the most indispensable member of the FBI program here at the embassy. Jennifer Rocharde. Anything on any of our databases you need to find, Jennifer is the person to find it. We'd be quite lost without her."

"Pleasure to be acquainted with you, miss." Gurley nodded toward Jennifer and immediately her cheeks flushed bright pink.

"Now, where were we?" Sol sat on the edge of Jennifer's desk and folded his arms.

Ingrid continued to tell him what she'd discovered, turning to the Major sporadically for his input.

It never came.

"You haven't said very much, Major. What's on your mind?" Sol said when Ingrid had finished.

"May I speak frankly, sir?"

"Wouldn't have it any other way. And please—call me Sol."

"I'm concerned we're wasting time. The clock's running down. We should be out there searching for Foster. We're making polite conversation while the trail's going cold."

Ingrid wondered why the hell Gurley had even agreed to come to the embassy if he felt so strongly about it.

"We should be following standard US Air Force procedure: apprehend the man who's gone AWOL, ASAP. Foster's had survival training—in the event of being shot down in enemy territory. If he's gone to ground, it's going to be one hell of a job to track him down."

"And you feel you're the man for the job?" Sol's tone was patient, if a little condescending.

"Due respect, sir. I know I am."

Sol smiled up at Gurley's blank face. "As a matter of fact, I've spoken to your superiors at the base and they agree. They have full confidence in your abilities. They want you and Agent Skyberg to share your expertise with the Met. But you have to understand, the Met does have some experience in apprehending fugitives."

"To be truly effective, I've found it's better if I work alone."

He glanced at Ingrid. "No disrespect, agent. I'm making no comment on your skills in these matters."

For a man who didn't mean to disrespect anyone, Gurley was doing a good job at demonstrating the complete opposite. Why was he making things difficult when the investigation had barely begun?

"Working alone just isn't practical on this case," Sol said. "I was under the impression that had been explained to you. The Pentagon has agreed to Bureau involvement."

Gurley shook his head and stared down at the floor.

"But both you and Agent Skyberg must work closely with the Metropolitan Police Force. They have the best intel in this kind of situation. Their PR department are liaising with the major news outlets to get the story out there. The officers manning the phones in the police incident room have already received calls from people claiming they've seen Kyle and Tommy Foster."

"Claiming? What does that mean?"

"None of the sightings has been confirmed at this time."

"You see? Their intel isn't worth a shi—" Gurley glanced at Jennifer and didn't finish his sentence.

"Is Carrie Foster making a statement herself?" Ingrid asked.

"At the press conference. Hopefully that'll happen tomorrow morning. She'll be pleading for the safe return of her son. Trying to appeal to her husband's sense of duty, loyalty. Playing on his conscience—if he has one. And if all that fails to elicit the desired response, she'll be appealing to the great British public."

"So that more crackpots and loony toons call the police and waste even more time? You really think that's gonna help any?" Gurley thumped the desk with his fist and made Jennifer jump. "I'm sorry, miss."

Ingrid could see Sol struggling to control his reaction to Gurley's obstructiveness. "I know this operation is outside your normal working procedures, but we have to be flexible and adapt. We've got to pull together." He looked from Gurley to Ingrid. "Can we agree to that at least?"

"Not a problem for me," Ingrid said.

"I don't have any choice, do I?"

"We'll reconvene here tomorrow after the press conference."

The muscles in Gurley's jaw were working overtime. "Where is this police incident room?"

"Holborn Police Station," Jennifer told him.

He looked at her blankly.

"Around two miles from here," Ingrid said.

"If that's where all this valuable intel will come from, why are we here instead of there?"

Ingrid supposed it was a good point, but knew that Sol would have had his own reasons to bring Major Gurley to the embassy, presumably to get some measure of the man.

"I'm sure that will be your next stop, Jack—may I call you Jack?"

Gurley nodded but didn't seem enthusiastic about the idea.

"But first I'd like to discuss First Lieutenant Foster's service history with you."

"I don't actually know the man."

"But since you were informed of this morning's tragic events, you must have read his personnel file?"

"I've perused it. Dry facts and figures tend not to help in these situations."

"Before you left the base, I'm guessing you had a chance to speak to the doctor who's treating him for PTSD?" Ingrid asked.

"She wasn't available. I'm still waiting for a call."

"But you've read his medical report?"

Jennifer handed Ingrid a sheaf of papers held together in the top left-hand corner by a paperclip.

"What's this?" she asked the clerk.

"I only just finished putting it together. It's everything we have on Kyle Foster."

"That's Defense Department classified information. You have no authority to look at that." Gurley reached out a hand, but Ingrid was too fast for him, she snatched away the report.

"I can print you one too, if you'd like, Major?" The clerk smiled at him.

Gurley hadn't taken his eyes off Ingrid as she leafed through the pages. "That won't be necessary, thank you, Miss Rocharde."

"Did you know Foster has been flying drone missions for the last two years?" Ingrid said. She scanned down to the bottom of the page.

Dear God.

"You've read this, Sol?"

Her boss nodded gravely at her.

"It says he was responsible for the deaths of at least twenty-two women and children in a single mission in February 2011." She swallowed and turned the page. The more she read, the more she wished she hadn't. "The targets were meant to be arms silos and fuel depots, but the missiles ended up hitting a school in a village just outside Hajjah. She looked directly at Gurley. "You knew about the civilian casualties in the drone attacks?"

Gurley let out a breath and clenched his jaw, as if he'd been expecting the question. "You're always going to get collateral damage in a war situation."

"According to the report these people were on their way to a family *wedding*."

"You know as well as I do that shit happens."

"Did you tell Radcliffe about all this?"

"It wasn't relevant to his investigation."

"How can you say that? The police need to know what kind of man they're dealing with." Ingrid flipped through the pages to get to Kyle Foster's medical reports and discovered his PTSD was formally diagnosed at the end of 2011. She remembered Carrie Foster telling them he'd been suffering for quite a while longer than that. She skimmed through the remainder of the report. "It doesn't say what caused his condition," she said when she'd finished. "Was it his time in Afghanistan, or the drone missions he's carried out since moving to the UK?"

Gurley shrugged. "It's not likely to be one isolated incident. How is that relevant, anyway?"

"It might help us work out what his triggers are likely to be."

"You heard what his wife said—loud noises, crying,

screaming—that's what set him off this morning. God knows what little thing might trigger the next attack. We've just got to hope Tommy is behaving himself." He glanced at Jennifer before continuing. "We have to accept the longer they're out there, the more chance there is Tommy will be his next victim."

9

Ingrid stared at her vibrating phone, suspecting it was Svetlana rather than Mike Stiller, wondering whether she could face speaking to her. She answered just before the call diverted to voicemail. "Hi, Mom. Before you ask, I don't have any news yet. And yes, I did put in a request with one of my old colleagues." She hit the speakerphone option on her cell and rested it on the counter between the sinks in the ladies' washroom. "All we can do now is wait." She put her hands under the faucet then ran her wet fingers through her messy hair in an attempt to restyle it.

"Oh we can do plenty more than just wait," Svetlana said. "You think you know what I'm going to say before I get a chance to open my mouth? Well you're wrong. I'm calling to beg you to speak to Kathleen. She's been talking about you all day. She got out the photograph albums this morning. She showed me the pictures of you and Megan. The two of you looked so happy."

We were. But I ruined all that.

"I can't go through this again with you, Mom. Please stop asking me. My answer isn't going to change."

"Where's your conscience?"

Locked in a secure file cabinet at the bottom of Lily Lake, just where the psychotherapist told me to put it.

"I didn't raise you to be so heartless."

You didn't raise me at all.

Ingrid hung up and tossed the phone into her purse. The door into the restroom opened and a uniformed policewoman walked in. Ingrid reapplied her lipstick and gave herself a long hard stare in the mirror. She was looking tired. Her eyes were a little bloodshot and dark shadows had started to appear underneath them. She ran her fingers though her short blond hair again, but it was well past restyling. She could take some consolation from the fact she was spending the evening in Holborn Police Station rather than on a much anticipated date with Detective Constable Ralph Mills—at least he wouldn't see just how crappy she looked. She corrected a smudge of lipstick with the tip of her little finger and fished around in her purse for some concealer to deal with the dark circles beneath her eyes. Before she found the tube of makeup her phone started to vibrate again. She pulled it out, saw it was Ralph calling and couldn't decide whether or not to answer.

What the hell.

"I just got your message," he said, as soon as Ingrid picked up.

"I'm really sorry. I wouldn't cancel if it wasn't important."

"That's why I'm calling. There's no need to cancel. I'm walking up Theobalds Road as we speak."

That was just around the corner. "I really can't leave right now."

"That's why I'm coming to you. I've got two pizzas and half a dozen chilled beers. I went for a quattro formaggi and pancetta with mozzarella and rocket. How does that sound?"

"I don't know—I really need to work."

"I can help. I do know my way around an incident room. See you in five." He hung up.

Ingrid stared at her phone. She was tempted to call him back, but she was ravenous, and a big part of her really wanted to see him. She'd been on a few dates since she'd ended her fourteen month engagement with Marshall Claybourne. Feeling a little on the rebound, she'd wanted to get Marshall out of her system, so she'd dated men who didn't really mean that much to her. But Ralph was different. She'd wanted their first date to go well. For once she actually cared what impression she made. But an impromptu meal in a busy corner of a station house? It wasn't an auspicious start to a relationship. Not that Ingrid was even sure that was what she wanted from him. She dug into her purse again, found the tube of concealer she'd been looking for, plus some mascara and eyeshadow. She did the best she could to enliven her tired features. The female PC emerged from one of the cubicles just as Ingrid put the final flourish to her eyelashes.

"Are you working the abduction case?" Ingrid asked her, feeling she couldn't exactly ignore the woman in the cramped restroom.

The policewoman nodded at her via the mirror.

"Taken any promising calls yet this evening?"

"Not so far. I have had two proposals of marriage, a heavy breather and a shed load of abuse though."

"What gets into folk?"

"Your guess is as good as mine."

Ingrid headed for the door. "See you back in there, I guess."

"I've just finished a double shift. I'm going home. If I'm lucky I might just get there before it's time to come back again." She smiled at Ingrid. "Good luck."

"Thanks." Ingrid had a feeling she might need it.

10

Ingrid returned to the incident room. It seemed even busier than when she'd left it. The forty-foot square, open-plan office was jammed with desks, two people answering phones at each one. The large room was brightly illuminated by unflattering fluorescent overhead lighting, more than bright enough to expose all the flaws in her hasty repair job.

She saw Ralph Mills sitting on the edge of a desk, chatting to a detective whose name Ingrid had forgotten. Ralph was dressed in combat pants and a vintage tee shirt, a pair of Timberland boots on his feet. He must have been home to get changed after work. He looked restless, nervously picking the label off a bottle of beer. She was relieved he seemed just as anxious as her about their 'date'. She took a deep breath and marched toward him.

A moment later Ralph spotted her and his anxious expression melted away as he smiled warmly at her. In that instant, Ingrid was reminded, just as she had been many times before when Ralph smiled at her, of Clark Swanson: her very first junior high school crush. Something about that smile made her stomach flip, as if she were thirteen all over again.

She gave him a little smile in return and he jumped up from the desk and hurried toward her.

When he reached her, a long, awkward moment passed, both of them unsure how to greet one another. Finally they simultaneously opted for a safe peck on both cheeks, a sanitized European-style 'hello' that couldn't carry any subtext. He stood back and beamed at her. "You look fantastic."

His dopey grin was infectious. She found herself grinning back at him so hard her cheeks started to ache. "You too."

"I've managed to commandeer a spare desk in a relatively quiet corner of the room."

"Hey, I'm really sorry about this."

"I completely understand. You can't just drop everything. But I've had a quick chat with the incident room manager, I've wangled you the next twenty minutes off."

"A man with influence, huh?"

"I have my uses. Why do you think the boss has put up with me for so long?"

Ralph's senior officer, DI Natasha McKittrick, was the nearest thing Ingrid had to a good friend in London. In fact, Natasha was pretty much the closest friend she'd had in her adult life. After Megan Avery had disappeared, Ingrid had made it a rule not to get too close to people. In each of the field offices she worked in her eight years in the Bureau, she'd done no more than made acquaintances. No real friends. She was grateful Mike Stiller still took her calls.

"Which reminds me," Ralph said, breaking into her thoughts. "The boss says 'hi'."

"You told her about our… this… I mean, tonight?"

"Didn't you?" When he took in the appalled expression on her face, he made a silent 'o' with his mouth. "I just assumed you chatted to her about everything. Thought I'd get in early, try to prevent some of her piss-taking." He sighed. "Needless to say my strategy didn't work—she's been ribbing me about it all day."

Even before Ingrid had made the break from Marshall, McKittrick had done her best to act as Cupid. The detective inspector seemed determined to get the two of them out on a date together. Now McKittrick had finally gotten what she wanted. In the end it was easier for Ingrid to give in to her friend's ham-fisted attempt at matchmaking than continue to pretend she wasn't interested.

"She just won't let up," he said. "She's been worse since you broke off—" He stopped himself, no doubt encouraged to by the admonishing look Ingrid was giving him. "That was out of order. Shouldn't have mentioned it. Sorry."

"It's not like it's a taboo subject or anything. But I'd rather not spend whatever time we've got this evening talking about my ex."

Ralph turned away, suddenly unable to look her in the eye. He ducked between desks, not stopping to look back until he'd reached the promised 'quiet corner'. The small desk was flanked on both sides by long tables occupied by a half dozen cops speaking loudly into their phones. Ingrid joined him and they perched on the edge of the desk, facing toward the wall. Ralph set down the two pizza boxes and pack of beers between them. Ingrid flipped open the lid of the top box.

"So, Natasha's been working you hard today, huh?" She pulled out a wedge of cheesy pizza.

"She's a tough boss. Fair, but tough."

"Sounds like she told you to say that." She smiled. "And is that OK with you? Working hard all the time? No chance for a little fun every now and then?"

"We're having fun now, aren't we?" He pulled off his own triangle of pizza and took a large bite. At the next desk a female cop slammed down the phone and muttered, "bloody pervert". Ralph raised his eyebrows. "Ah, the joys of a public appeal. Shame it has to involve the public." He picked up a bottle of beer, pushed off the top on the side of the desk and handed it to Ingrid. They clinked bottles and Ingrid raised a toast to law enforcement officers everywhere.

"Hear, hear." Ralph took a swig of beer. "I might moan about it, but I do seriously love this job. It's all I ever wanted to do. I suppose it's in my genes."

"Really?"

"My dad was a copper. Detective Inspector Charlie Mills." He picked another corner of the label from his bottle. "In his heyday that name sent chills up and down most old lags' spines." He took another swig. "If he could see me now, eating fancy pizza and drinking beer out of a bottle."

"Pizza too fancy for him is it?"

"Too foreign, definitely."

"A traditional guy, huh?"

"In every sense of the word. Especially at work. Not always a good thing. He wouldn't hesitate beating a confession out of a suspect if he needed a swift conviction. They really were the bad old days."

Ingrid raised her eyebrows.

"Don't get me wrong, I know there are still problems that need sorting inside the Met, but we've made a hell of a lot of progress."

Ingrid hadn't envisaged talking about work quite so much on their first date, but given the surroundings, she didn't really see how they could avoid it. "The guy I'm working with on this case, Jack Gurley?" She turned and looked around the office, expecting to see Gurley standing over someone's desk, waiting to pounce on a confirmed sighting and leap into action, but couldn't spot him anywhere. "I get the impression he's beaten up plenty of prisoners in his time. Different rules in the armed forces, I guess."

"How long are you going to be working with him?"

Was that a fleeting flash of jealousy she detected in Ralph's expression?

"Until we locate the suspect. I guess it could be a while."

"Oh."

"It's OK—I know how to handle the Jack Gurleys of this world."

"I wasn't saying you didn't, I just—"

Ingrid grabbed his hand. He looked down at her hand covering his then looked up into her eyes. He opened his mouth to say something else and Ingrid shoved a corner of her pizza slice into it. She opened the other box and pulled out another slice. "You want some of this too?" she said, waving the triangle of dough laden with thick cheese and pancetta.

Ralph's nose twitched. "Not for me, thanks. Not a big fan of pork."

"You're not?"

"Been that way since I was a kid."

"Come on—not even crispy bacon?"

He shook his head firmly. Ingrid noticed he'd gone a little pale. "Not since half a rotting pig carcass was dumped on our doorstep when I was six years old," he said.

"Who would do a thing like that?"

"Dad never found out. He suspected it was someone he'd put away. Too many potential suspects there to actually pin it on someone." He shook his head. "My God, it was disgusting."

Ingrid looked down at the pizza slice. Ralph's story hadn't put her off one bit. She took a bite. "I was raised on the stuff," she said, in between chews. "My dad was a hog farmer."

"He's retired now?"

"He's dead."

"I'm sorry. What about your mum?"

"Oh she's very much alive—powered by vodka and nicotine."

"Are you close?"

"Not at all. I was a real daddy's girl. He was the kindest man you could ever meet."

"The complete opposite of mine then."

"Do you get along OK?"

"He's dead too."

"Sorry. How did the conversation get so morbid? Let's change the subject, shall we?" She raised her bottle, couldn't think of anything to toast, then took a sip. "Here's to good beer and fine dining."

Ralph raised his bottle too. "And beautiful company." When he realized what he'd just said, his cheeks bloomed crimson. He looked away.

Ingrid couldn't help but smile to herself. It wasn't much of a date, but she had the feeling they would manage to make the best of it.

Across the room someone hollered. Ingrid turned around to see a uniformed cop waving a piece of paper in her hand and running toward DS Tyson who was just coming through the door. Ingrid jumped up and zig-zagged between the tightly arranged desks.

"Cab driver, picked up a man and a boy this morning in Judd Street. Just a couple of hundred yards from the hotel. He said he didn't get a good look at the boy, but the man more or less fits Foster's description," the breathless PC said.

"And where did he drop them?" Tyson asked.

"The man told him to head north. Then asked him to stop just before they reached King's Cross Station."

Gurley appeared in the doorway. "We have a sighting?"

"It looks promising," Tyson told him. "I'll get on to Transport Police, they can check CCTV at the station." He looked at the PC. "What time was this?"

"Around nine a.m."

"We should get down there," Gurley said.

"That was over twelve hours ago." Ingrid shook her head. "He could be anywhere by now. But at least we know which direction Foster was headed. It's a damn sight more than we had five minutes ago."

"She's right," Tyson said. "Let's see what the CCTV comes up with before we go racing round. We can make a start on mapping his movements after he left the hotel."

Ingrid glanced over to the corner of the office. Ralph shrugged back at her and closed the lid of the pizza boxes.

11

The news conference had been arranged by the Metropolitan Police press office, with a lot of unhelpful interference from the embassy and the US Air Force. As Ingrid waited on the steps outside the conference hall just around the corner from New Scotland Yard, she let her mind wander to the end of her 'date' with Ralph Mills.

They had said their goodbyes at Holborn Tube station. Ingrid had explained she had a really early start and Ralph said he did too, even though, by the expression on his face, he looked a little crushed by her announcement. Just as she was about to turn away, Ralph pulled her toward him and planted a kiss on her lips. He tasted of oregano and beer. She felt a rush and flutter in the pit of her stomach, like some schoolgirl on a first date, not an until recently engaged-to-be-married thirty-one-year-old woman.

When they pulled apart again, he looked her square in the eye and for once, he wasn't blushing.

Every time she had remembered that kiss subsequently, Ingrid experienced the same flutter radiating out across her body. So what if it made her feel like a lovestruck teenager?

The sight of Jack Gurley ducking out of a taxi wrenched her from her romantic musings. She was relieved to see he was wearing civilian clothes: a pair of brown pants and a beige shirt with a button-down collar. He still looked like an off duty military cop, but at least it was better than the battledress of the previous day. He spotted her, nodded a restrained 'hello' and paid the cab driver.

They entered the building in silence and followed the last of the journalists and photographers into the main hall. There had been a couple more promising sightings the previous evening, one at the London Aquarium, the other near the London Eye—both locations close to one another on the south bank of the Thames—but as the day approached its end, the number of calls dwindled and eventually stopped. The hope was that a personal appeal by Carrie Foster herself would get more media coverage and in turn lead to a surge in reported sightings.

As the doors closed behind Ingrid and Gurley, Carrie Foster appeared at the other end of the hall, walking unsteadily along a low stage, assisted by a plain clothes female cop—the family liaison officer Ingrid had seen at the hospital. Foster looked more drawn, and much paler than she had the previous day. She was trembling as she placed her bottle of water on the long table. She sat down next to a gray-haired cop in his late fifties who was wearing full ceremonial dress uniform. The Metropolitan Police were obviously very keen to show the world just how seriously they were taking the situation. Next to the uniformed cop sat DCI Radcliffe, looking every bit as sleep-deprived as Foster.

The guy in uniform introduced himself as Assistant Deputy Commissioner Trevor Twyford, then went on to explain how Detective Chief Inspector Paul Radcliffe would be leading the investigation. Twyford outlined the details of the case, referring regularly to a stack of printed notes sitting on the table in front of him, reading from them as if he were discovering the information for the first time. When he was done he opened the floor for questions.

"I hope putting Carrie Foster through this ordeal pays off," Gurley whispered to Ingrid as a dozen arms went up at the front of the hall. "Look at her. She's close to collapse."

"I expect she's tougher than she looks." In Ingrid's limited experience, military wives had to be resilient in order to survive. "Besides, she knows this might really help locate Tommy."

"As long as this press conference doesn't just generate a shit storm of unverifiable sightings."

"Do you have a better strategy?"

"I have some ideas."

"However we may feel about the way the police are handling this, we have to play along. It's delicate politically—you heard what Sol Franklin said yesterday. We're guests in this country and right now one of our compatriots is wanted for attempted murder and abduction. I think, on the surface at least, we follow the Met's lead."

"On the surface? What's that supposed to mean?"

Before Ingrid had a chance to respond, a voice she recognized hollered a question from somewhere near the back of the hall. She might have known Angela Tate would turn up at such a high profile media conference. Ingrid desperately scanned the room to pinpoint the journalist's exact location, just so she could avoid her later, but she couldn't see her anywhere. When Tate didn't get a response from the Assistant Deputy Commissioner right away, she hollered her question again even louder.

"Is the man armed?" she yelled. "You just warned that the public should not approach him—does that mean he's carrying a weapon?"

"We very much doubt that's the case." DCI Radcliffe answered.

"Doubt? You don't know for sure?"

"Kyle Foster wouldn't have had an opportunity to obtain a firearm."

"But you don't know for sure?" she said again.

"Who is that lady?" Gurley asked, "and why the hell doesn't she just shut up and sit down?"

"She's an investigative reporter working for the Evening News—the main London newspaper. She has the ability of a bloodhound to sniff out a story and the tenacity of a Russell Terrier not to let go once she's found it."

"You know her?"

Tate had crossed her path more times than Ingrid would have liked. But she wasn't about to give Gurley a potted history. She raised a finger to her lips. A hush had descended on the room as, with trembling hands, Carrie Foster shuffled through a stack of paper in front of her. She cleared her throat.

"Jesus Christ." Gurley shook his head.

"Yesterday morning, Molly, my beautiful baby girl, almost died. Right now she's hooked up to a hundred and one machines that are helping to keep her alive. But at least I know she's safe. My boy, Tommy, is out there somewhere and he's in danger. I need everyone out there to help the police find him."

Mrs Foster was reading from a sheet in front of her. It seemed so emotive, Ingrid wondered if someone had written the statement for her. It was certainly having the desired effect on the cynical reporters present: they hadn't made a sound.

For the next five minutes, Carrie Foster explained, blow-by-blow, exactly what happened to her and her children the day before. It was the same account she'd given the detectives. Her voice cracked and quavered as she spoke, but she carried on, describing Kyle Foster's PTSD and making it plain just how unstable he had become in recent months.

"But he's still my husband," she said. "I didn't feel I could tell anyone that his condition was getting worse. I so deeply regret now that I didn't. Worst decision of my entire life. If I'd thought for a moment that... that..." Her final words got caught up in a sob. The bottle of water was shoved in front of her. She ignored it and stared directly toward the bank of television cameras. With tears streaming down her face, she said, "Please bring him back to me, Kyle. Please don't hurt my precious boy." Those were her final words before she started to sob uncontrollably.

The family liaison officer jumped up, helped Foster to her feet and led her out of the hall by a side exit.

"We need to get back to the hospital," Ingrid said. "I won't get the chance to speak to Carrie Foster here."

"Is that really necessary? Don't you think she's been through enough already this morning?"

"We still don't know how she got that bruise on her leg.

There's something she's not telling us about what Kyle did. Maybe she's protecting him somehow." Ingrid turned towards the exit, eager to make her escape before the few dozen journalists rose from their seats.

But she wasn't fast enough.

"Agent Skyberg!" Angela Tate hollered at her. "I was hoping to bump into you here." The journalist hurried towards them. "My God, you're big," she said to Gurley, uncharacteristically stating the obvious. "So, you're traveling with your own personal bodyguard now, are you, Ingrid?"

Gurley bristled, clearly offended.

"No?" Tate looked from Gurley to Ingrid.

"I'm working with Major Gurley on this case."

"Are you military police?" Tate asked.

"Security Forces, US Air Force, ma'am."

"For God's sake, don't 'ma'am' me! Please, call me Angela." She laid a hand on one of Gurley's forearms.

Was Tate flirting with him? For some reason, the thought appalled Ingrid so much she felt a little nauseous. She started to edge away.

"Would either of you like to give me a quote for the West End Final edition?"

Ingrid arched an eyebrow.

"Oh, please yourself. 'Sources close to the American embassy' it'll have to be then." With that she marched away. "Until next time, Ingrid," she shouted over her shoulder as she pushed through the door.

"Trouble, huh?" Gurley said.

"With a capital 'T'."

"Nothing you can't handle."

Ingrid didn't know quite how to respond. In the day or so that she'd known him, that had to be the nicest thing he'd said to her.

"Let's get to the hospital before Tate and the rest of the pack, shall we?" He strode to the door and held it open for her.

Ingrid led them down a side street she'd discovered cab drivers used as a short cut. As soon as they saw a taxi approaching, Gurley stepped into the road, waving and flapping his long arms. He had to have a wing span of close to seven feet. Not someone to be ignored. The cab screeched to a halt and they jumped in.

Just as they settled back into the seat, Ingrid's cell phone started to ring inside her purse. She yanked it out and peered at the screen and was relieved to discover it wasn't an international call. She answered and turned away from Gurley. "Jennifer, what do you have for me?"

There was silence at the other end as if the clerk were waiting for a formal greeting.

"Jennifer?"

"Hi."

"I'm in kind of a hurry here."

"Sure, sorry. The police have contacted me, they didn't want to disturb you in the middle of the press conference. But I thought you'd like to know right away."

"Yes?"

"There's been another sighting. As a result of Carrie Foster's appeal."

"Already?"

"I guess the story has really captured the public's imagination. I was watching it on the news. She looked so frail. I felt so sorry for—"

"This sighting, the police think it's genuine?"

"Seems that way. A woman working in a laundromat saw a man with a boy dressed in Spiderman pajamas. They were hovering around the driers for a little while, then the man opened one, grabbed some clothes and ran out."

"And the man and boy match Kyle and Tommy Foster's descriptions?"

"I think it was the pajamas that convinced the witness." She paused.

"I guess that's good news, isn't it?" Ingrid said. "Getting warmer clothes for the boy, means his dad is caring for him at least."

Jennifer swallowed noisily. "I wouldn't jump to that conclusion, I haven't told you everything yet."

"What is it?"

"The witness said she thought the boy might be injured."

"What?"

"She was pretty sure she saw blood on his face."

12

Ingrid relayed the details of the call to Gurley. "We should be out there looking for him," he said. "At least get to the laundromat and speak to the witness."

"Don't you see? Speaking to Carrie now is even more important. I want to find out if Tommy was hurt before he left the hotel room or after."

"What difference does it make?"

"If it's happened since it might mean Tommy's in more danger than we thought. It might change how we handle the case."

"As far as I'm concerned Foster's capable of anything. It must have happened after—Carrie Foster would have mentioned it otherwise."

"We speak to her first then work out our next move. Agreed?"

Gurley gave her a begrudging nod and didn't say another word all the way to the hospital.

When the elevator doors opened on the eleventh floor of UCH, Ingrid and Gurley stepped out into the lobby area to discover DCI Radcliffe speaking to a constable in uniform, a grave expression on his face. They waited until he was done before approaching.

"Chief inspector," Ingrid smiled as she strode toward him. "I'm a little surprised to see you here," she said.

"Why wouldn't I be here?" His tone was unmistakably defensive. He shoved his hands in his pockets and leaned toward her.

"I thought you would have handed over the day to day running to a deputy by now." In Ingrid's experience most of the investigative work was done by a team of detective constables led by a detective sergeant or inspector.

"Not this case. Too high profile."

Ingrid glanced behind her as the elevator doors opened again. "The press haven't arrived here yet?"

"I'm in the process of posting officers at the bottom of all the stairways and on each of the lifts on the ground floor, checking visitors' credentials. I'm not having those vultures roaming around, upsetting people."

"Good, you might want to look out for a woman in her fifties with frizzy hair wearing a raincoat and shiny knee-length boots."

"Tate's here?"

"You know her?"

"It's hard to avoid the woman."

Gurley cleared his throat noisily then made a point of looking at the oversized diver's watch on his wrist.

"We really need to speak to Mrs Foster again," Ingrid said.

"She's in with Molly. I don't want her disturbed."

"It wouldn't take longer than five minutes."

"I suppose you've heard about the sighting in the launderette yesterday?"

Ingrid nodded. "We'd like to speak to Carrie about Tommy's injury."

"So would we."

"You haven't yet?"

"She's only just back from the press conference, for God's sake. She needs time with her daughter."

"How is Molly?"

"No change. Which the doctors are taking as a good sign, apparently."

"We can wait to speak to her," Gurley said, much to Ingrid's surprise. "If Tommy sustained his injury after he left the hotel, it could mean Kyle Foster poses a greater threat than we thought."

"You think we haven't worked that out for ourselves?"

"So why wait to speak to her?" Ingrid asked.

Radcliffe bit his top lip as he considered Ingrid's question. "I'll get the FLO to bring Mrs Foster out in ten minutes. I'm not questioning her at Molly's sick bed.

Fifteen minutes later Radcliffe, Ingrid and Gurley were sitting in a cramped room tucked away at the end of a long corridor, opposite Carrie Foster who now looked so pale her skin appeared almost translucent.

"Thank you for speaking to us again, Mrs Foster," Radcliffe said. "I realize reliving your ordeal this morning in front of all those people had to be very hard for you." He leaned in a little closer to her. "Something new has come to light that I really need to speak to you about."

The woman searched the detective's face. "What?"

"Can you recall whether or not Tommy was struggling when Kyle grabbed him yesterday morning?"

Carrie Foster widened her bloodshot eyes. "Why? What's happened?" She held onto the sleeve of Radcliffe's jacket. "Have you found him?"

"Please, there's no need to be alarmed. We haven't located Tommy, not yet. But we have received some information from someone who believes they saw Tommy and your husband yesterday."

"Did he seem OK?"

"The eye witness said she saw blood on Tommy's face."

"Oh my God!" Mrs Foster raised a hand to her mouth. "How bad is it?"

"It really doesn't seem to be that serious. Please—I'm sure there's no need to worry yourself about it."

"How can you say that?" She jumped to her feet.

Ingrid stood too. "Please, Carrie. What you tell us now could really help us find Tommy faster. We all want that."

Mrs Foster's gaze dropped to the floor and she sank back onto her chair. "My poor baby."

"Can you remember if Tommy was hurt *before* he left the hotel room?" Ingrid asked her, keeping her voice quiet and gentle.

Foster continued to stare at the floor. She started to shake her head slowly. "I don't think so. Kyle just scooped him into his arms. Tommy didn't struggle. Why would he? He loves his daddy. I'm pretty sure he was OK. I would have noticed if he'd had blood on his face, I'm certain." She fell silent for a moment then stared up at Ingrid, a look of panic on her face. "Does that mean Kyle has hurt him since then? Is that what you're saying?"

"We don't know that for sure. Maybe he had an accident." Even as Ingrid said the words she realized just how unconvincing they must have sounded to the distraught mother sitting in front of her.

Tears were falling down Foster's face. "What happened? Kyle used to be so kind. I just can't believe what he did to Molly. He was a good man, you know? No one can change that much, can they?"

Ingrid felt Gurley tense slightly as he sat next to her.

"Thank you for your time, Mrs Foster." Radcliffe stood up. "It's been a great help." He waited for Ingrid and Gurley to get to their feet.

Ingrid hadn't had a chance to ask Carrie Foster about the bruise on her leg, but it didn't seem appropriate to bring it up now. She led the way into the corridor, relieved to get out of the airless room.

"After what he did, how can she even think he was a good man?" Gurley said when he'd closed the door behind them.

"It's complicated for her," Ingrid said. "She still remembers the man he was. Before the PTSD. I guess she doesn't want to admit she's married to some kind of monster." She started to head back down the corridor toward the elevators.

"You can find your own way out," Radcliffe said once they'd reached the set of doors leading into the ICU. He disappeared through the doors without waiting for a reply.

"We need to map out Kyle Foster's movements from the time he left the hotel, to see if we can predict where he'll head next." Gurley said.

"I'm sure the police are doing exactly that."

"You heard Radcliffe just now—he pretty much dismissed us.

We're meant to be providing our expertise. He doesn't seem that interested in what we might have to offer."

"You're right." Ingrid found herself reluctantly agreeing with Gurley. "We should get back to the embassy and try to convince Sol it's better for us to break free of the Met's investigation. We can be more effective working our own line of inquiry."

"Agreed. Right now I feel like the cops are tolerating us at best."

Welcome to my world.

As they approached the elevator, the doors opened and two uniformed policeman ran out. Ingrid and Gurley looked at one another for a moment, then hurried after the two men. They hung a left, toward the ICU.

The door leading into Molly Foster's room was wide open. There was no sign of the cop who should have been on duty outside.

The two cops ran into the room, with Ingrid and Gurley right behind them. A third cop was inside, anxiously watching the nurse Ingrid had seen the day before check the various machines Molly was hooked up to.

"Is she OK?" the cop asked.

"She's fine. Absolutely fine." The nurse had a worried look on her face.

"I thought he was a doctor. He was dressed in scrubs. He had a stethoscope around his neck."

"What happened?" Ingrid said.

All three cops now turned toward Ingrid and Gurley. "Who the hell are you?" one of them demanded.

Ingrid quickly retrieved her badge. "FBI, American embassy. We've just been interviewing Mrs Foster." She strode toward the bed. "What happened?" she asked the cop again, this time more firmly. She glanced quickly back at the door, wondering where the hell Radcliffe was.

"A man walked right up to the door. He had a hospital ID badge clipped to his pocket. I suppose I should have checked it more closely. I came into the room with him—it's protocol when the nurse isn't around. I was standing next to him the whole time." He lifted a hand to his face. He was trembling. "Have the exits been secured?" he asked the other cops.

One of them nodded. "We've got people at the front and rear. He won't get out of here."

Ingrid stared into the nervous cop's face. "What made you think he wasn't a doctor?"

"There was something about him. Most of the consultants I've seen in here are... you know, cocky. He seemed more unsure of himself. He grabbed the charts attached to the end of the bed, but it didn't look like he was actually reading them. He was too busy looking up at Molly, then at me."

"Who do you think he was?"

"I can't say. For a second I thought it might be her dad. But he didn't look like the photographs I've seen of him."

"Wait a minute," Gurley said. "Are you saying Kyle Foster was right here, in Molly's room?"

"I couldn't say. The man was dressed as a doctor."

"How long ago?"

"Five minutes."

"What did he do?"

"Nothing—he couldn't, could he? Not with me standing right next to him. Like I say, he just looked at her, then glanced at me. Then the nurse came in and he ran for it. It was only then that the penny finally dropped and I realized he wasn't one of the team."

"Why would Foster risk coming here?" Ingrid asked Gurley.

"To finish what he started." Gurley moved toward the door.

"Where are you going?"

"If they've got cops at the exits, I want to be there when they pick the son of a bitch up."

Ingrid ran after him. "You seriously believe Kyle Foster has so completely lost it he'd come into the hospital to try to murder his daughter?"

He paused at the door. "If he has lost it, one thing's certain."

Ingrid tensed, knowing what Gurley was likely to say next.

"We can assume Tommy is already dead."

13

"Wait up a second," Ingrid told Gurley.

Jack Gurley was already halfway through the door. He stopped. The two uniformed cops they'd followed into the room pushed past him and hurried away.

"You know for sure this guy wasn't part of the medical team?" Ingrid directed her question toward the concerned nurse, who was stroking Molly Foster's forehead.

"No one I've seen before in ICU."

"But we don't know for sure it was Kyle Foster. Did you get a good look at his face?"

"Not that good. If it was him, he didn't look like his photo, that's for sure."

"We've just come from the press conference," Ingrid said. "The place was full of unscrupulous reporters looking for a scoop. Any one of them might stoop so low they wouldn't think twice about impersonating a doctor." Ingrid thought it was amazing Angela Tate hadn't already tried something along the same lines. "Describe the man to me."

"About five foot nine or ten, slim build, mid to late thirties," the cop said.

"Did he say anything to you?"

"No, I don't think so."

"You're sure?"

"Erm..." The cop paused, his face had taken on a sudden panicked expression.

A moment later Ingrid discovered why.

DCI Radcliffe was standing in the doorway. "For God's sake, Barlow—he was right here and you let him get away?" Radcliffe didn't bother to even acknowledge Ingrid and Gurley's presence. "Well?"

"That's what we're currently trying to establish," Ingrid said, getting a little frustrated she couldn't get a straight answer from the cop.

"And what the bloody hell is that supposed to mean?"

"Can you please keep your voice down or leave the room?" the nurse said.

"Barlow, come with me."

The hapless cop followed Radcliffe outside. As did Ingrid and Gurley.

"Did the man speak to you?" Ingrid said again.

"He might have said 'good morning'."

"So did he have an accent?"

"Not really."

"So he sounded English?"

"Yes, I suppose he did." He glanced at his superior officer. "The more I think about it... I'd say it was definitely an English accent."

"Just now you weren't even sure whether he'd spoken to you or not, for Christ's sake," Radcliffe said, not bothering to disguise his contempt.

"I've had a moment to think. It was an English accent, sir."

"So it might not have been Foster?" Ingrid asked.

Gurley pulled a folded sheet from the back pocket of his pants. He smoothed out the paper and showed the cop a full color, full length photograph of Kyle Foster dressed in camouflage pants and a light gray tee shirt. The cop turned his head this way and that as he stared at the picture.

"The man I saw had darker hair."

"For God's sake, could it be him?" Radcliffe said.

The nurse came to the door and glared at them. "How do you expect this little girl to recover with all this shouting?"

Gurley showed her the photo too. "Is this the man you saw?"

She stared at the picture for a few moments then said, "I barely got a glimpse of him. The general outline is right, but the man I saw was paler."

"I've got officers stopping people from leaving the building and you're saying it might not even have been Foster?" Radcliffe shook his head. "Un-bloody-believable."

"You got that right." Gurley folded the sheet and returned it to his pocket. "You should still have your officers check any thirty-something males, under six-foot tall, around one hundred sixty pounds, who try to leave the hospital."

"Thank you so much for telling me how to do my job. I would have been quite clueless without your invaluable input."

Ingrid's phone started to chirrup quietly in her purse. She hurried down the corridor before retrieving it. "Sol, if you're calling for an update, we're on our way back to the embassy now."

"No you're not."

"We're not?"

"Another confirmed sighting has just been reported. St Thomas' Hospital. Emergency room. I'll text the address just as soon as I hang up. I want you to speak to the staff there, get some kind of idea of Foster's state of mind."

"Won't the police be doing that anyway? The way things are between us and the cops at the moment, I don't want to tread on anyone's toes."

"Are they giving you a hard time?"

"I've had better."

"Then this break might be just what you need. The doctor who called it in couldn't get through to the incident line at the station house. Luckily for us he's a US citizen, so rather than just giving up and trying again later, he called the embassy. Jennifer spoke to him just a little while ago."

Ingrid hurried back to Gurley as her phone beeped with a

new text message. She grabbed his arm. "We have to leave. Right now. I'll explain on the way."

———

———

———

One of the receptionists on the front desk of the Accident and Emergency Department led Ingrid and Gurley to a small room to one side of the main waiting area. This hospital seemed a lot older than the one they were just at. The walls were scuffed at the bottom and paint was flaking off some of the windows.

But the smell was just the same.

Three chairs were arranged around a desk on one side of the room. On the other side was an examining table covered in a long strip of blue paper towel, ready for the next patient. At one end of the table was a lamp attached to the wall on an extending arm. Next to that was a large round magnifying glass. Ingrid saw Gurley looking at the equipment and thought she heard him gulp.

"I hate these places," he said.

The door opened and a young bearded man came in and introduced himself as Dr Daniel Obermast. "I hope I did the right thing calling the embassy." He sat in the chair immediately in front of the desk and gestured for them to take a seat.

"Completely," Ingrid reassured him.

Ingrid sat down but Gurley seemed reluctant to. Maybe he wanted to ensure he could make a fast getaway. He leaned up against a wall.

"You saw the man we want to question with his son?" Ingrid kicked off the interview. There was no point in wasting time on social niceties.

"I did. I'm certain it was him."

"When was this?"

"Yesterday morning. Eleven-fifteen."

"And you treated the boy?"

"I cleaned up his nose a little better than his dad had managed to and put two stitches into the poor little guy's bottom lip."

"Did his dad tell you how he sustained those injuries?"

"Skateboarding."

"You had no reason to doubt that?"

"Not at all. I see so many cases each week. Badly scraped elbows and knees. Dislocated shoulders. And that's just the adults!"

"Any other treatment?"

"I gave him a tetanus shot, as a precaution. Standard procedure."

"And apart from his injuries, how did the boy seem to you?"

"Fine. I guess."

"He didn't seem scared at all? Coerced in any way? He was happy being with his dad?"

The doctor raked his fingernails through his beard and thought for a moment. "There was nothing obvious in his behavior to suggest he was here under duress."

"Could he have been drugged?" Gurley asked.

"Drugged? No way. He was a little tired, I guess."

Gurley pushed himself from the wall and paced across the room. The doctor twisted in his chair to look at him as Gurley then leaned against the other wall.

"Is everything OK? Have I done something wrong?"

"Not at all." Ingrid glanced at Gurley, who had an unmistakable scowl on is face. "What about his dad? How did he seem?"

"Stressed, I guess." The doctor turned back to face Ingrid. "Worried about his son. He said he'd managed to stop his son's nose bleed, but the lip just wouldn't quit. He seemed sorry he hadn't brought him in sooner."

"So he was nervous? Maybe a little jumpy?" Gurley said.

"Yes, but I assumed that was because he was worried about his son." Obermast bent his head closer to Ingrid, almost conspiratorially. "Which is why I doubted myself when I saw the report on the news this morning. I don't normally watch TV, but there's a big screen in the waiting area. It's there to keep the patients occupied. Sometimes they have to wait quite a long time before they get treated," he explained.

"You doubted yourself?"

"The picture they showed on the news only looked a little like the guy I saw. So I talked to Margaret, on reception? She was pretty certain it was the same person. So I called. It was the presence of the boy that convinced me."

Something about the doctor's account didn't feel right to Ingrid. Why would Foster risk taking Tommy to a hospital? He must have known Carrie would get the police involved. He had to have realized by then he was a wanted man. "You said he seemed concerned," Ingrid said.

The doctor nodded.

"In your medical opinion, do you think he could have been suffering from the effects of post traumatic stress disorder?"

"I'm not expert in the field, I can't really say..."

"How about you give us your best professional guess?" Gurley said.

"Well, if you're forcing me to make an assessment..." He glanced at Gurley uncertainly.

"Please—if you wouldn't mind." Ingrid wished Gurley would wipe the frown off his face and sit down. He was clearly spooking their witness.

"If you'd asked me that yesterday, I would have said he just seemed like an anxious parent, worried about his son. Without hesitation."

"But now?"

"Now I know what the man is capable of, it puts his behavior in a whole different light. Maybe he was worried about getting caught. Maybe that's why he seemed so twitchy."

Gurley pushed himself from the wall and stepped toward the doctor, his eyes narrowing. But before he could say anything, there was a loud knock on the door.

"Come in," Obermast said quickly, clearly relieved the interruption had stopped Gurley in his tracks.

The door opened and a nurse dressed in an old-fashioned

pinafore dress hovered in the doorway. "So sorry, Daniel, I really didn't want to disturb you, but things are getting a little hectic out there." She threw an apologetic smile in Gurley's direction. "We really need you back on duty."

"I have to go. Was there anything else?"

"Do you think the boy is in danger?" Gurley asked.

The doctor nodded regretfully. "I just wish I'd known about the situation at the time. No way would I have let him take that child anywhere."

14

On their way back to the embassy, Ingrid called Radcliffe to let him know what Obermast had told them. She had to hold her cell away from her ear during his rant about agreed protocol being 'willfully ignored' and how she should understand it was imperative his team were kept in the loop at all times. "It's not your bollocks on the chopping board, Agent Skyberg."

"We do all want the same thing here."

"Really? You're not more interested in point scoring?"

Ingrid decided it was time to do a little ranting herself. "If you think for one second that anyone is treating this as some sort of competition, then you are sorely mistaken. Feel free to make an official complaint about my conduct with the embassy."

Gurley raised his eyebrows and gave her a silent round of applause.

"Dr Obermast and the other clinic staff are ready to speak to your officers, just as soon as they arrive." A moment after she ended the call her phone rang. She glanced at the screen. It was Angela Tate, the demon journalist of Blackfriars Road. Ingrid dismissed the call.

When they got back to the office they found Jennifer standing behind her desk as if she'd been waiting for them to arrive. "I thought we could go through Kyle Foster's last known movements," she said, and pointed to a pile of rolled paper tubes. "I got hold of Ordinance Survey maps of the Greater London area all the way to the M25," she explained. "Plus satellite images of the same region in various resolutions."

"Paper maps?"

"It's quicker than setting up a projector and booking a conference room. Sol requested we go low-tech—he likes maps he can draw all over."

"Where is Sol?"

"He said he'll be here soon."

"We're assuming Foster's still in the area?" Gurley asked.

"We have to start somewhere," Jennifer said.

Gurley started to unfold the maps, while Jennifer unrolled the satellite images.

Once the first map had been smoothed flat on one of the unoccupied desks, Jennifer stuck bright yellow stars onto the few positive sighting locations: the laundromat in King's Cross, the London Aquarium and London Eye on the South Bank and St Thomas' Hospital, less than half a mile away.

"Should I add one to University College Hospital?" She looked from Gurley to Ingrid.

"Radcliffe's team will check the CCTV footage from inside the building and the surrounding streets," Ingrid said. "It's possible we'll never know whether or not it was Kyle Foster in Molly's room."

"So what do we have?" Gurley asked, walking around the desk, staring at the map.

"After they left the hotel, Kyle and Tommy Foster walked just around the corner to Judd Street and hailed a cab heading north but got out after a few blocks at King's Cross," Jennifer said. "Then they went into the laundromat."

"Then there's quite a gap between the laundromat and the next sighting," Ingrid said. "It's what... maybe three miles between King's Cross and the South Bank?"

The clerk nodded. "A little less, maybe."

"And we don't know how they traveled there. On foot, public transport..."

"He wouldn't risk that, not with Tommy's lip bleeding. Safer to get another cab," Jennifer said.

"But we don't have another sighting from a taxi driver." Gurley had started pacing up and down.

"After the aquarium, Foster took Tommy to the hospital, so we have to assume his injury was getting worse by then. And Tommy must have sustained the injury some time between leaving the hotel and arriving at the laundromat."

Gurley stopped suddenly. "What the hell happened to him?"

"Maybe Foster got angry and lashed out?" Jennifer said.

"Or maybe Tommy had an accident," Ingrid suggested, not wanting to dwell on the worst case scenario. "And there haven't been any reliable sightings after Tommy got his lip stitched up at the hospital?"

"None yet," Jennifer said.

"Unless it *was* Foster in Molly's room earlier." Gurley started pacing again. He interlaced his long fingers on the top of his head, flattening the blond buzz cut and somehow making himself look ten years younger.

"It couldn't have been Foster at the hospital," the clerk said, still staring blank-eyed at the map. "That man was alone. If it were Foster, where was Tommy all the time he was there?" Jennifer looked up at Ingrid expectantly, as if she might actually be able to answer that question.

"I guess there are three possible explanations," Ingrid said, "Kyle is alive and Tommy's dead..." She sensed Jennifer stiffen. "...They're both alive and Kyle's found some place safe to stash Tommy..."

Jennifer exhaled.

"Or they're both dead," Gurley said, helpfully providing scenario number three.

Jennifer swallowed hard. "I really don't want to believe that."

"I know this is difficult. Anything involving kids always is." Ingrid had had more than enough experience in her years at the VCAC. "We need you to hang in there."

"I'm sorry, it's just that my baby brother is only ten years old," Jennifer said, her voice shaky. "Mom calls him her little miracle." She sniffed. "Dad calls him his gigantic mistake—but I know he's only kidding. If anything happened to him I don't know what I'd do. Carrie Foster must be going through hell." She sniffed, her eyes had started watering.

"Hey, Jennifer, we're relying on you to be strong for us," Gurley said. "The best way you can help Tommy is by being right where you are and working your butt off." He pulled a folded handkerchief from the back pocket of his pants and handed it to her. "Can you do that for us?"

Jennifer dabbed her nose and nodded rapidly. "Of course I can."

Ingrid caught Gurley's eye and mouthed 'thank you' at him. Maybe the gruff MP wasn't quite as insensitive as she'd thought. "OK," she said, and clapped her hands together. "Let's assume for the sake of argument that both father and son are still alive. If that's the case, Kyle would need to find some place safe for Tommy. So maybe he's taken a cheap rental somewhere, or a room in a budget hotel. Somewhere he could pay with cash without raising suspicion." She turned back to Jennifer. "Do we know how much cash he has on him?"

"Whatever he had in his wallet plus £500 he withdrew from the ATM at Barclays Bank on Russell Square, near the hotel."

"No other traceable activity?"

"No cell phone use, no credit cards. His bank account has now been frozen."

Ingrid looked at another map showing London and its surrounding counties. "Can we even assume he'd stay in the capital? Surely there's too much police activity for him not to leave? Is he familiar with any other location in the UK?"

"As far as we know, he's never been out of Suffolk before," Gurley said. "The only area of the country he really knows is within a forty mile radius of the base."

"I thought we might be needing this." Jennifer unfolded another unwieldy map. This one displayed the whole of England and Wales.

Ingrid studied the distance between central London and mid

Suffolk, the location of RAF Freckenham. She was so used to checking dinky little local maps on her GPS app, it was good to get a sense of perspective and distance. Judging by the scale, the Air Force base was around fifty miles from London as the crow flies, which didn't really help any, so Ingrid tapped the details into her trusty app to get the distance by road: seventy-two miles. "That's an awful long way to travel undetected with a small boy when the whole nation is looking for you."

"It would be plain dumb for him to return to the base. What possible reason could he have?" Gurley sucked his teeth.

"A network of people he can trust?" Ingrid suggested.

"Not after what he did," Gurley said.

"I expect Radcliffe has asked the Suffolk cops to watch the train and bus stations close to the base, but it's worth checking, I guess."

"I'll get onto it," Jennifer said.

Gurley returned to studying the map of England and Wales. "If he is on his own..." He lowered his voice. "And if he's gone to ground, living off the land, we might not get any more sightings. We'll just have to track him the old fashioned way."

"Which way is that?"

"Weighing up all the possibilities, trusting your gut, and hoping like hell it doesn't let you down."

"And what's your gut telling you right now?"

"He's going to return to what he knows."

"The base?"

"Not necessarily, but some place related."

Ingrid stared into Gurley's piercing blue eyes. He obviously had a theory. Why didn't he just come right out and tell her? She thought about it for a moment. If Foster returned to what he knew, what was it he knew better than anything else? "Airplanes," Ingrid said, after a beat.

A corner of Gurley's mouth curled into something close to a smile.

"Jennifer, we need a list of all the small airstrips within a..." Ingrid paused, looking at Gurley, "sixty mile radius of London."

"You can't visit every one of them," the clerk said.

"We don't intend to. You're going to call them for us," Gurley smiled at her. "Find out if they've seen anyone hanging around acting suspicious in the past twenty-four hours. If maybe any of their aircraft have been tampered with."

"So I should start from the center and work outwards?"

"See," Gurley said. "I said we couldn't do this without you."

Jennifer beamed up at him then set to work.

Gurley strode to the door.

"You're not staying?" Jennifer's disappointment was obvious.

"I need to get a tracker survival pack together. Want me to get one for you too?" he asked Ingrid.

"This isn't the wilds of Wyoming. You can't go too far in this country without passing a McDonald's or a Domino's Pizza."

"Please yourself. Don't come running to me when you don't have a ground sheet or a bed roll."

"You're suggesting we track him on foot, like stalking a deer or something?"

"It might come to that. Nothing wrong with being prepared." He set off down the corridor for a few steps then hurried back again. "Jennifer? Where should I head for a camping supply store in this city?"

Jennifer frowned at him. "Try Selfridges—on Oxford Street. They sell pretty much everything."

"Is that on the Tube?"

Ingrid found the location quickly on her GPS app. She showed Gurley. "It's just a few blocks away." He stared at the route for a few seconds, nodded his thanks, then disappeared back out the door.

"What do you make of him?" Jennifer whispered, staring at the vacant doorway.

"I really don't know." It was true. Ingrid had assumed he was an unfeeling, tough, arrogant son of a bitch. But he'd shown a different side with Jennifer just now. Maybe she needed to keep an open mind.

Jennifer returned to her mammoth task and Ingrid sat at her desk, hating the fact that all she could do right now was wait for information. From Jennifer's inquiries… from the police… She blinked. There was some other information that she'd already waited far too long for. She shoved her purse over her shoulder, pulled her jacket from the back of her chair and told Jennifer she was going for a walk to clear her head.

15

As Ingrid waited for Mike Stiller at FBI HQ to pick up, she soon discovered she was headed not to the main entrance of the embassy as she'd previously intended, but downstairs toward the underground parking lot. Somehow, on autopilot, her brain had found something useful for her to do while she waited for more news. The call to Mike diverted to his voicemail and she left a terse message.

She was climbing off her Triumph Tiger 800 outside the Fosters' hotel off Russell Square less than fifteen minutes later. She swapped her motorcycle helmet for her purse and locked the box on the back of the bike. Her cell started ringing as she ran up the front steps to the entrance. The call displayed on the screen was an out of area number. An international call. She hoped it was Mike Stiller calling back and not Svetlana on a mission to guilt trip her.

She answered and waited.

"Ingrid? Are you there?" Mike sounded tetchy.

"Did you find anything for me?"

"Not much. I was going to call when I had more information. They found three women in the property, two in their twenties, the third they're guessing is in her thirties."

"Guessing? They don't know?"

"If you let me explain all will become clear. Clearer, at least."

He took a deep breath. "So, two women have identified themselves. At present those IDs are being verified. They're not from Minnesota, it's taking a while to track down their next of kin."

"What about the third woman?"

"I'm just coming to that."

Ingrid skipped back down the steps and started to pace up and down the sidewalk.

"The third woman hasn't said a word. She looks older than the other two, and has been there the longest. Neither of the other two women knows anything about her."

"I need to get pictures of the third woman sent to someone in my home town—a lady called Kathleen Avery. She'd recognize Megan in a heartbeat."

"You know the drill. It doesn't work like that. Maybe the local feds can arrange for this Avery lady to visit the medical center the victims are staying at."

"That's not possible. Kathleen Avery hasn't left her house since 1999."

"What is she, sick or something?"

"It's complicated. Ever since Megan disappeared her mother has suffered from agoraphobia. Plus she's morbidly obese. She has serious mobility issues. For her, leaving home just isn't an option."

"Jeez. I don't know what else to suggest."

"There must be something the Bureau can do. What about a DNA test? They could take a sample from Kathleen, compare them with this woman's." Ingrid knew that eighteen years ago, taking DNA samples hadn't been part of regular police procedure in a missing person case. If it had been, making a match now would have been straightforward.

"I'll make some calls."

"And what about the interviews? Can you get me the video recordings?"

"I'm still working on that. It may take a while."

"Can you at least send me a photograph of the mute woman?"

"Sure. I'm attaching it to an email as we speak. But this is for your eyes only—at this stage I can't have you distributing it to anybody else. Is that clear? I shouldn't even be sending it to you."

Ingrid's breath caught in her throat. She wasn't sure she'd recognize Megan after so many years. "Mike?"

"You get it yet?"

"I'm not at my computer—it'll come through on my phone—I'll look at it later. The woman who's not speaking. Is she… heavy?"

"You mean like, morbidly obese?"

"Just heavy?"

"No. All three women were fed strict rations in captivity. Their abductor had specific tastes when it came to body shape and size. They're all pretty skinny."

"Thanks, Mike. You will keep me posted, won't you?"

"Sure—don't I always keep my word?"

"Eventually."

"Harsh! Why do I continue to come to your rescue? You cruel woman."

She appreciated Mike trying to lighten the mood, but she couldn't manage an appropriate retort before she hung up.

As she navigated to the email app on her phone, her mouth became very dry. She found a half bottle of Evian in her purse and finished it. She stared at her phone, paralyzed with dread.

She couldn't bring herself to look at the attachment. She wasn't ready. Not yet. Not to see Megan's face staring back at her after all these years. Instead, she hurried into the hotel.

DS Tyson was inside, chatting to the receptionist. Beyond him Ingrid saw several tables in the lounge-cum-bar area occupied by plain clothes cops interviewing a handful of guests.

Ingrid waited until the receptionist had to answer the phone before she approached Tyson. "Hey, detective, how's it going?"

Tyson spun around and took a moment to respond.

"Agent Skyberg. From the US embassy?" Ingrid prompted.

"Oh I hadn't forgotten you, believe me." He peered toward the hotel entrance. "Where's Lurch?"

"If you mean Major Gurley, he had business elsewhere."

"What can I do for you?"

"Have your CSEs finished up?"

He nodded. "Just this morning. Hotel room door has been secured."

"Made any new discoveries since yesterday afternoon?"

"You will be sent the forensics report when it's ready, you know."

"I can't wait that long."

The receptionist finished her call and Tyson led Ingrid away from the desk, past the groups of guests and cops and through to the empty dining room. He pulled out a couple of chairs and waited for Ingrid to take a seat.

"I thought you interviewed the guests yesterday," Ingrid said and pointed toward the lounge.

"This is the mop-up operation. Mainly the people who weren't around during the first round." He looked at her expectantly.

"The forensics?" Ingrid reminded him.

"You know about the blood in the bathroom?"

Ingrid sat up straighter. "What?"

"Across the tiles above the sink. It was only a trace—someone had obviously tried to clean up. But they didn't manage to get it all."

"Has anyone questioned Carrie Foster about it?"

"Last time I heard, she'd been sedated."

"Sedated?"

"She got wind of the impostor—whoever he was—getting into her daughter's hospital room. She became hysterical, apparently. Can't blame her. What if it was her old man come to finish poor little Molly off? Makes my skin crawl."

"How is Molly?"

"She still hasn't regained consciousness. But the doctors are hopeful."

Ingrid didn't know what a prolonged period of unconsciousness meant in terms of the child's recovery. She decided not to dwell on the subject. "Did the CSEs find anything else?"

"Nope. It's possible the trace of blood belonged to a previous guest—it all depends how well the staff clean the rooms, I suppose."

Ingrid looked through the doorway into the lounge area. Most of the guests had completed their interviews and were starting to leave. Except for one. A purple haired senior was leaning forward in her chair. She'd grabbed the detective's arm sitting opposite her and was squeezing it hard.

"She seems to have something to say for herself."

Tyson followed her gaze. "We haven't gleaned much so far from the other guests. No one seems to have spoken to the Fosters. I think people prefer to keep themselves to themselves in such an intimate sized establishment."

Ingrid rose from her seat. "Let me know if this latest round of questioning uncovers any interesting information." She pulled a business card from her purse and handed it to him.

"Sure, why not? It's not as if I'm busy."

"I really would appreciate it."

He gave her a begrudging smile.

As Ingrid walked toward the dining room exit, the purple haired woman looked up at her. "Good afternoon, ma'am," Ingrid said when she drew level.

"You're American."

"Yes, ma'am. From the US embassy." She extended her hand. "Agent Skyberg."

"Agent? That sounds official. Maybe you want to hear about what I saw yesterday. I'm not sure this young man is taking me at all seriously. It's my age, I expect." From the definite twang in the woman's accent, Ingrid supposed she came from one of the Carolinas.

The woman struggled to her feet, grabbed Ingrid's arm and led her away to another table. She sat down and encouraged Ingrid to do the same. "My name's Merle Simmons."

Tyson walked past their table and pulled a face at Ingrid behind the old woman's back. She ignored him.

"I saw him, you know!" The woman's voice came out in an excited whisper. "He was as close to me as you are now."

"Do you mean Mr Foster?"

"Of course I do!"

"When was this?"

"Yesterday morning. I was on my way down to the dining room. It was clear he'd been too mean to pay the extra supplement."

"I'm sorry?"

"For breakfast. He was carrying a large McDonald's bag. Bringing back food for his whole family, I suppose."

"What time was this?"

"Eight forty-five."

"You're sure?"

"Jim, my husband, and I go down to breakfast the same time every morning."

"I mean you're sure about the McDonald's bag?"

"Why wouldn't I be? Quite unapologetic about it too. He smiled right at me."

"Perhaps I could speak to your husband, confirm the details with him?"

"You don't need to do that, I'm quite in control of my faculties. Besides, Jim's having his nap."

"You didn't see Mrs Foster or the children?"

"Not until we all watched the ambulance people take that poor little baby away." She looked down at Ingrid's hands. "Shouldn't you be making notes? The policeman had a notebook, but once I'd told him what I'd seen, he didn't seem to want to write anything down."

"I have perfect recall." Ingrid smiled and started to get up.

"Is that it?"

"Did you see anything else of the family yesterday morning?"

"Only what I've told you already."

"Then I think we're done—thank you so much for your time."

"What's happening with the little boy? Have you found him yet?"

"Not yet, ma'am, but I'm sure we will real soon." Ingrid wished she could believe that herself.

She left the woman sitting in the lounge and went looking for Tyson. Why would a man who fled his hotel room in a panic, after shaking his baby senseless, return via the nearest McDonald's? It didn't make any sense. She was inclined to believe the old woman had been mistaken.

She found Tyson speaking to the receptionist again.

"You managed to escape her clutches, then?" he said, smirking slightly.

"A quick question. Did the CSIs find any evidence of a—"

"McDonald's bag?"

"Yes—how did you know I was going to say—"

"I've just spoken to the DC who interviewed the batty old cow. No they bloody well didn't find a McDonald's bag. That old lady's got a screw loose."

16

Natasha McKittrick grabbed the last corn chip from her plate as Ingrid started to clear away the dishes. "Any more of that margarita in the fridge?"

"You just drank the last of it."

"Time to break this open then." McKittrick waved the bottle of tequila she'd brought to Ingrid's for their now regular monthly Tex-Mex night. "I can't believe it's this late and you still haven't given me what I came here for."

Ingrid hurried into the kitchen with the dirty dishes to avoid what she knew was coming next. She probably should have canceled dinner with her friend, but after the frustrating afternoon she'd had—they still hadn't come up with a fresh lead by the time she'd left the embassy after nine p.m.—she felt a real need to vent. Now McKittrick was trying to change the subject, Ingrid wished she'd canceled after all.

"You can't escape that easily," McKittrick shouted from the living room. "I mean, fascinating as your new case is—and you must admit, I have been listening patiently—I would like to move on to the main feature."

Ingrid opened the freezer section of the refrigerator and luxuriated in the cool air for a moment.

"You can run but you can't hide." McKittrick appeared at the kitchen door, waving the still unopened bottle of tequila in her fist. "I need shot glasses."

"Maybe you should take it home with you."

"Not until you tell me how your date with Mills went."

"Coffee? Tea?"

"Come on. Spill."

"There's nothing to tell."

"Well he seemed pretty pleased with himself at work this morning, so there must be something."

Ingrid opened a cabinet and retrieved two mugs. "I can't imagine why. We had a bite to eat then said goodbye at Holborn Tube."

"He didn't come back here afterwards?"

"No he didn't. Not that it's any of your business." Ingrid filled the kettle and flipped on the switch.

"I didn't actually think you were serious about the tea." McKittrick slid the unopened tequila bottle onto the kitchen counter. "What's the point of being a matchmaker if I can't even get to enjoy a bit of gossip now and then?"

"Sorry to disappoint you."

Ingrid's cell phone started to vibrate against the kitchen counter. She glanced at the screen, saw it was an out of area number and dismissed the call.

"That's not Mills, is it?"

"Why do you care so much?"

"I've got to work with the grumpy old bugger. Do you know how miserable he's been the last couple of months? When you agreed to go out with him he was like a changed man. Suddenly he was the most attentive detective on the team. Nothing was too much trouble."

"So glad to have helped with morale." Ingrid shoved the phone in a pocket.

"Was it Mills?"

"It was my mom."

"I thought the two of you didn't speak."

The kettle boiled and Ingrid made them both a peppermint tea. "We don't. Only in… special circumstances." She dunked the teabag slowly in and out of the tall mug, staring at the ripples she was creating on the surface of the water. A sudden, overwhelming need to talk about what was going on back home overcame her. "Have you seen the news reports about the three women who were being held captive in Minnesota?" she blurted.

"That's one way of changing the subject."

"I'm serious."

"I'm vaguely aware of it. I try to avoid the news whenever I can. I see enough stuff to depress me at work, without exposing myself to it when I'm off the job."

"The house where they were being held is just thirty miles from my home town. That's why my mom keeps calling me."

"Oh my God—you think one of those women is your school friend?"

Ingrid had told McKittrick about what happened to Megan on one of their drunken nights out, but only given her the sketchiest of details. Now she was regretting bringing the subject up. If she continued, she may never get to sleep tonight. "That's what I'm trying to find out."

"How are you coping?"

"Mostly by trying not to think about it. But the memories keep worming their way into my head, no matter how hard I try to shut them out. Certain sounds and smells take me right back to the moment she was taken and there's absolutely nothing I can do about it."

"Like your runaway pilot." McKittrick peered into her mug at the darkening liquid. She shoved it across the kitchen counter.

"Pilot?"

"Sounds like you're telling me you're suffering from PTSD yourself."

"It really doesn't compare to Foster's. According to his wife, any loud noise can trigger a reaction in him."

"You mean like the crying of his own child?"

"I know—it's tragic." Ingrid took a sip of her tea, decided it wasn't at all what she wanted, and threw the reminder into the sink. She opened another kitchen cabinet and retrieved a couple of shot glasses.

McKittrick grabbed the bottle from the counter and opened it. She poured out two measures. They both downed them in one and she refilled the glasses.

"That's the thing that's been troubling me about his meltdown," Ingrid said.

McKittrick gulped down her second shot.

"Kyle Foster developed his PTSD long after his return from Afghanistan. He was flying search and rescue missions there. His symptoms didn't show until after he started operating drones."

"So?"

"So you'd think his triggers wouldn't be loud noises. It's got to be pretty quiet in some isolated room in the middle of the Air Force base."

"I don't think you can say that. The mind's weird—maybe the drone missions reminded him of his earlier ones in the field and everything's got mixed up in his head. Who knows?"

"Still doesn't seem to fit." Ingrid removed her phone from her pocket and started turning it over and over in her hand, waiting for Svetlana to call again. She couldn't put off speaking to her forever.

"Maybe you should call her back." McKittrick refilled her own glass.

Ingrid put the phone on the counter.

"It was just a suggestion."

"There's something else. On my cell phone. I've been avoiding it since this afternoon. But I need to check it out before I talk to Svetlana."

"Do you have any idea how little sense your making?"

Ingrid took a deep breath and started again. "When I found out about the house in Minnesota, I put in a call to a contact I still have in D.C. This afternoon he sent me a photograph of one of the women. The only one who hasn't been identified."

"Are you telling me you haven't looked at it yet?" McKittrick shoved Ingrid's glass at her.

"What if it's Megan?" Much to her surprise, Ingrid's voice came out in a whisper. "What if it isn't?"

"You have to find out. God, Ingrid, you just have to." McKittrick snatched up the cell phone before Ingrid had a chance to. "Where is it? In your picture roll? Email?"

Ingrid plucked the phone out of her friend's hand. "You don't need to bully me into it." Holding her breath, she scrolled through to Mike Stiller's email and clicked on the attachment. She closed her eyes. She could hear McKittrick's breath quickening beside her. She opened her eyes and stared down at the image. All she saw was a jumble of random features—somehow the picture wouldn't resolve into a face. It seemed her brain was refusing to analyze the information it was receiving.

"Well?"

Ingrid blinked hard, as if she had grit in her eyes. She continued to look without being able to see. She stared at the image a little longer. Finally the random parts settled into a whole. The woman looking back up at her had drawn features, her face framed by lank, dark hair, her eyes lifeless with dark circles underneath. Ingrid shook her head. "I don't know. It's been so long."

McKittrick shuffled closer to her and peered at the image.

"Eighteen years since she was abducted. At least a decade since I last saw a photograph of her." She shoved the phone back into her pocket. "I can't tell. Jesus Christ, I can't even tell." Hot, unwanted tears sprang into her eyes. She turned away. She didn't want to cry in front of McKittrick.

"Bloody hell, it's hardly surprising. God only knows what that woman's been through over the past however many years. She probably looks completely different to the way she looked five years ago, even." She put an awkward arm around Ingrid's shoulders and squeezed. "You've got nothing to beat yourself up about."

If only you knew.

Ingrid emptied her glass and screwed the lid back on the bottle. "You want to take this with you?"

"Let's save it till next time. I might drink it on the way home otherwise."

McKittrick left a quarter hour later and Ingrid felt so restless she considered following her out the door—walking the dark summer streets for a while until she felt able to calm down. Instead she stepped out onto her roof terrace and drew the night air deep into her lungs. After three or four big breaths she pulled her cell from her pocket and called Svetlana.

"So, at least you listened to my message," her mother said in place of a greeting.

Ingrid hadn't. She didn't even realize her mother had left one.

"What have you found out that we don't already know from the TV?"

Ingrid relayed most of what Mike Stiller had told her. She didn't mention the photograph.

"This girl must come see Kathleen."

"That's not possible."

"Then I should go see her."

Ingrid was regretting telling Svetlana as much as she had. "Please, Mom. You have to trust that I know what I'm doing with this. I'm working on something that's going to help. I'll let you know just as soon as I make some progress."

"What? What are you working on? What aren't you telling me?"

"I've told you as much as I can. More than I should have. You have to promise me you'll tell Kathleen and no one else. What I'm doing is strictly unofficial. I could lose my job."

At the other end of the line Svetlana made a grunting sound. As if Ingrid losing her job wouldn't be the worst thing in the world. She'd never thought much of Ingrid's work at the Bureau.

"Is that it?" her mother asked after a long pause.

"There's one more thing." Ingrid hesitated. She wasn't sure whether it was the fact she was asking her mother for a favor—something she'd managed to avoid since elementary school—or the thing she was asking for that was making her feel so damn uncomfortable. "I need you to send me some photographs of Megan. The most recent ones you have. Go to the copy shop and have someone scan them in for you. Then get Bob or Harry to email them to me, can you?"

"You think I don't know how to scan and email? You think I need the neighbors' help for something like this?"

Ingrid dug the fingernails of her right hand into the fleshy part of her palm. It was amazing how the most innocuous of statements could insult Svetlana, then how easily Svetlana's indignation could upset Ingrid. Why wasn't she immune to it by now? "Great, even better, you can do it yourself."

"So, you're finally admitting you've forgotten what your best friend looks like? You wouldn't be having this trouble if you came back every year for the vigil at Kathleen's."

How could she deny what was true? "It's for the investigation, not me personally." As the words came out of her mouth she could plainly hear just how unconvincing they sounded.

"Oh sure."

"Listen, I have to go—there's someone at the door," she lied. "I'll call you again when I have news." She ended the call and went back inside. Without thinking about it, a minute later she was pulling on her running shoes. Two minutes after than she was sprinting down Sutherland Road.

No matter what the time of day, the neighborhood she lived in always felt pretty safe, but even if it hadn't, Ingrid knew she had the speed and skills to get herself out of trouble if she had to. It was something she'd forced herself to get good at after she lost Megan. She pushed her legs a little harder and pumped her arms a little faster, hoping to outrun the memories swarming in her head. Sometimes the technique actually worked.

Tonight it was futile.

She eventually returned to the apartment, her muscles exhausted, but her mind still racing. She went to bed, not hopeful she'd get any sleep, all too aware the alarm would wake her in less than four hours.

Amazingly, she did manage to finally drift off.

Only to be woken by angry banging on the apartment door just two hours later.

17

When Ingrid had asked Gurley exactly how he'd managed to get into her building he'd been evasive, mumbling something about the super letting him in. Except the building didn't actually have staff on site twenty-four hours a day. Ingrid had decided to let it go, concentrating instead on selecting some suitable clothes to throw on when she couldn't quite fully open her eyes.

"Are you drunk?" Gurley had asked when he saw the tequila and glasses on the kitchen counter. He dumped a large backpack by his feet. Its contents clanked and jangled when it hit the tiled floor.

Although Ingrid didn't dignify Gurley's accusation with an answer, she doubted she would have been safe to drive. Mercifully, he told her there was a cab waiting for them. "Where are we headed? An airstrip?" she called through the bedroom door. "Did Foster try to steal a plane?"

Gurley cleared his throat. "I still think that theory was a good one. But no—the sighting was in some place called Willesden. I checked on the map—it's not that far from here. If you could just hurry it up."

They'd made the trip in a little over ten minutes through the empty streets of northwest London. During the cab ride Ingrid had fired questions at Gurley he couldn't answer.

"I just got a call telling me the location. You would have too, if your goddamn phone hadn't been switched off."

Now, at just after four-thirty a.m., they were both leaning against an unmarked police car in a side street just off Willesden High Road that had been sealed off at either end. They'd both refused DCI Radcliffe's offer of a seat inside a car parked further away from the property the team was staking out, not wanting to be so far away from the action. They still felt the police were trying to sideline them.

After fifteen minutes of being ignored by pretty much every law enforcement officer in the vicinity—and there had to be at least two dozen uniformed officers and another dozen detectives—Ingrid was beginning to regret her decision not to wear a sweater beneath her jacket. Eventually Radcliffe approached them, a grim expression on his face.

"We're waiting for the hostage negotiator to arrive." Radcliffe looked as if he hadn't made it into his bed at all the night before. The shirt beneath his crumpled jacket was badly creased and there was a long greasy mark snaking down his tie.

"Why?" Gurley snapped.

"Because none of us has had the appropriate training," he answered in a dismissive tone.

To his credit, Ingrid thought, Gurley didn't react. "I meant, why aren't you just going in? You've evacuated the neighboring houses, right? Foster isn't armed, so why not storm the place with all the manpower you've got?"

"We don't know he isn't armed. Just because he's not likely to have a gun, doesn't mean he hasn't got a weapon. You are a little gun-focused."

Ingrid had to admit Radcliffe had a point. Foster could have easily purchased knives and other tools to use as weapons. They didn't know what they might be dealing with. "Have you made any contact with him at all?" she asked.

"We've got a couple of tech guys inside the property right now, rigging up a speaker system so that we can communicate without the whole street hearing." Radcliffe glanced up at the nearest cordon, just fifty feet or so from where they were standing. A few people had started to gather, eager to know what was going on. So far no journalists appeared to have heard about the incident. "The vultures are circling," Radcliffe said. "I expect pictures have already been sent from onlookers' mobile phones to all the major news outlets. The camera crews will be setting up before you know it."

"All the more reason to settle this swiftly. You have a SWAT team ready to go?" Gurley had started pacing. It seemed to Ingrid that he might go in himself if Radcliffe continued to refuse to.

"We have two vans of Specialist Firearms Command officers at the ready."

"So do it now."

"Save your breath. We're not going in now. And we won't until we've exhausted all other options."

Ingrid shuffled sideways so that she was standing between Radcliffe and Gurley. "Who called it in?"

Radcliffe looked at her, non-plussed for a moment by her question. "One of the other residents in the property. It's an HMO—house of multiple occupancy," he explained. "Houses crammed with lots of rooms that have basic cooking facilities—usually a two-ring hob and a kettle—but with shared bathrooms. They used to be called boarding houses in the old days. Or bedsits. Anyway, some bloke saw the boy coming out of the bathroom on his landing wearing a pair of Spiderman pajamas."

"I assumed Foster had dumped the boy's pajamas when he stole the clothes from the laundromat," Ingrid said.

"Well then you assumed wrong. They haven't been found anywhere."

"Is that resident still around? Can we speak to him?"

"He's been taken to the local leisure center—it's where we're keeping all the people that have been evacuated. I could arrange for a car to take you down there, if you like." He nodded a little too enthusiastically about the idea of sending them some place else.

"You can go, agent," Gurley told Ingrid. "I'm staying right here."

"These... HMOs," Ingrid said, "would the landlords rent the rooms out for cash? No questions asked?"

"Most of the tenants are on benefits... you know, welfare. So generally the rent would be paid by the local council. If any of the landlords can get their hands on actual cash up front, I expect they jump at the chance."

"But how would Foster have gotten the boy in with him, without arousing suspicion? God knows their pictures have been all over the news."

"That's what we'd like to ask the landlord. We're still trying to track him down."

A detective who had been hovering nearby whispered something in Radcliffe's ear.

"Oh—it's a landlady, apparently," Radcliffe said. "At least we're making some progress—we know the gender, if not the location of the owner."

Gurley was shaking his head. "How long before the negotiator arrives? How many hostage situations you got going on this morning, for crying out loud?"

"She'll get here when she gets here."

"A woman?"

Ingrid wheeled around and stared up into Gurley's face accusingly.

"Hey, take it easy, agent. I'm not commenting on her abilities as a negotiator, but don't you think after what happened with Foster's wife and daughter... guys in the military don't exactly have a *progressive* attitude when it comes to equality."

"She's the most experienced negotiator on the team." Radcliffe ducked around Ingrid just so he could square up to Gurley, even though he was a good eight inches shorter than the Air Force policeman. "This is my investigation and we're following Met protocols. Is that clear?"

Gurley shook his head resignedly. "Fine. You don't want my help, I'll keep my opinions to myself."

"At last," Radcliffe muttered.

They waited around for another five minutes until eventually the Met negotiator arrived. She disappeared with Radcliffe and two other detectives into a nearby unmarked van.

"Is that it? We don't get to hear what she has to say? Oh come on! What happened to close liaison?" Gurley started to make his way toward the van.

"Sir! Please stop," an officer called from a nearby patrol car. "You need to stay where you are."

Gurley ignored him and marched on.

"Hey, come on," Ingrid said. "We can speak to the negotiator later."

Gurley turned and said, "I'm sick of being ignored. I'm making a perfectly reasonable request here. I'm just going to speak to the negotiator. Discuss strategy."

"Please, I have to ask you not to get any closer to the surveillance van," the cop called out.

Gurley spun on his heels. "What you gonna do about it?" He continued toward the van.

With just a nod from the officer, three more cops ran toward Gurley.

"Watch out, Jack!" Ingrid warned.

Gurley glanced over his shoulder, then picked up speed until he was running flat out, his long gangly arms and legs seeming not quite under his control. Just as he was reaching a hand out to the door at the back of the van, one of the cops launched himself at him. The cop flung his arms around Gurley's shoulders, but the big MP barely lost any forward momentum. His fingers wrapped around the handle of the door.

Two more cops landed on him, each one grabbing one of Gurley's arms. With the help of his colleagues, the cop who'd shouted the warning slapped a pair of cuffs on Gurley's wrists. All four of them then proceeded to lead him to a patrol car, even though he wasn't putting up any kind of resistance.

Ingrid ran over to them. "Come on, guys... cuffs? Is that strictly necessary? Tempers just got a little out of control," she said, not quite believing the cops' overreaction. "We'll make sure it doesn't happen again."

But the officer in charge completely ignored her.

Gurley and the group of policemen surrounding him arrived at the car. One of them opened the door and reached up to place his hand on top of Gurley's head. The MP ducked down, bending his knees low and shouted to Ingrid, "For God's sake, Skyberg, don't let them screw this up."

18

As the officer who'd cuffed Gurley walked past her, Ingrid reached out and grabbed his arm. He looked down at her hand and raised an accusative eyebrow. She quickly withdrew it.

"I do hope you're not thinking of giving us any trouble, miss." His tone was patronizing, his demeanor dismissive. Ingrid detected a faint Scottish accent. Edinburgh, if she wasn't mistaken.

"My title is 'agent', and I'm not sure what you've just done to my colleague is entirely legal. Is he under arrest?" She noticed the officer had three stripes on his epaulet. A couple of ranks below Radcliffe.

"Why create all that paperwork for ourselves?" he said, an inappropriate smirk on his face. "We're just letting your friend cool off a wee bit. When this situation is resolved and we no longer consider him a threat to its successful conclusion, he'll be free to go."

"You do know he's a major in the military police? He's a cop, just like you. Can't you show the guy a little more respect?"

"If he'd shown us the same courtesy, you and I wouldn't even be having this conversation." He held her gaze for a long moment, making sure he'd made his point clear, then turned away to speak to a nearby constable.

Ingrid had been dismissed. As she was considering her next

move, a loud bang echoed from across the street. She looked toward the source of the noise: a sash window had been flung open in the house under surveillance. A dirty nylon curtain fluttered through the gap. Ingrid stared at it for a while, expecting more activity. None came. Presumably the police negotiator had made contact with Foster and that had sparked a reaction. Everyone in the street was craning their necks up toward the window, all holding their breath, waiting for the next move.

For a full five minutes Ingrid continued to watch nothing happen at the open window. She imagined how frustrated Jack Gurley had to be feeling, handcuffed in the patrol car, watching police officers run up and down the street, and not knowing why. He was so close to apprehending his fugitive and yet not allowed anywhere near the action.

The frustration was getting to Ingrid too. She felt useless. Tommy was less than two hundred yards from her and she couldn't help save him. She hoped he was all right and that Foster wouldn't decide to make some final stand and take his boy down with him if he thought all was lost.

Did the Met negotiator really know what she was doing? Was Kyle Foster even making demands? Maybe they should get Carrie Foster to speak to him. Hearing a familiar voice might make all the difference. Ingrid released the breath she hadn't realized she'd been holding. Kyle Foster talking to his wife could also make matters a whole lot worse. Besides, Ingrid wasn't even sure whether or not Carrie Foster was still under sedation.

She tried calling Radcliffe and wasn't surprised when his cell went straight to voicemail. As approaching the surveillance van to try to speak to him wasn't an option, she walked over to one of the uniformed officers. The man was wearing a Kevlar vest and had an earpiece in his left ear. She showed him her badge. "Any chance you know what's going on in there?"

He shook his head and said, "I'm just waiting for orders." Then he walked away.

Ingrid looked toward the crowd standing at the nearest cordon. Previously silenced by the recent activity at the house, they had started murmuring quietly amongst themselves again.

Except for one woman.

One woman standing close to the barrier had just shouted something at the cop manning the line. Ingrid jogged down to the cordon to see what the woman's problem was.

"I'm seventy-eight years old!" she hollered. "My husband fought for this country. You have no right keeping me from my home."

The cordon cop leaned close to the woman and said something very quietly in her ear.

"What would I do on the hard floor in the leisure center? With my hips? What is the matter with you, suggesting such a thing?"

Ingrid detected the merest hint of a Polish accent, almost eroded away after many years living in London. "Hello, ma'am. Has the officer explained what's going on to you?"

"He says I can't go back to my own house. I've been sitting in the hospital all night at my husband's bedside, on the most uncomfortable chair ever made, and now this policeman wants me to stand in the street for God knows how long."

"It's not safe for you to return right now." Ingrid pointed to the open window. "You see that curtain blowing there? Inside that house is a man the police need to speak to. He has a little boy with him. He's holding the boy hostage." As Ingrid made the statement she realized it wasn't strictly accurate. As far as she knew, Foster had made no demands. And it wasn't at all clear his son was being held against his will.

"Hostage? The poor man has just lost his wife. He's done nothing wrong."

Ingrid stared into the woman's face, realizing she had to be suffering from some form of dementia. She was about to suggest to the cop that he really ought to get the confused old lady somewhere she could rest up until the situation was resolved, when a loud crash sounded from the sidewalk outside the house. A bottle had smashed on the hard pavement.

"Dear God." The old woman crossed herself. "I hope he's not smashing the place up. I didn't take a deposit."

Ingrid had already started to walk back toward the house. She stopped. "You know the man in that apartment?" she said, turning back.

"Didn't I just say that? He's lost his wife. That is my house. I want to get back there."

"You rented the room to the man with the boy?" Ingrid asked.

"Who are you anyway? You don't look like a police officer, and you have an American accent. What has all this got to do with you?"

"I work for the American embassy. I'm here because the man and boy are American."

The woman wheezed out a cackling laugh. "Sure they are… and I'm Peruvian."

"What did he tell you?"

"That his wife died and he'll be taking his son back home, just as soon as his family send him the money for his plane ticket."

"And where did he say home was?"

"He did tell me… Iran maybe… or Turkey. I don't remember. And I don't care, as long as I get my rent."

"What does the man look like?"

"I don't know, average. Dark skin, dark hair, average height."

"And the boy?"

"Similar, except his hair is very curly."

Ingrid lifted the blue and white police tape high in the air and guided the old lady beneath it. "I need you to come with me."

"I can go home?"

"You have to speak to some people first."

The uniformed cop ran from the other end of the cordon towards them. "What do you think you're doing?"

"I'll take full responsibility. Call DCI Radcliffe if you don't believe me." The tape had gotten caught in the woman's hair, Ingrid gently lifted it off. But before she got a chance to start walking her down the street, a car screeched to a halt on the other side of the cordon. A familiar figure climbed out.

Ingrid's heart sank.

19

As ever, Angela Tate had managed to arrive at a crime scene ahead of her competitors. Though the sun hadn't yet risen and the street was bathed in a grayish half-light, the journalist spotted Ingrid immediately. She pushed her way to the front of the cordon. Just getting out of the taxi was the overweight photographer who seemed to accompany Tate on most of her assignments. He started arguing with the cab driver.

"Don't run away, agent. Not without a quick comment for the *Evening News*." The reporter stuck out an arm and shoved her digital recorder into Ingrid's face.

"No comment." Ingrid tried to move away but the old woman resisted.

"You're from the newspaper?" She looked Tate up and down. "My husband always used to read the *Evening News*, before his eyesight failed him. So much better than the free papers they give away everywhere now."

"I couldn't agree with you more." Tate gave her an uncharacteristically genuine smile, which faded quickly as she turned back to Ingrid. "Given that you're here, I can only assume the man inside that house is First Lieutenant Kyle Foster."

Ingrid shook her head. "You're wrong."

"How wet behind the ears do you actually think I am? I thought you knew me better than that by now."

"OK—I'll give you a comment," Ingrid said, "but then I really have to go."

Tate looked at her suspiciously.

"Neither Kyle Foster nor his son are in that house."

Tate narrowed her eyes. "You really expect me to believe that?"

"Believe what you like. I've got to get this lady home."

"Yes—yes that's right," the woman said. "I need to go to bed."

Ingrid led the woman to the first patrol car, explained to the cop there that she had new information for DCI Radcliffe about the hostage situation, then waited while he ran to the surveillance van and banged on the door. Radcliffe's pale, sleep-deprived face was thunderous when he emerged from the back of the truck. Nevertheless, he hurried to Ingrid, frowning at the old woman as he approached.

"It's not Foster," Ingrid said, cutting straight to the chase.

"Who's this?"

Ingrid realized she'd never asked the woman her name.

"Katarzyna Tysowski," the old lady said.

"Mrs Tysowski is the landlady of the property. The man she rented the room to looked nothing like Kyle Foster."

"Is that all you have?"

"There's more, but first of all, tell me what was thrown out of the window just now."

"A bottle of whiskey."

"Whiskey? Maybe it wasn't Iran—where he came from," Mrs Tysowski said. Then, at Ingrid's prompting, repeated to the DCI exactly what she'd just told her.

When she was done, Radcliffe let out a low groan. "You're certain?" he asked the old woman.

"I'm not senile."

Ingrid turned to her and smiled. "Please excuse us for a moment, ma'am." She walked up the street a few paces and Radcliffe joined her a moment later. "You have to go in there. Put an end to this now. The press have already arrived. The longer you leave it, the worse—"

Radcliffe cut her off with a raised palm. "Thank you for pointing out the obvious for me." He lifted both hands to his face and stood there in the middle of the street, rocking back on his heels. "This bloody case. I swear to God…"

Five minutes later a team of twenty officers dressed in riot gear stormed into the property. Five minutes after that one of them emerged with a boy in his arms. A female cop wrapped a blanket around the boy's shoulders and carried him to a waiting police car.

"Have you found someone to look after him?" Ingrid asked Radcliffe.

"His mother's on her way." He saw Ingrid's puzzled expression. "Alive and well. Estranged from the boy's father, waiting for the divorce to come through."

"So he had abducted his son?"

"We got that much right, at least." He shook his head. "The whole thing's been a bloody fiasco from start to finish."

Jack Gurley couldn't have put it better himself, Ingrid thought. "I'm guessing you don't have a problem releasing my colleague now?"

"God no—you're welcome to him." He stopped a passing constable and requested Gurley be released immediately.

Jack Gurley emerged from the patrol car, stretching his arms and legs, rubbing his wrists where the cuffs had been. Ingrid quickly brought him up to speed.

"The guy in the house sounds nothing like Foster."

"I think the witness' description relied a little too heavily on the Spiderman pajamas," Ingrid said.

"You're kidding me." Gurley glared at Radcliffe who was now standing on the other side of the street, issuing orders to a group of uniformed officers. "All this manpower for nothing?"

"I know—it's frustrating as hell. But what else could the police do? Ignore it? This was just an unfortunate case of mistaken identity. God knows it's happened to me before."

"But we're no further forward." Gurley shook his head. "I've got to get out of here." He strode across the street, grabbed his heavy backpack, then headed at speed towards the cordon. Ingrid ran after him.

As they reached the line of police tape at the end of the street, Ingrid could see Angela Tate moving fast in her direction, an angry expression on her face.

"Do you think I like standing around in the cold for no bloody reason at all?" the reporter said.

"Not my problem. I gave you a statement—you chose to ignore it," Ingrid told her.

Gurley's cell phone started to ring. He answered the call and turned away, leaving Ingrid to deal with Tate on her own.

"Tell me one thing," Tate said, "off the record."

"You think I'm ever going to believe that, coming from you?"

"I swear."

Ingrid pursed her lips. When she tried to move away, Tate quickly wrapped her fingers around her arm.

"Do you think Tommy Foster is still alive?"

"No comment." She peeled off the reporter's hand only to be grabbed again around the wrist. This time by Gurley. He yanked at her arm and dragged her under the police tape and through the crowd of onlookers.

"What is it, for God's sake?" Ingrid pulled her arm out of his grasp.

Gurley said nothing until they were safely out of Tate's earshot. "We have a lead. A sighting. And this time I can actually trust the intel."

"Why?"

"It came from one of my men at the base."

20

Jack Gurley was forced to duck very low as he ran across the helipad to the waiting Pave Hawk helicopter the US Air Force had sent from RAF Freckenham. Slung across his shoulder was his clanking backpack. Ingrid couldn't help wondering what he'd purchased the day before at the department store. He hadn't volunteered the information and she didn't want to seem so curious that she needed to ask. With just a spare pair of panties, a tee shirt and a toothbrush stuffed into her purse, she was starting to feel a little under-equipped for their trip.

She followed him to the dove-gray chopper. As she approached the big helicopter—it was easily over fifty-foot long—she was reminded of the last time she had flown in one. It was during her first ever case at the embassy. Her stomach lurched a little as she recalled the turbulence they'd endured on the flight back to London, as they tried and failed to outrun a big winter storm. She swallowed hard. At least the weather today was a lot calmer.

Once they were safely harnessed inside, the helicopter rose into the air, and Ingrid spotted Angela Tate standing in the road that led to the helipad in Battersea, looking disheveled and maybe even a little defeated. Ingrid felt a twinge of pity for the reporter.

The feeling soon passed.

The journalist must have followed them all the way from Willesden, no doubt determined to get a better story for the front page of the *Evening News* than a child being snatched by a disgruntled father from his estranged wife. Tate would be on the hunt for bigger headlines and wouldn't stop until she got them. Ingrid was pretty sure that the reporter's expense account wouldn't stretch to hiring a helicopter of her own. For a while at least, their destination would remain classified information.

Gurley tried to fit his long legs into the cramped space, twisting his body one way then the other. He finally resorted to resting his feet on the backpack with his knees up somewhere around head height.

"Maybe you didn't need to bring all that gear," Ingrid said, adjusting her headset so it sat more snugly on her head.

"I wasn't going to leave it behind—I just bought this stuff. Besides, we don't know how Foster is surviving. He's probably living off the land, sleeping outdoors. You might find some of this stuff useful if we have to track him."

"*I* might?"

"I can get all the supplies I need from the base." He thudded the backpack with the heel of his boot. "Think of this as a small gift from me to you."

Gee, I'm touched.

"On that subject—tracking—I want to make it clear now, I can't have you slowing me down," Gurley told her, his expression solemn. "No offense. It could get very physical."

"I run five miles most days—do you?"

"It's not just about stamina, you need strength too."

"Don't you worry about me." She managed to resist the urge to have him squeeze her biceps just to prove her point.

Gurley didn't comment. His silence told her plenty. Although she might not be capable of overpowering him in an arm wrestling contest, she was damn sure she could outrun him. But there was nothing to gain in getting pissed at his attitude, so she got back on topic. "Assuming this sighting is reliable—"

"It is."

"OK—I guess we'll find out soon enough. Assuming it was

Foster, why would he return to Freckenham? Why get anywhere near the base? Do you think he's planning to turn himself in?"

"He could have walked into any station house to do that."

"Not if he thinks he can be tried in the US if he surrenders to US personnel. Maybe he just wants to go home."

"You're still making the mistake of assuming he's thinking rationally. He's gone postal—nothing he does now can be predicted with any measure of accuracy. We don't know what's going through the crazy S.O.B.'s head."

Something didn't fit with the crazed airman picture Gurley was painting. Right now Ingrid couldn't put her finger on it. "So why do you think he's here?"

"Maybe to seek revenge?"

"On who?"

Gurley shrugged.

"You think he really might want to hurt the people on the base?"

"Worst case scenario—maybe some folks in the village too."

"Then we really should inform the local cops." Ingrid didn't want get the Suffolk force involved, but wasn't sure she could keep the new intel from them.

"The local cops were supposed to be keeping the train and bus stations under surveillance. They didn't do a real good job, did they?"

"Assuming this sighting is reliable."

"Like you say—we'll find out soon enough."

The journey from London to Suffolk was uneventful. Ingrid's attempts at engaging Gurley in any conversation that wasn't directly connected to the hunt for Foster were either ignored completely—more than once Gurley feigned sleep—or slapped down as either irrelevant or too damn personal. Silence was just fine with Ingrid. It was a relief to concentrate on the view out the window than make excruciating small talk.

The chopper landed in a designated helicopter zone on the base and a jeep arrived within moments to convey them to a windowless low-rise block situated at the edge of the complex. One of Gurley's sergeants escorted them to a stuffy room at the end of a long corridor. Inside was a man in his late thirties or early forties, a little overweight, dressed in civilian clothes. He was pacing up and down behind a table and four chairs.

"Is that it? Am I going to the police station now?" He had an English accent, with a slight lilt to it. Ingrid supposed he was a local. The man had directed his question at Gurley, ignoring Ingrid completely.

"Mr Cooper?" Gurley said, "Mr Glen Cooper?"

"You know who I am, for God's sake. What's going on here?"

"We need to speak to you, sir."

"Christ, what do you think you're doing? You have no right to hold me like this. Where are the police? I asked the other bloke I spoke to—Lieutenant Grayson—to call them. Where the hell are they? Finally he turned his attention from Gurley to Ingrid. "And who the hell are you?"

Ingrid showed him her badge. "I'm from the American embassy. We're very interested in finding out exactly what you saw this morning."

"Oh, is that right? Well maybe I don't want to tell you. I've done nothing wrong. I've got other deliveries to make. You can't keep me here. It's not legal."

"Why don't you let us worry about what is and isn't legal?" Gurley pulled out a chair from the table and sat down.

"Piss off."

Ingrid sat down too. "The faster you tell us what you saw, the faster you'll get out of here." Ingrid felt sorry for the guy, locked up for the past two hours as if he were a criminal. What the Air Force was doing was illegal, but if it meant that they tracked Foster down sooner, she was willing to be party to a little bending of the rules.

"I know you, I've seen you around the base, you look different out of uniform. Smaller somehow."

"My name's Jack Gurley—I'm a Major in Security Forces. I need you to tell me everything you saw."

"I can't hang around here. I thought I was going to speak to the police. Not bloody Mulder and Scully. I've got a business to run. Deliveries to make."

"You've made that quite clear. Why don't you sit down and tell us what you know?" Gurley folded his arms and tilted his head to one side, the picture of a patient interrogator.

"I'll talk just as soon as that door's unlocked and the armed man outside has been dismissed."

"Not possible." Gurley scraped back his chair and stood up. He hurried around the table and squared up to Cooper. He towered over the man.

Cooper flinched, and raised his arms across his face.

"What? You think this is going to get physical?" Gurley said.

"I know what you Yanks are like, Guantanamo and all that."

"Then you must know how determined we are to get the information we need." Gurley forced a smile.

Ingrid got to her feet, staying on her side of the table, but preparing to launch into action if Gurley did overstep the line. "You say you have a business to run, Mr Cooper?" She maintained a quiet and even tone, despite being sorely tempted to holler at him. "You deliver supplies to the base?"

"And I have been doing for years. You really shouldn't be treating me like this."

"So I'm guessing you rely on the base for a large part of your income. I'm guessing it'd be... significant, in terms of your... profitability, if you lost the RAF Freckenham contract."

Cooper lowered his arms and his shoulders drooped. He stared into Ingrid's face, then down at the floor and shook his head. "That's how you're going to play it. Threatening my business." He looked at Gurley. "She's good. You could learn a thing or two from her, Mulder." He shuffled to the table and sat down opposite Ingrid. "Let's get on with this bloody interview, then, shall we?"

Gurley gave her a begrudging smile as he returned to his seat.

Cooper interlaced his fingers and flexed them outwards, forcing the cartilage to pop noisily. "What do you want to know?"

21

They had been at the base for over thirty minutes, and still hadn't gotten the first nugget of intel from the eyewitness. It was clear to Ingrid that Cooper had been locked up and isolated to maintain first mover advantage. She suspected Gurley wanted to bring Kyle Foster in himself, single-handedly, if he had a choice.

If he thought for one second he could shake her off, he needed to think again.

After Gurley had made a show of rolling up his sleeves, to reveal remarkably pale, almost hairless arms, he planted both elbows on the table and leaned forward. "When did you see him?"

"Just before six o'clock. I was only a few miles from here. Running a bit late… that's a bloody joke, considering what time it is now… anyway, Foster was standing outside the post office, next to the pillar box. Looked as if he was waiting for something."

"Or someone?" Gurley asked.

Cooper shrugged. "How am I supposed to know that?"

"So you recognized him? From the TV reports?"

"I know him. Not well, but enough to recognize him in the street."

"What did you do then?"

"I pulled up and got out of the van."

"Why?"

Cooper paused for a moment. "Actually, I'm not sure. I didn't think about it. By the time I was out of the cab, he was gone."

"Why didn't you call the police right away?" Ingrid asked. Gurley threw her an irritated sideways glance.

"I tried. My phone battery was out of juice. I need to get a new phone, it runs right down after a couple of calls. I just haven't got round to it."

"There are public pay phones in the village. I've seen them," Gurley said.

"But have you ever actually seen anyone use one? You won't have—they've all been vandalized. Quick as BT send an engineer round to fix them, so some little bastard smashes them up again."

"So you continued your journey into the base?" Ingrid asked.

"Seemed like the smart thing to do. I told Lieutenant Grayson I'd seen Kyle. He said he'd phone the police and I should sit tight and wait for them to come out to question me. That was bloody ages ago. And then you two turn up."

"Was Foster alone when you saw him?" Ingrid said. "Was his son with him?"

"Alone. I expected to see Tommy close by, but there was no sign of him. That's not good, is it?" He popped his knuckles again. "My youngest is so upset by it all he's refusing to go to school. Probably just an excuse to bunk off, but you can understand he'd be feeling scared."

"Your son knows Tommy?"

"Lewis plays footie with Tommy every Saturday. It's a little local league, nothing to get excited about, but that doesn't stop some dads taking it very seriously."

"And was Foster one of those dads? Did he push Tommy to do well?"

"God no. He was just pleased Tommy had made a few friends outside of the base."

"Why's that?" Gurley's upper body tensed defensively.

"You'd have to ask him. But I think I know what he meant.

Village life can get like that too. Seeing the same people all the time isn't healthy for anyone, is it? That's how tempers fray and arguments start. Well, you tell me, Major. I bet it's like a pressure cooker in here sometimes, isn't it?"

Gurley didn't respond. He just narrowed his eyes and set his jaw.

"So Tommy and Lewis play soccer together. How about you and Foster—are you close?" Ingrid asked.

"What are you getting at?"

"How well do you know him?"

"We have a pint after the match on a Saturday afternoon. But if you're implying that I've done anything wrong... that I'm such a close friend I'd protect him or something... then you're totally barking up the wrong tree. I reported seeing him just as soon as I could."

Ingrid wondered why Cooper had become so defensive. Could he be hiding something? "What was Foster wearing when you saw him?"

"Dark trousers, a pale shirt. Bloody big boots on his feet. US Air Force issue, they looked like."

"Was he clean shaven?"

"He looked like he hadn't had a shave for a day or two. But he didn't exactly have a beard. His hair was greasy, lying flat against his head."

"So maybe he hadn't had access to a bathroom, the past forty-eight hours?" Ingrid asked.

"I suppose not."

"Did he look as if he'd been sleeping outdoors?" Gurley said.

"He looked bloody rough, so he could have been."

"Rough?"

"His clothes were creased and muddy. He seemed exhausted."

"Sounds like you got a pretty good look at him. How long were you staring at him before you opened the door of your truck?" Gurley's tone had changed from general hostility to outright mistrust.

"Wait a minute, I don't like the way this is going."

"What were you planning to do?"

"I wasn't planning anything, I told you, I wasn't thinking at all. I just jumped out of the van."

Ingrid leaned forward, closer to Cooper than Gurley was. She felt as if she needed to get between the two men before tempers flared even more. "Is there anything else you can tell us about the way he looked?"

It took Cooper a moment to tear his gaze away from Gurley's face. Ingrid wasn't even sure he'd heard her question.

"I told you, one second he was there, the next he was gone. I've told you everything there is to tell."

Gurley suddenly stood up and ducked around the table. He crouched next to Cooper, their heads at the same level. "I'm going to ask you this once and I'd advise you to think very carefully before you answer."

Cooper frowned at Gurley, then turned toward Ingrid. She managed to keep her face expressionless. What the hell was Gurley doing?

"Do you know where Kyle Foster is right now?"

"Of course not! How could I? I've been in this place for over two hours."

"Are you protecting Kyle Foster?"

"No! I barely know the bloke. I wish I didn't, now I've found out what he's capable of."

"Did you give him money, or any other kind of assistance when you saw him earlier?"

"What's going on here? I reported the sighting, didn't I? Why would I do that if I wanted to help him?"

"I don't believe you."

"But I'm telling you the truth. For God's sake, what do I have to do to convince you?"

Gurley moved closer to Cooper. "Who then? Who else would want to help him? Who was he waiting for when you saw him?"

"How would I know? I'm not a bloody mindreader." Cooper tried to move his face away, but Gurley clamped a hand around the back of his neck. "Ask Yvonne if she knows anything about it," Cooper said, his voice coming out in a strangled whisper.

"Yvonne?"

"Yvonne Sherwood. The landlady at the Hare and Hounds—the pub I go to on a Saturday afternoon with Foster. She's decidedly chummy with the bloke. If you know what I mean."

22

Ingrid jogged to keep up with Gurley as he strode down the corridor and back outside. "We have to let him go," she said.

"Do we?"

"He's a witness, not a goddamn criminal—he could make a lot of trouble for the embassy if he decided to go to the press. You know how sensitive this whole situation is."

"We will let him go. But there's no harm in having him stew a little longer before we do. That way he might be more reluctant to go to the police when he gets out of here. He won't want to waste any more of his precious time being questioned." Gurley stopped abruptly and called over a Security Forces sergeant who was coming out of the adjacent building. "That guy—Cooper—make sure he gets his phone back and is released in thirty minutes. No, make it an hour. If he talks about filing an official complaint, remind him how valuable the US Air Force contract is to him." He glanced at Ingrid. "That was a nice touch, by the way."

The sergeant saluted Gurley and disappeared into the building they'd just exited.

"Thank you," Ingrid said.

"I had no intention of detaining him. I wouldn't want to make any trouble for you and the embassy."

Ingrid wasn't sure she entirely believed him. She suspected

he'd make just as much trouble as he needed, if it got him the right result. "You do know we're supposed to keep DCI Radcliffe informed of what we're doing, if we discover anything new," she reminded him.

"So far we've had an unconfirmed sighting. Geographically we might be a little closer to Foster, but practically? We're no further forward than we were two hours ago."

It seemed like a fine line they were walking, but for the time being, Ingrid was prepared to go along with Gurley's approach. It wasn't as if Radcliffe could offer them much assistance right now, and involving the local cops would only slow them down. "OK—let's go talk to Yvonne Sherwood. Then we can make a decision whether we pass on the information. Maybe she'll tell us nothing useful. No point in wasting anyone else's time."

"Couldn't agree more. We'll take my car. We don't want to roll into the village in an Air Force vehicle. No need to announce our arrival." He set off at top speed once again.

"Do you know her—the manager of the Hare and Hounds?" Ingrid asked, breaking into a jog to catch up with him.

"Never been in there. It doesn't do for members of Security Forces to fraternize with servicemen. Or rather, if any of us showed up, the place would clear in two seconds flat." He smiled at her. Ingrid could have sworn she saw the hint of a twinkle in his eye.

Was Jack Gurley starting to enjoy this mission?

They returned to the jeep and Gurley's sergeant drove them to a large parking lot behind Gurley's quarters. Gurley's car was a pristine condition maroon Oldsmobile. Ingrid would have guessed he'd had it especially imported if she hadn't seen a few of them on the streets of London. She couldn't understand the appeal of something so solid and cumbersome. Until she climbed inside. It was like stepping into an air conditioned ranch house. She sank into the gray and maroon upholstery of the passenger seat and did her best to keep her eyes open.

The eight mile drive into the village took no time at all. Gurley parked on the street rather than using the parking lot of the Hare and Hounds. How he thought the Oldsmobile was any less conspicuous than a regular US Air Force issue jeep, Ingrid hadn't been able to work out during the ride over. On the street or in the parking lot, the car positively glowed with its American credentials. They might as well have made an announcement on a bullhorn when they drove into the center of the village.

"You ready for this?" Gurley asked as he put on the handbrake.

Why was he even asking her that? She wondered if maybe she had fallen asleep at some point during the trip from the base —after all, she'd only managed a couple hours' sleep the night before. "Me? Ready for anything. Always."

"That your personal motto?"

Ingrid smiled. She hadn't thought about it that way before, but maybe it was. Maybe she should get some bumper stickers printed.

When they got inside the Hare and Hounds they found a young bearded man serving drinks. The place was pretty empty —but then it was only eleven-thirty a.m. Ingrid scanned the room. It was decorated in a traditional English country style, horse brasses and leather tack hung from the dark, wooden beams and silver-colored tankards lined high ledges around the walls. She thought it was trying a little too hard to look authentic and wondered if maybe the pub had opened just a few years ago.

"We're looking for your boss, Yvonne Sherwood?" Gurley said.

The man gave him a wry smile. "She's not my boss." He came from behind the bar and hollered into the adjoining room. "Mum! There's some tall bloke asking for you."

"Is he dark and handsome too?" came the muffled reply.

"Well, he's not my type—you'll have to judge for yourself."

Gurley shifted his weight from one foot to the other. He cleared his throat.

The barman returned to the bar. "She'll be with you in a minute. Can I get you a drink?" He glanced at Ingrid and smiled broadly at her, as if he hadn't noticed her before. He leaned his elbows on the bar and rested his chin on a fist. "Now my day just got a whole lot better. What can I get you?"

"Nothing, we're fine, thank you," Gurley said.

A forty-something petite woman with a nice smile and a pink flush to her cheeks appeared at the bar, drying her hands on a dish towel. "You are tall." She looked up into Gurley's face. "And handsome enough, I suppose." She smiled more broadly. "What can I do for you?" She laid her bony hands flat on the bar.

Ingrid stepped forward, her badge already in her hand. "Good morning, ma'am. I'm Agent Skyberg from the US embassy and this is Major Jack Gurley—he works in Security Forces at RAF Freckenham. We'd like to speak to you about Kyle Foster."

The nice smile disappeared so quickly it was as if it had been slapped off the woman's face.

"Why? Has something happened?"

"You know the police are looking for him?"

"Yes, of course I do. I mean has anything new happened. Is he all right?"

"Is who all right, ma'am?"

The two old men drinking nearby had stopped their conversation and shuffled a little closer.

The woman hesitated. "Well, Tommy, of course. Do you have news about Tommy?"

Ingrid stepped right up to the bar and rested her hands very close to Sherwood's. "Is there some place a little more *private* we can speak?"

A flash of panic flitted across the woman's face. "Something has happened, hasn't it?" She lifted a hand to her mouth. "Oh my God!"

Sherwood's son supported her arm and led her into the other main room of the pub—a dining area. He indicated to Ingrid and Gurley to follow. Gurley glanced at Ingrid. Ingrid shrugged back at him. The woman's response had seemed a little extreme, in the circumstances. They hadn't actually explained what it was about Foster they wanted to discuss. She was leaping to her own negative conclusions. Ingrid wondered if that meant the woman had a guilty conscience.

Once they were settled at a corner table, well away from any curious customers, Ingrid started over. "We'd like to speak to you about Kyle Foster because we believe he may try to contact you."

The woman said nothing. Her gaze was focused in the middle distance.

"Has he made contact with you since yesterday morning?"

Yvonne Sherwood's eyes opened wide, her lips parted slightly. After a beat she seemed to recover. "Why would he contact me?"

"We have reason to believe you know First Lieutenant Foster quite well," Ingrid said, not wanting to reveal the details of Glen Cooper's sighting just yet.

"Who told you that?"

"Do you know him?"

"He comes in for a drink now and then. But that's true for a lot of men from the base. Doesn't mean I know them all." She started to scratch her forearm as if something was irritating her skin.

"We believe he may try to return to the area."

"Surely he knows this is the worst place he could come."

"Can you explain what you mean by that?"

"If he doesn't want to get caught, why would he come back here?"

"Perhaps he wants to give himself up."

Sherwood shook her head. "Why would he?"

"But surely that would be better for Kyle, better for Tommy. Better for everyone. Don't you want to see him safely in custody?" Ingrid did her best to keep her expression as neutral as possible. She didn't want to influence the woman's response.

The bar manager swallowed. "Of course. We all want to make sure Tommy's safe. But I was just trying to put myself in Kyle's position."

Gurley leaned back in his chair. His gaze hadn't left the woman's face.

"Can you think why he might come back here?" Ingrid continued.

"I can't imagine, that seems like a stupid thing to do. Are you sure you've got your facts straight? Who told you he was going to come back?"

"We can't share that information with you, I'm afraid, ma'am." Ingrid leaned in a little closer. "How well do you know Kyle Foster?"

Sherwood stopped scratching her arm. Her nails had left long red marks. "I told you. I don't really know him at all. He comes in here every Saturday with some of the other dads from football. They have a couple of drinks. Maybe play some pool. The kids amuse themselves outside—we have a climbing frame and swings in the garden. My son plays for the team too."

Ingrid glanced over her shoulder toward the bar in the other room.

"Not Marcus! My youngest, Luke."

"So does your husband take Luke to the match every week? Maybe he knows Kyle a little better? Maybe we should speak to him."

"I don't have a husband."

"Oh, I'm sorry."

"No need to be sorry—he's not dead or anything. A dead weight, maybe. That's why I got rid of him. Useless lazy sod." Her nostrils flared slightly. "I take Luke to football, Marcus looks after everything here."

"Did you ever get a sense from Foster or Tommy that there might have been problems at home? Anything that might have indicated a recent change in Kyle Foster's state of mind?"

"No, I'm sure everything at home was fine. There's nothing wrong with Kyle Foster's mind." She answered emphatically, without a moment's hesitation.

Ingrid wondered how Sherwood could be so sure if she hardly knew Foster. She glanced at Gurley.

"I know what they keep saying on the news about all that post traumatic whatnot, making a big thing of it," Sherwood said, unprompted. "I heard one of the other dads talk to Kyle about it once. There'd been documentary on the television about PTSD. How it was under-diagnosed in the army. Kyle said he'd seen a few of his Air Force buddies really get it bad." While she was talking about Foster the expression on her face had softened. It was obvious to Ingrid that she liked the guy.

"Kyle Foster was seen in the village early this morning." Gurley blurted, no doubt getting impatient with the way Ingrid's questioning was going. "There's no point in protecting him, it'll only make things worse. Did he contact you?"

What the hell did he think he was doing?

"I've already told you that he hasn't!"

Ingrid glared at Gurley.

Sherwood stood up. "I think I've answered enough of your questions. I'd like you to leave now."

Reluctantly, Ingrid rose to her feet. She held out a business card to Sherwood, who folded her arms and looked away. Ingrid slipped it onto the table instead. "If he should contact you, it really would be in his best interests if you told us about it. Or the police."

They left the bar and Ingrid strode back to the car. For once, Gurley ambled. Then he turned around and stared at the doorway of the pub, where Yvonne Sherwood and her son were standing, defiant expressions on their faces. He walked the remaining few steps backwards, keeping his gaze fixed on them.

"Thanks for your input," Ingrid said, using all her will power not to raise her voice. "I think we really made some progress with her."

"You know as well as I do she's lying. You saw how uncomfortable she got. Foster could be holed up in her basement right now for all we know."

Ingrid watched Sherwood and her son turn away from the door. There was definitely something about the woman's demeanor that didn't feel right. She seemed too eager to come to Foster's defense. "OK—let's say you're right. Let's say she has heard from Foster."

"You're actually agreeing with me?"

"If you are right, there's only one option open to us."

"I can have a half dozen men here in under fifteen minutes."

"That's not the option I had in mind." Ingrid retrieved her cell from her purse. "I'm calling the local cops."

23

Ingrid and Gurley were waiting outside the Hare and Hounds when the detective sergeant heading up the search of the pub appeared at the door, his head down, his hands buried deep in his pockets.

"Nothing," he said as he approached them.

The search warrant had been arranged quickly. Ingrid and Gurley had stayed in the Oldsmobile, watching the exits of the pub while they waited for the police to arrive. The search itself had taken less than thirty minutes.

"Nothing at all?" Gurley said.

"I did spot a couple of pork pies in the kitchen well beyond their 'best-before' date that environmental health might want to know about. But I don't suppose that's something you'd be interested in." He wrinkled his nose as if the aroma of the offending pies was lingering in his nostrils. "You still haven't told me—what made you think Foster had come back to the area in the first place?"

Gurley shot Ingrid a look. He really should learn to trust her. As if she would say anything to contradict him. She waited with anticipation for his reply.

"A policeman's hunch. I guess you get them all the time too, huh? The key thing is to determine which ones you should pay any attention to. On this occasion I called it wrong."

Ingrid could see Gurley struggling to maintain a light tone. She knew he still thought he was right about Yvonne Sherwood harboring a fugitive.

"Is it possible something could have been missed? Another room inside that your men haven't seen? You were awful fast in there." Gurley asked.

"Do you know how much pressure is on us to track Foster down?" The cop's previously jovial tone disappeared in an instant. Ingrid couldn't blame him, Gurley was more or less accusing his team of being incompetent. "Are you seriously suggesting we wouldn't do a thorough job?"

Gurley held up his hands. "OK, OK—you made your point already."

"We're sorry to have wasted your time on this," Ingrid said, hoping a little polite interjection might diffuse the tension between the two men.

"Do you think maybe I could take a quick look around inside before you pack up and go?"

Gurley just wouldn't quit.

"Unless the proprietor invites you in especially, you're not getting anywhere near the place." The detective shook his head in disbelief and walked away.

"What were they looking for in there? A man hiding in a closet?" Gurley said when the cop was still well within earshot.

"They know what they're doing. Can you just admit that maybe you misjudged Sherwood?"

"And you didn't?"

Ingrid watched the last of the cops trudge out of the pub and back to the police vehicle. "OK—I admit there was something about her that didn't feel right. Maybe she's importing liquor without paying taxes. It's possible she was hiding something. It just wasn't Foster." Ingrid walked around to the passenger side of Gurley's car.

"Are we going somewhere?" he asked her.

"Back to the base."

"What for?"

"There's something I want to take a look at."

Back at RAF Freckenham, Gurley parked up behind his quarters. The jeep was already waiting to convey them to the family quarters on the far eastern side of the compound.

"I had my team search the house yesterday, as soon as I was told what Foster had done. They didn't find anything." Gurley said as they stepped inside the Fosters' dinky little two-story house. "What are you looking for?"

"Not a man in a closet."

Ingrid headed for the living room first. A worn couch and armchair took up most of the space, both were angled towards a forty-eight-inch flat screen TV. Framed pictures of the two children adorned the walls. A large plastic crate stuffed with kids toys was shoved in a corner. Beyond the living area was the kitchen. It was big enough to incorporate a small dining table and four chairs. A refrigerator stood in one corner, so tall it almost reached the ceiling. Ingrid pulled open the door. It was pretty much full of groceries. Strange that the Fosters had such a well-stocked fridge when they were planning to go away for a few days. Ingrid wondered if the trip was a last minute decision. Something else they should ask Carrie Foster.

Ingrid opened up the freezer. Apart from the usual cartons of ice cream and frozen vegetables, containers of what she supposed was frozen breast milk were stacked inside.

"How old is Molly?" she asked Gurley.

"Fourteen months," he said quickly.

"Isn't that a little old for breast feeding?"

"Hey—don't ask me. I've managed to avoid that kind of knowledge my whole life." He pulled out one of the containers and held it up to the light as if it might yield some clue. "It looks almost green. Maybe it's really old."

Ingrid checked another container for a date. Stuck on the bottom was a little strip of tape with the digits 07-24 written in thick black Sharpie. "Last month. I guess it keeps frozen as long as any other kind of milk." She screwed up her face. She felt sorry for Carrie Foster having to express the stuff, then label up the container and carefully place it next to the frozen dessert. Ingrid's mom had given her formula just as soon as she could. She grabbed the pot from Gurley's hand and shoved both containers back in the freezer drawer. Then she turned around and headed toward the front door. She paused at the foot of the stairs leading up to the second floor. "Are you OK?"

Gurley nodded back at her unconvincingly.

"Your face looks a little pale. Was it handling the breast milk?"

"Not at all. Just remembered the sight of little Molly lying in that hospital bed."

"We should check to see how she's doing—it's possible Radcliffe wouldn't bother to keep us informed." Ingrid pulled out her cell. She needed to call Radcliffe anyway to give him an update on the local situation. Better that he heard it from her rather than the Suffolk cops. Just as she opened her contacts list the phone vibrated in her hand. An out of area number. She looked at Gurley.

"Hey—you go right ahead. It's not as if we have a man to hunt down here."

Ingrid hesitated for a beat. *Screw Gurley.* She answered the call. Thankfully her gamble paid off: it wasn't Svetlana. "Hey, Mike. I'm in the middle of something right now, can I call you back?"

"It won't take a minute, I was just checking you got the mp3 files I sent you."

"You did?"

"Yep—audio interviews of the two women. I finally got a hold of them. Thought you'd want them right away."

"Thanks Mike. I'll check my email account later. I really appreciate your help."

"Hey—glad to be of service."

She said goodbye and hung up.

"You all done?"

"It's another case I'm working on—I can't just drop everything else."

"You should feel free to go right back to it. I have everything under control here."

Ingrid decided not to remind him about the fruitless search of the Hare and Hounds. She wasn't sure he had anything under control at all. She bounded up the stairs. At the top, straight ahead of her, was the open door leading into the bathroom. The room was small by US standards, but big compared to the tiny shower rooms she'd seen in people's apartments in London. There was a bathtub and a separate shower cubicle, and a sink beside the toilet. Above the sink was a mirrored cabinet. Ingrid opened the door. Inside were the usual items: shaving paraphernalia, deodorant, painkillers, and a small unlabeled bottle of pills. Ingrid reached in for it and checked the reverse—no label there either. She opened the childproof cap and shook a few pills into her hand. Small blue and white capsules rolled around her palm. She returned all but one of them to the bottle and screwed on the lid. She held the capsule between thumb and forefinger, trying to read what was printed in tiny letters on the side. After some serious focusing, she made out a manufacturer's name, a four digit number on one side and a dosage: 30mg, on the other. There was no indication what the drug was called.

"Do you know what it is?" Gurley asked her.

Ingrid had no idea. But she knew a woman who would. Meanwhile, she didn't want Gurley jumping to any conclusions about what they'd found. They didn't even know if the unmarked bottle belonged to Kyle Foster or his wife. "It's a medication for…" She wanted to choose something Gurley wouldn't question. "For severe menstrual cramping."

"Really?"

It seemed Gurley questioned everything no matter what.

"Sure. I take them myself sometimes." She waited for Gurley to turn away before she slipped the single pill into her pants pocket, then followed him into the next room—the kids' bedroom. On one side of the room was a narrow single bed, a Spiderman comforter cover draped over the edge. On the other was a wooden cot, a furry animal mobile suspended above it. On a dresser next to the cot was a baby monitor.

It all seemed so regular. So normal. How could it have gone so wrong?

The final room was the master bedroom. Gurley hesitated at the door. "What was it you were hoping to find in here, anyway?" he asked.

"Don't you think it's worth looking? Just in case we uncover something your team may have missed?" She pushed past him into the room and opened up the closet. Carrie Foster had a lot of shoes, or at least, a lot of shoe boxes. Ingrid glanced along the row of rectangular cardboard containers. The box furthest away from her had a dark stain in one corner. She reached into the closet and grabbed it. The cardboard was wet. She pulled off the lid. Inside was a bottle of vodka, its top a little loose.

Gurley finally made it into the room. "Kyle Foster is a secret drinker?"

"I found it on Carrie's side of the closet."

"Where better for him to hide his nasty little habit?"

"I would think pretty much the worst place ever." Ingrid had no reason to believe it didn't belong to Carrie Foster.

A bang sounded downstairs. "Hello? Carrie? Are you back? Did you know your door is wide open?"

Ingrid shoved the bottle back in its box and shoved the box back in the closet.

24

A few seconds later, a youngish, dark-haired, pale-skinned woman dressed in a light summer dress and baggy cardigan appeared in the hallway.

"Jesus Christ! Who the hell are—" She turned her head and saw Gurley. "Oh, I see." She wrapped her arms around the cardigan, hugging herself as if a sudden chill had blown into the room. "Does this mean? Is Molly…?"

"As far as we know Molly's condition hasn't changed." Ingrid reminded herself again to check in with Radcliffe.

"Should you even be in here? What are you doing here anyhow?" The woman's accent was pure south Boston. "Is this even legal?" She marched over to Gurley. "You can't go rummaging through people's private, personal stuff." She held her head up high. "You got no right to do that."

Ingrid introduced herself quickly, then explained, "We're only here because it may assist us in finding Tommy. Anything that helps track him down is worth doing, wouldn't you say?"

The woman hadn't taken her eyes off Gurley. "I want Tommy to be found as much as anyone. I'm just looking out for Carrie."

"We appreciate that—I'm sure Carrie does too. Maybe I could ask you a few questions?" Ingrid was careful to use the singular pronoun. As she did, she made sure to stare at Gurley and raise her eyebrows, hoping he'd take the hint.

He stood his ground. It was obvious this woman wasn't going to speak freely in front of a member of Security Forces, why wouldn't he just accept that?

"Major Gurley, I don't want to keep you any longer than necessary," Ingrid said. "I can make sure the property is secure when I leave." She nodded expectantly at him. "Didn't you say you had to report to the… ah… general with an update?"

Gurley finally tore his gaze from Carrie Foster's friend and gave Ingrid such a disdainful look it was as if she'd just insulted his family going back three generations.

"Sure—I'll be right back." He slipped past the woman who was now practically scowling at him. She watched him leave before she said another word.

"I don't know what I can tell you that'll help find Kyle and Tommy." She walked over to the window and watched Gurley stride back to the jeep. "Arrogant bastard," she murmured under her breath. She smoothed down a corner of the lilac and pink throw that covered the bed. "I don't know what's gotten into Kyle." She shook her head. "How could he do a thing like that?"

"Did you know they were planning a trip to London?"

"Carrie never mentioned it."

"But you'd say you and Carrie are quite close?"

"I'm the closest thing she's got to a best friend. I don't understand why she never told me about the trip. It's been bugging the crap out of me."

Ingrid was surprised the women were so close: judging by their accents alone they were from different social classes. But she supposed the Air Force threw people together that wouldn't normally mix in civilian life. "You haven't spoken to her since she left?"

"I tried calling when I saw what happened on the news. But I think her cell must be out of juice. It goes straight to voicemail." She shook her head again. "She must be going through hell."

"She's coping. Spending most of her time with Molly."

"Can you get a message to her from me?"

"Sure."

"Tell her we're all thinking of her. We're all praying Molly pulls through."

"I'll let her know." Ingrid smiled at the woman. "It'd help if you told me your name."

The woman opened her eyes wide. "I forgot you didn't know it. Rachelle. Rachelle Carver."

"Shall we go downstairs, Rachelle? Sit down and get a little more comfortable?"

"I can't stay long. My eldest is looking after his two sisters. I only left the house to pick up a few groceries from the commissary."

Ingrid led the way downstairs to the living room.

"Do you mind if we step outside?" the woman asked. "I need a smoke." She was out of the front door and pulling a pack of cigarettes from the pocket of her cardigan before Ingrid had a chance to answer. "Can't do this at home. Mustn't set a bad example, huh?" She offered Ingrid a cigarette.

"Not for me, thanks."

"You can judge me all you like. Doesn't bother me."

"I wasn't judging at all. Every time I tried smoking when I was a teenager, I just threw up," she lied.

"I need all the help I can get." She drew deeply on the cigarette and blew smoke from her nostrils.

"Help?"

"Getting through the next eighteen months of Billy's tour of duty in this shit hole of a country."

"You're having a tough time?" It wasn't the way Ingrid would have described the UK. So far she had a pretty good impression of the place. But then she'd spent most of her time in the capital. Freckenham seemed a nice enough village. She wondered if Rachelle Carver had actually ever ventured far beyond the base.

"I miss my friends, my family. A decent pizza."

"I guess every military wife posted abroad feels the same way."

"You think I'm whining about it?"

"Not at all—I can imagine how difficult it must be. Is it like that for Carrie too?"

She puffed smoke over Ingrid's head. "That's not for me to say."

"I'm just trying to get a picture of her life here."

"Maybe you should ask her."

"She has other things on her mind right now."

Rachelle Carver narrowed her eyes as she exhaled again. She stared at Ingrid through a cloud of smoke. "Carrie doesn't talk about home a whole lot."

"Yet she seems like such a family-oriented person."

Rachelle continued to puff on her cigarette as if she were in a race to finish it, but didn't comment.

"How well do you know Kyle?"

"I only know him through Carrie. So not really that well at all."

"But well enough to form some kind of opinion of him?"

"What are you getting at?"

"Did you like him?"

"I think he must have fooled a lot of people. He seemed like a regular, straight-up kinda guy. If anyone had asked me two days ago, I'd say he adored his wife and kids. Couldn't do enough for them. Just shows you how wrong you can be about somebody." She took another long pull on her cigarette then flicked the glowing butt away. "Maybe he went on one mission too many. Maybe something cracked inside him that couldn't be fixed."

"But you can't blame him for that."

"If you've got a nervous disposition, you shouldn't join the military. My Billy went on three tours in Afghanistan. He's just fine. You can't blame the job for something that happens in your own head."

Ingrid thought Rachelle's little speech sounded less than convincing. As if she were reciting a script rather than telling her what she really thought. Maybe she was just repeating what her husband had told her. "But up until what happened on Monday, Kyle seemed like one of the good guys?" Ingrid asked.

"A regular superhero. For a while there, Carrie and Kyle

seemed like the perfect couple. If you want the truth… I was a little jealous of their relationship. I thank God now mine is nothing like theirs."

"Perfect in what way?"

"Every way. Kyle doted on Carrie and Tommy."

"And Molly?"

Rachelle considered her answer. "Sure—I guess. But now that Kyle hurt her so bad… Jeez, I don't know. Who am I to make a judgment?"

"You think maybe Kyle was closer to Tommy than Molly?"

"I've been going over things in my mind since it happened—driving myself half crazy trying to work out why he did what he did. Looking for clues in his behavior, you know?"

"And have you come to any conclusions?"

Rachelle shook her head. "Not really. Except maybe… It's not my place to comment."

"Whatever you tell me is in the strictest confidence."

"I don't know. Feels like I'm betraying Carrie's trust."

"What if you don't tell me something that could have helped find Tommy? Whatever you tell me can only help Carrie right now."

Rachelle took a deep breath. "You swear this is between you and me?"

"You have my word."

The woman raised her eyebrows as if Ingrid's word meant nothing to her.

"After Molly was born I noticed a change in the way Carrie and Kyle were with one another. It was a gradual thing, like they just grew apart. New babies can do that to people sometimes. If I'm completely honest? I guess Carrie started to withdraw from Kyle. I figured they'd work through it. I think Carrie did too. Turns out we were both wrong." She played with the pack of cigarettes, turning it over and over in her hands. "You will give Carrie that message, won't you?"

"Absolutely."

"Maybe I should send something to the hospital. A card or something, can I do that?"

"I think she'd like that. If you want to really help, maybe you could arrange for all the fresh produce in Carrie's refrigerator to be disposed of?"

"The fridge is full of food?"

Ingrid nodded.

"Why would she go grocery shopping if she was going away?"

"I asked myself the same question. Maybe Carrie knew nothing about the trip. Maybe Kyle surprised her."

"I guess." Rachelle shoved the cigarettes into a pocket. "I should be getting back to the kids. Before the third world war breaks out."

Ingrid handed her a business card. "Any time you want to speak to me, if you think of anything that might help us locate Kyle and Tommy, just call."

Rachelle stared down at the card. "You know, Kyle really was a good husband. And a good dad. I can't believe what he did." She glanced over Ingrid's shoulder and tensed for a moment.

Ingrid turned around and saw Gurley approaching. "MPs really are as unpopular as their reputation, huh?"

"I just don't trust the guy."

"Gurley? Why?"

She shrugged and slipped Ingrid's card into her pocket. "Forget I mentioned it. I spoke out of turn. OK?" She hurried away.

25

"What were you talking about?" Gurley eyed Ingrid suspiciously as he approached.

"Do you have a problem with Rachelle?"

"No, why would I?"

"Earlier, upstairs... the atmosphere seemed a little tense."

"Don't know what you're talking about." He stared at Rachelle as she scurried away. "What did she tell you?"

"She just wanted to know how Carrie and Molly were doing. She's concerned."

"And what did you tell her?"

"That Carrie was doing OK, in the circumstances."

"You think so?" He started chewing the inside of his lip.

"I had to be a little upbeat."

"Did you find out anything from her that might help locate Foster?"

"Not really. But she did tell me Carrie and Kyle were the perfect couple before Molly was born."

"She did?"

"Maybe Carrie spent a little too much time with the new baby and Kyle felt excluded. Maybe that was when Kyle's problems started."

Gurley shoved his hands in his pockets.

"Where have you been?" she asked him.

"Speaking to the medical officer."

"The one treating Foster's PTSD?"

He nodded.

"What did she tell you?"

"Not much more than what was in his medical report."

Ingrid wasn't sure she believed him. "Maybe I should speak to her too."

"We're not supposed to be duplicating work."

"She must have been able to give you some background."

"Do you know how many service personnel and their families she treats in a week?"

"Surely not that many suffering from PTSD."

"Foster's been going to regular counseling sessions, making good progress, she said."

"And that's all she had to say?"

"There was nothing more to say."

"What did she make of what happened in London?"

Gurley looked away.

"Major?"

He screwed up his face. "She was surprised. Shocked. He seemed to be doing fine, she said. She thought he had his anger issues under control." He folded his arms. "Just shows you how anyone can make mistakes."

Ingrid wasn't happy that Gurley had interviewed the doctor without her. Was there something he wasn't sharing? "Does the doctor have any inkling what his next move might be?"

"I didn't bother to ask her. I knew she wouldn't know a damn thing about it."

"So, what's next?"

"We both know the manager of the bar was lying."

"About something, maybe."

"So we go back to the village and watch her for a while. See where she goes. See who visits her."

It wasn't the dumbest idea, and in the absence of anything better, Ingrid couldn't really object. "OK—but we limit the surveillance to a couple of hours."

"How about six hours and I'll buy you dinner after?"

"How about four and you promise me you weren't actually asking me out."

"Have no fear of that. You're really not my type. No offense. Four hours and you can buy yourself a pizza, eat it all on your lonesome."

"Deal."

After Ingrid had updated both DCI Radcliffe and Sol Franklin, she and Gurley returned to the village in a less conspicuous vehicle than his Oldsmobile. Gurley had somehow managed to get hold of a beat up Land Rover that blended right into the rural surroundings. Ingrid insisted she drive and that Gurley slide down in the passenger seat as far as he could and wear a dark knitted hat over his bright blond crew cut. He was a difficult man to disguise.

Ingrid parked forty or so yards from the Hare and Hounds, making sure they had a clear view of the front and rear exits. Unless the pub had some kind of tunnel leading from its basement to a neighboring property, they'd be able to observe anyone leaving or entering the premises. She looked at her watch. "Four hours."

Half an hour into their surveillance, Ingrid's cell phone beeped with a text message. It was from Ralph Mills. She'd been letting his calls go to voicemail since their date on Monday night—she didn't want to be distracted by him in the middle of a manhunt. Not that he'd called her that often. In fact, he'd probably judged the amount of attention he was giving her just about right. His messages had been sweet and funny. He wasn't hassling her for another date, just letting her know she was on his mind. Given she had nothing better to do for the next three and a half hours, she couldn't see any reason not to reply. She didn't want him thinking she wasn't interested. She quickly tapped a message into her phone:

Good thnx, u? on stake out w/ gurley need entertainment

She could sense Gurley was glancing toward her. He was somehow managing to demonstrate his disapproval merely by altering the pattern of his breathing.

Only jokes i know are infantile or adolescent… sorry to disappoint

How about a poem?

There was a young lady from minnesota, who... used up the state's hog feed quota

Is that it?

Her pigs were so big, she needed to dig...

Huh?

Nope sorry... run out of rhymes

Gurley let out a long sigh and shifted in his seat. "If this mission is getting in the way of something more important, I could just complete it without you."

Ingrid turned to look at him. His expression was fixed in a grimace. He really wasn't joking. "From now on, it has my undivided attention. How about that?" She tapped another quick message to Ralph:

Expect u to get it finished by next time i see u

She hesitated before sending. That reply would mean she was suggesting another date. She considered deleting it, but with Gurley breathing down her neck, she hit send before she got to the end of the thought process. Ralph had almost written her a limerick, for God's sake. No one had ever done that for her before. That fact alone was definitely worthy of a second date.

I'll do my best... good luck with mission/gurley

Ingrid's phone buzzed again twenty minutes later: Natasha McKittrick calling. She dismissed the call, not wanting to give Gurley another excuse to question her commitment to the case. Her phone vibrated again to let her know she had a voice message. Dammit, Gurley was making her feel like a misbehaving schoolgirl. She turned away toward the driver window, shoved the phone against her right ear, and listened to the message.

"What have you done to my detective?" McKittrick said, her tone completely deadpan. "He's got the stupidest grin on his face and is practically bloody useless. I've had to send him out for coffee in the hope that the fresh air might blow some sense into him. Call me as soon as you pick this up."

Smiling to herself, Ingrid deleted the voicemail and slipped the phone into a pocket.

"Whoever that was, she has a voice that carries," Gurley informed her. "You might want to let her know."

"Thanks for the tip."

"I'm so glad this operation is giving you plenty of time to organize your social engagements."

Why was Gurley so pissed at her? She wondered if maybe he didn't have much of a social life himself. Working in Security Forces on a base in the middle of the English countryside had to be a pretty lonely existence. Maybe she should feel sorry for the guy.

Three and three-quarter hours later, just as the daylight was starting to fade and Ingrid's behind was aching due to the thin layer of foam between the worn upholstery and the rock hard driver's seat, she turned to Gurley. "I think maybe we should call it a day."

Gurley tapped a big forefinger on his watch. "Fifteen more minutes."

"Nothing's going to happen now." Ingrid adjusted her position and tried to shake some feeling back into her numb right foot.

"You agreed to four hours."

"OK!" She threw up her hands in surrender.

A few minutes later, Yvonne Sherwood appeared at the door of the pub. She was carrying a large sports bag. The woman struggled with the bag to a nearby car and dumped it on the passenger seat.

Gurley mumbled something about patience being a virtue and slid a little further down into his seat. "Remember not to get too close." There was a definite smug tone to his voice.

"I have tailed a few vehicles in my time." Ingrid could tell Gurley was frustrated not to be sitting behind the wheel.

The pub manager's dinky silver car pulled away from the curb and Ingrid started up the Land Rover once there was a distance of fifty or so yards between the two vehicles.

The silver car stopped a minute later outside the convenience store and Yvonne Sherwood jumped out. She looked up and down the street, her gaze lingering in their direction for more seconds than was comfortable.

Ingrid held her breath.

A moment later Sherwood turned away and disappeared inside the store. She re-emerged after a few minutes with a bag of groceries. She shoved the bag onto the passenger seat of the car. Then, instead of getting back behind the wheel, she returned to the store. She pulled something from her purse and headed for the ATM next to the door. She removed the thick wad of cash that came out of the slot, found another card in her purse and repeated the process. They watched her do the same thing with another two cards, then shove all the cash into a pocket.

"Goddammit," Gurley said, when Sherwood headed back to her car. "I knew I was right about her."

26

In the deepening gloom Ingrid and Gurley trailed behind Yvonne Sherwood for fifteen minutes, not daring to put on the headlights of the Land Rover, edging along the narrow country lanes.

"We're going to lose her, put your foot on the gas." Gurley was leaning so close to the windshield, his nose was practically pressed up against the glass.

"Maybe now's the time to call the cops. Get some backup."

"They made their attitude quite clear this morning. I won't have them swarming all over the countryside and screwing everything up. We call them when she's led us to Foster."

"If that's where she's going. We're still working on a hunch here. What if we lose her?" They turned a sharp bend in the road and Ingrid could just make out the beams from Sherwood's headlights in the distance. It felt more like luck than judgment.

"Maintain this speed and we won't lose her. We don't need backup. I'm not sure the local cops could find their own asses with a— What the f—"

Ingrid yanked the steering wheel hard right and stamped on the brake as an overhanging branch loomed up at the windshield in the twilight. She yanked the wheel in the opposite direction just a few inches from a dense thicket on the far side of the road. Her heart lurched in her chest. She felt as though Gurley was watching her every move, waiting for her to make a mistake. She was determined not to give him the satisfaction. "You must work with the cops here all the time. Are you seriously suggesting they can't do their job?"

"I don't work with them a whole lot. They leave us to deal with our men as the Air Force sees fit. They get on with their business and leave us to ours. And that's just the way I like it."

"I'm sure they're really not as bad as you make out." Ingrid didn't know why she was defending the local force, but now she'd started she felt as though she had to follow through. "I've worked with a lot worse police departments Stateside."

"Then maybe the whole world is screwed."

"Yet military cops remain shining examples of perfect policing that everyone else should emulate? You don't have such a great record yourselves. Maybe you should think twice before you start throwing stones."

"I can only judge on what I've seen so far. And it don't impress me much."

"As long as you know I'm calling the cops as soon as we get Foster." Ingrid squeezed the steering wheel harder.

"That's just fine with me."

"Good."

"Great."

After another couple of minutes twisting around tight bends, the road straightened and Ingrid could clearly see the taillights of Sherwood's little Nissan a hundred or so yards ahead of them. Fifty yards later the silver car slowed right down and took a left. Ingrid drove past the dirt track Sherwood had disappeared down and stopped on the other side of the road. As she came to a halt, the driver side wheels sank into a ditch and the Land Rover lurched sideways.

Gurley huffed out a sigh.

"Maybe you should have brought along the night vision goggles." Ingrid used the flashlight function on her phone to avoid landing in the ditch herself as she climbed out.

They both closed their doors quietly and jogged back to the dirt track. "She might be driving miles down here," Ingrid whispered.

"Lucky we're both in such good shape, wouldn't you say?" Gurley lengthened his stride.

Unlike Gurley's, Ingrid's boots weren't designed for uneven terrain. She did her best to tread carefully and avoid the worst of the exposed stones and random divots underfoot. Right now, straining or twisting her ankle would be nothing short of disaster. Forced to make two strides for every one of Gurley's, she felt a little like a small child trying to keep up with its older sibling. After a few more strides she picked up pace a little and overtook him. As she passed, she noticed his breathing seemed labored. Maybe he wasn't as fit as he'd claimed.

Less than two hundred yards down the track, Ingrid saw the Nissan parked up close to a wide wooden gate. The interior light was on, but there was no sign of Sherwood inside the vehicle. Ingrid shoved out her hand in front of Gurley, who had already slowed down. They ducked sideways into a nearby hedge.

"Where the hell is she?" Gurley whispered.

"Wait a second."

A moment later, the top of Yvonne Sherwood's head appeared above the headrest of the driver's seat. As Ingrid had suspected, the woman had been bending low over the passenger seat, where she'd dumped the heavy sports bag and the groceries earlier. She then climbed out of the car, ran around to the passenger side and, with some effort, heaved the bag out. She hauled it onto her back and immediately seemed six inches shorter.

"What does she have in there?" Gurley leaned out of their hiding place to get a better look. "We have to move in closer."

"Can we just wait for a moment?" Ingrid grabbed his arm and pulled him toward her.

They watched in silence as the petite manager of the Hare and Hounds struggled to the wooden gate with the bag. She fumbled with something where the gate met the gate post, then shook the gate with both hands in frustration. With great effort she heaved the bag over the top of the gate and let it fall on the other side. It landed with a loud metallic clank that echoed down the track. Sherwood then climbed the gate and swung one leg over, sitting on the top for a few seconds, staring toward the muddy field beyond.

She awkwardly swung her other leg over and jumped down the other side. Then she grabbed hold of the heavy bag and dragged it behind her as she stumbled toward the middle of the empty field.

Crouching low, Gurley quickly slipped across the dirt track. He reached the fence that ran alongside the field, and, still keeping his head low, headed toward the gate. Ingrid followed him. Although her eyes were adjusting to the gloom, the darkness seemed to be closing in on them fast. If it hadn't been for the light pink sweat top Yvonne Sherwood was wearing, Ingrid might have lost sight of her all together. She strained her eyes a little harder and managed to figure out the bar manager's destination. Two-thirds of the way across the field was a small trailer. It looked like it had no wheels. Its windows were boarded with wooden planks and the door was hanging half off.

A few feet ahead of Ingrid, a good thirty or so yards from the gate, Gurley stopped. He pulled a small pair of binoculars from a pocket.

"Can you see any sign of life inside that trailer?" Ingrid asked. "Can you see anything at all?"

"I can't see anything happening on the inside and Sherwood is at least fifty feet away from it."

Ingrid peered into the grayness of the night. She could just about make out a lonely figure standing completely still in the middle of the field. "What's she doing?"

"Looking around. Waiting." Gurley moved in closer to the fence and lowered his head. "Stay very still. She's more likely to notice movement."

"Is that so?"

"She's walking again. Headed straight toward the trailer." He slowly scanned the field with the binoculars. "No signs of life anywhere else. She's opened the trailer door now and she's putting the bag inside."

Although Gurley's running commentary was starting to

grate, Ingrid wouldn't have known what the hell was happening without it.

"She's not climbing inside the trailer," he continued. "She's walking around it." Gurley watched for a few more moments then, grabbing Ingrid by the arm, dropped suddenly to the ground. "Dammit. She's headed back toward the gate." He lay flat on his belly and dragged Ingrid closer to him.

"We can't stay here. We're too exposed. She'll see us when she drives past," Ingrid hissed at him.

"We can't exactly get up and hightail it back down the track either."

Ingrid peered through the fence into the churned up field. Running along the length of it, parallel to the fence, was a trench, two-foot wide. "Can you wriggle under this wooden bar?" She hit the bottom of the fence with a fist.

"It'd be tight."

"I figure if we time it so that we roll into the ditch when she's climbing over the gate and stay low, she won't notice us."

"You're suggesting we roll into a ditch?"

"You have a better suggestion, then make it fast." Even without binoculars, Ingrid could see Sherwood was striding quickly across the field. She'd reach the gate in no time.

Gurley was already slithering toward the bottom of the fence.

"Deep breath in, Major."

"It's not my stomach I'm concerned about."

As Gurley wriggled closer to the fence, Ingrid noticed for the first time just how big his ass was.

Sherwood grabbed the top of the gate and started to climb.

"OK, you've got to go now," Ingrid told Gurley and watched with alarm as his buttocks got wedged beneath the low wooden strut. "Relax your glutes," she told him.

"Don't you think I'm trying to?"

Ingrid grabbed his ass and started to push.

"What do you think you're doing?"

"Helping." She shoved harder. "Come on, she's on top of the gate now. I've got to get under there too." She took hold of his hip with both hands and pushed with all her strength. Gurley's ass finally submitted and he slid the final few inches into the field. Ingrid quickly followed behind him, rolling into the ditch and onto Gurley's back. She shuffled backwards fast, into her own section of the trench, and was rewarded for her haste with a mouthful of dirt. She spat it out. She was grateful there wasn't a pool of stagnant water at the bottom of the ditch. In fact it was remarkably dry. She exhaled.

They stayed exactly where they were, not daring to move a muscle, until they'd heard the Nissan chug along the track a couple of minutes later. Ingrid lifted her head and shook dirt from her hair. Gurley adjusted his position so that he could prop the binoculars on the edge of the trench and train them toward the trailer.

"I guess all we can do now is wait."

As the cold, silent minutes passed, Ingrid wondered if she should make the most of the forced intimacy and try to get Gurley to open up a little. There was something going on with him that she couldn't put her finger on. But staring at his impassive, motionless back, she quickly decided she'd need a crowbar and a dose of sodium pentothal to make him tell her anything about himself. "Do you think Foster is hiding in an identical ditch on the opposite side of this field, watching the trailer just like us, making sure Sherwood wasn't followed?"

"We can't rule that out."

"That's got to be difficult, with an eight-year-old boy in tow."

"You're assuming Tommy's still alive."

"I'm certain he is." Something about the way Rachelle Carver spoke about Foster had convinced Ingrid that the boy was safe with his dad. She hoped to God she wasn't wrong.

"Must be nice to be so sure about things." Gurley started to lift his head, then froze. "Did you see that?"

"How can you see anything in the dark?"

"Ten o'clock, movement in the bushes. There it is again."

Ingrid saw it this time. A gray shape about a hundred yards away, making a beeline for the trailer. When the figure was just a few dozen feet from the door, Gurley lurched to his feet. He started to race across the field in the darkness, stumbling and tripping as he went, somehow managing to stay upright.

What the hell did he think he was doing? Why hadn't he waited until Foster had disappeared into the trailer? His impatience had completely blown their cover.

Ingrid scrambled to her feet, but rather than follow behind Gurley, she ran in the opposite direction, aiming to approach the trailer from the other side. Hopefully she could stop Foster if he ran away across the field.

She ran as fast as she could without losing her balance. When she was just thirty or so yards from the trailer, Gurley started yelling.

"Stop right where you are, Foster. Put your hands above your head."

From her position, the trailer was now obscuring Ingrid's view. She accelerated forward, stumbling as she went. Just a few feet away she saw a figure come hurtling around the side of the trailer.

It wasn't Gurley.

She picked up speed and hurled herself at the running man, grasping his legs and bringing him crashing to the ground in a classic quarterback tackle.

Gurley caught up with them a few seconds later. "Got you," he yelled. "You sonofabitch!"

27

The man on the ground reared up against the pressure Ingrid was applying to his butt and lower back. Gurley stamped a boot between his shoulder blades.

"You stay just where you are."

He moved his foot upwards and pressed on the man's head, forcing it further into the ground.

"Who the hell are you?" the man managed to say before his voice was muffled by the dirt.

Gurley glanced at Ingrid. The man had spoken with an English accent.

Holy crap.

Ingrid scrambled to her feet. Gurley released the man's head, grabbed his upper arms and hauled him upright as if he were as light as a child. Once he was vertical the man started to cough violently. Grabbing his knees he bent forward. He vomited onto the ground, retching for long moments. Finally he stopped, wiped a sleeve across his mouth and, gasping for breath, managed to stand up straight.

Ingrid grabbed her cell phone, found the flashlight app and shone it into the man's face. He had dark hair and dark eyes, a two inch diagonal scar across his left cheek.

"What are you doing here?" Gurley yelled into his face.

"You're American. Are you from the base?" He wriggled his

shoulders. "I think you might have broken something, you know. I could sue."

"We had reason to believe you were a known fugitive." Gurley's tone was unapologetic. "Tell us what you're doing in the middle of a goddamn field in the middle of the night."

"I live here." He pointed toward the dilapidated trailer.

"You do?" Ingrid said.

"I just needed somewhere to put my head down for a couple of nights." He turned more toward Gurley. "The missus chucked me out."

"This is your trailer?"

He shook his head, cleared his throat and spat onto the ground. "I suppose it belongs to the farmer who owns the field. Not sure who that is. But it's not as if I'm doing any harm. He won't even notice."

"So no one knows you're staying here?" Gurley started walking around the trailer.

The man followed him. Ingrid brought up the rear.

"It's not exactly something I want to broadcast. I am squatting, after all. And... well, I don't want my kids to find out. It is a bit of a shit hole." He wiped his mouth again.

Gurley had reached the front of the trailer and was inspecting the door, it was hanging from one hinge. He grabbed it with both hands and yanked it from its flimsy mooring. The door snapped off like a piece of cardboard. Gurley picked up the bag Sherwood had left inside.

"Hang on," the man said, a note of panic in his voice. "That's nothing to do with me. I've never seen it before. If you're trying to plant some evidence on me... you can—"

"Yes?"

"This is my country. You can't just come over here and act as if you own the place. Bloody hell." He started rubbing his back. "You know, I think I am going to make an official complaint. What's your name?"

"I'll tell you when we get to the station house."

"The what?"

"I'm sure the police will want to speak to you. At length."

Gurley smiled. Even in the dark, Ingrid could see his even white teeth gleaming. "On the plus side, at least you'll have a leak-proof roof over your head."

"Wait a minute." He peered at the bag in Gurley's hand. "You've got to believe me, that's not mine."

Gurley just stared at the man, clearly enjoying his discomfort.

"Really—I wouldn't lie to you."

Gurley reached up a hand toward the guy's head. The man immediately flinched. Gurley placed his hand on the man's shoulder and squeezed. "I'm feeling generous. So I'll give you the benefit of a doubt."

"And there's no need to tell the police anything, is there?"

Gurley turned his head toward Ingrid. "The police? No—I don't think we need to get the police involved at this stage."

"Cheers, mate—I owe you one."

Ingrid and Gurley left the man where he was and trudged across the field back to the track, Gurley keeping a tight hold of the sports bag. When they returned to the Land Rover, he unzipped it. Ingrid found a pair of nitrile gloves in her purse. She didn't have a pair large enough to stretch over Gurley's hands, so she searched the bag. Inside she discovered a small tent, two bed rolls, bread, cheese and a pint of milk, a change of clothes and a folded wad of bills.

"Seven hundred," Ingrid told Gurley after a quick count.

"Wouldn't get him that far."

"We don't know how much he has on him already. But I guess we can assume he must be running out of cash."

"And maybe getting a little desperate."

"There are kid's clothes in the bag," Ingrid said, doing her best to sound upbeat. "So maybe that means Tommy is still alive."

"Or maybe that's just what Foster wanted Sherwood to believe."

28

Ingrid parked the Land Rover right outside the entrance to the Hare and Hounds. It was just past closing time, so she was forced to bang on the door for a good minute before it opened. Marcus Sherwood stood in the doorway, arms folded defiantly across his chest.

"Jesus. Look at the state of you." He looked Ingrid up and down then past her toward Gurley, who was standing on the sidewalk, the sports bag grasped firmly in his hand.

Ingrid shook the remaining dirt from her clothes. "We're just here to return some property of your mother's."

The young barman glanced down at the bag. "Mum hasn't lost anything. I think you've made a mistake." He started to close the door.

Ingrid shoved her foot over the threshold and grabbed the doorframe with her hand. "We could do this the friendly way, or I can call the police. It doesn't actually make much difference to me. But your mom might prefer to keep this just between ourselves. Why don't you go ask her?" She stepped through the doorway, forcing Sherwood's son backwards.

"There's no need for that." Yvonne Sherwood appeared at the open interior door, a resigned, disappointed expression on her face. "You'd better come in."

Once they'd settled themselves at the same table in the dining area that they'd occupied earlier, Yvonne Sherwood told her son to go to bed.

"I'd rather stay with you. Make sure you're OK," he said.

"I can look after myself. I'll be up soon. If I'm not you can send the search party. All right?" She grabbed his hand and kissed the back of it. It seemed a peculiarly intimate gesture for a middle-aged mother and her grown-up son. But then Ingrid didn't have much to compare it to. Svetlana had never been the demonstrative type.

Once the son was gone, Gurley dragged the heavy bag around the table and unzipped it. "I guess Foster could really have used this stuff, huh?" He gently kicked at the bag with the tip of his boot. "What did he do—give you a list?"

"I don't know what you're talking about." Sherwood scooped a stained cardboard beermat from the table and started to pick at a corner of it.

"Man, it's been a long day," Gurley said. "Why is it so many people don't know what it is I'm talking about?" He turned to Ingrid. "Is it something to do with my accent? Do I talk too fast? Maybe it's my pronunciation?"

The bar manager said nothing, just peeled off a shred of the printed layer from the surface of the beermat.

"Yvonne, you are aware that aiding and abetting a suspect is a criminal offense?" Ingrid kept her voice low. "Perverting the course of justice carries a maximum sentence of life imprisonment."

"That isn't my bag. I've never seen it before."

"Your prints are all over it. And all over the seven hundred pounds inside. We saw you withdraw the cash from the ATM." Gurley sat back in his chair and interlaced his fingers across the back of his head.

"You can't threaten..." Sherwood looked from Gurley to Ingrid.

"There really is no point continuing this charade, ma'am," Gurley told her.

"Where did you find it?" Sherwood stared down at the bag.

"Right where you left it."

"I've never seen it before." She was sounding less convincing each time she repeated the lie.

"Someone got to the trailer before Foster. Seems you didn't choose your drop-off location carefully enough—someone's living there."

"What?"

"Somebody is living in the trailer."

"They've got no right."

"But it's OK for you to drop stuff there for a wanted man, huh?"

She didn't respond.

"Kyle Foster didn't get a chance to pick up what you left him," Ingrid said.

Sherwood closed her eyes.

"Are you ready to start leveling with us?" Gurley kicked at the bag again. Metal clanked against metal.

Sherwood snapped open her eyes at the sound. "The money's still inside?"

At last.

"Everything's inside." Gurley said. "I guess Kyle really needed that cash."

"Have you any idea how much trouble you're in?" Ingrid asked. "You were helping a man accused of attempted murder escape arrest, Yvonne."

"Attempted murder? That's ridiculous. Kyle wouldn't hurt a fly. He's not that sort of man."

"He's a First Lieutenant in the US Air Force. He's flown on dozens of missions. Conducted countless drone attacks. Over the years he must have killed hundreds of innocent civilians. The guy's hardly a peace loving hippy." Gurley jabbed the bag with the heel of his boot.

"He was assigned to search and rescue missions in Afghanistan. And the drone operations are for reconnaissance purposes only."

Gurley gave her a wry smile. "That's what he told you. He couldn't say anything else even if he wanted to."

"OK! But he wouldn't hurt his own flesh and blood. No way.

He loves his kids. He'd do anything for them."

Gurley sat up straight. "I'm sure under normal circumstances, he wouldn't deliberately set out to hurt anyone. But under pressure, in the middle of an anxiety attack… in a blind rage? That's a whole different ball game."

"You don't know what you're talking about. Kyle just isn't like that. I've seen him have an attack. Have you?"

Gurley fanned out his thick, long fingers in the air. "Please, enlighten me."

"He doesn't go on the rampage, if that's what you're getting at."

"Really?"

"He gets very subdued, withdrawn, even."

"What brings on an attack—do you know?" Ingrid asked, wondering whether the screaming of his children would have been the thing that triggered the episode on Monday.

"Stillness. Quiet," Sherwood said without hesitation. "He can't stand it. Always has to have the radio on in the car. Or he's constantly whistling some annoying tune. Anything to fill the silence." Sherwood flipped over the beermat and started to peel the printed design off the other side. "He told me that sometimes he even goes into Tommy's room at night just to listen to his noisy breathing. He's a bit of a snorer, Tommy. My Luke is always complaining about him whenever he comes here for a sleepover."

Ingrid glanced at Gurley, wondering if he'd remembered that part of Carrie Foster's account. She had definitely told them it was the noise that triggered Kyle's extreme reaction.

"It's just Kyle's way of handling the problem, I suppose. His coping mechanism," Sherwood continued. "And he has been handling it. He's been doing really well."

"Until Monday morning," Gurley said.

"No!" Sherwood stood up and threw the beermat on the table. "Haven't you been listening to a word I've said? He wouldn't hurt Molly. He couldn't. It's just not in him."

"Due respect, but none of us know exactly what we're capable of, ma'am." Gurley picked up the shredded beermat and folded it in two. Then four. "I mean, I bet before today you had no idea you'd help a suspect evade the law."

Yvonne Sherwood looked to Ingrid, as if she might offer some support. When she said nothing, the woman slumped back into her chair. "He's an innocent man. I'm only interested in justice. You all seem to have made your mind up about him."

"Why are you so certain he's not guilty?" Ingrid said.

"I've already told you—Kyle's just not like that."

"When did he first get in touch with you?" Ingrid leaned further forward in her seat, trying to encourage Sherwood to confide in her.

"Why does that matter?"

"We're trying to piece together his movements. To be frank, we're also trying to work out what might have happened to Tommy."

"Nothing's happened to him. Tommy's fine."

"Have you seen the boy?" Ingrid asked.

"No."

"Spoken to him?"

"No—Kyle told me Tommy wanted to know if Luke was playing football on Saturday. I get the impression Tommy doesn't even realize anything is wrong. You know what boys are like—he probably thinks it's all some big adventure."

The way Sherwood was speaking, it sounded as if Tommy might still be alive. Unlike Gurley, Ingrid didn't believe Foster would lie to Sherwood if he'd seriously hurt the boy. A wave of relief passed over her. Maybe Rachelle Carver's assessment of Kyle Foster was accurate. Perhaps he did still care about Tommy.

"A big adventure huh?" Gurley threw the beermat back onto the table. "Including the part where Tommy gets a bleeding nose and split lip, courtesy of his father?"

"What?" Sherwood stared at him wide-eyed.

"I thought Foster may have neglected to mention Tommy's injuries to you." Gurley flared his nostrils.

"There has to be some innocent explanation." Despite her words, Sherwood looked genuinely shocked by the news. "Tommy must have had a fall."

Ingrid felt the need to move the conversation in another direction, just in case Gurley's revelation stopped Sherwood talking. "Did Kyle call you on your cell phone?" Ingrid asked.

"He called the public phone, here in the bar."

"And was he using a cell phone?"

"I don't know. Why?"

"It's a way we might be able to trace him." Ingrid leaned even closer to Sherwood. "You do know his best option is to give himself up?"

The woman nodded meekly. "I was hoping to talk him into doing just that. I thought I'd get a chance to speak to him."

"Oh really?" Gurley kicked at the sports bag again. "Would that be before or after you gave him the money?"

"I just want to help him."

"He can't escape, you do realize that?" Gurley said. "There's no place for him to go. The longer this goes on, the worse it gets for him."

Ingrid wished Gurley would shut up, he wasn't helping any. "What was next for Kyle, Yvonne? What was he going to do with the money? Where was he planning on going?"

Sherwood pursed her lips and shook her head so rapidly it looked as if she'd developed a sudden tremor. "He never told me his plans." She looked Gurley square in the eyes and folded her arms. "And that's the God's honest truth. You can arrest me if you want. Threaten me with whatever you like. I still won't tell you anything—I can't tell you what I don't know."

Ingrid glared at Gurley. He didn't seem to notice. He was deliberately ignoring her. His bombastic approach had gotten them nowhere. "Major Gurley, would you mind leaving Yvonne and me to speak alone for a moment?"

He frowned at her, completely taken aback by the suggestion.

"Please?"

"I'll go check on the car," he finally said, and slowly got to his feet. At the door he stopped and turned around, taking a moment to glower at Ingrid, just in case she hadn't picked up on his annoyance.

29

"You're wasting your time if you think I'm going to tell you any more now that he's left the room." Sherwood said. "I don't know where Kyle and Tommy Foster are."

"When he called you, did you hear Tommy in the background?"

The woman thought for a moment, finally uncrossing her arms and relaxing just a little. "I can't be sure, I don't think so."

"But you didn't ask to speak to the boy?"

"Why would I?"

"To check he was OK."

"I had no reason to think he wouldn't be." She let out an irritated sigh. "Kyle Foster is a good man. You don't work in this trade for twenty-odd years without being able to read people."

"Even good people break down. I've been working at the Bureau for long enough to see it happen plenty of times. The nicest folk can do stuff that's completely out of character."

Sherwood shook her head adamantly. "Not Kyle. Molly must have had an accident or something."

"Did Kyle tell you that?"

"He hasn't told me anything about what happened. Only that he didn't hurt Molly."

"Why didn't you try to persuade him to give himself up to the police when he called?"

"Because he told me he didn't do it."

"But he could explain all of that to the police."

Sherwood was shaking her head. "He has Tommy to think about."

"Don't you think Carrie might want Tommy with her?"

"I saw how she was on the news. She doesn't look capable of looking after herself, let alone Tommy."

Ingrid didn't believe what Sherwood was telling her. There was something more to it. Was it possible Yvonne Sherwood was having an affair with Kyle Foster?

"You OK, Mum?"

Ingrid looked up to see Marcus Sherwood standing at the door.

"I thought you'd gone to bed," his mother said.

"As if I'd do that, with you being interrogated down here." He stared at Ingrid. "Where's the other one? Snooping around somewhere?"

"Major Gurley is outside," Ingrid told him.

"Go back upstairs, Marcus. I'll be up soon. I promise." She stared at Ingrid. "I'm sure we're almost finished here."

"Sodding bastard, putting you through this," he said.

"I can assure you Major Gurley was just doing his job. We have to ask these questions," Ingrid said. "The police won't be any different."

"I wasn't talking about Gurley."

"Marcus! Can you please go upstairs?"

"For God's sake, Mum. He's not worth getting into trouble over. Think about Luke. What if you're arrested?"

His mother said nothing. Marcus Sherwood stormed out of the room.

Ingrid sank back in her chair, her eyes wide, her eyebrows raised. She remained silent and waited for Sherwood to comment. After what seemed a very long few moments, she finally did.

"Marcus isn't a big fan of Kyle's."

Ingrid didn't respond.

"Marcus thinks I flirt with Kyle." She tucked a few stray

strands of hair behind her ear. "Silly sod. I flirt with every bloke who comes into this place. It's part of the job. It doesn't mean anything. Especially not with Kyle."

Ingrid wriggled forward in her seat again but didn't speak.

Sherwood looked towards the door. "I don't want Marcus to find out about this." She tipped back her head and stared up at the ceiling for a few moments. "I feel so stupid about it now."

Ingrid maintained her silence.

Sherwood puffed out a steadying breath. "A few months ago… Oh God. I'm only telling you this because it might change your opinion of Kyle…" She took another deep breath. "A few months ago I made a pass at Kyle. I was a bit tipsy. The kids had finally won a match and everyone was celebrating. Kyle and I were getting on really well. I misjudged the situation." She put a hand across her eyes. "I can still picture the shocked expression on his face. He didn't need to say anything—it was clear I'd crossed a line. Kyle might join in with a bit of banter now and then, but he only has eyes for one girl."

Ingrid made no comment.

"You do know I'm talking about Carrie? That's why Kyle arranged the surprise trip to London for her, just to show her how much he cares."

"Actually I'd heard things had been a little… difficult between Kyle and Carrie since Molly was born."

"Who told you that?"

"I really can't divulge—"

"No—I don't suppose you can."

"You don't agree?"

"Kyle mentioned it a few times. He confided in me, I suppose. It's what made me think that he might be interested in…" She shook her head. "What a bloody fool I was." Sherwood leaned in towards Ingrid. "Can this stay just between you and me? I'm only telling you because I want you to understand that Kyle and I became quite close. That's how I know he couldn't do what you say he did."

"Tell me what happened between Carrie and Kyle after Molly was born." While Sherwood was in a confessional mood,

Ingrid hoped she could squeeze a little more information from her.

"I'm not a doctor, I couldn't tell you. But I suppose Carrie had a touch of the baby blues. I know she didn't sleep much when they brought Molly home from the hospital. Not for months. I think the sleepless nights took their toll."

"Do you know if Carrie went to see the doctor about it?"

Sherwood was just about to answer when Gurley strode back into the room. Why couldn't he have stayed in the car?

"Yvonne?" Ingrid said gently.

The woman was clearly distracted by the sight of Jack Gurley heading toward her. "What?"

"Did Carrie visit the doctor?"

"Why don't you ask her about it?" she snapped.

Ingrid knew that the interview had come to an end. Gurley's reappearance had seen to that. She got to her feet. "Thank you for your frankness."

"What happens now? Should I expect a visit from the police in the early hours?"

Ingrid was inclined to keep the police out of the picture for now. She was pretty sure they wouldn't get much more out of Sherwood than she had. Although the prospect of prosecution might make the woman more forthcoming, Ingrid decided to hold the threat of police involvement in reserve.

"Not at all. We'll be in touch."

30

On the drive back to the base Ingrid got Gurley up to speed with what Sherwood had told her. "You agree we hold back on informing the police about her involvement?" she asked him when she was done.

"I'd like to keep them out of the picture until we've come up with our own strategy for what we do next."

"We will have to tell them something, though."

"Let's sleep on it, deal with that whole pile of crap in the morning. Agreed?"

"OK." The idea of getting some sleep was suddenly so appealing to Ingrid, right then she might have agreed to anything Gurley suggested. But she knew her day wasn't nearly over. She still had a whole lot of her own crap to confront.

When they reached the base, Gurley personally escorted her to a guest room he'd had prepared for her in advance. As soon as she closed the door behind him, Ingrid collapsed onto the single bed and took a moment to focus on her next task. It was already well after midnight. If she didn't act now, her first chore would have to wait until the morning.

She eased herself upright then carefully retrieved the pill she'd found in the Fosters' bathroom cabinet from her pocket. She then grabbed her cell phone from her purse and called Natasha McKittrick.

"Bloody hell—what time do you call this? Is everything all right?"

"I need a quick favor."

"Where are you?"

"I need you to identify a drug for me."

"Me?" McKittrick exhaled noisily. "What makes you think I can help you?"

The hostility in her friend's tone took Ingrid by surprise. "You told me you were on a prescription drugs bust a little while ago. Sounded to me as if you knew a little something about the subject. Did I get that wrong?"

The line went quiet, but Ingrid could hear McKittrick breathing. "Natasha? Have I said something out of line?"

"No—you woke me up—that's all. I can get a bit tetchy. Sorry."

"Hey, no problem. I'm sending you a photo of the pill now." Ingrid found a sheet of plain white writing paper on the bureau next to the door, carefully placed the small capsule on it so that the writing printed on the side was clearly visible and snapped a couple of shots with her phone. She sent them to McKittrick. "You get them yet?"

"No—where did you find this pill, anyway?"

"Bathroom cabinet of Kyle Foster."

"What does it say on the bottle?"

"The bottle was unmarked—you think I'd be calling otherwise?"

"OK—the pictures have arrived. Give me a second." A few moments later she was back on the line. "It's an anti-depressant. A bit like Prozac with knobs on. You think Foster was taking them for his PTSD?"

"The therapy he's been getting is the cognitive behavioral kind. Do you know if there are any common side effects to these drugs?"

"Like most of this class of drugs: disorientation, fainting, drowsiness maybe."

"Not exactly ideal if you're a pilot."

"Maybe that's why they were in an unmarked bottle. Perhaps he's been getting some unofficial *extra help* with his problem."

"How easy are they to get 'unofficially'?"

"If you have the contacts, it's no problem at all."

Ingrid couldn't imagine how Kyle Foster would have the right connections to get hold of prescription drugs and wondered what other secrets he might be keeping.

"Are they something he'd need to keep taking? Are there any withdrawal symptoms?"

McKittrick paused a beat before answering. "You can't just stop them dead. Otherwise you might suffer severe mood swings, maybe even suicidal thoughts."

Ingrid thought about Tommy. If Kyle Foster were that volatile, it wasn't surprising he'd lashed out at his eight-year-old son. "I don't think the police found any drugs in the hotel room."

"Maybe Foster keeps some with him all the time."

"But if he has stopped taking them… does that mean Tommy is at risk?"

"Foster might not even have any withdrawal symptoms. But it could affect his stability, his judgement." McKittrick yawned.

"I really did wake you up." Ingrid glanced at her watch.

"Nothing shameful about getting to bed early on a school night."

"Sorry to disturb you."

"It's OK. Try not to make a habit of it, will you. Do keep me posted, though."

"We're not making much progress."

"I don't mean with the bloody case. I want to know what's happening with you and my detective constable. What kind of spell have you put on him?"

"I genuinely do not know what you're talking about."

"Oh yeah, right."

"Look—I've got to go. Pleasant dreams." Ingrid hung up before McKittrick had a chance to protest. As she sat staring at the phone, she wondered if she should tell Gurley about her discovery. She quickly decided it was something that could wait until the morning.

She put the phone on the nightstand and started to get ready for bed. In the bathroom she was pleasantly surprised to discover toothpaste, soap and shampoo. The US Air Force knew how to treat their guests.

While Ingrid cleaned her teeth, hoping to let her mind drift, she started to think about the mp3 attachments Mike Stiller had sent her. She'd managed to keep any thought of them buried all day, but now she was on her own, with nothing else to distract her, their presence on her phone was harder to ignore.

She thought about the phone sitting innocently on the nightstand. Now she'd started to consider the content of Mike's email, she knew it would be impossible for her to get to sleep until she'd at least listened to one of the interviews.

She quickly finished up in the bathroom, changed into her tee shirt, turned off all the lights except the one on the nightstand and picked up her phone. Mike's email was easy to find—it was the only one in her private mail account flagged as both urgent and important. She stared long and hard at the mp3 attachments before summoning the courage to open one of them. When she did, the recording started playing automatically. She hit the pause button, not quite ready for what she might hear.

She grabbed a bottle of water from the nightstand, slowly drank a third of it, then hit 'play'.

The first voice she heard was a man's. He had a thick Kentucky accent. He introduced himself, a colleague, and the interviewee for the purposes of the recording. The sound quality wasn't good. There was a low background hum and the voices sounded distant. As Ingrid strained to make out the words, she jotted down a few notes. The start of the interview merely covered the basics: name, date and place of birth and date of abduction. The twenty-eight-year-old woman, Karla Anderson, then quickly went on to describe the basement where she'd been held captive, unprompted by the two agents. She seemed anxious to convey just how bad her living conditions had been for the last fifteen years.

It took Ingrid a little while to notice she had started to cry. It wasn't until tears had actually started to dribble around her jaw and down her neck that the dampness registered. She found a Kleenex in her purse and dabbed her eyes. She wasn't sure whether she was crying in sympathy for the woman's plight or if she'd been imagining Megan Avery in the same house, forced into the same deprivation and depravity.

When the interview moved on to the other women and girls being held, Anderson had nothing to say at all. "First I knew I wasn't there on my own was when I was taken to the hospital in the same ambulance as another girl. Soon as I laid eyes on her I knew she'd been through the same things I had. The pain in her eyes, you know? I could see it plain as day."

"You thought you were alone in the property with your abductor?" a female agent asked.

"He was the only person I spoke to in fifteen years."

"Did you see him?"

"He didn't wear a mask, if that's what you mean."

"Can you give us a description?"

"Why do you need me to do that? You know what he looks like. I can identify him no problem—just tell me when."

The recording fell silent.

"What, what is it?" Anderson asked, the panic in her voice building. "Wait a minute. You have arrested him, right? You do have him locked up?"

"At this time, the suspect is not yet in custody."

"Sweet Jesus. How could you let him get away?"

"Have no doubt, Miss Anderson, we will arrest him. How quickly depends in part on the detail of the description you can give us."

Ingrid heard a muffled sob, then a louder one.

"Please, Karla. We know you've been through so much. But the sooner you give us the information, the faster we can get him behind bars."

"OK. Where should I start?"

"How about height and build?"

"He's skinny… wiry, I guess, only a few inches taller than me, I'm five-foot-six. No, wait. That's how tall I was when I was fourteen. Maybe I grew since then."

Ingrid heard a distant rustling of paper.

"You're five-foot-nine."

"I am?"

"You don't remember the nurse measuring you during the medical exam?"

"I guess I had other things on my mind."

"What else can you tell us about him?"

"He's white, but tanned, like he's spent a lot of years outside. He has tattoos on his arms, from the middle of his forearms right up almost to his shoulders. Old style ones, like you'd see on some old sailor or something. He has greased-back dark hair, going gray a little above his ears. Long sideburns."

"Does he have an accent?"

"Southern. Couldn't say which state, though."

"Did he ever talk about where he came from, originally?"

"He always said he was from everywhere. Real proud of the fact he lived like a gypsy."

"A gypsy?"

"He traveled around the country, always moving from state to state, he said. Until he came here. And decided to settle down."

"What was he? Some sort of salesman?"

"No! He told me he managed the roller coaster at a traveling carnival."

Dear God.

Ingrid closed her eyes. Her head started to buzz. An intense heat rose from the middle of her chest up into her neck and head. She couldn't breathe.

A traveling carnival?

It had to be the same man who took Megan.

31

The next day Ingrid rose early. She was dressed and making her way to the officers' mess for breakfast before seven.

The previous night she had continued to listen right to the end of the mp3 recording, then listened to the whole thing again, just to make sure she hadn't missed anything. Then she'd called Mike Stiller, impressing upon him once again the importance of the DNA test for the third woman.

"I'm still working on it," he'd said. "You have to trust that I'm doing everything I can here." He'd sounded pissed that she'd interrupted the ball game he was watching.

"The more I hear about this case, the more convinced I am that this guy took my friend. Is the investigating team getting any closer to finding him?"

"They're making some progress. That's all they can tell me."

By the time she'd hung up on him and laid her head on the pillow, her mind was swirling with images of carnival men, tattoos, bright lights and contorted half-smiling, half-grimacing faces. She could taste the sweetness of cotton candy at the back of her throat and hear the off-key steam organ music all jumbled up with the screams of people on the roller coaster. It hadn't taken much to transport her back eighteen years and four thousand miles. Mike Stiller had to come through with more information for her. He just had to. The waiting and not knowing whether or not the third victim was Megan was getting harder with each day that passed.

Halfway through breakfast a Security Forces sergeant came to her table and told her Gurley was waiting for her in his office. Five minutes later she arrived at a single-story cinder block building that looked like a bunker from WWII.

She was met at the door by another uniformed sergeant, this one a woman, and led through an outer office to an interior door. The sergeant knocked twice and opened the door without waiting. As Ingrid stepped inside the inner office she saw Gurley sitting behind a wide metal desk, his back to her, his chair facing the wall. He was on the phone, but he wasn't speaking. After a moment he swung around to face her and held up a forefinger indicating he'd be another minute. Ingrid decided to fill the time by looking at the framed photographs hanging on the wall next to the door. They all featured Gurley posing with high ranking officers, various Secretaries of Defense, and even one or two ex-presidents. Gurley hadn't struck Ingrid as the boasting kind, so an array of his claims to fame arranged on the wall like a collection of hunting trophies seemed a little out of place.

Gurley slammed down the phone. "Sonofabitch!" He took a breath. "Him, not you," he said, staring at the phone.

"Something to do with the Foster investigation?" Ingrid asked.

"No—Air Force bureaucratic bullshit. I should be used to it by now, but it still pisses me off. It's a waste of time and money." Gurley stood up and stretched his arms above his head. For a moment Ingrid was sure his knuckles would graze the ceiling. "I didn't ask you last night," he said, "did you get a sense from Sherwood that she thinks Foster is likely to stay in the area?"

"I don't think she was lying when she told us she has no idea what Foster's plans are. Without the supplies and the cash from Sherwood, I guess Foster has fewer options."

"I wouldn't be taken in by her story."

"I have done this before, you know. I can get a sense when somebody is lying to me."

"Well, I don't trust her. I'm planning on keeping her under

surveillance today, just in case she gets any ideas about helping Foster again."

"I'm not staking out the pub. It'd be a waste of time."

Gurley folded his arms across his broad chest. "I had no intention of asking you to. I'll get a couple of my team to check it out."

"Good, waste their time instead of mine."

The landline on Gurley's desk started to ring. Its tone sounded particularly shrill as the noise bounced off the cinder block walls.

"Excuse me." Gurley snatched the handset and turned away from her. "You're saying he's on the line right now?" He glanced over his shoulder at Ingrid. "Of course you should patch him through. Set up a trace on the call, as fast as you can."

Ingrid ran around the desk. "Is it Foster?"

Gurley nodded.

"Put the call on speaker phone."

Gurley narrowed his eyes, clearly reluctant to comply with her request. "He called to speak to his superior officer. His superior officer has transferred the call to me. Foster doesn't know who the hell you are."

"You want me to escalate this? With the embassy? With the Pentagon?"

"This is Major Gurley, Security Forces." He turned another few degrees away from her, the handset pressed hard against his ear. "Major Brown thought it best you speak to me."

Ingrid scanned the phone on the desk and stabbed at the only button that looked remotely like the right one. A crackle of static filled the room. Followed by an irritated sigh from Gurley.

"I know what you're doing. I know you'll be tracing this call, so I'm going to be quick. You have to listen to me without interrupting." Foster's voice was deeper than Ingrid had expected.

"Go on."

"You have to believe that I didn't hurt Molly. I could never hurt her. I love her and Tommy more than anything in the world. Jesus, until I saw the news reports, I thought she was dead.

That's why I panicked and took Tommy. I had to get him out of harm's way."

"Tell me what you've done to him," Gurley said.

"I told you not to interrupt. I haven't done anything. Tommy's right here with me. He's safe. I want him to stay that way. In order for that to happen, I need your help. I want to get him to my parents back home. You can arrange that for me, I know you can."

"Let me at least speak to Tommy, know for sure he's all right."

"I don't have time for that. I want him on a flight to the US by the end of tomorrow. He'll need a chaperone. Maybe one of your female officers. My mom and dad will take good care of him."

"We know Tommy was injured. We spoke to the doctor who treated him. What did you do to him?"

"I didn't do anything. Aren't you listening to me? I love my kids."

"I think it's best for Tommy, for you… for everyone… if you give yourself up. We can hear your side of the story then. Take all the… ah… mitigating circumstances into account."

"Story? What do you think this is? I'm not telling tales. Jesus. Why won't you listen to me? I want to make sure Tommy's safe. And Molly. She looked so tiny wired up to all those monitors. I just wanted to scoop her into my arms and protect her. Take her away with me. But I saw the cop guarding her. I figured she was in the best place. That she was safe. But as soon as she can travel I want her to go to my mom and dad's too."

The door opened and the female sergeant from the outer office held up a sheet of paper with the words: *keep him talking, partial location only* scrawled across it.

"A flight to the US and a chaperone will take some organizing, Kyle. It'd be much easier if you and Tommy come to the base, then we can start to put those wheels in motion for you."

Foster didn't reply.

"Kyle?"

"You're lying," Foster said, eventually. Then the line went dead.

"Goddammit!" Gurley slammed down the handset.

A moment later another MP ran in. "He's in northeast England, within a ten mile radius of the center of Newcastle."

Gurley considered the information for a moment. "A ten mile radius?" He paused a beat, glancing up at the ceiling. "That's an area of over three hundred square miles. For crying out loud, you couldn't do any better than that?"

"It took a little while to set up the trace. He hung up too soon."

"I want a trace ready to go next time."

"You think he'll call back?" Ingrid asked.

"We have something he wants: a plane ride home for his son. Of course he'll call back."

"What did you make of all that? He seemed genuinely concerned for Tommy's safety. And his daughter's, for that matter. Do you think he was suggesting they're not safe with Carrie?"

"Yes—I do think the sonofabitch was suggesting that."

Ingrid remembered what Sherwood had told her about Carrie Foster's 'baby blues'. Maybe they were a lot more serious than she'd realized. "At least we solved the mystery of the impostor in Molly's hospital room."

"We were so close to him."

"And now he's over two hundred fifty miles away."

"How'd he get to Newcastle so fast?" Gurley's face had reddened.

"I'd say train, but the local cops should have been liaising with British Transport Police, watching all the local stations and train lines."

"*Should* have been."

"We need to check out the CCTV footage they have, maybe we'll see something they missed."

"So damn close," Gurley said again and thumped the desk with a fist.

The female sergeant ran into the room again, stopped abruptly in front of Gurley's desk and stood to attention.

"Tell me you've pin-pointed his location," Gurley barked.

"No, sir. It's something else." The sergeant glanced at Ingrid, her lips pursed.

"For God's sake, you can speak freely in front of Agent Skyberg!"

"The munitions store have just contacted me. A hand gun and ten rounds of ammunition are missing from their inventory."

32

Ingrid managed to run after Gurley and climb into the passenger seat of the jeep just as he stamped his foot on the gas. He hadn't invited her to join him, but she'd be damned if she let him shut her out. They made the three minute journey in silence—Gurley clearly too mad to talk.

The munitions store was on the other side of the base, a single-story concrete bunker with no windows and one double door made of steel. Gurley stopped the jeep without bothering to park it in the demarcated bay and jumped out. Ingrid made sure she was hot on his heels as the metal door opened and an MP stepped out.

"Sir!" The MP stood to attention.

"At ease. Show me where the gun was taken from," Gurley said, stooping low to get through the doorway.

The MP stepped in front of Ingrid. "I'm sorry, ma'am. Authorized Air Force personnel only."

"Hey, Major Gurley!" she called after him as he disappeared inside. "Tell him I have full authority."

"Not Air Force authority," Gurley shouted back at her.

The MP followed his superior inside and shut the door in Ingrid's face. She slammed a hand against it. Then she took a deep breath and, eager not to feel completely useless, pulled her phone from her purse. She put in a call to Mike Stiller to find out what was happening with the abductee case, got his voicemail and left a curt message, taking her anger with Gurley out on Mike. Which wouldn't help her get the information she wanted any faster. Then she put in another call to the local cops, requesting they make the CCTV footage from the local train stations available for viewing.

After that all she could do was pace up and down outside the steel doors waiting for Gurley to re-emerge. When he eventually did, ten minutes later, he ignored her completely and marched back to the jeep.

"Well?" Ingrid said, running after him. "What did you find out?"

Gurley crunched the gearshift into reverse and drove a fast wide loop to turn the jeep around. "The last inventory was taken at seven p.m. yesterday evening."

"So that means the gun and bullets went missing some time last night."

Gurley didn't respond.

"Then it couldn't have been Foster," Ingrid continued. "He had to be staking out a muddy field in the middle of nowhere last night."

"Sherwood didn't get there until eight-thirty. Foster had plenty of time."

"Oh come on, how could he have entered the base without anyone seeing him and then break into the locked munitions store? Stuff must go missing here all the time."

"We can't rule out the possibility that the suspect is now armed."

"You just spoke to him—did he sound like a man who'd break into an Air Force base? He's just interested in looking out for his kids."

"I don't know what's gotten into you. Why are you so keen to believe Kyle Foster is innocent?"

After talking to Rachelle Carver and Yvonne Sherwood, Ingrid wasn't entirely sure what to think, but she was determined to keep an open mind. "You must have CCTV cameras on the base. Check the footage. You'll see Foster had nothing to do with it."

"The two most useful cameras are out of action. The lenses have been smashed. Glass and small rocks were found at the base of the poles they're mounted on. Foster could easily be responsible for that."

"It still doesn't explain how he got onto the base in the first place."

"What is it with you? Why have you started defending him?" Gurley stamped his foot on the gas and the car lurched forward.

"I'm not—I just don't see why he'd do something like that. Has he even had small arms training?"

"He's a first lieutenant in the US Air Force—of course he has." Gurley took a sharp left turn, slamming Ingrid hard against the passenger door.

Slightly winded, Ingrid grabbed onto the dash and righted herself. "Tell me how he got past the guards on the security gate."

"How big do you think the perimeter fence is here?"

Ingrid shrugged. "A mile… two miles?"

"Ten. We check and repair it on a regular basis, but it's possible there's a hole some place."

"A place that Foster just happens to know about?"

"I'm treating Kyle Foster as an armed suspect who kidnapped his own son. If you want to cast him in a different light, fine. But I'm warning you—I won't have your out of whack judgment affect the way this operation moves forward."

"Guilty till proven innocent, huh?"

"It's the military way."

"Foster has no reason to arm himself."

"Leverage."

"What?"

"You heard what he said. He's started making demands. Making them in possession of a lethal weapon is a whole different ball game."

"But he wants to protect his son, not threaten to hurt him."

"Who says he'll threaten Tommy? Besides, you didn't believe

that bullshit just now, did you? He's trying to pin the blame for what happened to Molly on her mother. Sonofabitch. The 'making sure Tommy's safe' line is a smokescreen. He's just trying to protect his own ass. Please tell me you didn't fall for it."

They drove back the rest of the way to Gurley's office in silence. When they arrived, Ingrid followed him into the building even though he hadn't bothered to invite her. He was on the phone requesting a helicopter to take them to Newcastle before she'd even sat down.

"You think that's really the best way to use our resources?" Ingrid asked when he hung up. She was doing her best not to scream at him for being so gung-ho he hadn't even considered the facts.

"There's no point in looking for him here, is there?"

"But you said yourself—it's a lot of ground to cover. The Northumbria police are in a much better position to search for him."

"While we sit around doing nothing?"

"As soon as they have something solid, then we follow up. In a chopper it wouldn't take that long to get there." Ingrid wasn't sure she was getting through to him at all—his expression was completely blank. "Besides, I'd like to see the CCTV footage from the local train stations. I've already arranged for the force here to make it available to us."

"Why?"

"I'd like to at least check if he has Tommy with him. Wouldn't you?"

Gurley opened his mouth, but couldn't come up with a counter argument. Instead he picked up the phone and barked at his sergeant to find out who the highest ranking police officer in Newcastle was and to get the sorry-assed bastard on the phone.

33

In less than a half hour Ingrid and Gurley were sitting in front of a bank of TV monitors at the local railway hub station. Lined up for their scrutiny on two larger monitors was the footage from the two closest train stations to Freckenham between the hours of eight p.m. and two a.m. the night before. Ingrid had chosen the timeframe without consulting Gurley. She figured Foster was probably watching a muddy field until around nine p.m. and the last scheduled train at either of the local stations was just after midnight. She'd requested a wider timescale for the footage just to play it safe.

"We don't have a lot of time here," Gurley told the technician assigned to operate the equipment for them. "We have some place else to be."

The technician said nothing but made a point of exhaling noisily and shifting in his seat.

"OK, then why don't we start with the footage from nine p.m. onwards?" Ingrid suggested. "We have a pretty good idea where Foster was before that."

The technician quickly found the right point in the footage and hit play on both monitors. The left hand one showed all activity around the entrance of Newmarket station, the other at Kennett, a much smaller station that was closer to the base. At first Ingrid switched her attention between both screens, but as the uneventful scenes played out for half a minute or so, she started to feel a little nauseous. "Let's play these at eight times normal speed, I'll keep my eyes peeled on the left hand monitor, you take the right. OK?"

Gurley grunted his agreement and folded his arms.

After running the footage through from nine p.m. to the final trains at both stations with no sign of a man and a boy, Ingrid asked the technician to stop the playback. "Is it possible for someone to get onto the platforms without using the main entrance at these stations?"

"Possible, but not likely. Security's been tightened up in the last couple of years—to prevent fare evasion. I suppose if someone is really determined to get in they still can, but it'd mean scaling a ten foot wall with barbed wire strung along the top of it."

"Can you get on a train without a ticket?" she asked.

"If you've bypassed the ticket barriers at the entrance you can. The conductor on the train checks that passengers have valid tickets, but he'll also sell you a ticket if you don't have one."

"Can we get a record of any tickets sold on trains last night?"

"You can, but it might take a while."

Gurley let out another grunt. "We're wasting our time here. There's no sign of Foster and Tommy in this footage. Either he didn't use the main entrance—which seems unlikely—or Foster doesn't have Tommy with him anymore." He clapped a heavy hand on the technician's shoulder, making the man jump in his seat. "Thanks for your time. We won't take up any more of it."

"Maybe we can extend the window, start the footage a little earlier," Ingrid said, not wanting to give up just yet.

"I'm leaving, if you want a ride back to base, I suggest you come with me right now."

"Let's give it another fifteen minutes—how will that make a difference to today's schedule?"

Gurley shook his head and frowned at her. "Fifteen and no more."

"So—you want to see the footage from six? Five p.m.?" The technician looked up at her.

"No, same time frame as before—start it at nine but play it at four times normal speed. I saw something early on that bugged me for some reason and I'm not sure why."

The technician did as he was told. Under twenty minutes into the recording Ingrid asked him to freeze the footage on the left hand monitor. She jabbed a finger at the screen. "There, you see that?"

Gurley leaned in closer and peered at the blurry image. "What am I looking for?"

"This guy with the backpack. Can you rewind a few seconds and play at normal speed?"

The technician complied.

"See the way he's walking? Staggering might be a more accurate description. Either he's so drunk he can't walk straight, or that pack on his back is throwing him off balance. He's really struggling to get around."

They all continued to watch the man awkwardly make his way to the ticket counter. His right hand flew up and backwards and he seemed to slap the side of the backpack. He then readjusted the weight on his back.

"Can you get a close-up of his face?" Ingrid asked.

"Sure."

Although the image wasn't clear, what was evident was the color of the man's hair—much darker than Kyle Foster's.

"Could that be him?" Ingrid asked Gurley. "He's the right build and height. He could have dyed his hair." Ingrid stared hard at the screen. "Pull back again, so we can see his whole body." She leaned further forward. "Did you see that?"

"Something moved in that bag," the technician said, a little excitedly, when Gurley didn't respond.

"Hit the pause button again, will you?" Gurley ordered the technician. He turned to look at Ingrid. "Are you seriously suggesting this is Foster and he's stuffed Tommy into the backpack?"

"It could be, couldn't it? The timing fits. Can we get footage from the platform cameras? Which platform would he need if he were planning to head north?"

The technician took a few minutes to cue up the required recordings and fast forward to the correct timestamp. "There are four cameras on the right platform." He tapped the four split screen images in turn with a pen.

They watched in silence as the footage played in real time. They continued to scrutinize the recording for ten minutes until the first train arrived. The man they'd identified hadn't appeared on the platform in that time. At quadruple speed they watched for another five minutes. Another train arrived. Still no sign of the man with the wriggling backpack.

"Where'd he go?" Gurley sounded curious and impatient at the same time.

"Maybe he wanted to cover his tracks a little, took a train some place else, then backtracked," Ingrid suggested.

"We can check the other platforms, give me a second to bring up the relevant recordings."

"What are we trying to prove here?" Now Gurley just sounded pissed. "This guy may or may not be Foster. Tommy may or may not be inside that bag. It doesn't get us any closer to finding him." He shook his head. "Jesus, what kind of man stuffs an eight-year-old kid into a bag anyway?"

"You're right," Ingrid conceded.

Gurley opened his eyes wide. "I am?"

Ingrid realized she wasn't going to get more definite proof that the man with the backpack was Foster, so decided to withdraw as gracefully as she could. Better to make a concession to Gurley when there was nothing much at stake. "We should try to figure out why Foster's decided to head north. Who does he know up there? Why make such a long journey?" Ingrid was hoping a conversation about Foster's motives might help pinpoint his possible location.

"Let's ask those questions on the way, shall we?"

Ingrid thanked the technician, requested he send her as good a close-up still image of the man with the unwieldy backpack as he could, then she and Gurley made a swift exit.

Halfway back to Freckenham, Gurley's phone rang. He

answered on hands-free. A hesitant voice the other end crackled into the car.

"Major Gurley?"

"Yes?"

"Sergeant Willis here, sir. We've had a report sent to us from the local police department in Northumbria that I thought you should know about right away."

"What is it, Willis?" Gurley didn't bother to mask his impatience.

"A flying club in Felton—about twenty miles north of Newcastle—has reported one of their aircraft is missing."

"Missing?"

"Stolen. Must have happened in the last two hours they think."

"And they've only just noticed?" Gurley glanced at Ingrid. "What kind of aircraft?"

"Helicopter, sir. A Eurocopter EC120. First Lieutenant Foster flew choppers in Afghanistan as part of his search and rescue missions."

"Thank you, Willis. I'm well aware of that fact." Gurley ended the call and pulled the car over to the side of the road. He slammed his fists against the steering wheel. "Goddammit! The goddamn sonofabitch could be anywhere by now."

34

After Jack Gurley agreed with Ingrid that a trip to the airfield in Northumberland was a waste of time, he drove her to Bury St Edmunds railway station and left her to get back to London by her own devices. The train journey was a little uncomfortable, and took longer than she would have liked, but she was relieved to be headed back to the embassy without Gurley breathing down her neck.

When she finally returned to her desk, late afternoon, she discovered a rectangular, Fed-Ex labeled box sitting beside her computer monitor.

"Hey, Ingrid, I didn't expect you back so soon," Jennifer said when she walked into the office a moment later, a steaming cup of something herbal in her hand. It smelled as if the clerk had gathered up a few blades of grass from Grosvenor Square and poured boiling water over them.

"When did that arrive?" Ingrid nodded toward the parcel, a hand shoved into each armpit. She circled the desk, not wanting to get anywhere near the package. Certainly not intending to touch it.

"It's OK—security have scanned it," Jennifer told her. "It won't puff white powder into your face when you open it. Or explode. Did you see it's from Minnesota?"

Ingrid didn't need to check the 'from' address—she knew

exactly who had sent it and what was inside. Which was why she was so reluctant to touch it and why she had such a sick feeling in her stomach. Jennifer continued to look at her expectantly.

"Aren't you going to open it?" she said, her eyes wide in anticipation.

"Nah, I know what it is."

Jennifer nodded excitedly.

"Just a pair of shoes I asked my mom to pick up for me."

"Oh."

"Sorry to disappoint."

"I didn't mean to pry… I just thought…"

"It's OK, Jennifer. No problem." Ingrid took a deep breath and, using just thumb and index finger, transferred the box from the desk to a drawer beneath it. No wonder Svetlana hadn't sent her the photographs she'd asked for. Not with this ticking time bomb about to arrive any minute. What did she hope it would achieve?

Aware Jennifer's gaze was still trained on her, Ingrid concentrated on keeping the expression on her face as neutral as possible. She'd deal with Svetlana's surprise package when she got home. She grabbed a clean shirt from the bottom drawer of her desk and hurried to the ladies' restroom to change into it, all the time trying to keep thoughts of Svetlana's parcel from her mind. Then she retrieved her cell from her pocket, found DCI Radcliffe's number and hit the call option. As she wasn't sure about the theory she'd come up with on the long train journey back to London, she wanted to speak to the detective in private—and the ladies' restroom was as good a place as any. Radcliffe picked up after several rings.

"You've got a bloody cheek calling me," he said before Ingrid got a chance to say hello. "Why is it I find out Foster's called the base from one of Gurley's men hours after the event? What happened to the timely exchange of information?"

Ingrid silently cursed Gurley. He could have at least warned her one of his team would be speaking to Radcliffe. If she hadn't needed a favor from the chief inspector she would have been tempted to find an excuse to hang up on him. Instead she'd need to beg for forgiveness. "I guess I got a little too involved on the ground to consider the bigger picture. I'm sorry. I assumed Major Gurley would inform you about the situation sooner. It was just a case of miscommunication." The words sounded pathetic enough to her. She could imagine the look of contempt on Radcliffe's face. "There is a bright side," she added.

"Really?"

"Kyle Foster's request for a safe passage for Tommy back to the US at least means the boy is still alive."

"But we don't know that for sure. Without concrete proof I can't tell Mrs Foster."

"What do you make of Kyle Foster's request?"

Radcliffe didn't answer right away. Ingrid couldn't judge if it was because he was carefully considering her question or was too mad at her to respond. "The man is deluded if he thinks anyone will agree to something like that," he finally said.

"But when he calls back, we should at least play along."

"When he calls back I want to be part of the conversation. Do you understand?"

"Of course. Timely exchange of information. I won't let you down again, chief inspector."

"Make sure you don't."

Ingrid pulled the phone away from her face and puffed out a breath. Why did working with local law enforcement always have to be this hard? It was just the same Stateside. She put the phone back to her ear and did her best to stay calm.

"Why are you calling, anyway? Do you have another update for me?"

"I need a favor." She paused a beat and braced herself for his response.

"Of course you bloody well do. I should have guessed."

"Please—just hear me out. I've been working on a theory." Ingrid hesitated. She hadn't said it out loud to anyone yet, and she wasn't sure just how screwy the idea would sound.

"Spit it out, for God's sake—I don't have all day."

"I've talked to a few people now about Kyle Foster and they

all tell me what a great dad he is. How they can't imagine him doing anything to hurt his kids."

"So what? We know he flipped. His PTSD got the better of him. Doesn't matter how good a dad he's been in the past."

"But I've seen cases like this before. Usually the father wipes out the whole family then takes his own life. Why bother to take Tommy with him? Why get him treated at the hospital?"

"Why cause Tommy's injuries in the first place?"

Ingrid sucked in a long breath.

Here we go.

"We don't know for sure Kyle was responsible for hurting Tommy."

"What?"

"Shouldn't we at least consider the possibility that Carrie could have hurt him?"

Radcliffe didn't answer, but Ingrid heard him expel an exasperated breath. "You're basing this theory on what exactly?" He didn't wait for a reply before continuing. "Nothing more than a few good words about Foster's character?"

Ingrid hesitated again. She wasn't sure whether she should bring it up, but Radcliffe clearly needed to be persuaded. "We searched Foster's house," she said, quickly.

"We?"

"Major Gurley and I. It's on the base, Gurley has full jurisdiction."

"And?"

"Hidden away in a dark corner of Carrie Foster's closet was a bottle of vodka."

"That's the best you can do? So she likes a drink now and again."

"Hiding booze? Surely that's got to set alarm bells ringing."

"Tell me you've got more than that."

"Someone told me Carrie's been having a hard time since Molly was born. The baby blues, they called it." Ingrid waited for a response, but it didn't come, so she plowed on. "Isn't it worth investigating? Can we really just ignore the possibility Carrie might have hurt Molly too?"

"You're very free and easy with the 'we' pronoun, aren't you? Does Major Gurley agree with your theory?"

I don't give a rat's ass what Gurley thinks.

"I haven't discussed it with him. I thought I'd run it past you first."

"I'm honored."

"I'd like to talk to the consultant at the hospital to discuss Molly's injuries in detail. I was hoping you could arrange an appointment for me—it might speed the whole process up."

"He's a very busy man."

"I'm sure he'd make the time if you convinced him how crucial it was to the ongoing investigation."

Radcliffe let out another exaggerated sigh. "It's too late to set up a meeting for today. And I want to make this quite clear—I'll lead any interview with him. This is my investigation."

"I know that." Ingrid was determined not to apologize to Radcliffe again.

"I'll call you tomorrow and let you know what I've managed to arrange."

Ingrid was just about to hang up when Radcliffe said, "Molly regained consciousness half an hour ago."

"She did? That's fantastic."

"I wouldn't celebrate just yet. It's not clear if any permanent damage has been done."

He hung up before Ingrid had the chance to thank him for letting her know. She made her way back to the office, tapping Gurley's number into her phone, to let him know the good news. She even had a little bounce to her step.

But as she reached the door of the office, she remembered the package her mother had sent, nestling innocently in her desk drawer.

A shiver went up her spine.

35

Ingrid was relieved to finally return home after her sojourn in Suffolk. She didn't leave the embassy until after eight and was looking forward to a good night's sleep in her own bed. Even though she had a feeling she was unlikely to get it. Not with Svetlana's parcel sitting on the coffee table in the living room. She wanted to ignore it, to open it tomorrow. Or the next day. But she knew she couldn't. She knew she wouldn't be able to get any peace at all until she unwrapped the box and inspected each item inside.

First, though, she needed to get changed. She threw on some sweat pants and a baggy tee shirt and left her running shoes by the apartment door. After she had dealt with the package, she might feel the need to hit the well-lit and empty sidewalks of Maida Vale and St John's Wood.

For a moment she pictured herself running across the street in Abbey Road. Her dad had been a big Beatles fan. He would have loved a photograph of her sprinting over the black and white stripes of the crosswalk.

Her breath caught in her throat. She could go for days, or even weeks without missing her dad, but every now and then, a memory of him would catch her off guard and knock her sideways. How she wished he was still around. He'd know exactly what to say when she opened the Fed-Ex box.

Ingrid knew she couldn't ignore it any longer.

She padded slowly into the kitchen, her feet feeling cool on the tile floor, grabbed a bottle of Finnish vodka from the freezer compartment of the tall refrigerator and a glass from the cabinet above the sink, and shuffled into the living room. She slumped down onto the couch and stared at the box in front of her. As she opened the icy bottle of vodka and poured herself a generous measure, she wondered how much of it would be left by the time she'd finished going through the contents of the parcel.

The perforated strip pulled off easily enough and the outer cardboard container peeled away to reveal exactly what she was expecting: a beaten up old sneaker box decorated with hand-drawn flowers and hearts on the lid and around the sides. Very gingerly she lifted one corner of the lid and slid it onto the table.

She took a deep breath and forced herself to look inside.

Lying on top, as if Svetlana had strategically positioned it there, and despite the fact that the parcel had been air freighted all the way from Minnesota, was the most difficult item Ingrid knew she'd have to confront. Using just the tips of her fingers, she pulled out the photo booth strip of four color photographs. Each one was posed individually. Each one featured Ingrid and her best friend in the whole world. She and Megan were pulling faces, sticking out their tongues, tugging on each other's braids and collapsing in fits of laughter as the final flash clicked.

Tears sprang into Ingrid's eyes at the sight of Megan. Especially Megan laughing. The last time Ingrid had seen her face it had been contorted with fear. Tears streamed down Ingrid's face. There was no stopping them. It was the effect Svetlana had probably been hoping for when she'd arranged the contents of the box. It must have taken a while for her mother to unearth it, buried in an unused corner of the basement.

But what did her mother hope would happen when the tears stopped? Did she suppose Ingrid would be calling her right away, desperate to speak to Kathleen Avery? Didn't she know her better than that? She wiped her cheeks with the bottom of her tee shirt and dabbed at her eyes.

Dammit.

She wasn't going to let Svetlana orchestrate her reactions from over 4000 miles away. She picked up the box and shook its contents to get a better look at what was inside without having to actually touch anything. She spotted two of her favorite Mickey Mouse hair grips, Megan had a pair just the same. Then she saw three large metal pins, one featuring Erasure and two decorated with images of a very young George Michael. To one side of those was a length of red and silver ribbon Megan had tied around one of Ingrid's birthday gifts. She shook the box again to see, right at the bottom, wrapped in an almost translucent layer of tissue paper, a lock of Megan's curly brown hair.

A sudden wave of nausea swept up from the pit of Ingrid's stomach. She grabbed the vodka bottle and took a large mouthful, waiting for the burn of the alcohol to extinguish the taste of vomit at the back of her throat.

Ingrid had snipped off a lock of her own bright, almost white, blond hair and given it to Megan. They had decided exchanging locks of hair was a more meaningful and permanent gesture than mingling blood from cut fingers. They both agreed they should do something that would last forever.

Ingrid took another swig of vodka then slowly reached into the box. But she couldn't bring herself to touch even the tissue paper that surrounded the lock of hair. She wondered if Kathleen Avery still kept Megan's treasure trove contained within a shoe box. Whether she had seen the lock of Ingrid's hair wrapped in tissue paper. The thought of Kathleen sifting through Megan's prized possessions set off another deluge of uncontrollable tears.

When the tears subsided, Ingrid sat very still for a few moments, not quite knowing what to do next. Svetlana was probably waiting for her call. But there was no way she could speak to her mother the way she felt right now. She knew she'd say things she'd regret. She retrieved her cell from the coffee table and scrolled through her contacts list until she found Mike Stiller's number. She hit the call button and waited, hoping she would be able to control any tremor in her voice.

"Hey, Mike. Tell me you have some news. I really need some good news. Tell me the DNA test has been arranged."

"Are you loaded?"

"What?"

"You're slurring your words."

"I am not."

"Have it your own way."

"Well?"

"I don't have any good news to share with you."

"What is that supposed to mean? You have bad news?"

"I planned on calling you tomorrow. What time is it there now?"

"Tell me the news, for God's sake."

"The third woman started talking. She's from Indiana, she's twenty-nine years old. She claims her name is Brenda Lohan." He paused for a moment. "I'm sorry, Ingrid. She's not your friend."

"What do you mean she 'claims' her name is Brenda Lohan?"

"The investigating agents think she may have lifted the name from a magazine they'd given her to read."

"What?"

"They can't find a record of any Brenda Lohan of the right age."

"If she's lying about her identity, maybe she's made up the other stuff too."

"A twelve-year-old girl went missing from Columbus, Indiana in 1995."

"That was the year Megan disappeared."

"Trust me—this woman is not her. Too much of what she said was accurate. About her home town, her school. Everything."

"Except her real name."

"After so many years, maybe she forgot her real name."

"Yeah and maybe she's lying."

"It's not your friend, Ingrid. I know you don't want to hear that but—"

"I'm sorry, Mike. I have to go." She hung up. She couldn't listen to any more. She poured herself another large vodka and drained the glass. Finally she slumped back onto the couch, still clutching her cell phone. She wanted to tell somebody what Mike had told her. But she couldn't tell Svetlana. Not yet. She scrolled to Natasha McKittrick's number and called her. The call went straight to voicemail. She didn't bother leaving a message. She went through the remainder of her contacts list. There were so few people she could share this with. She stopped scrolling when she reached the entry for Ralph Mills. He was a good listener. But could she really burden him with all of this? Could she risk being that vulnerable with him? They hardly knew one another. She hit the 'call' option before she could talk herself out of it.

He answered right away.

"Are you back from the wilds of East Anglia?"

"Uh huh. Listen, do you have a few minutes? I really need to talk something through with you."

"Jesus, what's wrong? You sound awful."

"Do you have the time to—"

"I'm coming over." He hung up.

Ingrid called him back. A phone conversation was one thing. But face to face? She wasn't ready for that. The call diverted straight to voicemail.

Twenty minutes later the intercom was buzzing insistently in the hall.

36

Immediately after Ralph's call, Ingrid drank another glass of vodka then brewed herself a strong coffee. She had just started to drink it when he arrived. She padded unsteadily from the living room to the hall, coffee cup in hand, concentrating hard on walking in a straight line. Although the room wasn't exactly spinning, she was aware her senses were a little dulled. After what Mike Stiller had told her she should have been grateful for the sensation, but she needed to be alert enough not to let her guard down with Ralph. She didn't want to risk doing or saying something she may regret.

As she slowly opened the apartment door she wondered whether it would be best to tell him to turn right around and go back home. But Ralph's anxious expression took her by surprise. She tried to smile at him, hoping to prove he really didn't need to be quite so concerned. But the muscles in her face refused to cooperate.

"It's late," Ingrid said, "I didn't mean for you to come over. We both have work in the morning."

"Actually, I don't start until midday. I can stay up as late as you need me to."

Should he really be staying at all? He followed her inside and closed the door. She stopped at the kitchen.

"Can I get you anything? A coffee? Tea?"

"A cold beer would be great."

"Go on through to the living room. I'll be right in." Ingrid set her coffee cup on the counter and opened the refrigerator. She stood there for a while breathing in the crisp air, wondering again if she'd made a mistake phoning him. She would ask him to leave after he'd finished his beer, she decided. Before would just seem rude.

She shuffled slowly into the living room, bottle of Mexican beer in one hand, her coffee in the other, to find Ralph standing by the window looking out at the view south toward the center of town. She joined him and handed him the beer. He clinked it against her mug.

"Cheers. Great view you've got up here."

Ingrid's apartment was only six floors up, from the end of the roof terrace she could make out some of the major London landmarks. She'd only moved in three months ago and the novelty of the view still hadn't worn off.

"It's my favorite thing about the place."

"Beats my one-bedroom basement flat, that's for sure. I really like the minimalist interior design."

Ingrid glanced at the few items of furniture: the couch, the coffee table and the low, freestanding bookshelf on the other side of the room. "I guess I need to do a little shopping. All this stuff was already here when I moved in."

Ralph took a swig of beer, then said, "So. Tell me what's wrong."

"It doesn't seem so bad now. I feel guilty you've come all the way here."

"No distance at all. Honestly. Any time you feel like you want to talk, I'll be here." He looked toward the couch. "Shall we sit down?"

He pushed off his shoes and curled his long legs under him as he sat down. He patted the leather couch with the flat of his hand. "Come on, sit down and tell me all about it." As Ingrid lowered herself onto the couch she noticed Ralph was staring at the shoebox and its contents on the coffee table.

"What's all this?"

Ingrid blinked. "It's… ah… it's…" Tears prickled her eyelids. *Dammit.* She couldn't cry in front of him. She squeezed her coffee cup a little tighter, sucked down what she hoped was a silent deep breath.

"Bloody hell." He slipped an arm around her shoulders, pulling her toward him until her head was nuzzling his neck. He smelled fresh, an aroma of soap rather than overpowering cologne. She liked it. She let herself be held for a few moments longer, then gently pulled away, her tears now safely under control.

"You remember a little while ago I told you I lost a friend when I was a teenager?" Ingrid said, aware she'd have to continue now she'd started, but not entirely sure how.

Ralph nodded and put his beer on the table. He twisted on the couch to get a better look at her.

"Pretty much ever since it happened I've been hoping that Megan would be discovered some day, alive. For a long while I fantasized I'd be the one to rescue her. But over time I realized that she was most probably dead, killed not long after she'd been abducted."

Ralph held his tongue. Ingrid was grateful he had the sense to know not to speak.

"A few days ago, three women were discovered in a house just outside Jackson, Minnesota. That's only thirty miles from where Megan disappeared." Ingrid drew in a snagging little breath. She wrinkled her nose and swallowed, trying hard to keep fresh tears at bay. "One of the women couldn't be identified. I found out tonight that even though she was abducted the same year, even though her description roughly matches Megan… Oh God… it's not her. It's not my friend." Ingrid sniffed. "I knew it was a long shot. I knew that. But it didn't stop me hoping." She picked up Ralph's beer and took a swig. Then she handed it to him. He hesitated before taking it. "I can get you another," she told him.

"I think maybe you might need it more than me." He put it back on the table. "And these things in the box, they're from your childhood? They remind you of Megan?"

Ingrid nodded. "My mom sent them to me. I think she's trying to make me feel so bad I'll agree to do what she wants."

"And what's that?"

"For years she's tried to bully me into having a long conversation with Megan's mom, Kathleen. But I just can't. I can't face her."

"You don't want to relive it. I understand." Ralph put his hand over Ingrid's. His fingers felt warm and strong.

"It's not that. I relive what happened most days. I can't avoid it. A sound or a smell can trigger the exact same feeling I had at the time. The sickness in my stomach. The fear. The guilt I felt afterwards."

"Guilt? It wasn't your fault."

"But it was."

"Some sick bastard took her. How could you be to blame for that?"

"I ran. I thought she was right behind me. I was slow, but she was even slower. I abandoned her. If I'd stayed I could have protected her."

"You have no way of knowing that. What if he was armed? He might have snatched you both."

"But I *ran*. Don't you get it? I didn't look back. I just kept on running until I was so out of breath I couldn't take another step." An involuntary sob burst out of her mouth. She took a moment to recover. "It was only then that I turned around. And she wasn't there. She wasn't a few steps behind me. She'd gone. And it was my fault." It was the first time she'd admitted that to anyone. Now she had, she wished she could take it back. What must he think of her? "How can I speak to Kathleen when it was all my fault?"

"You can't keep saying that."

Ingrid jumped to her feet. "Why not?"

"Because it's not true. You were just a girl. You did the only natural, instinctive thing you could have done. You expected Megan to do the same."

"But she was heavier than me. And slower. It wasn't as if I didn't know that." She hurried over to the door that led out onto the roof terrace and unlocked it. She stepped outside and immediately the cool breeze enveloped her. August nights in London had been a lot cooler than she was expecting, but she was grateful for that now. She breathed in deep, expecting the tears to come again. But mercifully they didn't. After a moment Ralph stepped out onto the roof. He reached her in a few long strides, wrapped his arms around her and held her tight.

"It's not your fault," he said again, whispering into her ear.

"But it is. How can I face Kathleen when I know what I did? What I didn't do."

Ralph squeezed her tighter. "I lost someone too," he said, continuing to speak in a whisper. "I was even younger than you were when it happened. And for years afterwards I blamed myself."

Ingrid pulled away from him so she could look up into his face. "Who?"

He shook his head. "I shouldn't have brought it up. Totally different circumstances." He started to chew at his bottom lip.

"Who was it, Ralph?"

He wandered over to the edge of the roof, looking out at the view. Ingrid followed him.

"Who, Ralph?"

"My sister." He rubbed his eyes, keeping his face turned away from her. "She killed herself. I was the one who found her in the bathroom."

Ingrid slipped her hand into his and interlaced their fingers. "I'm so sorry."

"I was twelve. For years and years I thought that if I'd come home from school just a few minutes earlier, if I hadn't messed around with my mates in the park first… I could have saved her."

"But you stopped blaming yourself?"

He nodded.

"What changed? What made you think about it differently?"

"Another suicide. I was still a uniformed officer—it was just a few years ago. I was trying to convince a woman that she couldn't have done anything to change the outcome. That if someone is determined to end their own life, there's nothing you can do to dissuade them. Not in the long run."

"And telling her that, you convinced yourself?"

"Not right away. Took a long time before I came round to that way of thinking." He squeezed her hand and started to pull her toward the door. "Let's go back inside. You're shivering."

Still feeling light-headed from the vodka, Ingrid allowed herself to be led through the door and back into the living room. Ralph sat her on the couch and disappeared into the hall. He came back a few moments later with the vodka bottle and two glasses. He poured two generous measures and forced a glass into Ingrid's hand.

"I think you might need this." He watched as she took a sip. He didn't drink anything himself.

Ingrid leaned her head against his shoulder and closed her eyes. "Thank you for listening."

"It's what I came here for." He put an arm around her shoulders, his hand caressing the top of her arm. "You can tell me anything." He hauled her legs over his so that he was cradling her in his arms. He stroked her hair and kissed the top of her head.

Ingrid nodded, her eyes filling again. She raised the glass to her lips, trying to hide her face with it. Ralph settled back on the couch, his arm wrapped around her, his hand stroking her hair.

The insistent ring of Ingrid's cell phone woke her. It took a moment before she managed to open her eyes. Her mouth was dry. She was curled up on the couch, wrapped in a woolen throw.

Alone.

She sat up quickly and wished she hadn't. Her head started to pound. She found her phone by her feet. It was four-thirty in the morning. She recognized Gurley's number and quickly swiped the answer button.

"They found the chopper," he said brusquely.

"Have you any idea what time it is?"

"It was abandoned in a field in a place named Aylesbury—that's only forty miles from central London. He's come back to the capital. I was thinking maybe we should stake out the hospital."

Ingrid ran a hand through her hair. She was barely awake. No way was she rushing to UCH on a hunch of Gurley's at this time of the morning. "The location of the helicopter probably isn't even relevant. Foster could be anywhere." She tried to sit tall and straighten out the crick in her neck. Her whole body was sore as hell. "You should get some sleep. We'll think about a strategy in the morning."

"I'm not going to sleep until I have that sonofabitch locked in a cell."

37

Ingrid was early for her meeting. She'd arranged with DCI Radcliffe to meet in the café in the main University College Hospital building. She grabbed herself a half decent Americano and sat at a table by the window hoping to see Radcliffe when he arrived. The café was busy, mostly occupied by patients and visitors, no doubt grateful to escape the wards and consulting rooms for a few brief moments.

With a quarter of an hour to fill, Ingrid's mind naturally returned to the events of the night before. Or rather, the non-events. After she'd put the phone down to Gurley, she'd discovered a hastily written note Ralph had scrawled on the back of an envelope, explaining how it had gotten late, she had fallen asleep and he thought it best to leave, in the circumstances. He'd signed it with his initials. It seemed a little formal, given she'd pretty much poured her heart out to him. Ever since she'd read it she'd been worrying something had happened that she had no memory of. Had she really been that wasted? The vodka bottle had been half full when she started drinking. When she woke up at four-thirty it was empty. Had she just passed out? What did he mean, 'in the circumstances'? Had she said or done something embarrassing? Offended him, maybe?

She buried her head in her hands. She was driving herself crazy asking the same questions over and over. The more she tried to remember of the night, the more her brain stubbornly refused to recall anything more than the feel of his hand on her hair. Or the smell of his skin.

Good God. Had she blown her chance of starting something serious with the only man she'd met in a long time that she actually gave a damn about?

She retrieved her phone from her purse, and, not for the first time that morning, scrolled to his number in her contacts list. Her finger hovered over the call option.

She couldn't do it.

Instead she called Mike Stiller.

"Jesus, Skyberg. It's not even seven a.m. What's the matter with you?"

"Are you seriously telling me I woke you up?"

"As it happens, I'm on my way to the office. But I coulda been wrapped up in bed."

"Sure. You'd live at Bureau HQ if someone put a cot next to your desk."

"I guess you're calling for another update. Even though the woman isn't your friend."

Ingrid took a sip of coffee. "I can't let this one go now. I owe it to Megan's mom to see it through." She owed her a whole lot more besides.

"I do have more news, but you might not want to hear it."

"Nothing you tell me can be worse than what I've been imagining."

"You might want to brace yourself anyways."

Ingrid put down the coffee cup.

"They've started to recover some remains buried underneath the basement floor and in the backyard."

Ingrid swallowed. She'd figured the perp wouldn't have been satisfied with just three abductions. "How many?"

"So far they've identified bones from three different bodies. All female. All probably under forty years of age."

"So far? There could be more?"

"Maybe close to a dozen, according to my sources."

"Jesus, Mike."

"I know."

"And they're still no closer to tracking him down?"

"Getting closer. Maybe. The theory is that somebody's protecting him. When the details about the buried bodies hits the news channels, the hope is whoever's sheltering him will get a bad conscience and come forward."

"That's not much of a lead."

"They're working some other angles—I just don't know what they are yet."

"When you find out, will you tell me right away?"

"I'll do my best." He drew in a sharp breath. "Listen, I know this matters to you, but you gotta keep a little perspective, OK? Don't get obsessed with it, you hear?"

"Don't lecture me, Mike. Just give me what you've got just as soon as you get it." She hung up and shoved the phone back in her purse.

"You're keen."

Ingrid looked up to see Detective Chief Inspector Radcliffe looking down at her. "Can I get you a coffee?" she asked.

"I'm awash with the stuff. I had my first at half-six this morning and I haven't stopped since." He glanced at his watch. "Professor Glynde is expecting us."

"Sure." Ingrid drank the last of her Americano and pushed out her chair. "I really appreciate you setting up this meeting so fast."

"I'm still not entirely sure why I agreed to it."

"You don't want to leave any stones unturned any more than I do."

Radcliffe marched them down to the main reception area of the hospital and they took the elevator to the third floor. He led the way along a corridor with closed half-glazed doors on both sides. Ingrid supposed this floor housed the majority of the administration department.

"Glynde says he can spare us twenty minutes. He's due in theater in just under an hour."

"Busy man."

"Aren't we all." Radcliffe knocked on the door and pushed it open.

Inside, a young woman was standing behind a very organized desk, just a phone, computer and keyboard sitting on top. "DCI Radcliffe?" she asked.

Radcliffe nodded.

"Professor Glynde's expecting you." She grabbed a large gym bag from beneath the desk. "I'm off to lunch now—you'll be taking your own notes at the meeting?"

"We're fine, no need for you to stay." Radcliffe smiled at her and knocked on the interior door just to the right of her desk. This time he actually waited for a response before barging in. "Professor Glynde, thank you for your time." He extended his arm and the two men shook hands. It wasn't until Glynde looked expectantly at Ingrid that Radcliffe remembered his manners. "This is Agent Skyberg, from the American embassy."

"A pleasure." The professor shook her hand, scrutinizing her as closely as she was him. His auburn wavy hair was graying at the temples, he had a pair of wire-framed glasses perched on the end of his nose and his skin was ruddy rather than tanned, as if he sailed on the weekend. His red bow tie completed the hospital consultant look.

He let go of Ingrid's hand and turned to Radcliffe. "I must admit, I thought we'd been through everything in detail during my previous interview, chief inspector."

"Agent Skyberg has some additional questions."

"Fire away. I have to warn you though, I am quite pressed for time."

"I've seen a list of Molly's injuries and there's one in particular that I'd like to speak to you about."

Glynde raised his eyebrows.

"The bruising on Molly's upper arms."

"Consistent with a shaking injury. The child is grabbed by the arms, the attacker squeezing hard against the soft flesh between elbow and shoulder joints. The flesh there bruises fairly readily without too much pressure being applied."

"Have you seen many head injuries caused by shaking?"

"Nothing that's led to a police inquiry."

"But you would definitely say the injuries in this case are consistent with a shaking incident?"

"They are. But I don't have much experience in these kinds of cases. Which is why I invited Dr Ryland to speak to you. He's rather an expert in the field. Given evidence in court and so forth."

"Dr Ryland?" Ingrid said.

"Yes—he should be here any moment. You can continue speaking to him when I duck out. He really is the man who knows all there is to know about cases similar to this one."

"And Dr Ryland is familiar with the details of this case?"

"I've briefed him."

Ingrid was beginning to feel she was being fobbed off. "Do you have Molly's file here?"

Glynde reached over his desk and retrieved a slim folder from the top of a tall pile. He opened it and started to flip through the few pages inside. He stopped at a color photograph of Molly's arms. "What did you want to know about the bruises?"

Ingrid noticed a scale printed at the side of the photo. "Can you tell me the size of the bruises?"

He turned the file around so that it was facing Ingrid. "You can see for yourself. This photograph has recorded the injuries at life size."

Ingrid studied the purple and red marks on Molly's pale arms. "These are finger marks caused by pressure applied to the flesh?"

"They are indeed." The professor glanced at the clock on the wall.

"Wouldn't you say the finger marks were a little small for a man's hands?"

Radcliffe, who had previously been leaning back in his chair, sat forward to get a better look at the photograph.

"It's impossible for me to form an opinion—after all, I don't know the size of the suspect's hands. Perhaps his fingers are abnormally small."

"As far as I can recall, Kyle Foster is average height, average weight." She looked directly at the DCI. "Surely if there were anything abnormal about his hands you would have been made aware of it?"

Radcliffe thought about it for a moment. "The crime scene manager will compare the injuries with Foster's fingerprints in due course."

Ingrid was amazed it hadn't been done already. But then there was no doubt in Radcliffe's mind that Kyle Foster was responsible for his daughter's injuries. Why should there be? All the evidence pointed to Foster. Why would he question the testimony of a distraught mother when the case seemed so cut and dried?

Glynde was looking at the clock again. "Look, I'm sorry I've had to cut this meeting short, but I'm sure Dr Ryland will arrive any moment. Perhaps you could speak to him in the café downstairs?" He stood up.

Reluctantly, Ingrid got to her feet only after Radcliffe had slowly risen from his chair. She could see he was pissed at being asked to leave.

Glynde led them to the door just as a man on the other side opened it.

"Ah... Geoff! I'm afraid I can't stick around. Do you mind taking the reins?"

Ingrid and Radcliffe exchanged an uneasy glance: if anyone was in control it should be one of them.

"Not at all, Roger. Only too pleased to help. It's why I'm here, after all." He turned to Ingrid and Radcliffe.

"You'll have to introduce yourselves. My apologies." Glynde ushered them out of his office, firmly closing the door and then herded them through the outer room and into the corridor beyond. He then practically sprinted away.

"It's all go!" Glynde's colleague stuck out a hand. "Geoff Ryland, at your service." Ryland's appearance was the opposite of Glynde's. He was balding, bearded, gray-skinned and tieless.

Radcliffe quickly introduced himself and Ingrid. He clearly wanted to ensure Ryland knew exactly who was leading the investigation.

"You work here at UCH?" Ingrid asked.

"Did my training here. But no—I'm based at King's College now—the college itself rather than the hospital. I'm involved purely in research these days." He gave Ingrid a sad smile. "Now, Roger tells me you want to discuss shaken baby syndrome." He let out a sigh. "Not that we should call it that, of course. That particular theory has been widely discredited. And my reputation along with it."

38

Rather than have their meeting in the café within the hospital, Dr Ryland suggested they adjourn to a nearby pub. "It is practically lunchtime," he said, as he led them across Tottenham Court Road and down a side street leading to an area that Ingrid had discovered had been dubbed "NoHo" a few years ago.

Once they'd found the pub and Ryland had ordered beer battered fish with thick-cut French fries, a pint of bitter and two orange juices from the bar, they all headed for a corner seat of the large dining area. Ingrid sat down next to Ryland on the dubiously stained upholstery while Radcliffe pulled up a low wooden stool from a nearby table.

"So, little Molly Foster," Ryland said and gulped down a few mouthfuls of beer. "Such a tragic case."

"Professor Glynde suggested you were quite an expert in the field," Ingrid said.

"Certainly I was. As I mentioned before, the subject has been quite controversial over the years. In the mid-2000s a number of cases went to appeal and the original convictions were overturned. Which reflected very badly on me, unfortunately."

"How?"

"I was an expert witness for the prosecution. All the evidence I provided was scientifically sound at the time. But the science itself changed in the intervening years."

Ingrid wondered just how reliable Ryland's opinion was now. Were they wasting their time talking to a doctor about a discredited theory?

"The Crown Prosecution Service changed its guidance on the subject only a couple of years ago—but I'm sure you don't need me to tell you that, chief inspector."

Ingrid looked expectantly at Radcliffe for an explanation. The DCI shifted uncomfortably on his stool. "The CPS guidance says a charge of homicide or attempted murder can't be justified by the presence of head injuries alone. Other evidence needs to be present," Radcliffe told her.

"Such as?"

"Such as an eye witness account of what happened. In this case, Carrie Foster's." The DCI sounded irritated.

Ingrid turned away from him. "How strong would someone need to be to do this kind of damage?" Ingrid was frustrated not to have Molly's file in front of her. "You are familiar with the details of the case?"

"I am—Roger brought me up to speed." He suddenly seemed distracted by something.

Ingrid followed his gaze and saw a waitress approaching with a large oval plate piled high with chunky fries and an enormous hunk of fish covered in dark orange batter. Ryland's eyes widened as he shoved his pint glass out of the way to make room for his lunch.

"Another pint of bitter would go down a treat too." He winked at the waitress then turned to Ingrid and Radcliffe. "Would you like another drink?" He eyed their untouched glasses sitting on the table. "Something stronger than orange juice perhaps?"

"We're both fine." Radcliffe dismissed the waitress with a wave of his hand.

The interview wasn't going the way Ingrid had envisaged. She'd have to keep Ryland on track. But now he had beer battered Moby Dick and two pounds of deep fried potatoes to distract his attention, she wasn't hopeful she'd manage it.

"The person responsible for the attack wouldn't need to be

that physically strong at all," Ryland said after he'd thoughtfully chewed and swallowed a large mouthful of greasy fish. Ingrid was surprised he'd even remembered the original question. "Although the infant brain is pretty well protected by the skull at fourteen months, there's still space inside the cranium to allow significant movement of the fragile organ with only the gentlest of shaking. It would need to be prolonged, however." He speared three fat fries onto his fork, dipped them in tomato ketchup and shoved them into his mouth.

"And would prolonged shaking indicate more… premeditation… more intent?" Ingrid waited for him to repeat the chewing and swallowing procedure.

"Impossible to say."

"Really?"

"I would have suggested that in the past, but I've had my fingers burnt making those kind of assumptions."

"So it's possible in a moment of weakness, a fit of rage… in a desperate attempt to stop a baby crying, for example, someone could inflict those injuries *accidentally*?"

"It has been known."

Ingrid stared pointedly at Radcliffe, who took a moment to look up at her. He'd previously been mesmerized by Dr Ryland's eating habits, an expression of mild disgust on his face. He gave her a shrug, his eyebrows raised as if to suggest what Ryland was telling them was of little consequence.

"Though in those cases, in my experience, additional head trauma has been present," Ryland said.

"Meaning?"

"The head has made contact with a hard surface."

"Is there evidence of that in this case?"

"There is some external bruising at the back of the skull. So it's certainly possible."

"Could that kind of injury be the result of an accidental knock to the head?" Ingrid asked.

Ryland nodded thoughtfully. "Though I'm not sure where you're going with this."

"If you wouldn't mind bearing with me just a little longer."

"Not at all." He shoveled more fries into his mouth.

"What if someone were suffering from postpartum depression? Would that make the possibility that the injuries were inflicted without premeditation more likely?"

"Most definitely. In the majority of the cases I've studied, post natal depression has been present. And proven to be a contributory factor."

"Equally, some other type of mental health condition could also trigger this kind of attack, isn't that true?" Radcliffe said, obviously keen to derail Ingrid's theory that Carrie Foster might have been responsible.

"What sort of condition are you talking about?"

"A bout of rage caused by post traumatic stress disorder?"

"Not something I've come across personally. Not really my area. But yes, of course, there have been cases. I've read about them in the papers, just like everyone else."

"But again, that wouldn't point to premeditation," Ingrid suggested.

Ryland put down his cutlery for the first time, picked up his glass and drank the last inch of beer just as the waitress arrived with a fresh pint. He looked from Ingrid to Radcliffe. "Are you two hoping to prove opposing theories?"

Neither of them answered.

"Only, I wouldn't rely on anything I tell you. In these cases I've learnt to have a completely open mind. It has been rather forced upon me by past experience, but nevertheless... either or both of those two syndromes could have triggered an incident of shaking that might have caused Molly Foster's injuries."

"But you wouldn't rule either of them out?" Ingrid pressed her point.

"No—I'm not one for ruling anything out. Not anymore." He stared into space for a moment before quickly recovering to turn his attention back to his now half empty plate.

Radcliffe got to his feet. "Thank you for your time, Dr Ryland. Good of you to come over."

"No trouble at all. Nice to have been asked!" He stood up and slowly reached his right hand behind his back, presumably to grab his wallet from a pocket. He was so slow, in fact, that he still hadn't retrieved it before Radcliffe offered to pay.

From the expression on his face as he called over the waitress and settled the check, Ingrid knew the DCI was seriously pissed.

39

Once they were outside the pub the DCI let rip. "I don't know what you hoped to achieve with that exercise, but I think you'd have to agree your plan failed abysmally. That man is a washed-up excuse for a professional. He's a joke."

"I didn't plan to speak to 'that man' at all—that was Glynde's idea. But you can't totally disregard what he told us. Carrie Foster is strong enough physically, and maybe mentally… compromised enough to have inflicted those injuries on Molly herself. You can't ignore it any longer. You have to at least rule her out of any involvement before you can make any assumptions about her husband."

"We interviewed her extensively. Her statement hasn't wavered."

"You were questioning her specifically about Kyle. About his actions. Have you closely examined hers?"

"She's in no fit state to be put through that kind of interrogation. She wouldn't cope with the ordeal."

"Come on, you know you have to question her again. Kyle Foster insists he didn't hurt Molly."

"Of course he does. He's abducted his son and is evading arrest for the attempted murder of his daughter. What else would you expect him to say?"

"What about the size of the bruises on Molly's arms? How do you explain those?"

Radcliffe didn't answer.

"And there's the vodka hidden in her closet, the fact that people close to her said her mood worsened after Molly was born."

"People? Unless you have medical evidence proving that fact, I'm not interested."

"There's something I haven't told you."

Radcliffe shook his head. "What desperate piece of insignificant information are you going to dredge up now to support your case?"

"I have nothing to gain by proving or disproving Kyle Foster's guilt. How could I? I just want to make sure we look at his side of the story before totally dismissing it. I just want to get at the truth."

"And you think I don't?" He started to walk away.

Ingrid reached out and grabbed his sleeve as she drew level with him. They walked back toward Tottenham Court Road and the hospital. "I don't think that for a second."

"What, then? What haven't you told me?"

"When Major Gurley and I were searching the Foster house we found a bottle of pills in the bathroom cabinet. I've since had them identified as anti-depressants. There was no label on the bottle, so I presume they weren't officially prescribed."

"You're saying they were obtained illegally?"

"That's my presumption. What if they're Carrie's?"

"Why didn't you tell me about them before? Oh wait, I was forgetting, you're somewhat selective with the information you pass on."

"I'm telling you now."

"Because it suits your purpose. They still might be his."

Ingrid threw up her hands. Maybe Kyle Foster had shaken his daughter so hard she lost consciousness, but since Ingrid had spoken to Carrie's friend on the base and Yvonne Sherwood, both telling her what a good father Kyle had been, she felt she should give the guy the benefit of a doubt. He'd seemed so concerned about Tommy's safety when he called the base, wasn't the possibility that his wife was responsible worth at least a little investigation?

As she and Radcliffe walked across the busy intersection, Ingrid tried desperately to come up with something she could tell the DCI that might convince him she wasn't wasting his time.

Nothing came to mind.

They reached the other side of the street and Radcliffe turned to her. "I'm going back to the station. So I suppose this is goodbye." He shook her hand and turned away.

As she watched him walk up Euston Road she saw a steady stream of slow moving pedestrians making their way to the entrance of the hospital. Some of them were in wheelchairs, some using strollers, crutches, a lot of them frail, most of them old.

Then she remembered something. Maybe Radcliffe would dismiss it as irrelevant just as soon as she told him, but she couldn't not mention it. It could make a sliver of difference—and right now she was dealing in tiny increments. She ran after him.

"Hey, chief inspector!"

He didn't hear her, just carried on marching. Or maybe he did and was ignoring her. She picked up her pace and reached him in a matter of seconds. "Please, DCI Radcliffe. There's something else."

He stopped dead and turned to her, a scowl on his face. "Something else you neglected to mention previously?"

"I pretty much dismissed it before, but now maybe it makes more sense."

"Be quick. I really don't want to waste any more of my day."

She snatched a breath and launched into her unprepared speech. "There was a witness at the Fosters' hotel, an American woman. She saw Kyle Foster return to his room when she was on her way down to breakfast on the morning of… the incident."

"The attempted murder, you mean."

"She said she distinctly remembered Foster was carrying a large McDonald's bag."

"I do hope this is leading somewhere."

"According to Carrie Foster, Kyle grabbed Molly from her arms and shook her, violently, flung her onto the bed and stormed out of the room."

"Yes?"

"He was mad. Out of control. He ran. Maybe she thought he wouldn't come back. But he did. Not only that, he came back with *breakfast* for the whole family?"

"According to this witness."

"Why should we doubt it? She was very clear. She said Foster *smiled* at her as he passed. Does that describe a man who practically shook his baby daughter to death only fifteen minutes earlier?"

"I've seen all the evidence collected from the scene. There was no McDonald's bag."

"OK, I don't know what happened to the bag. But I'm sure there must be some CCTV footage from inside the restaurant showing Foster buying breakfast, if you doubt the witness' account."

"You know I can actually hear the faint sound of rustling, you're clutching at straws so desperately."

"I'm just saying Carrie Foster could have hurt Molly while Kyle was out fetching breakfast. She had the opportunity."

The DCI didn't respond.

"Come on—we have this, the hidden booze, the illegally prescribed pills, the small bruises. Doesn't it all add up?"

Radcliffe closed his eyes and shook his head. "Dear God, you just don't give up, do you?"

"Is there any other way to be?"

"All right. But I'm doing the questioning. I'll try to arrange for an interview with Mrs Foster sometime later today."

"Can I observe?"

"I don't want you in the room with me."

"From another room, then."

"We'd need to conduct the interview at the police station for that to be possible."

"Surely you'd want to do that anyway—to record the interview?"

"She won't be answering questions under caution. Let's be quite clear about this—I am *not* arresting her."

"No—of course not."

At last. Ingrid felt she was beginning to get somewhere.

40

"What the hell do you think you're doing?" Jack Gurley towered over Ingrid, she felt his hot breath on her face. His cheeks were scarlet with rage.

Two seconds earlier he'd burst into the observation room next to interview room five in Holborn police station, slamming the door behind him. The uniformed officer assigned to sit with them jumped up from his seat and forced himself between Gurley and Ingrid.

"Take it easy!" he said and raised his hands to Gurley's chest, taking care to leave a good two inches of air between his palms and the angry MP's shirt.

The door opened and another uniformed officer hurried into the room. She had an embarrassed expression on her face, clearly she'd just had the door slammed on her by Gurley.

"Thank you, constable," Ingrid said. "But I think I can manage the situation myself."

"How is it I find out about this interview from your clerk at the embassy?"

"I thought your priority was seeing Kyle Foster behind bars, I didn't imagine you'd be interested in anything more his wife had to say."

"Where's Radcliffe?" he yelled at the male PC standing just inches away from him. "I have to get this thing stopped."

"No way," Ingrid said. "DCI Radcliffe agrees there are enough anomalies in the case to make another interview necessary. With respect, Major, the decision to interview Carrie Foster again wasn't yours to make."

Gurley swore under his breath and kicked a nearby chair. It clattered into the table that was supporting an array of TV monitors. The monitors shook, one of them threatening for a moment to topple onto the floor.

"Take it easy," the male PC said again.

"For crying out loud, is that all you can say?" Gurley marched toward the door, turned, then marched back again. "I want you to know I strongly oppose what you're doing here."

"I think you've made that quite clear."

"Oh I can make it plenty clearer, believe me." He pulled out the chair he'd just kicked and sat down.

The far left-hand monitor on the table showed activity in the interview room. The door opened. The family liaison officer they'd seen at the hospital walked in a few paces ahead of Carrie Foster. They both sat down on a low-backed couch, Carrie Foster leaning forward, her forearms resting on her knees. She looked as exhausted as she had during their previous meeting. After a few moments, DS Tyson and DCI Radcliffe entered the room and shut the door behind them. They sat on a matching couch arranged opposite the other, with just a few feet between the two. It almost looked as if Tyson's knees might bump against the FLO's. Ingrid understood the furniture and ambience of the room was meant to feel casual and unthreatening, but the forced intimacy seemed almost oppressive.

"Look at her," Gurley said, tapping the screen of the next monitor along. It showed a close-up of Carrie Foster's face. "She looks ready to collapse. They shouldn't be putting her through this." He balled his hand into a fist and banged it against his knee. "This shouldn't be happening."

Ingrid pulled out the chair next to him and sat down. The male PC sat next to her. The female PC took up position by the door, presumably ready to hinder any attempt by Gurley to interrupt the interview in the next room.

"Let's just listen to what she has to say, shall we?" Ingrid said.

Gurley didn't answer, just flexed his jaw muscles in response.

Radcliffe's voice boomed through the speakers in the observation room. "Thank you for agreeing to come into the station like this, Mrs Foster. We really appreciate your cooperation."

The PC stretched across Ingrid and lowered the volume control on the small amplifier sitting on the table.

"Do I need a lawyer?" Carrie Foster glanced at the FLO, who gave her a reassuring smile. She ignored it. "I mean, you're all cops after all. Maybe I should have somebody here looking after my interests."

"Good," Gurley muttered. "She won't be a pushover. Radcliffe won't be able to bully her."

"You're not under arrest, Mrs Foster," Tyson said in a soft voice. "You can get up and leave anytime you want. This is just an informal chat."

"Are you recording this?" she looked up toward the ceiling. "Filming it?"

"Only for your benefit. We wouldn't want to mis-remember anything you told us. We don't have to record a single word, if you'd rather have it that way."

Mrs Foster hesitated before answering. "I suppose it's for the best. I wouldn't want you twisting my words."

"We have absolutely no intention of doing that. Why would we?" Radcliffe said, his tone acquiring a harder edge.

"Look—I can't stay here long. I still can't sleep without medication, I've hardly eaten. I don't feel well enough to answer a lot of questions. I shouldn't be away from Molly."

"We only really want you to tell us what happened on Monday morning."

"Again?" Carrie Foster and Gurley said in unison.

"What is this? Anomalies my ass," Gurley said. He started to get up, then changed his mind.

Ingrid did her best to ignore him, concentrating instead on what was going on in the room next door.

"I know it's traumatic for you," Radcliffe was saying, barely managing to sound sympathetic. Ingrid supposed he was eager to get the whole thing over with. "But now that Molly is on the road to recovery, we thought you might feel more able to speak to us."

"The doctors don't know if she'll make a full recovery. There may be long term issues. What if she's permanently brain damaged? What if she can't hear or see properly?" She clasped her hands together. "What am I even doing here? I should get back to the hospital." She stood up.

"We won't keep you long, I promise." Radcliffe managed a faint smile. "Something you tell us now might help track down Kyle."

"Why is it taking you so long to find him?"

"It's just as frustrating for us, believe me. Our priority is to locate Kyle and get Tommy back to you. That's why it's important for us to talk again. You do understand?"

Carrie Foster sat back down. For the next ten minutes she proceeded to list the same sequence of events that she had in her earlier interview.

In the observation room, Ingrid was willing Radcliffe to interject, probe Carrie Foster's account of what happened little more rigorously. But he just sat there nodding silently.

"When you say you attempted to grab Molly back from Kyle, can you describe how you tried to do that? I'm having trouble picturing it," the DCI finally said.

"I pulled at his arms. He was holding Molly close to him while he was shaking her. His grip on her was too tight."

"Where was he holding her, exactly?"

Carrie Foster paused, closed her eyes, as if trying to remember the scene in detail. "He was squeezing her arms."

"At the shoulders? The elbows?"

She lifted her hands in the air, her fingers curled, supposedly miming the actions of her husband. "Upper arms, between her elbows and shoulders."

"That would certainly be consistent with the bruising there," Radcliffe said.

Ingrid thought she saw a flash of panic cross Mrs Foster's face at the mention of Molly's bruises.

"How long was your husband shaking Molly?" Radcliffe asked.

Foster looked down at her hands. She shrugged. "I don't know, a long time maybe. It felt like a long time."

"And all the while you were grabbing at his arms, to try to get Molly back?"

She nodded slowly. "Every time I reached out for her he swung her away from me."

"Still shaking her?"

"Yes! How many times do I have to tell you? He didn't stop shaking her."

The FLO rested a calming hand on Mrs Foster's knee. She angrily batted it away.

"I'm sorry. I really don't mean to upset you," the DCI said. "But you must realize, if we're to build a solid case against your husband, we do need to know even the smallest of details."

"You've got to catch him first. Maybe you should be spending your time doing that."

"Believe me, we are. We've devoted considerable manpower to the operation."

"Oh sure." Gurley said. "And look where it's gotten you."

The uniformed PC sitting next to Ingrid huffed a disapproving sigh.

"You got something to say, officer?"

The PC didn't reply.

"Then keep your goddamn mouth shut."

"Shhh," Ingrid said, still watching the monitors intently.

"What happened next?" Radcliffe said. He had leaned both elbows on his knees, his hands grasped together in front of him.

Carrie Foster let out an unexpected high pitched sob. "Molly went quiet."

"She'd been crying all this time?"

"That's why he was shaking her. To make her stop."

"And then what happened?"

"He shoved her back at me."

The image on the far right-hand monitor showed Radcliffe's

forehead pucker into a severe frown. "I thought you said your husband threw Molly onto the bed."

"What?"

"In your earlier statement."

"He did."

"But you just said—"

"He shoved her toward me, I wasn't expecting him to do that, I wasn't ready to take her, so she landed on the bed."

"So he was more throwing Molly at you, rather than deliberately hurling her towards the bed?"

"I don't know what he was doing." She leaned forward, her face inches away from the detective's. "You'd have to ask him that."

41

Without being asked, the family liaison officer got to her feet. Radcliffe glared at her. "Sir, I think it might be time for a break now."

"I'll decide when a break is called for."

"But, sir, Carrie's clearly distressed. Let me at least get her a glass of water."

Carrie Foster started to cry.

"I can't let this go on a minute longer." Gurley got to his feet.

Ingrid grabbed his arm. "Let's wait a few moments, can we? I think Radcliffe might be getting somewhere."

"Sure, if harassing an innocent woman was his aim, he's doing real well."

Ingrid stood up too. "Just a little while longer. Please, Jack."

They both turned their attention back toward the monitors to see the FLO hand Carrie Foster a bottle of water. Mrs Foster's hands were trembling too much to unscrew the top, so the FLO opened the bottle for her.

"Jesus, look at what he's done to her," Gurley said, sitting down again.

"We are grateful for you answering our questions like this, Mrs Foster, I can't express that strongly enough," Radcliffe said gently.

"Are we nearly through?"

"Almost, just another couple of questions and we'll be done." Once again, Radcliffe glanced up at the camera, an admonishing look on his face, as if he were holding Ingrid personally responsible for Carrie Foster's current condition. "In your earlier statement you said that Kyle pushed you away so violently that you bruised yourself on an item of furniture."

"Yes?"

"You didn't mention it just now. When exactly in the sequence of events did this happen? And can you describe the furniture in question?"

"It was... I guess it was the bureau, the wooden bureau set against the wall."

"Really?"

"I think so."

"Only that seems a little high to cause a bruise on your thigh. How tall are you, Mrs Foster?"

"Five-six."

"Exactly, far too high."

Carrie Foster frowned at him. "Maybe it was something else. I wasn't really paying attention to the furniture. Kyle was hurting Molly, it was all I could think about."

"And you sustained this injury when?"

She thought for a moment. "When I tried to grab Molly from him."

"So he what, let go of Molly with one hand to push you?"

"No, he didn't stop shaking her. He kind of... he shoved me with his hip and thigh, sent me off balance and I crashed into something —I guess I don't remember what that was." She raised the bottle of water to her lips with a trembling hand and took a sip. "Is that it?"

"Just one final thing." Radcliffe tilted his head sympathetically. "It has been brought to my attention that you are in possession of a prescription drug—an anti-depressant—that has been illegally obtained."

"What?"

"A bottle of pills was discovered in your bathroom cabinet at home."

"What the hell have you been doing in my house?"

"Strictly speaking, the house is the property of the RAF, leased to the US Air Force. Our American colleagues authorized the search."

Carrie Foster lifted a hand to her mouth.

"Are the pills yours, Mrs Foster?"

"I… don't know anything about any pills."

Ingrid was surprised at her answer. She'd assumed Carrie Foster would say the pills were Kyle's right off the bat.

"Do they belong to your husband?"

Slowly blinking away her tears, Carrie Foster wiped the back of her hand across her cheeks. "I guess they could be—I've never seen any pills."

"The hell with this." Gurley started towards the door. "I'm stopping it right now."

"There's no need," Ingrid called to him. "It's over."

Gurley turned abruptly. "What did you think you were doing?" He pointed a finger into Ingrid's face, his fingertip just a fraction of an inch from her left cheek. She reared backwards, almost losing her balance.

The PC stood up.

"Tell me to take it easy one more goddamn time and I swear…" Gurley yelled at the officer. "You told Radcliffe about the pills?" he said, lowering his hand. "You said they were for menstrual cramping. What's all this anti-depressant crap?"

"Hey—I made a mistake. They were the same color as something I've taken before."

"How'd you even know what they were?"

"I did a little research."

"And when were you planning on sharing that information with me?"

"I guess it slipped my mind."

"Un-fucking-believable."

It was the first time she'd heard Gurley swear. "I'm sorry, OK?"

"You thought they belonged to him, didn't you? But you

didn't want to believe he was taking anti-depressants. Didn't fit in with this new theory of yours, huh?"

"Why do you refuse to even question Carrie's innocence?"

Gurley glanced at the PC standing close by. "I'm not having this conversation with you now."

"I just want the truth. Nothing more, nothing less. I thought that's what you wanted too."

"Don't even try to suggest that I don't. How dare you—" He was cut off by the door opening.

Ingrid turned to see Radcliffe standing in the doorway. "Well?" she said. "What are you going to do about her?"

"Give her a lift back to the hospital."

"She contradicted her earlier statement."

"Not significantly."

"She was uncomfortable when you brought up the subject of the bruising. And how could she not know about the pills in her own bathroom cabinet?"

"What do you want me to do?"

"Don't you have enough to arrest her? Insist she answers more questions. You didn't even bring up the issue of the breakfast from McDonald's."

"The what?" Gurley said.

"Nothing—an unconfirmed witness statement. I didn't bring it up because it wasn't relevant," Radcliffe snapped. "I've just put that woman through hell, and wasted my own time in the process. Are you satisfied now?" He stared at Ingrid accusingly.

"Not in the least," she said, holding his gaze. "But I guess that's my problem." Dissatisfaction with Radcliffe's interview technique wasn't the issue. She was frustrated as hell nobody wanted to consider another explanation for Molly's injuries.

Without saying another word, the chief inspector left the room. Gurley followed him out, with Ingrid just a couple of steps behind them.

"Tell me I'm not going to witness a repeat of that performance," Gurley said. "Tell me you have no plans to question Carrie Foster again."

"Perhaps you should be talking to your colleague about that, rather than me." Radcliffe marched away.

"What's going on with you?" Ingrid asked Gurley.

"With me?" He shook his head. "You just don't know when to stop, do you? When to admit you're wrong."

"There's something you're not telling me. How can you be so sure Carrie Foster had nothing to do with her daughter's injuries?"

"You seem to be the only person who isn't. As far as I can see you're in a minority of one."

As they stood in the gleaming, white-walled corridor, the door to the interview room opened and Carrie Foster emerged. She was hanging on to the arm of the family liaison officer for support. She looked from Gurley to Ingrid. "What are you doing here? Was this your idea? I thought you were supposed to be supporting me."

Gurley reached out a hand to her. Carrie Foster ducked away.

"We are here for you," he said, his voice gentle.

"You make me sick. All of you."

The FLO led Mrs Foster away. DS Tyson appeared in the doorway of the interview room. He ignored Ingrid and Gurley and walked away, shaking his head as he went.

"You've managed to alienate just about everyone," Gurley said, contempt in his voice. Then he called after Tyson. "Hey, wait up. I'd like to see the latest intel you have."

Tyson slowed. "I'm on my way to the incident room now."

Ingrid was left stranded in the middle of the corridor. She grabbed her phone and called Sol Franklin.

"Hi Ingrid, any developments?" he said as soon as he picked up.

"No. Nothing worth reporting. I'm calling about something else. I want to make a formal request to investigate this case solo. Major Gurley and I have very different, incompatible methods. His attitude is affecting my ability to do my job."

There was silence for a few moments on the other end of the line.

"Sol?"

"I wanted to talk to you about Major Gurley, as a matter of fact."

Another pause.

"You did?"

"He contacted Louden earlier today. Major Gurley has requested you're taken off the case."

42

Ingrid emerged from Holborn police station in a daze. The rest of her conversation with Sol Franklin had not gone well. She'd let loose a series of grievances about Gurley's behavior that just made her seem whiny and unprofessional. Sol listened patiently to all of her complaints, finally telling her they'd speak in more detail after he'd tried to smooth things out with Louden. She hoped Sol could work his magic and keep her on the case. She'd come too far now not to see it through to its conclusion.

On the other side of the sidewalk she noticed a small gathering of people. It took her a moment to realize they were reporters. A moment after that a familiar figure stepped out of the crowd.

"Ingrid. I'm so glad I didn't miss you." Angela Tate hurried toward her.

Tate was the last person Ingrid wanted to see. She considered making a dash for it. "How did you know I was here?"

"I have my spies at the hospital. They told me Carrie Foster was on the move, accompanied by her FLO and two detectives. It didn't take a genius to work out she was being brought in for questioning. Has she been arrested?"

"How did your… colleagues find out about it?" Ingrid pointed to the handful of journalists, some of them talking on cell phones, others enjoying a cigarette. She saw Tate's photographer chatting to a man holding a large microphone covered in a furry windshield.

"News travels fast, unfortunately. I was rather hoping for an exclusive." She smiled at Ingrid. "Still am, as a matter of fact, with your help."

"No way."

"You haven't answered my question: has Carrie Foster been arrested?"

"I have no intention of speaking to you."

Ingrid could only suppose Foster had been escorted back to the hospital using an alternate exit. Through the parking lot, most probably. Thank God. At least Tate wouldn't get the chance to fire questions at her. "How long have you been waiting here?"

"Long enough to get bloody cheesed off. Come on, Ingrid—throw me a crumb."

"You're wasting your time. There's no story for you."

"Then why are you here? I'm guessing your tall friend is somewhere in the vicinity too." She peered into the entrance of the police station. "Perhaps he'll be a bit more talkative."

"Carrie Foster has not been arrested. That's all you're getting from me."

"Then why bring her to the police station at all?"

"There's no story," Ingrid said again. "Nothing to splash across the front page of tomorrow's *Evening News*. Sorry to disappoint."

"Oh I'm sure you are." Tate pulled a pack of cigarettes from her purse, shook one out and lit it with an antique silver lighter. She exhaled, blowing the smoke behind her. "I do have something else in mind for the headline tomorrow, as it happens."

"I'm not interested."

"No? How about I run it past you? I was thinking of focusing on your absolute lack of competence. Your inability to track down a man and his eight-year-old son. You can't blame this one on the boys in blue. You're all equally culpable. And as far as I can see, equally useless."

Ingrid started to edge away. She was actually inclined to agree with Tate. They had failed at every turn. Especially after getting so close to Kyle Foster in Suffolk. It was pitiful. How was he managing to keep Tommy so well hidden?

"Still nothing to say? Don't you have some embassy approved excuses to reel out?"

Ingrid's phone started to ring. Relieved, she dug it out of her purse and glanced at the screen. It was Natasha McKittrick. "I have to take this."

"Of course you do."

Ingrid answered the phone as she hurried up Lamb's Conduit Street. She wanted to get away. From Tate. From Gurley. If she hadn't felt Tate's gaze boring into her back, she might even have broken into a run. "Hey, it's good to hear a friendly voice."

"I haven't said anything yet." McKittrick sounded decidedly downbeat.

"You just saved me from the clutches of Angela Tate."

"What's that old hack after now?"

"The usual. My soul."

"Tell her nothing." She let out a long sigh.

"What's wrong with you?"

"Mills. Have you seen him recently?"

Ingrid wasn't sure how to answer. She said nothing.

"I'm taking your silence as proof that you have. What happened? I've never seen him like this."

"Like what?" Ingrid worried again that something had happened the previous night that she had absolutely no recollection of.

"I'm used to him moping about when he's seen you, like a lovestruck teenager, too embarrassed even to take the mildest of piss-taking. But today he's just been… weird."

"How?" Now Ingrid was getting really concerned.

"It's hard to describe. He seems… resigned somehow. That's the only word I can come up with."

"About what?"

"About you, I suppose. Like the life's drained out of him. What on earth happened between the two of you?"

"Nothing."

"Something must have. Did you dump him?"

"No! Really—nothing happened. As a matter of fact…" Ingrid wasn't sure she wanted to share this with McKittrick. She certainly didn't want to be teased about it. She wasn't in the right frame of mind.

"What? You have to tell me now."

"Nothing happened between us and I'd really hoped it might."

"Whoa! You're telling me neither of you made a move? Where was this?"

"My apartment, late last night."

"I had no idea you planned to get together yesterday."

Ingrid turned right into Great Ormond Street, not entirely clear where she was headed. "It wasn't planned. I needed someone to talk to, your cell went straight to voicemail. So I called Ralph. It was a spur of the moment thing. He came over. We talked." She picked up speed, hoping to walk off the awkwardness she was feeling.

"And?"

"And nothing—I told you already—nothing happened. I woke up a few hours later and he was gone." She reached the end of the street and stopped.

"You fell asleep on him? As insults go, that's pretty damning."

"I was drunk. He knew that. I hoped he wouldn't take it personally." Ingrid looked up and down the street, unable to decide which direction to take. If she turned right she would loop back around to the police station. "I think I may have blown it with him. That the moment has passed. Like we're destined to be friends and nothing more. He was a shoulder to cry on when I needed it."

"Maybe you should give him a call. Let him know how you really feel."

"The mood I'm in right now, that is the last thing I should do."

"Tate really got to you that badly?"

"No, not Tate. This whole investigation. It's stalled and I'm not sure how to fix it."

"You'll think of something. You always do."

"Gurley's asked Sol to take me off the case."

"That's a bit extreme.

Ingrid's phone beeped in her ear. "I have another call. I should probably get it. Maybe we can talk later?"

"Let's make it over a coffee, I don't want you falling asleep on me."

Ingrid hung up and answered the other call. "Yes?"

"DS Tyson here. We've had a number of new sightings. One is particularly interesting. DCI Radcliffe thinks you should come back to the station straight away."

Ingrid took the right hand turn. "Can you meet me at the entrance out back, in the parking lot? There's somebody I need to avoid."

43

When Ingrid arrived at the incident room she found Gurley leaning awkwardly over a low desk, deep in conversation with DS Tyson. They seemed to be getting along just fine without her. She felt as though she was on the outside, looking in. Gurley's attitude toward her in the observation room made more sense now she'd discovered he was doing his best to have her removed from the investigation. He could cozy up to Tyson all he liked: she wasn't about to let either of them shut her out.

As she approached the desk, Tyson acknowledged her with a nod, and although Gurley turned to face her, he didn't say a word.

"Tell me about the sightings." She addressed the detective sergeant, as if Gurley wasn't there. If Gurley wanted to play games, she would too.

"We've had quite a few conflicting reports. If we took them all seriously we'd have to assume Kyle Foster had perfected the ability of being in two or three places at once. Some of them are from opposite ends of the country."

"And the most promising one?"

"The owner of a convenience store. Said he served a young boy, just over four-foot tall, light brown hair, dressed in clothes that looked a bit too big for him. He was buying milk and Frosties and some paper dishes. The thing that got the shop owner really suspicious was the way the boy spoke. Bloke said he thought the kid had an American accent. Plus the fact he wanted to buy a disposable mobile phone."

Ingrid raised her eyebrows. "It's the first sighting we've had of Tommy in a long while. The boy's still alive." *Thank God.* "Where was this?"

"We're in the middle of trying to trace the call. The caller rang off suddenly. Before he told us his location."

"Do you know why?"

"No idea—I suppose it's possible Foster turned up and threatened him."

"How long ago did he call?"

"About fifteen minutes."

"So you should have a location soon. And Foster has to be pretty close by."

"The man who called in wasn't using a landline. It'll take us a bit longer to get the details of his mobile and address."

"Anything else to report?" Ingrid glanced at Gurley, who continued to ignore her.

"We're just waiting on this. Like I said, it's the most promising sighting we've had in a while."

It felt hot and airless in the incident room. Although the space was large, none of the windows was open. The hostility radiating from Gurley made the atmosphere downright oppressive. "Listen, I need a little air," she said. "I'll be out back. Can you come fetch me when you have news?"

Tyson looked at Gurley before answering. "Of course."

When Ingrid stepped outside she took a deep breath. She wasn't at all certain she could continue to work with Gurley if he carried on behaving the way he was. But she sure as hell wasn't going to leave the investigation without a fight. As she paced up and down between the parked squad cars, her phone chirruped in her purse. She snatched it out and answered without looking at the screen. "You have a location?" She moved toward the rear entrance of the police station.

"Nope. They still haven't found the guy." It was Mike Stiller. "That's not why I'm calling."

"Sorry, Mike. I thought you were somebody else."

"I figured that out already."

"The killer is still on the loose?"

"Yes, but like I said, that's not why I'm calling. They've recovered more bodies. A dozen remains so far. And counting."

The breath caught in Ingrid's throat. It was possible one of them could be Megan. "You have to try to get a match with Kathleen Avery's DNA. You need to get a sample from her."

"The local Feds did that already. Jeez, I was hassling so hard for it, they could hardly refuse."

"It won't be a 100% match—we don't have a sample from Megan's dad." Ingrid remembered the lock of hair at the bottom of the sneaker box. "If it looks promising I can get you a better sample."

"You can? How?"

"Don't worry about that for now. Just look out for a Fed-Ex package from me." A familiar shiver ran up her spine.

"You doing OK?"

"I'm fine. The job's a little... challenging at the moment."

"When is it anything else, huh?"

"I really appreciate your help with this, Mike. I think maybe I've been forgetting to tell you that, I've been so caught up in the detail."

"Hey, don't mention it. I'll call soon as I have more news." He rang off, leaving Ingrid standing in the middle of a police parking lot feeling more than a little lost.

She walked unsteadily to a low brick wall that separated the lot from the back of the police station and sat down, reflecting on what Mike had just told her.

So many bodies.

The killer must have been adding to his collection for at least eighteen years. Ingrid wondered how long his victims had survived before they ended up buried in the yard or beneath the floor of the basement. How much they had suffered before that. She prayed Megan wasn't one of them.

The door to the parking lot opened and Tyson stuck his head

through the gap. He stared at her for a moment, a shocked expression on his face. "Are you OK?"

Ingrid stood up, relieved to discover her legs were strong enough to carry her weight. "I'm fine." She swallowed. "Did you get a location for the store?"

"Better than that—Foster's on the phone right now to your tall friend."

Ingrid ran to the door and pushed Tyson aside in her hurry to get back to the incident room. "Can you get a trace on the call?" she said, striding down the corridor.

"We weren't exactly set up for it—we're trying to get something fixed up as quick as we can."

Ingrid slowed to let Tyson catch up with her. "It's OK—the base is monitoring all calls coming into Major Gurley's phone. I'm guessing it was patched through from his landline at Freckenham?"

"No idea—Jack didn't exactly get a chance to tell me."

Tyson's use of Gurley's first name didn't pass Ingrid by. The two of them were getting a little too pally for her liking.

A few moments later, she burst through the incident room door, with Tyson close behind. Gurley turned sharply and glared at her. A plain clothes cop Ingrid hadn't seen before was sitting at the desk next to him with the handset of a landline pressed hard against her ear. She made a circling motion with an index finger, encouraging Gurley to keep Kyle Foster talking. But Foster knew what he was doing—he wouldn't stay on the line for long.

"Sonofabitch!" Gurley exclaimed. "The bastard just hung up on me. Said he'd call back tomorrow." He looked at the detective sitting at the desk. She was nodding and making approving noises into her phone.

"They traced the call to Tring," she said when she'd put down the phone.

"Where the hell is that?" Gurley said.

"It's a village just north of London," the detective explained.

"So he's maybe on his way back to London? To the hospital?" Gurley asked.

"He wouldn't risk it," Ingrid said. "Too many cops."

"Then why come south at all?"

"What did he say to you?" Tyson asked.

"He was making demands again—that Tommy be put on a plane to the US. The guy's got a screw loose."

"What did you tell him?" Ingrid asked.

"What I did before," Gurley said without looking at her. "To give himself up before he made things even worse for himself."

"Why would he change his mind now?"

"I'm not giving in to him."

"We need to at least pretend to agree to his demands—how else are we going to track him down?" Ingrid moved closer to Gurley until he had no choice but to look at her. "What else did he say?"

"He wanted to know how Molly was. I refused to tell him unless he put Tommy on the line."

"You actually spoke to Tommy?"

"No. Foster went quiet after that. Then hung up."

"Couldn't you have given him the information first, then asked to speak to Tommy? The guy's clearly concerned about his daughter." Ingrid felt like shaking Gurley.

"How is that relevant? I kept him on the line long enough to trace the call to some village. How hard can it be to find him there?"

"Except that he's probably already on the move." Ingrid walked away, just in case the temptation to slap Gurley in the mouth became too overwhelming to resist.

She wheeled back around when the landline on the desk rang. Tyson grabbed it. He nodded a couple of times, thanked the caller and threw the handset back onto the cradle. "Unsurprisingly, we've just had confirmation the convenience store is also in Tring."

"How quickly can we get there?" Gurley asked the detective sergeant.

"With blues and twos? Rush hour traffic? It's going to take the best part of an hour. Maybe more."

"We don't have that much time. I'll call the base, get a chopper."

"I can get in touch with the Hertfordshire force. At least get some bodies on the ground." Tyson was already reaching for the phone. "Maybe get the traffic cops in the air too."

"If we're going we should get down to the helipad," Ingrid said.

Gurley scowled at her, but said nothing. She'd expected him to refuse to take her, point blank.

"I'm coming with you." she said, forcing the issue.

"I guess so," Gurley said, reluctantly. "Foster asked for you by name."

"He did what? How does he know my name?"

"He didn't say."

"I don't understand."

"Is there anything you need to tell us, Agent Skyberg?" Tyson took a step toward her.

"No! Why would he ask for me specifically?"

"Has Kyle Foster made contact with you before?" Tyson asked.

"What is this? Of course he hasn't. He must have called the embassy or something—I can get the phone logs checked—see who's been making inquiries in the Criminal Division in the past twenty-four hours." Although she was desperate to find a reasonable explanation, the likelihood of Kyle Foster calling the American embassy seemed pretty remote, even to Ingrid. "Maybe he's been back in touch with Yvonne Sherwood. She could have mentioned my name to him."

Gurley glared at her. "Maybe you can give Sherwood a call. See what she has to say for herself."

44

Even though Gurley's suggestion was clearly meant to be sarcastic, on the way to the helipad in Battersea, Ingrid did try calling Yvonne Sherwood. As soon as she'd introduced herself, Sherwood hung up on her. Each time Ingrid tried after that, her calls went straight to voicemail.

"That's your answer right there," Gurley snapped at Ingrid after her third attempt. "She must have heard from Foster and now she's avoiding you."

"On the plus side, maybe she told him he could trust me. It's possible, isn't it? If he's asking for me specifically."

She and Gurley were sitting in the back of a Metropolitan Police patrol car, the driver and Radcliffe sitting up front. Tyson and another uniformed driver were following behind. Both cars had sirens wailing and blue lights flashing, trying to get through the evening rush hour traffic as fast as possible. Gurley had reluctantly agreed to let the two detectives ride in the US Air Force helicopter to Tring. He couldn't really refuse.

Gurley was still pissed at Ingrid over the Carrie Foster interview and she was mad as hell that he'd tried to have her removed from the investigation. But for the time being at least, they were stuck with one another.

Ingrid decided it was time to clear the air. "Sol told me you've been talking to the chief at the embassy."

"I pretty much guessed that."

"Can we agree on a truce for tonight?"

Gurley continued to stare out the window as the car swerved and slalomed through the heavy traffic.

"Come on, Jack. Meet me half way here. I'm just as pissed as you."

He snapped his head around toward her. "What have I done?"

"If you have a problem with me, you should tell me to my face. Not report me to the boss."

Gurley exhaled noisily through his nose. "I was frustrated. Sometimes it feels like you can be more of an obstruction than a help."

"Is that what you really think?"

"Why have you started taking Kyle Foster's side?"

"I haven't. I told you already. I just want to find out the truth."

"Everyone else accepts Carrie Foster's version of events. They seem happy with the truth as it stands."

Ingrid noticed that DCI Radcliffe had tilted his head sideways into the gap between the passenger and driver seat, obviously trying to listen in. She dropped her voice. "I can't ignore it when things don't add up."

"You are incredible."

"I'll take that as a compliment."

Gurley shook his head. But Ingrid thought she detected the slightest of smiles play across his lips.

"We both want the same thing: to find Foster and recover Tommy, safe and sound."

Gurley nodded.

"So," she said, sticking out her hand, "a truce?"

After a moment's hesitation, Gurley wrapped his hand around Ingrid's and shook on it. "For tonight."

The helicopter ride to Tring lasted only fifteen minutes. They landed in a park that had been closed to the public about a half mile from the convenience store Tommy had been in. The area of parkland was enclosed on all sides by stands of tall trees. Through a gap between two of them, Ingrid could make out the main highway that skirted around the little town.

A whole team of detectives and uniformed officers were there to meet them. Ingrid and Gurley were forced to wait around while DCI Radcliffe was debriefed by his opposite number on the Hertfordshire force. When the conversation passed the five minute mark, Gurley lost his patience. He strode over to the two men and stood between them.

"Sorry to break up your cozy chit-chat, detectives, but wouldn't it make more sense to say everything once?" He turned to Ingrid who had followed him over. "After all, my colleague and I are going to be asking you the exact same questions."

The Hertfordshire cop looked at Radcliffe, who gave him a nod.

"What do you have on the ground?" Gurley asked.

The cop stuck out a hand. "DCI Strickland."

"Major Jack Gurley, this is Agent Skyberg, FBI."

Strickland shook Ingrid's hand too. "Pleasure." He gave them both a little smile. Ingrid could sense Gurley's impatience increasing. "We're conducting door to door inquiries on the High Street—where the convenience store is situated. We've got officers—in plain clothes—patrolling the local bus and train stations. Plus a dozen squad cars cruising the vicinity."

"Any new sightings from the public?" Ingrid asked.

"Nothing that's proven particularly reliable."

"What resources do you have in the air?" Gurley asked.

Strickland glanced up at the darkening sky. "Traffic have put a helicopter at our disposal for the rest of the night. It's equipped with powerful searchlights and infra-red equipment. At the moment we've got it flying low over open ground within a five mile radius of the last confirmed sighting."

"Has anyone spoken to the owner of the convenience store?" Gurley asked. He pushed up his sleeves.

"We've interviewed him extensively."

"Did he tell you why he hung up? Did Foster threaten him?"

"Nothing that extreme. Apparently a couple of schoolboys were acting suspiciously at the back of the shop. The owner's had a lot of trouble with shoplifting of late. He rang off so that he could deal with the two lads."

"And you believe him?" Gurley didn't seem convinced.

"I've no reason to doubt him."

"Have you searched his premises?" Ingrid asked.

"We did. Nothing to report."

"What about roadblocks?" Gurley was shifting his weight from one foot to the other, glancing around the park, finally fixing his gaze on a large clump of trees.

"We can't close the roads," Strickland said firmly.

"Why not?"

"Foster's not exactly a threat to the general public."

"What if he's armed?"

"What makes you say that?" Radcliffe suddenly started paying attention. "Is he?"

"I think Major Gurley is just saying that we don't know that he isn't," Ingrid interjected. She attempted to change the subject. "You've got a trace on the cell phone Foster used to call us earlier?" she asked Radcliffe.

"There's no signal. Presumably he's started using a new burner phone and switched the other one off."

Gurley glanced back at the trees. "What if he's gone to ground? You have a lot of woods round here?"

"A fair amount."

"The chopper won't help you find him there. Are you using dogs?"

Strickland let out a snorting laugh. "We really don't have those kind of resources. If we knew where to start looking I could get a couple of dog handlers involved. But without an approximate location they'd be totally wasting their time."

"Jesus." Gurley walked away.

Strickland looked at Radcliffe who shrugged back at him. They both looked at Ingrid. "He's a little frustrated right now," she said, unsure why she was making excuses for his rudeness. "He feels personally responsible for getting Foster back." She gave both detectives a weak smile and hurried after Gurley. "You can't speak to them that way," she said when she caught up with him. "We're all on the same side here. Doing our best with the resources we have."

"We're looking for a man and an eight-year-old boy. How hard can it be? If it were Foster alone I could understand it—the man's been trained to evade capture. But Tommy must be slowing him down, holding him back."

"We must work with the cops now, or risk getting shut out of the investigation completely. They still have access to intel we need."

Gurley rubbed a hand across his face. "Foster's probably miles away by now. Headed God knows where."

"We don't know that. We have to accept the local cops are doing everything they can."

"It's not enough."

Ingrid could quite easily have slapped Gurley across the face. What did he think could be gained by bitching about the cops? It wasn't as if he was coming up with a better strategy of his own.

Out the corner of her eye, Ingrid noticed some activity among the uniformed officers. One of them ran over to Radcliffe and Strickland, who had now been joined by DS Tyson. She started to jog toward the little group. "What's happened?" She made sure to address DCI Strickland, out of courtesy, given this was his patch, and in the hope he might react favorably to the gesture. He didn't answer right away. He was too busy scowling over her shoulder, presumably at an approaching Jack Gurley. "Chief inspector?" she prompted.

"We have CCTV footage of a man and boy, fitting the basic description of Foster and his son, boarding a London-bound train."

Ingrid turned to Radcliffe. "How quickly can you get a team down to the station in London?"

"I'm afraid we're too late for that, agent," Strickland said. "The train was due in at Euston over an hour ago. The best we can do now is get personnel looking at the CCTV recordings for the surrounding area. We might at least be able to discover which direction he was heading in when he left the station."

Behind her Ingrid heard Gurley exhale noisily. She was grateful he didn't make any comment.

"Well, there's no point staying up here," Radcliffe said. "Thanks for all your efforts, Ted. I think it might be time for you to get the troops to stand down." He shook Strickland's hand. "Really appreciate your help."

When just Tyson and Radcliffe remained, Gurley said, "I guess you'll be wanting a ride back?"

"Actually we've arranged alternative transport. Thanks all the same." With that the DCI walked away, closely followed by his number two.

"Wow—I really pissed them off, huh?" Gurley shook his head.

Ingrid was about to reply, when she was interrupted by the trilling of Gurley's cell. He peered down at the number. It was clear he didn't recognize it. He stabbed the answer key. "Major Gurley," he said, "who is this?" He quickly turned away and started walking.

Ingrid ran after him.

"It isn't that straightforward," she heard him say. "What the…?" He glared at his phone.

"Was it Foster?" Ingrid asked him, grabbing his arm.

"Sonofabitch is still making demands."

"The demands haven't changed? He wants safe passage for Tommy?"

"He said he's calling again tomorrow with 'full instructions'. He made one thing very clear."

Ingrid watched the expression on his face turn from anger to something approaching satisfaction. "Well?"

"On no account should we get the police involved."

45

After a restless night, Ingrid arrived at the embassy ahead of Jack Gurley. They had arranged to meet there so that Foster's call could be more easily traced. The technical team assured her the tracking process would kick in just as soon as he called. All she could do now was wait.

She sat at her desk in the Criminal Division for a few minutes enjoying the silence. No phones were ringing, Jennifer wasn't bombarding her with questions, even the air conditioning seemed uncharacteristically quiet. She rested her chin on her hands and closed her eyes, then tried to make her muscles relax and her mind go blank.

It was a mistake.

A sudden image of the house in Jackson filled her mind. She snapped her eyes back open. How many more bodies were they going to recover? What kind of monster were they dealing with? Immediately her head was full of all the messages she'd ignored from Svetlana. Of the shoebox crammed with memories from her past. Of Ralph's silent departure in the middle of the night.

Maybe silence was overrated.

Much to her relief, it was shattered a few moments later by the ringing of her cell. It was DCI Radcliffe.

"You're at work early," she said in lieu of a greeting.

"Did I wake you?"

"Not at all—I'm at the office."

"Is Gurley there with you?"

"No. Why?"

There was a pause. As if Radcliffe didn't believe her.

"What is it?"

"I got back to my desk last night to discover a preliminary forensics report. There's been a new development."

"Forensics? From the hotel? What is it?"

"I don't want to tell you over the phone. Face to face. Without Gurley."

"I can't exclude him from something like that."

"You've had no qualms about excluding us. Gurley's a royal pain in the arse. If you want the information, you meet me on your own. Can you get down to the station now?"

"I have a meeting this morning... with my boss," she lied. "It's the reason I'm here so early."

"Call me when you're out of it. This new evidence—it could be a game changer."

"Can't you even give me a clue?"

"Not over the phone."

"I swear he's not here."

"Call me later." He hung up.

"Who's not here? Who was that?"

Ingrid swiveled in her chair to see Gurley standing in the doorway. She felt her cheeks warm and hoped to God they weren't glowing red. How long had he been standing there? "Radcliffe. You're not too popular with him right now."

"That's why he was calling? To bitch about me?"

"Sometimes it helps to let off a little steam. Unfortunately, he chose me to listen to him vent."

"You want me to call him?"

Ingrid flinched at the thought. She hoped Gurley hadn't noticed. "Best leave him to calm down."

Gurley grabbed a chair from the other side of the office and dragged it to Ingrid's desk. He slumped down on it. Ingrid thought it might collapse under his weight.

"Foster gave no indication what time he'd call?" Ingrid asked Gurley, even though she already knew the answer.

"No. I guess all we can do now is wait." Gurley rested his chin on a fist. "Seems to me it's all we've been doing. Foster has made us look like fools."

"He's a man determined to stay hidden. There's not much anyone can do about that."

Gurley pulled his cell from a jacket pocket and slid it onto the desk. Both he and Ingrid stared wide-eyed at it for the next few minutes in silence. There wasn't anything else to say or do.

When the phone finally rang, the vibration buzzing it across the desk toward Ingrid, she involuntarily jumped in her seat.

"The trace is set up?"

"We've been ready since six a.m."

Gurley snatched up the phone, hit the answer key, and the speakerphone option, but said nothing.

"The silent treatment makes a change," Foster said. "Aren't you going to spend the next minute trying to persuade me to give myself up?"

Gurley cleared his throat. "I think we're beyond that now, don't you?"

"Pleased to hear it."

Ingrid leaned forward in her chair. It creaked noisily.

"Who's there with you?" Foster demanded.

"This is Agent Skyberg," Ingrid said.

"Good to make your acquaintance, Ingrid. I'm hoping you can drill some sense into Major Gurley's skull."

Ingrid didn't bother to reply.

"I've identified a location for you to pick up Tommy. You'll need to provide the paperwork for travel—I'm sure the embassy can work that out. I don't have his passport. I want Yvonne Sherwood to take him to the airport and ensure he gets on the plane."

"Yvonne is here in London?"

"I haven't told you the location yet."

"I can take Tommy to Heathrow," Ingrid said.

"All due respect, agent, I'd rather have someone I can trust."

"You can trust me."

"I know you're trying to keep me talking, so I'm going to go now. I'll text the location and time shortly. Remember—no police." He hung up.

"Has he lost it completely?" Gurley said. "He thinks we'll let that woman just walk away with Tommy? He's crazy."

The phone beeped. The text gave an address with a west London postal code, a time and another instruction:

Tommy in exchange for Skyberg

Ingrid stared at the words for a moment, unable to quite take in their meaning. A hostage exchange? It seemed almost a quaint notion. It was totally against Bureau protocol. Yet in the circumstances, it seemed like a logical option. If Foster wasn't armed, surely she'd be able to handle it?

"He has lost it," Gurley said, jumping up from his seat. "We can't agree to that. No way."

Ingrid watched him pacing around the room. He reached a bank of metal file cabinets and thumped the first one with his fist. Meanwhile Ingrid was trying to figure out how they could make the whole hostage switch work.

"We'd need to get the police involved," she said. "The Bureau doesn't have the resources here for that kind of operation." She stared at Gurley, as if she were willing him to disagree.

"I understand. But can we at least negotiate some measure of control over their operation?"

"Maybe you should leave that to me."

"Or get your boss involved? Maybe they'd take a little more notice of him?"

Ingrid shook her head firmly. "No way. This isn't something I want Sol to know about. If I do this, it's between you, me and the Metropolitan Police Service." She managed to smile at Gurley, even though a wave of anticipatory nausea was currently making its way from her stomach to the back of her throat.

Kyle Foster had chosen a disused industrial estate in Hounslow for their rendezvous. A location that was just three miles from Heathrow Airport. According to Radcliffe, it had been pretty much abandoned in the last recession. As yet, the slow recovery in the British economy hadn't encouraged new tenants to move in. It was so run down that as Ingrid sat next to Gurley in an unmarked embassy car on the main access road, she fully expected to see tumbleweed blow across the street.

"More waiting," Gurley said, not for the first time. They'd been parked there for less than thirty minutes. Ingrid hoped something would happen soon. Otherwise his complaining would become unbearable.

Her phone vibrated in her pocket. She snatched it out and answered quickly.

"All personnel are in position," Detective Sergeant Tyson informed her.

"You're sure everyone's well hidden?"

"It's a bit tricky getting bodies in place in such a deserted location, but we've got some men about to start digging up the road just northwest of your current position, and a fake estate agent and two clients heading for the other entrance right about now. Everyone else is keeping their distance. As promised." He paused. Ingrid could hear him breathing heavily, as if he'd been running. "Are you all right about this?" It was the first time anyone had actually asked her that outright. She was a little taken aback.

"I'm fine. I've worked this kind of operation dozens of times before. I'm an old hand, trust me." It was a gross exaggeration, and she hadn't done anything like it for more years than she cared to count. "Everything's under control my end." Just as she said that, a large muscle in her thigh started to twitch. She convinced herself it was because she hadn't had a long run for too many days now—nothing to do with her mounting anxiety at all.

A minute later Gurley's phone started to ring. He glanced at the screen. "This is it. You ready?"

"As I'll ever be."

Gurley answered, selecting the speakerphone option once again.

"You double-crossing bastards. Yvonne said I could trust you! What is it with you people?"

"You can trust me," Ingrid said, raising her voice.

"This place is crawling with cops!"

"Please, Kyle," Ingrid said. "It's just me and Major Gurley here."

"You think I'm blind? Or stupid?

"You have to believe me—I had no idea the police were involved." Ingrid winced at the weakness of her lie.

"Bull. Shit. You'll regret this."

46

Following Tyson's directions, Gurley drove quickly around the perimeter of the industrial units and out onto the main drag where they found the detective sergeant standing beside DCI Radcliffe at the open rear doors of a small, white unmarked van.

Ingrid jumped out the car before it came to a complete stop, eager to get to Radcliffe before Gurley had a chance to let rip. "What the hell happened?" she said.

"You tell us. What's he got, this bloke, some sort of sixth sense? You approved our positions before we went into this. What else could we have done?"

Ingrid shook her head. "Foster just told me we'd regret this. He sounded like a man who's been pushed too far. I'm really worried for Tommy now." It was the first time she'd even admitted that to herself.

"Jesus Christ?" Gurley yelled. "Can't you get anything right? You were supposed to be invisible." Gurley was somehow managing to square up to Radcliffe and Tyson simultaneously. Both detectives took a step backwards. Neither man seemed to have the energy for a fight.

"It happens," Radcliffe said resignedly.

"Is that it? We just walk away? Where are the roadblocks?"

"We've got officers trawling the area. If he's close by he won't get far," Tyson said, watching the retreating back of his senior officer as he disappeared into the van.

"OK—I'm getting back in the car, search for myself." Gurley said. He turned to Ingrid. "You coming?"

"Actually, I'd like to stay here, speak to the DCI," Ingrid told him. "Work out what went wrong."

"Fine—you do that. I have nothing more to say to that man."

Ingrid watched Gurley march back to the embassy car, hoping in his anger he wouldn't smash into anything. After he'd accelerated away, tires squealing, she stepped up into the van.

She found Radcliffe sprawled out on a hard bench inside. The man looked exhausted.

"The American Air Force must train their pilots extraordinary well," he said, rubbing a hand across his bloodshot eyes. "We really were careful about the placement of our officers. There shouldn't have been any way for Foster to spot them. You have to believe me." He pulled in his legs and shuffled sideways on the bench, patting the seat beside him. Ingrid perched on the edge.

"It's OK—I haven't come in here to question your tactics. What's done is done. I'm more interested in discussing the new forensics evidence. What exactly do you have?"

Radcliffe seemed a little relieved. "DNA results."

"It's taken this long to get them? I know there can be a backlog, but I thought this request was getting fast-tracked."

"It was fast-tracked. The problem was there were so many samples to analyze. It's been difficult for the lab to differentiate between them. The samples were from the drain in the bathroom sink. As you can imagine, lots of people pass through a central London budget hotel room over the course of a week."

"What exactly did you find?"

"Enough to arrest Carrie Foster."

It had taken Ingrid quite a while to convince DCI Radcliffe that Jack Gurley should be permitted to observe Carrie Foster's interview.

"Can you guarantee he'll behave himself this time?" Radcliffe had finally asked.

"I'll make sure of it."

She and Gurley were now sitting in a much better equipped observation room than before. This one had so many monitors and digital video recorders crammed inside, Ingrid felt as though she were sitting in a TV studio. There had to be at least a half dozen cameras in the interview room, each one trained on a different location.

Now that Carrie Foster was being questioned under caution, gone were the ambient atmosphere and soft furnishings. This interview room was starkly decorated: four whitewashed walls and a gray tile floor, the only furniture a wooden table and four chairs.

Sitting next to Ingrid in front of an array of monitors, Gurley turned to her and said, "Radcliffe didn't tell you exactly what they think the forensics will prove?" He kept his voice low so that the lone uniformed officer standing at the door couldn't hear him.

"Trust me, I'm not holding anything back. You know just as much as I do." Ingrid had tried to press Radcliffe for the details, but he'd refused to divulge any further information.

"He's grandstanding. He wants to make the big reveal the same time he confronts Carrie with it. The guy's playing with us."

"That's his prerogative, I guess."

Gurley glared at her.

"Hey—I'm not saying I agree with it." She stared back into Gurley's face. He looked pale. More distressed than angry.

Sudden movement on the monitor screen immediately in front of her refocused Ingrid's attention. Carrie Foster walked unsteadily toward the table. Behind her was the lawyer appointed by the embassy. Both women sat down at the table, tucking their chairs underneath. A close-up of Mrs Foster's face filled the screen directly in front of Gurley. He stared at it without saying a word. Carrie Foster had clearly been crying. Her eyes were red and puffy, the skin around her nostrils raw. Ingrid glanced from the screen to Gurley. He seemed to have grown even paler. She still couldn't shake the feeling he was holding something back from her. She hoped to God it wasn't what she was beginning to think it might be.

Radcliffe and Tyson entered the room and sat down. DS Tyson then proceeded to switch on a digital recorder. He leaned towards it stating the date, time and persons present. Then he sat back in his chair and fixed his gaze on Carrie Foster.

DCI Radcliffe placed both palms flat on the table top. He pursed his lips.

"Whatever it is you're about to say, don't bother wasting your time," Mrs Foster said. "I've told you everything that happened. There's nothing more to discuss." She narrowed her eyes, almost willing Radcliffe to snap back at her. To his credit, he merely slid his hands from the table and rested them in his lap.

"You have been arrested on suspicion of causing cruelty to a minor." He glanced at the lawyer. "Further charges may follow. You understand how serious this situation is?"

"I have made my position perfectly clear. I have nothing to say to you."

Given Carrie Foster's distressed appearance, Ingrid was amazed the woman was holding it together so well. Maybe the team of solicitors the embassy employed were a little too good at their jobs. This one had clearly coached her client very well.

"Of course, as we stated earlier, and as your solicitor has no doubt reminded you, you do have the right to remain silent. But that might not be the best course of action. We have new evidence that we'd like to discuss with you."

DS Tyson passed his superior a file.

"What new evidence?" Carrie Foster snapped. "I told you what happened. Kyle hurt Molly, then snatched Tommy and disappeared. And you still haven't found them."

"I haven't been informed of any new evidence. It should have been disclosed ahead of this interview." The lawyer nodded at the file in Radcliffe's hands.

Gurley shifted in his chair next to Ingrid. "What did I tell you?" He shook his head wearily. "The man's grandstanding." Sweat had started to prickle along his hairline.

"You did arrive rather late, Ms Welland. Perhaps you'd like a few moments now to go through it? We can leave you to discuss it with your client if you'd like?"

"It's OK," Carrie Foster said. "I just want to get this over with. Whatever they have won't change anything. I know what happened."

The lawyer took the slim file from Radcliffe and opened it. It seemed to have only one or two sheets of paper inside. Carrie Foster hadn't taken her eyes off Radcliffe's face.

"I can't imagine what you think you're going to prove, but would you please hurry. I want to get back to the hospital. If anyone's causing cruelty to a minor it's you. Molly shouldn't be in that place without me."

"There are a few… issues we're hoping you'll be able to clear up for us."

47

Ingrid noticed a flicker of emotion in the lawyer's previously mask-like expression as the woman continued to read the notes within the file. Was it surprise, disgust or resignation? Carrie Foster didn't seem to have noticed—she was too busy staring out Radcliffe.

"As I'm sure you know," Radcliffe began, "a number of forensic samples were taken from your hotel room by our crime scene examiners. We have just received an analysis of the DNA tested from the various samples taken from the bathroom. Of particular interest are those recovered from the drain beneath the sink."

Although the monitor Ingrid was staring at showed a close-up of Carrie Foster's face, she didn't react at the mention of the sink. Still the woman refused to look away from Radcliffe's face. But her neck and shoulders definitely seemed to be holding on to a lot of tension.

"It took a while to separate out the various samples. The most interesting results relate to the fine filaments of hair we found."

More tensing of Carrie Foster's neck. She swallowed, visibly but silently.

"You see, the hair samples are definitely yours, Mrs Foster, as we might have expected. But the traces of blood we found clinging to some of those hairs are Tommy's. Tommy's blood on *your* hair—odd isn't it? How do you explain that?"

There was a knock at the door of the interview room. A female detective Ingrid remembered seeing in the incident room appeared just within shot. She was carrying a clear plastic bag. An evidence bag.

"Ah, perfect timing, Alex." Radcliffe took the bag from her and laid it gently on the table. He waited for the detective to close the door behind her before continuing. "We retrieved this from your handbag earlier today."

Inside the evidence bag was a hairbrush. Just a regular hairbrush as far as Ingrid could make out, white plastic bristles, short blue handle. There were long, light brown hairs tangled in a clump at the base of the bristles. She wondered what it had to do with the evidence the police had found in the hotel bathroom.

"I'm surprised you didn't try to get rid of it," Radcliffe said. "I mean, given we didn't find evidence of Tommy's blood on any of the objects we retrieved from the room, and as his blood was attached to *your* hair, it wasn't much of a leap to suspect your hairbrush might have been the weapon used to cause your son's facial injuries."

Carrie Foster set her lips in a hard line.

"Obviously we haven't yet had a chance to analyze the brush for traces of blood, but perhaps you could preempt our findings, Mrs Foster?"

"I have nothing to say."

"It's the trace of Tommy's blood we found that's troubling me the most, as I'm sure you can imagine."

Finally Carrie Foster tore her gaze away from Radcliffe and looked to her lawyer for support.

"My client is asserting her right to remain silent."

"We know Tommy sustained injuries to his face—a split lip and a bloody nose. That much was confirmed by the A & E Department at St Thomas'. When we asked you about them previously you seemed adamant that your son remained unharmed at the time Mr Foster took him from the hotel room.

And yet, as I say, we've detected traces of Tommy's blood in the drain."

"No comment." Carrie Foster stared down at her hands. She was clasping them together on the table, as if she were praying.

"Maybe you'll feel more inclined to speak after we've analyzed the hairbrush. I mean, how would you explain any trace of Tommy's blood on that?"

"You won't find any. Why would you?"

"Oh I realize you must have cleaned it several times since Monday. That makes perfect sense. But you'd be surprised just how stubbornly small traces of DNA evidence can cling on to things. Fortunately we'll also be taking samples from the inside of your handbag. I presume that's where you shoved the hair-brush before you left the hotel room? Such presence of mind not to leave it behind. One might say it was calculated."

Ingrid stared at the monitor showing a close-up of Radcliffe's face. His expression seemed almost smug.

"Can we stop this now?" Carrie Foster turned to her lawyer. "I have nothing to add to my previous statement."

"I'm afraid we have more questions for you to refuse to answer." Radcliffe handed the evidence bag to Tyson, who hurried to the door and passed it to the female detective waiting on the other side for it.

"Perhaps you'll feel more like talking if we shift to a slightly different subject," the DCI said.

Mrs Foster frowned at him suspiciously.

"Tell me about the circumstances surrounding your husband's departure from the hotel room."

Her expression switched from suspicion to confusion in an instant. "He snatched Tommy and ran. What else is there to say?"

Radcliffe tilted his head to one side. "I mean his earlier departure."

"After he hurt Molly?"

Radcliffe said nothing.

"He threw Molly onto the bed and rushed past me. He nearly knocked me over. I've already told you that."

"And he returned less than twenty minutes later. A full seven minutes after you called for an ambulance."

"I wasn't exactly taking notice of the time."

"No—of course not. Let me run through some of the events of that twenty-five minute period. According to your account, and what we've been able to piece together with the aid of CCTV footage…" Radcliffe turned to the lawyer. "Details are on the second page." He straightened his spine and pulled back his shoulders, as if he were preparing himself for a long speech. "Shortly after Mr Foster allegedly shook your daughter and threw her onto the bed, he ran out of the hotel room—presumably in somewhat of an agitated state—and then down several flights of stairs, through the reception area and onto the street."

"I guess."

"It's surprising none of the other guests at the hotel can remember witnessing this hurried departure. Not a single one of them."

Carrie Foster shrugged. The tension in her shoulders increased as she leaned away from the table. She looked like a woman bracing herself for a blow.

"Anyway," Radcliffe continued, "Mr Foster then proceeded to walk half a mile south along Southampton Row and arrived at a McDonald's restaurant on High Holborn, where he ordered two breakfast wraps, pancakes and syrup, a raspberry and white chocolate muffin, two black coffees and three bottles of orange juice. He then returned to the hotel, a large McDonald's paper bag under his arm, and made his way to your room."

Mrs Foster dragged down her top lip with her bottom teeth.

"Seems a strange thing to do, really. Purchasing a family breakfast after his supposed violent outburst."

"You've made a mistake."

"CCTV footage from the restaurant in question confirms his movements. Fully time-stamped. No mistake, Mrs Foster."

In the observation room, Gurley had started to shake his head. He let out a long sigh. "Sweet Jesus," he whispered.

Carrie Foster's lawyer closed the file in front of her. "I need to discuss this evidence privately with my client." She glanced at

Mrs Foster, who was staring, wide-eyed at the table. She had bitten her top lip so hard it had started to bleed.

Radcliffe started to get to his feet. "Certainly. I'll get one of our constables to escort you to another room."

Tyson leaned toward the digital recorder.

"No!" Foster said and raised a hand to her mouth.

"We really need to talk about this Carrie," the lawyer insisted.

Carrie Foster shook her head. "I just want to get back to the hospital. Please. I need to see Molly."

48

During the unscheduled break, Ingrid and Gurley had sat in the observation room in silence. At one point DS Tyson stuck his head around the door, a self-satisfied grin on his face. Ingrid wasn't sure what he had to be so smug about—it wasn't that long ago he and Radcliffe were certain of Kyle Foster's guilt.

"Can I get you anything?" he asked.

"We're fine, thanks," Ingrid said, answering for them both, unsure if Gurley was capable of saying anything. His face had now lost all its color. He seemed really shaken.

"You're sure?" Tyson frowned at Gurley. "The next session might take a while."

"Really, we're OK." Ingrid just wanted Tyson to leave. His demeanor had started to piss her off.

After fifteen minutes speaking to her lawyer, an unsteady Carrie Foster was led back into the interview room by a female constable and helped onto a chair. She leaned back, tilted her head toward the ceiling and closed her eyes.

In the observation room Gurley murmured something so quietly Ingrid supposed she wasn't meant to hear it. She didn't bother asking him to repeat it.

Ingrid stared at the monitor that showed a close-up of Carrie Foster's face. Her skin was slack. Her eyes seemed blank, her expression resigned somehow.

The two detectives returned to the room and Tyson restarted the digital recorder.

"Now you've had a chance to discuss the new evidence with your solicitor," Radcliffe said, "perhaps you'd like to go over the events of Monday morning again? Tell us what really happened."

The lawyer turned to her client, gently laying a hand on her arm. "You don't have to do this."

"I do. It's been tearing me apart." Carrie Foster blotted her eyes and nose with a Kleenex. "Could I get a glass of water?"

In the next room Ingrid sat up straighter in her chair. She hadn't been expecting a change of heart from Carrie Foster. She craned her neck closer to the screen in front of Gurley. His face now wore a bewildered expression.

A few moments later, the female detective appeared with a plastic jug and four plastic beakers on a tray. She took her time pouring water into each beaker. Carrie Foster drank half a glass, waited for it to be refilled, then took a deep breath.

"It was an accident," she said. The muscles in her face tightened.

Both detectives leaned back in their chairs, a subtle but unmistakable sign that they didn't want to pressure Carrie Foster any further—they were happy to let her make her statement in her own good time.

"Molly just wouldn't stop crying. She's never slept well, ever since she was born. There was no escape from the noise in that tiny hotel room. On Monday morning Tommy was acting out too. I guess he was overexcited to be in a new place, looking forward to visiting the big toy store. He seemed to be making Molly worse. After a while she was pretty much screaming." She closed her eyes. Squeezed them tight shut. "I sent Kyle out to get us some breakfast—asked him to take Tommy with him. But Tommy wasn't dressed yet and Kyle said he'd be much faster if he went alone. We both hoped the promise of food might make Tommy quieten down a little. Tommy loves McDonald's." She drained her glass. Tyson refilled it for her. "Tommy started to bounce up and down on his bed. Higher and higher. I told him to stop, but he wouldn't. I guess I must have had the hairbrush in my hand. I don't really remember. I was just pointing it at him. Not in a threatening way, I swear." She looked at one detective then the other. "You have to believe me, I love my kids." She dabbed her eyes again and leaned towards Radcliffe. "When you have my statement, can I go back to the hospital? Molly really shouldn't be left on her own. She'll get upset."

"Why don't we see where we are when you've finished? Make a judgment then," the DCI said, careful not to make promises he wouldn't be able to keep. "What happened after that?"

"Then Tommy started shouting at me. Taunting me, I guess. Daring me to hit him, almost." She took another drink of water.

Ingrid glanced at Gurley, still he hadn't moved a muscle or said a word. She wanted to ask him what he made of Carrie Foster's statement, but doubted she'd get any kind of sensible response. It was as if he'd gone into a trance, his gaze fixed on the screen, his hands gripping his knees.

Something about the way Carrie Foster spoke was troubling Ingrid. The woman seemed to make every sentence into a question, as if she were doubting herself with each word she uttered. Perhaps she'd hidden the truth for so long, when she actually revealed what really happened, the facts seemed alien to her.

"And then?" Radcliffe asked, when Mrs Foster had returned the beaker to the table.

"Then Molly screamed even louder. I yelled at Tommy to stop shouting. Stop jumping. He wouldn't. Then the bed collapsed. I suppose I lashed out, you know? Forgetting the hairbrush was still in my hand. I caught him right across the face. A second later he was bleeding. Then he started to cry. Then Molly's screaming got louder still. I picked her up from our bed and jiggled her in my arms, but it didn't do any good. Then Tommy ran into the bathroom." She paused, staring down at her hands.

"Did you go after him?"

"Not right away, I wanted to settle Molly first. I couldn't think straight, she was making so much noise. I guess I must have started to shake her. I didn't mean to. I was out of my mind."

The interview room fell silent. All Ingrid could hear was the faint hum of the loudspeakers and the sound of Gurley breathing beside her.

"I'd like to take a break now." Carrie Foster looked at Radcliffe. "Can I take a break?"

"Has anything like this happened before?" Radcliffe asked quietly.

"It was an accident."

"Have there been other accidents?"

Carrie Foster shook her head.

"For the recording, Mrs Foster, I need you to answer verbally."

"No. I get angry sometimes, I suppose. Lose my temper now and then. Mostly I just get a little down."

"Depressed?"

"Doesn't everyone?"

"Those pills in the bathroom cabinet. They're yours?"

She blinked slowly at him. "Kyle got a hold of them for me when I refused to go see the doctor. I didn't ask how he got them. I didn't want to know. But I haven't started taking them. I was mad at him for even suggesting I should. I'm still breastfeeding Molly. I didn't want to have anything in my system that might hurt her."

But 60-proof vodka is just fine, Ingrid thought.

"You haven't seen a doctor about your depression?"

"I thought it would pass, you know? Just as soon as Molly started sleeping through. But I'm still waiting for that to happen." She shook her head. "You've got to believe me—I wouldn't deliberately hurt Molly for the world. It was a terrible, terrible accident." She buried her head in her hands and started to sob.

As Ingrid stared at her, the woman's shoulders and upper body convulsing with with each sob, she still couldn't shake the feeling there was something Carrie Foster wasn't telling the police. What was she hiding?

Radcliffe gave a nod to Tyson, who stated for the record that the interview session was being terminated.

The two detectives got to their feet and left Mrs Foster and Ms

Welland sitting silently at the table.

Ingrid slumped back in her chair, a sharp pain radiating across her shoulders where she'd been hunched over leaning forward on the edge of her seat for so long. She opened her mouth, about to make a comment about something in Carrie Foster's statement that really didn't add up, but took another look at Gurley's bereft face and decided to keep it to herself.

The door to the observation room opened and Radcliffe marched in, an almost triumphant swing to his arms. "It seems your suspicions were not unfounded after all."

"I guess I'm a little surprised she decided to confess. She could have chosen to tough it out."

"Perhaps the stress of the situation was just too much for her in the end." He glanced at the monitor. "Doesn't she look like a woman unburdened?"

Ingrid stared at Carrie Foster's face. She looked spent more than relieved. "Are you planning another interview today?"

"I think we'll reconvene tomorrow in all likelihood."

"There's something I'd like you to pursue," Ingrid said.

"Yes?"

"That whole deal with the hairbrush. If she lashed out at Tommy, in a fit of rage, then *accidentally* shook Molly, because she was so 'out of her mind', what compelled her to even think about washing the hairbrush? Trying to get rid of evidence? Doesn't that make her actions seem more premeditated?"

Before Radcliffe had a chance to consider her question, Gurley jumped up from his chair. "For God's sake, what's the matter with you?" he said, spitting out the words. "You got your confession. What more do you want?" He took a stride towards Radcliffe. The DCI stood his ground.

"Actually there's a lot more we need to speak to Mrs Foster about."

"Such as?" Gurley was stooping, his face close to Radcliffe's.

"The DNA analysis revealed something we'd very much like to discuss with her. Although given her confession, it's probably less relevant than might previously have been the case."

"What the hell are you talking about?" The color was creeping back into Gurley's cheeks.

"It seems Kyle Foster is not Molly's biological father."

49

"Can I speak to her?" Ingrid asked. "In my capacity as a representative of the American embassy? Just to let her know we're still here to support her."

"Not possible," Radcliffe said. "And I'm surprised you're even asking. You know better than that."

Ingrid glanced at Gurley. He was staring into space, his face flushed red.

"You're going to release her on bail." Ingrid made it a statement rather than a question.

"In her state of mind? I think it might be better to keep her in custody for her own protection," Radcliffe said.

"The embassy can give her all the protection she needs."

"The solicitor will make her case to the magistrate."

Ingrid felt the sudden need for air. She'd been cooped up in a stuffy room with Gurley for too long. "I'll be outside. I need a few moments to take all this in," she announced, and left the room.

Once outside she walked up and down between the parked vehicles, trying to get some blood pumping in her legs, and tried hard to work out why she wasn't feeling in the least bit satisfied her hunch about Kyle Foster's innocence had been proved right. Maybe there were just too many questions that remained unanswered, especially now, with Radcliffe's latest revelation. As she walked it occurred to her they needed to contact Kyle Foster urgently. He was so pissed at them the last time he called, Ingrid was worried what he might do next. She found Yvonne Sherwood's number in her cell and called her, but the call went straight to voicemail. She considered leaving a message to let Sherwood know about Carrie Foster's confession, but somehow it didn't seem right to tell Sherwood before Kyle Foster was informed. She needed to discuss what their next move should be with Gurley.

Ingrid hurried back to the observation room to find Gurley slumped against the corridor wall outside, hands on knees.

"Pretty intense, huh?" she said.

He looked her hard in the eye but didn't say a word. Ingrid suspected he was unable rather than unwilling to speak to her.

"I'm going back to the embassy," she told him, suddenly feeling more sorry for the guy than he deserved. He looked so devastated by what he'd just heard. "I think you should come too. We need to work out exactly what we're going to say to Kyle Foster the next time he calls."

"If he calls." Gurley's throat sounded dry as he spoke. He looked up and down the corridor. "Let's get out of here."

They'd exited the police station and had been walking for at least ten minutes before Gurley spoke again. "I guess I owe you an apology. You were right to keep an open mind. I just can't believe Carrie would hurt Molly like that."

"You heard what Carrie said—it was an accident."

"Her own mother?"

"You were prepared to believe her father could hurt her."

Gurley stopped suddenly in the middle of the sidewalk and grabbed Ingrid's arm. "You think Kyle Foster knew Molly wasn't his?"

Ingrid considered the possibility for a moment and quickly rejected it. "I don't think so—every time we've spoken to him he's always referred to Molly as his daughter. He wants to protect her just as much as Tommy."

"But maybe he had to say that. Otherwise we would have been even surer he had motive to hurt Molly."

"You seemed pretty sure he wanted to hurt her anyway."

"I'm not sure about anything anymore." Gurley shrugged his massive shoulders and started walking again. As Ingrid hurried after him her cell vibrated in her pocket. She grabbed it and stared at the screen: it was a cell number she didn't recognize. This time it was her turn to stop in her tracks, getting in the way of pedestrians hurrying along the sidewalk. She hit the answer option and waited.

"Agent Skyberg?"

Gurley mouthed "Who is it?" to her and she mouthed "Foster" back.

"Kyle?" she said.

"I told you no police—why did you go against my wishes? I thought I could trust you."

"Kyle, is Tommy there with you? Is he OK?"

"Tommy's just fine—why wouldn't he be?"

"Absolutely no reason at all. Everything's changed now, Kyle. Your wife has told the police exactly what happened. We know you didn't hurt Molly. We know that for sure now. You don't have to hide out anymore."

"You're lying. This is a trap to get me to give myself up."

"Truly, please believe me—I'm not. Just take Tommy to the nearest hospital, wherever you are, get those injuries looked at again. We can arrange for you both to see Molly. Wouldn't you like that?"

"You lied to me before. Why should I believe you now?"

"It'll be on the news soon, you don't have to take my word for it." Ingrid had no idea when Radcliffe would be making a statement to the media. Maybe she could persuade him to do it sooner rather than later. "Is Yvonne there with you? Maybe I could speak to her."

"She won't be any more convinced by what you're telling me than I am." Foster was starting to sound a little crazy now. Why wouldn't he just take her word for it? She supposed living on his wits, without much sleep or food for the last six days must have taken its toll.

"What can I say to convince you?"

"Nothing—I want to set up the exchange again. Though I swear, if you get the police involved again—"

"Please listen to me, Kyle. There's no need for any of that. Tommy doesn't need to go anywhere. He's safe now. So is Molly. Carrie's in custody. She can't hurt either of them now."

He hung up.

Gurley looked at her expectantly.

"He wants to set up another exchange."

"What's the matter with him?"

"He's just not thinking straight. It's OK—we do as he asks, then I can convince him face to face that he's not in any trouble."

"He abducted his son."

"He was clearly only trying to protect Tommy—he just wanted to get the boy away from Carrie."

"He stole a helicopter."

"In the scheme of things, I think the police might overlook that, don't you?" She was surprised Gurley hadn't brought up the subject of the missing gun and ammunition from the base. She sure as hell wasn't going to mention it.

Her phone beeped. It was a text message from Foster telling her to stand by for further instructions.

50

An hour later Ingrid and Gurley were hunkering down in an anonymous embassy car at another abandoned industrial park. This one was much more run down and older than the first—the buildings were made of red brick rather than prefabricated particle board. No doubt the architects had built them to last, even though by now many of them had started to fall down. Ingrid noticed some of the roofs had collapsed. Most of the windows had no glass in them.

"He'll be calling you, right?" Gurley asked. "My phone is low on juice."

"Mine too. Hopefully the battery will last long enough."

Gurley had pushed back the passenger seat as far as it would go, but his knees still seemed to be butted up against his chin. He adjusted the seat so it reclined at sixty or so degrees and tried to relax his head against the head restraint. He closed his eyes. He started to say something then stopped.

"He'll call when he's ready," Ingrid said. "We can summon a little more patience, can't we?"

"Seems this whole investigation has been about waiting."

"We're so close to the end now. I'm sure I can talk some sense into Kyle." She turned on the radio in the car, keeping the volume low, and retuned it to a news station.

She and Gurley listened in silence for the next five minutes, but there was no mention of Carrie Foster's arrest. The bulletins were full of eye witness reports from Jackson, Minnesota. As the body count increased, so the reporting seemed to get more ghoulish. Ingrid turned off the radio.

"Nothing about the Foster case," Gurley said. "Seems the British media are more interested in something that's happening 4000 miles away."

"Got to keep their audience happy." Ingrid hoped Kathleen Avery wasn't still watching every news report back home. She hated to think of her being exposed to the gruesome details of how each victim had died.

"I guess a head injury sustained accidentally doesn't make for exciting headlines."

"We don't know it was accidental. That's for a jury to decide."

"What?" Gurley turned awkwardly in his seat to face her. "You don't seriously believe Carrie planned to hurt Molly?"

"How can I possibly know one way or the other?" Ingrid really didn't want to have this argument now.

"Come on, you said yourself it was probably an accident."

"I'm not sure what to believe. You've obviously made up your mind." She paused a beat. "But then you were certain she was innocent. Until she confessed." Ingrid had her own suspicions why Gurley was so ready to accept Carrie's version of events, but now really wasn't the time to broach the subject. She reached for the radio dial again, hoping she might find some inoffensive pop station.

Gurley leaned forward and grabbed her hand.

"What the hell?" Ingrid snatched her hand out of his grasp.

"What are you getting at?"

"Can we just focus on the task ahead of us? I'd like a little time to prepare myself, if that's OK with you."

Gurley turned away and stared out at the street. "How long have you known?"

"Known what?" She *really* didn't want to have this conversation now.

"Did Rachelle tell you?"

If she hadn't been certain about her suspicions before, she

sure as hell was now. Ingrid stared out through the windshield too. Those street lights that were still working started to flicker into life.

"If you have something you want to confess, maybe you can save it for another time?"

"I know Carrie couldn't hurt Molly deliberately. I just want you to understand that."

"I'm not sure that's necessary."

"Kyle was on a training mission in Iraq. Carrie was lonely. I was in the right place at the right time, I guess." He put a hand to his forehead and sucked in a breath. "The whole thing ended a little under two years ago. It was over before it started. We both knew it was a mistake."

Ingrid didn't respond. What was there to say?

"I promise you I knew nothing about Molly. I had my suspicions, obviously—the timing kind of worked out—but when I asked Carrie about it, she swore to me Molly was Kyle's." He ran a hand over his short hair. "What a fucking mess."

Ingrid sat very still. She tried to recall their first meeting with Carrie Foster at the hospital. There had been something strange about it—a tension she couldn't identify at the time. Then there was Gurley's subsequent refusal to have any doubt about Carrie's account of the incident.

Gurley was right: it was a fucking mess.

"Say something for God's sake." Gurley twisted in his seat again.

There were no words of comfort or reassurance she could give him. She reached up and squeezed his shoulder, looked into his face, trying to muster an expression of sympathy, suspecting she was failing spectacularly.

Her phone beeped.

It was a text from Kyle Foster.

"We're on," she said, "I have the directions."

Gurley blinked hard a few times, as if he were trying to refocus his attention.

"I can't let you go in there on your own," he said after a moment.

"He's not going to hurt me. He has no reason to."

"He could be armed."

"Really?"

Gurley slammed a hand against the dash.

"I really don't think he had anything to do with the missing gun at the base. He didn't have the opportunity."

Gurley turned to the passenger door and opened it. "I'm going in."

"He didn't ask for you." She put a restraining hand on his arm. "Please, Jack. Think about it."

He glanced over his shoulder.

"Maybe Kyle knows about… Maybe you're the last person he wants to see." She braced herself, worried how Gurley would react. She needn't have. He just slumped back in his seat.

"I don't want you going in there without backup."

He still didn't trust her abilities. She would have gotten mad if she'd had the energy. "Tough—we're doing this my way."

"You should have some protection at least."

"I can look after myself."

"Why not have a little extra help?" Gurley shoved an arm behind his back, beneath his jacket. He yanked something from the waistband of his pants. Then held it out to Ingrid.

The Beretta M9 seemed small in his huge hand.

51

Recoiling from the gun, Ingrid pressed her back into the driver door. "What the—"

"Take it."

"No way. Do you have any idea how much crap I'd be in if anyone found me with that?"

"Same for me." He proffered the gun again.

"It's the missing pistol from the munitions store, isn't it?"

"We were hunting a man who tried to kill a fourteen-month-old and had abducted his son. I wanted a little backup."

"And how convenient, to blame Kyle Foster for the theft. You were actually prepared to *frame* him?"

Just when Ingrid thought she was getting a measure of the man, that maybe Gurley wasn't the dick she'd supposed him to be, he threw this at her. What was wrong with the guy? She wanted to punch him in the mouth now more than she ever had. How could he possibly think his actions were in any way justifiable? She was tempted to report him to his superior when this whole thing was done.

"I just wanted to get Tommy back safe and sound," he said. Then added, "By any means necessary." The gun was still balancing on his open palm, his arm outstretched towards her.

"Get that thing out of my sight." She thumped the steering wheel with a fist. "And find some way of returning it to the munitions store. You better make sure it's clear to everyone Kyle Foster had nothing to do with it."

Gurley reluctantly shoved the gun back into his waistband. "You said yourself he sounded like a desperate man. You can't go in there unarmed."

"That's exactly what I intend to do. Foster's instructions are quite clear. I have every intention of following them to the letter. If I can't convince him of Carrie's confession, that we finally believe his version of events, I can at least go along with his plan. That way no one has to get hurt."

Her phone beeped again. The message contained just one word: *now*.

Gurley started to open his door.

"Where the hell do you think you're going?"

"Let me at least walk you to the outside of the building, for God's sake."

"I go alone."

She climbed out the car and hurried to the second building on the right-hand side of the street, as per Foster's instructions. The darkness seemed to be falling more quickly now. She checked her watch: it was a little after eight-thirty. A distant street light was doing nothing to illuminate her path. She stumbled awkwardly over a brick or lump of masonry as she reached the curb. She glanced back towards the car. Much to her relief, Gurley hadn't decided to rush to her aid.

She reached the entrance of the dilapidated building, one of the rotten wooden doors was hanging off its hinges. She shoved it a few inches to one side and squeezed through the gap. As soon as she was through the other side, the light disappeared almost completely. Standing still for a moment in the dark, she hoped her eyes would adjust to the gloom, but apart from a pale glimmer from a distant window, somewhere way over to her left, which cast the faintest of glows onto the uneven, litter strewn floor, she couldn't really make out any detail. Even though she was reluctant to use her precious phone battery, she flipped on the flashlight app and quickly swept it in an arc in front of her. She spotted a doorway on the other side of the high-ceilinged, hundred-square-foot space, switched off the flashlight and slowly made her way towards it, each footfall landing on broken glass or rubble. After a few dozen more steps she reached out her arms, ready to touch the wall she'd been heading for. When she got to it she was surprised the doorway she'd seen wasn't immediately in front of her. She must have deviated from a straight line. She felt along the wall and edged sideways, frustrated progress was so slow.

Her phone beeped.

Another text message from Foster:

whr the fck ru?

Instead of wasting time fumbling with the phone to text a reply, she located the doorway and moved through it as fast as she dared. She hollered loudly, "I've just crossed the first big room. Can you hear me?"

"Hello?" a distant child's voice answered. "Who are you? Have you—" The child let out a muffled yelp, as if someone had put a hand over his mouth.

"Tommy? Is that you?" Ingrid shouted. "Are you all right?" She stared into a deeper darkness, relieved that Tommy was still alive, but worried now that someone was hurting him. "Tommy?"

As she stood perfectly still, trying to hear his reply, a loud noise, a shuffling, scraping sound, came from somewhere ahead of her. She switched on her phone flashlight again, but there was no one with her in the twenty-foot square room. In the far corner she saw another doorway. With the flashlight trained on the floor, she quickly picked her way over the debris. She reached the door. Through the other side she was relieved to discover a narrow corridor, just as Foster's instructions had described. She called out again, "Kyle? Tommy? I've reached the corridor now. Where are you?" She waited a moment for a reply, but didn't really expect one.

The corridor would be much faster than the previous two rooms to navigate in the dark. All she had to do was reach out both her hands to touch the walls on either side to guide her. She was pretty sure, according to Foster's instructions, her final destination was the room beyond this passageway.

She turned off the flashlight.

After a dozen or so steps another noise, much closer this time, forced her to stop in her tracks.

She felt something scurry over her feet. It was heavy. It had to be a rat.

She continued down the corridor, even faster than she had before. She reached the doorway at the far end and listened.

She heard only the rush of blood and beating of her own heart thump in her ears.

Concentrating hard, Ingrid tried to recall exactly what she was supposed to do once she'd come to the end of the corridor.

Through the doorway she turned right, and, with her fingers lightly touching the rough brickwork of the wall on her right-hand side, followed it until she reached another doorway.

Here she was supposed to wait. Though she was tempted to switch on the flashlight again, she resisted, concerned that in the pitch blackness she might startle Foster with the dazzling bright light.

He might be just feet away from her.

She held her breath and tried to make out the sound of Foster's breathing nearby.

"Kyle? Are you here? Is Tommy with you?" she said, after a few moments.

She listened again.

All she heard was scuttling behind her. More rats, she supposed.

She swallowed hard. The rats themselves weren't a problem. It was the fact she couldn't see them that really bothered her.

She turned her head to the left, then right. But the blackness was absolute.

Behind her the scuttling noise stopped. She exhaled.

"Kyle?"

A split second later she felt an intense pressure across her throat.

Before she could react, a violent shove from behind pushed her face into the rough brick wall. More pressure on her throat, swiftly followed by heavy weight pressing against her body, and she was pinned flat against the wall.

She couldn't move her arms or legs. She couldn't make a sound.

52

"Are you alone?" Though the words were spoken in a harsh whisper, the voice was unmistakably Foster's.

It was impossible for Ingrid to speak, the pressure against her throat was crushing her windpipe.

She managed to nod once.

"You'd better be." Kyle Foster quickly slipped his arm from her throat, grabbed her head by the hair and shoved her left cheek hard against the wall. The rough surface scraped against her skin.

With his spare hand he patted her down, lingering at the pockets. He located her cell phone and threw it onto the ground.

"Please, Kyle." Her voice came out in a murmur, her throat stinging. She coughed. "You're not in any trouble. Carrie has told the police exactly what happened. How she hurt Molly. Why don't you take me to Tommy?"

"You think I would trust you, after you betrayed me before?"

"The police insisted on being part of the operation. It was out of my control." She coughed again. "They're not here now—doesn't that mean anything?"

"Maybe it's a trap." He pressed a knee into her thigh.

"Where's Tommy?"

"You don't need to know."

"Is he with Yvonne?"

"Shut up!" He shifted his weight, leaning more heavily against her. His breathing was rapid and uneven.

Ingrid relaxed her muscles as best she could, hoping Foster might loosen his grip.

He didn't. After a few moments his breathing slowed a little.

"If what you're saying is true, why did Carrie decide to change her story?" he said.

"She had no choice." Ingrid coughed again, her throat felt raw. She tried to swallow. "The police found new evidence."

"I've said all along I wanted to protect Molly and Tommy from her and you didn't believe me. And now you're telling me she's confessed?"

"It's true."

"You'll say anything to get Tommy back. You make me sick."

She couldn't argue with him. The way he was talking, nothing she said would make him trust her. "OK," she said, "just tell me how you want this to work."

He shoved her harder against the wall.

For the first time Ingrid worried what he planned to do to her once he released Tommy.

"Where's Tommy?" she asked again, eager to focus on the reason she was there. "Is he safe? Is Yvonne here with him?"

"Do you have his papers? He needs them for the plane."

"We have an embassy car waiting outside. All the paperwork is inside," she lied. "We've done everything you asked." Ingrid swallowed again. She wasn't sure how much longer she could continue speaking. "You have me now. You can let Tommy go."

He shoved her again. "Shut up! We're doing this my way. When I say."

"You wanted an exchange. You got it. Please. I just want to help you."

"Stop lying to me!" He twisted sideways in an attempt to shove her even closer to the wall.

But this time Ingrid resisted with all the strength she had.

Her efforts threw Foster off balance. He stumbled.

She took her chance.

Driving back both elbows as hard as she could into his torso, she stamped down onto one of his feet. It was enough to knock him further off balance. She used the little momentum she'd gained to spin around and wrap both her arms across his body, pinning his arms to his sides.

He struggled against her.

Now she shoved him against the wall. She knew she wouldn't be able to hold him there for long. He was bigger than her, stronger.

"Kyle—listen to me. Tommy will be safe. We can work together on this."

"Why should I believe you?" He struggled against her grasp.

A strange, high-pitched gulping sound came from behind her. Then a bright light threw her shadow onto the wall. She couldn't turn to see what was there without loosening her grip on Foster. She heard the noise again. More of a sob this time. Then a scream.

Then something barreled into her at speed. The beam of a flashlight bounced around the room, momentarily blinding her. Weak punches hit at her lower back, followed by kicks to her calves. The flashlight clattered to the floor.

"Daddy's right! Stop telling lies!"

"Tom-my!" Her voice cracked between syllables.

"Stop lying." Even though the boy's punches and kicks weren't doing any real damage, they were making it much harder for her to contain Foster.

"Mommy didn't hurt Molly. You're telling lies. Stop it!" The punches came faster and harder for a few moments then eased and gradually stopped. The boy had exhausted himself. He slumped onto the ground. "It's naughty to lie. Mommy didn't hurt Molly." He started to cry.

"It's OK, Tommy," Foster said. "Everything's OK. I'm sure Mommy didn't mean to hurt her."

"Listen to your dad."

Tommy punched her weakly behind her knee. "Let Daddy go!"

Foster wasn't offering any resistance. Ingrid was tempted to release him. "What I said before, it was true. Carrie told the police it was an accident."

"That's true. It was an accident," Tommy said, then sobbed again. "I didn't mean to hurt her." He slid past Ingrid's feet and wrapped himself around his father's legs. "I just wanted to stop her screaming. She was making Mommy cry. She makes Mommy cry all the time. I didn't mean…" His voice was swallowed up by the sobs erupting from his throat, coming faster and louder with each snagging breath he took.

"What?" With his right arm Foster pulled against Ingrid and tried to reach down to his son. "What did you just say?"

Ingrid tightened her grip.

"For God's sake, let me hold my son." Foster strained against her.

"Where's Yvonne?" Ingrid asked.

"She's supposed to be with Tommy."

"I ran away from her," the boy said.

Ingrid let go of Foster and stepped away, out of her reach. Foster dropped to the ground and gathered Tommy into his arms.

"I'm sorry, Daddy."

"Shhh… there's nothing for you to be sorry about."

"But there is. Molly was on the bed, screaming. Like she always does. I could hear Mommy in the bathroom, crying. I told Molly to be quiet. But she wouldn't. So I grabbed her and shook her a little. But she screamed louder. So I shook her some more… I think maybe she hit her head on the back of the bed. I just wanted to…" His voice trailed away.

"It's OK. It's all right, Tommy," Kyle said in a soothing voice.

"That's when Mommy hit me. I let go of Molly then and I hit Mommy back. I punched her in the leg. She shouldn't have hit me. I was just trying to help. I didn't want to hurt anybody."

For the next few moments the only sound that echoed around the room was Tommy's violent sobbing.

"He's lying," Foster said eventually. "Trying to help his mom. He wouldn't hurt his baby sister. He's a good boy." Clearly Foster couldn't believe what his son had just admitted. His voice was shaky, uncertain.

Even in the near-dark, just from the sound of their breathing, Ingrid could tell Foster was squeezing the boy tighter to him.

"I didn't mean to hurt her so bad. It was an accident."

"Shhh, you don't know what you're saying. Be quiet."

"I'm sorry, Daddy."

"It was Carrie," Foster insisted. "It had to be. Molly was just lying so still in Carrie's arms when I got back to the room. But she can get help, right? She's been depressed. That will be taken into account, won't it? Temporary insanity. The stress... the depression she's been suffering from..."

"I'm sorry," Tommy said again between sobs.

"Shhh... I'm not going to lose him," he told Ingrid. "He doesn't know what he's saying."

Ingrid knelt down next to them. "You won't lose him," she said firmly. "That won't happen. Tommy's only eight years old."

"So? He's old enough to be prosecuted. I can't have him go through that."

"He doesn't have to. He's too young."

"You think I'm going to believe you?"

"It's different here than back home. The age of criminal responsibility in the UK is ten years old." She lowered her voice and leaned closer to Foster's head. "The police can't even arrest him."

"What?"

"I swear."

"I don't believe you."

"I wouldn't lie about something like that."

"Why should I trust you?"

"I can call a lawyer right now, if you help me find my cell."

53

A brilliant white light shone in Ingrid's eyes. She held up a hand to shield them from the glare and managed to make out Yvonne Sherwood heading towards them from the doorway, glowing cell phone in one hand, broken brick in the other.

"I'm sorry, Kyle," Sherwood said. "Tommy managed to wriggle out of my arms and run away. He knocked my phone from my hands. It took me a while to find it in the dark." She glared at Ingrid. "Is everything all right?"

"It's fine," Ingrid answered.

"Kyle? What's happened? Why's Tommy crying?"

"It was an accident. I didn't mean to hurt her," Tommy sobbed.

"It's OK, Tommy. It's OK. Shhh..." Foster wrapped his arms around his son more tightly, burying the boy's head beneath his jacket. "Carrie didn't do it," he told Sherwood. "She didn't hurt Molly."

The woman seemed bewildered. "I don't understand. If Carrie didn't—"

"It was Tommy," Ingrid said.

"Kyle?"

"He just said he was trying to make Molly stop crying. He shook her." There was still a tremor in Foster's voice.

"Dear God."

"She says he's too young to face any charges," Foster said, looking at Ingrid. "Do you know if that's true?"

Sherwood shrugged. "Might be. It rings a bell."

"How about you get rid of that brick?" Ingrid said, pointing at the potentially lethal weapon in Sherwood's fist. "Then maybe you can help me find my phone. We need to get out of here."

After locating her cell on the rubble-strewn floor, Kyle Foster gathered his son into his arms and they slowly picked their way across the room. They exited via another corridor and left the building using a different doorway, emerging onto a street on the north side of the derelict warehouse. Sherwood hurried ahead of them to her silver Nissan parked on the other side of the road.

Ingrid sat up front with Sherwood, while Kyle cradled Tommy in his arms on the back seat.

"Are we driving back to the base?" Sherwood asked, peering into the rear-view mirror.

"I want to visit the hospital, see Molly," Foster said. "Show Tommy his sister's going to be just fine."

Ingrid hoped to hell he was right. "I should call some people," she said. "That OK with you, Kyle?" When he didn't answer right away, she twisted in her seat to see him nodding at her, tears streaming down his face.

Ingrid found Gurley's number in her phone. "Jack?"

"What the hell is happening?"

"We've cleared the building. Everyone's just fine. I need you to meet us at the hospital."

"What went down in there?"

She gave him a quick account of what Tommy had admitted then hung up before he could ask her questions. Next she called DCI Radcliffe and repeated the same account.

"You believe him? You don't get the impression he's been coached to admit hurting his sister by Foster?"

Ingrid couldn't believe quite what a cynical bastard Radcliffe was. "I'm certain it's genuine. We're heading for UCH."

"We'll need to take a statement from him."

"Sure. Just not tonight, OK? The kid's exhausted."

Radcliffe reluctantly agreed, then hung up, just moments before Ingrid's cell finally ran out of battery.

Ingrid, Yvonne Sherwood and Carrie Foster's family liaison officer stood discreetly beside the door in Molly's hospital room as the little girl giggled and gurgled at the faces her big brother was making at her.

"See?" Sherwood said. "I told you he couldn't hurt either of them. He's a good dad."

"Maybe Carrie's a better mother than either of us have given her credit for too," Ingrid said.

Sherwood didn't comment.

After fifteen minutes, the ICU nurse ushered them all out of the room, insisting they let Molly sleep. Sherwood and the FLO took Tommy in search of something to eat while Ingrid stayed with Kyle Foster just outside the room.

"I think she's going to be OK," he said.

"Tomorrow morning you can speak to the doctors."

"When I saw Molly in Carrie's arms... in the hotel room, she wasn't moving. I just assumed that she was dead, that Carrie had... Carrie's been so down for so long now. I thought... I guess... I just had to get Tommy away from her." He rubbed the back of his hand against his forehead. He looked like he hadn't washed for days, his fingernails and knuckles were grimed with dirt.

Twenty yards or so down the corridor the double doors swung open. Carrie Foster, accompanied by DS Tyson, walked unsteadily towards them. Kyle Foster looked at his wife as she approached, but didn't move.

"I should go, give you a little time together," Ingrid said quietly.

"No, please stay."

"Why?"

"I'm not sure I'm ready to speak to her. A little support would be appreciated."

Carrie Foster quickened her pace. "I want to see Molly. And Tommy," she said as she got closer to the room.

"The nurse said Molly should rest for a while," Ingrid told her.

"Where's Tommy?" she asked.

"Getting something to eat. He's all right," Ingrid said. "Shaken, tired, but he'll be just fine. The FLO and Yvonne are with him."

After a long moment, Carrie Foster shifted her gaze from Ingrid to Kyle. She swallowed. "I'm sorry, Kyle."

They both turned toward the door of Molly's room and peered through the porthole window, saying nothing.

After a while Kyle Foster broke the silence. "Why did you tell the police I hurt her?" His voice was no more than a whisper.

Carrie Foster didn't answer.

"How could you do that?"

"I didn't know what else to do. I had to protect Tommy."

Kyle Foster shook his head. "So did I."

"I panicked. I'm sorry. I should have told them I was responsible right from the start. But I wanted to stay with Molly. If I'd said I'd hurt her they would have taken her away from me. When I saw that EMT staring at you in the hotel room, he had such a suspicious look on his face… the idea of blaming you was the first thought I had. It seemed the easiest option. I couldn't tell them what really happened."

"But you could have told me. We'd have worked something out."

"And what? Have the police arrest Tommy?"

"He's too young to be arrested."

"I didn't know that. You think I would have let all this happen if I knew that? You've got to believe me—I thought I was doing the best thing for everyone."

"Jesus, Carrie. You know how much I love them. How could you tell people I hurt them?" He sniffed. Tears were streaming down his face again.

"Why did you take Tommy?"

"What?"

"Maybe if you hadn't taken him… if you hadn't run…"

"I thought Molly was dead. Tommy had blood on his face… I had to get him away from you."

"I didn't mean to hit him. All I could think about was stopping him hurting Molly." She looked down at the floor. The expression on her face slowly turned from one of remorse to something closer to indignation. She stared up at her husband. "You really thought I'd killed Molly?"

"What else was I supposed to think? Especially when you blamed me for it." Kyle Foster glanced at Ingrid. She wasn't sure what it was he might want her to say, but there was no way she was getting involved. She started to back away.

"I told you already," Carrie said, "blaming you seemed the easiest option. The longer it went on, the more impossible it was for me to change my story. I was terrified of losing Molly."

"Me too." He stared through the window into Molly's room. "What did the doctors tell you? Is she going to be all right?"

"They're hopeful. She'll need more scans. She'll have to be monitored closely, but it's looking much better than it was."

"Thank God." He wiped his cheeks dry with the sleeve of his jacket. "The police need to interview Tommy. We should both be there when they do. He needs his mom and dad right now."

"Of course." She swallowed. "I want to try to put things right, Kyle." She reached out a hand, but he pulled away. "Tell me you want that too."

He shook his head. "Right now, I just care about the kids, OK? I'll do what I have to for them."

Carrie Foster took a deep breath. "There's something else I need to tell you, about Molly. Something you should hear from me, before you speak to the doctors."

"About her diagnosis?" He sounded panicked.

"No—nothing to do with her condition. Something else."

Ingrid had been slowly edging away from the couple, now she turned around and hurried along the corridor. There was no need for her to witness Kyle's reaction to the bombshell his wife was about to drop. She needed to get to Gurley, head him off at the pass before he came blundering in. As she approached DS

Tyson, who'd been keeping a respectful distance, she nodded and said, "Been a long week, hasn't it?"

The detective nodded back at her, his gaze fixed on the Fosters, a grim expression on his face.

"What'll happen to Tommy?"

Tyson hesitated before answering. "He'll need to make a formal statement. Then he might be given a Child Safety Order."

Ingrid looked at him blankly.

"If he is, he'll be placed under the supervision of a youth offending team. But that sort of approach is designed for persistent offenders. I'm not sure it can even be applied to foreign nationals. It's all a bloody awful mess, the whole thing."

Ingrid wasn't about to argue with his assessment.

Along the corridor, the double doors swung open again and Jack Gurley appeared, his face gray, his posture slumped. He looked like a defeated man.

"How's it going with the big reconciliation?" Gurley gestured in the Fosters' direction.

"Not great and I'd say it's about to get a whole lot worse," Ingrid said and quickly walked Gurley back through the doors. "I think Carrie is about to tell Kyle about Molly."

Gurley stopped. "Shouldn't I be around for that? To support Carrie? If Kyle wants to throw a punch at me, maybe I should let him."

"You really think Molly is yours?"

He nodded, letting out a long sigh. "I'll take a DNA test—prove it one way or the other. Maybe afterwards I should ask for a transfer back home."

"Shouldn't you stick around? For Molly's sake?"

"That's not up to me. I'll do whatever Carrie wants me to."

Ingrid wondered at Gurley's reluctance to get involved. He didn't seem like the sort of man who would run away from his responsibilities. "What did you do with the pistol?" she asked, keen to change the subject.

"It's in the glove compartment of the car. Don't worry—I'll deal with it, make sure no one can blame it on Foster."

"Good."

"I screwed up. Least I can do is put it right." He stuck out his hand. "Pleasure working with you, agent." He gave her a wry smile.

Ingrid took his hand in hers. "Likewise." It wasn't exactly a lie, but she wouldn't be in a hurry to repeat the experience. "But you're not quite free of me yet."

He raised his eyebrows.

"There's the whole Bureau debrief ordeal to get through."

"They need me for that?"

"Afraid so."

He shrugged. "Listen, that little chat I had with your chief, about getting you taken off the investigation?"

"It's OK—I won't bear a grudge."

He smiled at her again then led the way toward the elevators. "How about I buy you that pizza I promised you? Prove there's no hard feelings?"

"I'm real tired. Let's take a raincheck on that, shall we?"

He smiled again, his face a picture of relief.

54

The next day Ingrid didn't stir from her bed until noon. She hadn't set an alarm, assuming the bright morning light that streamed into her bedroom would wake her. But she'd slept right through. As she sat up and swung her legs over the edge of the bed, she wasn't sure the extra hours of sleep had been at all restorative. It felt a little shameful sleeping in so late. She reached down and grabbed her phone from the floor and discovered she'd missed a dozen or so calls. She quickly flipped through the list of text messages and worked out who she should call first.

Just as soon as she'd drunk her first cup of coffee.

As she staggered blearily into the kitchen, she listened to a long, rambling voice message from Ralph, telling her how relieved he was that she was safe and asking if she'd perhaps like to meet later, if she was feeling up to it. Ingrid saved his message, smiling stupidly at the phone, surprised at just how much the idea of seeing him appealed to her. She sent him a quick text message, promising to call later.

Then she made coffee.

Just as she was finishing her second large mug, sitting cross-legged outside on the roof terrace, her phone started to ring. It was an international call. Her mother or Mike Stiller. She wasn't sure right now if she wanted to speak to either of them. She drained her coffee and hit the answer button.

It was Mike. For him to be calling her this early D.C. time on a Sunday, it had to be something serious.

He took a while greeting her, asking how she was, how her case was going, was she busy, could she speak, until she had to shout at him to tell her whatever it was he'd called her about. Still he hesitated.

"For God's sake, Mike, all this prevaricating isn't actually helping. Just tell me."

Which was exactly what he proceeded to do for the next ten minutes. He spelled out in detail everything he knew, answering all of Ingrid's questions, even when she interrupted him—which would normally have gotten him so mad he would have hung up on her—and spoke in such gentle tones, at times she wasn't sure she was even speaking to the right man.

When she eventually hung up, even though she'd exhausted all her lines of questioning, drawn out every last morsel of information Mike had for her, Ingrid still couldn't believe what he'd told her. Or maybe she just didn't want to believe it. She stared down at her phone, watching it shake in her trembling hand, and felt her throat tighten. She stood up and walked unsteadily to the edge of her roof terrace. She stared out at the view across London, imagining another vista, another view. One she hadn't seen for many, many years. Maybe too many.

She closed her eyes. She knew what she had to do next, but wasn't sure if she was ready.

After a little while she opened her eyes, wiped the tears from her face and selected a number from her contacts list. She took a quick, deep breath before Svetlana picked up.

"Hey, Mom, it's me. I hope I didn't wake you." She braced herself for a torrent of insults and abuse, but it didn't come. Perhaps it was something about the tone of her voice, in those few words, that stopped her mother's complaints about unanswered calls and ignored messages.

Whatever it was, Svetlana simply said, "Tell me."

Ingrid swallowed and started to relay everything Mike Stiller had just told her. Unlike Ingrid, Svetlana remained quiet on the other end of the line, waiting for a natural pause in her daughter's account before she asked her first question.

"There can be no doubt?" she said, the inflection in the question suggesting she was hoping that there was.

"The samples they tested matched enough of Kathleen's DNA profile to prove the… victim is a close relative. As soon as they get a sample of Megan's hair to test, everything will be confirmed for sure. They found her, Mom. They found Megan."

Svetlana didn't say anything.

"She was so close to home, all this time. So close and we never knew." Ingrid was struggling to contain her tears. She pulled the phone away from her ear for a moment and sniffed sharply. "All these years I thought I could save her."

"Nobody could, Golubushka. Nobody." Ingrid couldn't remember the last time her mother used that name when she was talking to her. It sent a shiver up her spine.

"Are you with Kathleen right now?" Ingrid asked.

"No, I'm in the car on my way over to her house. I should call her."

Ingrid sucked in a breath. "No. Wait. Don't do that. Let me."

"You're sure?"

"I think it's the very least I can do. But she shouldn't be alone when she finds out. Will you call me when you get there, then pass the phone to Kathleen?"

"You don't even have to ask."

"We found her, Mom."

"I'll call you soon. Will you…" She paused.

"What is it?"

"Will you come home now?"

After a painful, but thankfully brief conversation with Kathleen Avery, Ingrid managed to book the last seat on the final flight to Minneapolis for the afternoon flight the following day. Then she called Sol Franklin at home to explain the situation, grateful to get through the whole story without breaking down.

"I hate to abandon my post, but I have to go back home. I'll need a week or so."

"Listen to me, you take as long as you need. We can cover for you here. I'll take on your caseload myself if I have to."

"I'm sorry, Sol."

"Nothing to apologize for—we'll manage."

"I need to write up my report on the Foster case."

"I'll speak to Major Gurley, I'm sure between us we can produce something to keep the chief happy."

Ingrid really did feel bad leaving a job half done. But doing the right thing for Megan Avery was more important than anything else.

"Just tell me you're planning on coming back," Sol said.

Ingrid hadn't been thinking that far ahead. She'd just assumed she would return to London. But now Sol had actually raised the possibility she might not, the idea didn't seem that outrageous.

"Ingrid? You are coming back?"

"Sure, sure."

"I'll keep the job open for you as long as I can."

"Thanks, Sol. I'll call you after the funeral, when I have a clearer idea of my plans. OK?"

Sol paused before answering. "That's fine. I know you won't let me down."

Ingrid said goodbye and hung up, feeling unsettled by the conversation. She looked around the living room of her sparsely furnished, rented apartment. She really hadn't personalized it at all. Did that mean in the back of her mind she hadn't been planning on staying? She shook the thought from her head and jumped up from the couch. *Now what*? She'd been working flat out the past week and now had no clue what to do with herself. Instinctively, she headed for the apartment door and found her running shoes there. A long overdue run would make things feel a whole lot better. She strapped her cell phone to her arm, stuck her earphones in her ears and left the building.

It wasn't until she reached the Outer Circle of Regent's Park, just a few dozen yards away from the official residence of the US ambassador, that she realized although her mind had been full of memories of Megan Avery during her run, not all of them had been painful. Thinking of her friend felt different somehow, but she couldn't quite pinpoint what it was that had changed. Previously she had tried and failed to outrun her memories when they came, but now she seemed more able to face them.

She stopped when she got to the entrance of London Zoo and called Ralph Mills.

"Hey, Ralph."

"Hi."

"You got my text."

"I did."

"Good."

"Thanks for getting back to me."

Ingrid had never heard him sound so awkward. She had a feeling the conversation was going to be harder than she'd imagined.

"Listen, about the other night," he said, then stalled.

"I'm sorry," they both said together.

"You have nothing to apologize for," he told her.

"And neither do you." She let out a breath, relieved to have cleared the air. "How about dinner tonight?"

"I was just about to suggest the same thing."

"Great. Pick me up at eight. We'll eat local."

"Look forward to it."

After dinner, which they spent talking about pretty much anything except the abduction case in Minnesota, Ingrid and Ralph strolled slowly back to her apartment. As they stood at the apartment door, and he leaned in to kiss her goodnight, Ingrid grabbed both his arms and dragged him over the threshold.

"I really don't want to be alone tonight," she said, then kicked the door shut and carried on through to the living room, figuring that heading for the bedroom right away might just freak him out.

They finished half a bottle of wine while talking about the Molly Foster case, until finally Ingrid had talked herself out. She put down her glass, got to her feet and, grabbing Ralph's hand, led him into the bedroom.

"You're sure about this?" he said, as she started to slowly unbutton his shirt. "I don't want you to think I'm taking advantage of the situation."

"Situation?"

"You're in a vulnerable place right now."

"Don't you think we've moved beyond that?"

"I just want to be sure—"

She put a finger to his mouth then kissed it. "Shut up, dammit."

The next morning, when Ralph left her apartment, his brown hair tousled, the left sleeve of his tee shirt ripped where she had tried to pull it over his head too fast, Ingrid was certain of one thing. She had definitely put her failed engagement to Marshall Claybourne firmly behind her.

A new start was just what she needed.

55

Standing at the end of the snaking security line in Terminal 3 of Heathrow Airport, Ingrid was determined not to get emotional. Ralph had insisted he take her to the airport, and though she hated lingering goodbyes, after the night they had spent together, she felt unable to refuse him. With dry eyes, she grabbed Ralph's face in both her hands, pulling his head toward hers, and planted a kiss on his partly open mouth. They stayed like that for a few moments before Ingrid tore herself away.

"I'll call you," she said.

"If I didn't know better, I'd say that sounded suspiciously like the brush off."

She smiled at him. He smiled his Clark Swanson smile back at her and she felt the inevitable adrenalin rush surge through her body. And it felt good.

On the other side of security, as Ingrid was stuffing her belongings back into her backpack following a particularly thorough search by an officious security employee, her phone started to ring. She retrieved it from her purse and hit the answer option.

"Hey, it's Mike."

Ingrid held her breath. "Tell me they've got him."

"Sorry, not yet, but I just spoke to one of the local agents. They've got a reliable tip-off. They're real hopeful it's gonna lead to something."

"That sounds like the kind of thing I used to say to console family members."

"I'm not bullshitting you. I wouldn't do that. They're real close to a breakthrough, they told me. I believe them, I really do. And you know what a cynical sonofabitch I am."

Ingrid didn't comment.

"As soon as I get any more news, I'll let you know."

"Thanks, Mike." Ingrid hung up wondering if this time she could risk allowing herself to hope for the best.

Before she proceeded to the departure gate, she made one more call.

"Chief inspector."

"Agent Skyberg, so good of you to check in."

"I'm on my way back to the US, I haven't had chance to—"

"It's all right, Sol Franklin has already informed me—a family emergency, I gather."

Ingrid swallowed. "SSA Franklin will be your main point of contact at the embassy in my absence."

"I'm sure we'll muddle through without you."

"Can you tell me what happened when you interviewed Tommy?"

"The boy was distraught, naturally. Clearly remorseful. The US Air Force have agreed to a program of extensive counseling, for both Tommy individually and the family as a whole. He'll be monitored closely, of course, but our forensic psychologist believes this attack was a one-off incident."

Ingrid hoped they were right.

"Have you heard from Major Gurley?" she asked the DCI.

"I haven't been able to contact him. I've been told by his superior officer that after his debrief he was assigned to another base."

"Here or in the US?"

"That wasn't entirely clear. Why?"

"No reason." Maybe Carrie Foster had suggested Gurley make the request for a transfer. She guessed it was something she'd never find out. "Thank you for the update."

"No problem. I hope your family issues are resolved soon."

It was a hope Ingrid hadn't dared wish for herself.

She changed planes at O'Hare International and when she finally reached the arrivals hall at St Paul Airport in Minneapolis, she spotted Svetlana standing at a low barrier, fidgeting with a pack of cigarettes.

In the three years since she'd last seen her, Ingrid's mother didn't seem to have changed at all. Her hair was still dyed bright red and she continued to wear the wiry locks piled high on top of her head. For Svetlana, the Soviet gymnast look was clearly impossible to shake. Ingrid surprised herself by smiling at her mother as she approached the barrier. Svetlana didn't seem to notice her own daughter until she was practically standing beside her. Two feet out Ingrid noticed her mother was wearing a pair of glasses on a chain around her neck. They were new. Perhaps she should try wearing them on her face instead, Ingrid thought.

She waved right at her mother. Svetlana jerked to attention, looked Ingrid up and down for a few moments, then said, "You've put on weight."

As soon as they got into the car her mother switched on the local news radio station. "We might hear something new," she explained.

"Nothing about the perpetrator yet?"

"Why?" Svetlana peered at her sideways, a suspicious look in her eyes. "You know something?"

"I just heard the local agents might have a lead."

"They have leads all the time. Each one comes to nothing." She started the car and they drove the next hundred and fifty miles without saying very much at all. But then there wasn't really anything to say. Catching up on each other's news didn't seem appropriate in the circumstances.

When they pulled into Kathleen's drive, just after five in the afternoon, Ingrid was amazed to discover how little the exterior of the house had changed. It must have been repainted over the years, but always in the same color: light blue clapboards with bright white trim. She wondered if time had stood still inside the house too. As soon as she set foot over the threshold, she could see that it had. She supposed Megan's room at the rear of the ranch-style single story building had remained untouched. She expected to find some sort of morbid shrine to her friend. The thought made her feel a little nauseous.

She hesitated in the hallway.

"Go on through," Svetlana told her, slipping a set of keys into her pocket. "Kathleen isn't going to rush out and greet us."

Still Ingrid felt unable to put one foot in front of the other.

"She's been talking about your visit non-stop since yesterday. For God's sake, at least go and say hello." Svetlana shoved Ingrid sharply in the back. Ingrid felt each one of her mother's bony knuckles press against her flesh.

She slowly walked into the living room, feeling all of fourteen again. The couch was pushed up against the wall on the left-hand side, just like it always had been. Kathleen Avery was sitting in the middle of it, her head turned toward the door. Suddenly her face broke into a broad smile.

"Come over here, honey."

Ingrid let out a silent breath of relief. Kathleen wasn't as big as she'd imagined. Morbidly obese, certainly, but it didn't seem she was totally immobile. Ingrid edged toward the couch, staring at Kathleen's flushed cheeks, her short light brown hair peppered with gray. She was wearing a long flowered smock dress over a pair of black leisure pants.

"Don't be bashful. Come sit right next to me." Her voice was just the same, thick like molasses, with a sing-song quality about it. A sudden memory of Kathleen singing lullabies to them when Ingrid stayed over as a child jumped into her head. Something she hadn't thought of in years.

After more coaxing from Kathleen, Ingrid did as she was told and eased herself down onto the soft upholstery of the couch, sliding sideways into the dip that Kathleen was creating in the middle seat cushion. A heavy arm wrapped around Ingrid's waist, pulling her further in. Kathleen planted a kiss on Ingrid's cheek.

"Don't you smell all grown up?"

Ingrid suspected it was the aroma of strong black coffee on her breath and the stink of Svetlana's cigarettes clinging to her hair that was creating the impression of adulthood. The last time Kathleen had laid eyes on her she was still firmly stuck in an awkward adolescence that threatened to go on forever.

Kathleen smelled the same as she always had: of sweet apples and fresh baked pastry. Immediately Ingrid was transported to the late eighties, sitting in the kitchen of this house, devouring a pile of pie and ice cream, wishing Kathleen was her mom and not Svetlana.

Maybe she still did a little.

Kathleen stopped squeezing her for a moment to point a remote at the forty-eight inch TV playing noisily on the other side of the room. "I pretty much have it on twenty-four seven—just in case there's any news." She looked toward the doorway at Svetlana who was hovering there.

"I'm going to the backyard," she announced. "I need a smoke." She marched through the room, glancing at Ingrid as she passed. It was the first time her mother had displayed any hint of tact. She must have guessed Ingrid needed a little privacy to speak to Kathleen. Their phone conversation the day before had been very brief.

"I guess you've been wondering why I haven't come to see you in all these years," Ingrid began.

"We all have our own way of dealing with pain." Kathleen wrinkled her nose, as if she was about to sneeze. Her eyes watered. "I'm not going to make any judgment about the way you dealt with yours." She smiled weakly at Ingrid. "I'm not saying I wouldn't have liked to see you. I'd have loved it, but I can understand how hard it was for you. I really can." Tears fell from her eyes.

"No—there's more to it than that. There's stuff you don't know."

Kathleen sniffed and dabbed her eyes with a lilac lace handkerchief. "Is it something you really need to tell me?"

Ingrid frowned into the woman's flushed face and noticed the deep lines around her eyes and mouth for the first time.

"I mean, it might very well be good for you to say what you've been keeping to yourself all these years, but do you think it would be good for me to hear it?" She wiped her nose with the handkerchief.

Ingrid had to look away. She gazed down at the swirling pattern in the textured carpet. It seemed to move somehow, like waves on the sea. It made her feel a little sick. She felt Kathleen's chubby fingers wrap around her hand. "I just thought I should tell you exactly what I remember," Ingrid said. "What I did." *And what I didn't do.*

"You were both not much more than babies." She sniffed again. "You can't be blamed for what happened."

"I'm so sorry, Mrs Avery."

"It wasn't your fault, do you hear me?"

Tears sprang from Ingrid's eyes and down her cheeks before she even realized she was crying. Kathleen pulled her toward her huge breasts and stroked her hair. She patted a hand against her leg. Sudden sobs issued from Ingrid's mouth, she was unable to keep them under control any longer.

"You let it all out, honey. You let it all out."

They stayed sitting like that for a few moments until Kathleen unexpectedly withdrew her hand and pushed Ingrid away. Ingrid tensed, bracing herself, worried what was going to happen next. What Kathleen might say. She looked at Kathleen's face, expecting to see an expression of disappointment. But Megan's mom turned her face away. She stared intently at the television on the opposite wall.

"Is that him?" Her ruddy face had grown pale.

Ingrid looked at the scene playing out on the huge screen across the room. Two tall FBI agents were bundling a wiry, balding man in his mid-fifties, a mass of tattoos on his scrawny arms, into a waiting police car.

56

Although Ingrid had booked herself a room in a local motel, somehow Svetlana managed to convince her to stay in the family home. Much to Ingrid's relief, her mother led her to a guest room on the top floor at the front of the house, rather than her old room in the attic.

After she'd unpacked, Ingrid checked her phone for all the calls and texts she'd been ignoring since she'd landed in the US. It took her a full fifteen minutes to plow through all of them and when she got to the end there was only one call she wanted to return. She hit a speed dial option.

"Hey, Ralph."

There was a pause at the other end—Ingrid wondered if she'd interrupted something. She hadn't quite oriented herself in terms of days and time. Had she called him in the middle of the night, London time?

"Hello. You arrived," he said.

"I did."

"I'm sorry if I left you a lot of messages. The Kyle Foster story hit the news here this morning and I thought you might want to know about it. Somehow Angela Tate managed to get a scoop. I don't know how she does it."

"Maybe she has friends in high places."

"More likely she has enemies and a lot of dirt on them." He

fell quiet again. "Listen, I should come clean—full disclosure and all that… I left you a ton of messages because… well I suppose I just—"

"Does it help to know you're the only person whose call I've returned?"

"It's good to hear your voice."

"I only saw you yesterday."

Another pause. She'd made him feel awkward—not what she'd intended. But to his credit he recovered quickly.

"You left just when things were starting to get interesting."

It wasn't as if she'd had a choice. No need to remind Ralph of that—she didn't want to make him feel uncomfortable.

He cleared his throat. "I saw on the news the police have made an arrest in Minnesota."

"Yes, I was at Kathleen Avery's house when I found out."

"Do you know if he's admitting anything?"

"According to my contact the sonofabitch won't shut up about what he's done."

"At least that'll make the whole process quicker."

"I guess."

"You've spoken to Megan's mum? How'd it go?"

"I think it was OK."

"Better than you were expecting?"

"Much."

"But it was still tough?"

"I didn't tell her exactly what happened—the fact that I ran. It wasn't until I was sitting right next to her that I realized that if I had I would just have been unburdening myself. It wouldn't have helped Kathleen any. It would have been plain selfish."

"You did the right thing."

"I think so. If she asks me for the details, I'll be honest with her. But now is not the right time."

He went quiet again.

"Ralph? Are you OK?"

"I feel like I want to wrap my arms around you, tell you it's going to be all right."

"I guess it never will be. But right now at least it feels a little less hard. I'll take that."

"Has a date been set for the funeral?"

"A week today. I was thinking I'd come back to London right after, but I might stay a while."

"Oh."

A single syllable could hardly ever have conveyed so much disappointment.

"I've got a lot of thinking to do. A lot of talking. And a hell of a lot of fences to mend." Ingrid had expected him to jump right in and tell her she should take just as long as she needed to. But he said nothing. Maybe he was even more disappointed with her decision to stay on than she'd realized.

They said a slightly awkward goodbye and Ingrid made sure she was the first to hang up.

The following Monday, with mechanical assistance from the local vehicle hire company together with her own determination, Kathleen Avery managed to get to the cemetery for her only daughter's funeral. It had been the first time she had set foot outside her home in over seven years. One of her six-foot, two-hundred-sixty pound sons pushed her along the paved path from the line of funeral cars to the grave in a super-sized wheelchair designed especially for heavy hospital patients.

Kathleen sat with her back straight and her head held high. She told Ingrid she wanted her to walk with the rest of the family to the graveside, seeing as Megan loved her like a sister. It was all Ingrid could do not to break down into floods of tears every time Kathleen mentioned Megan's name. She'd been feeling a little better with every conversation she'd had with Kathleen over the past week, but the guilt that had burned in her belly for the last eighteen years wasn't going anywhere. She held onto Megan's youngest brother's arm with a tight grip, not completely trusting that her legs would be strong enough to carry her to the mound of earth she could see fifty yards away.

When they reached the graveside, the assembled mourners arranged themselves around the eight foot by four foot hole in strict order of intimacy with the Averys. Even though she hadn't spoken to Kathleen since she'd left home, Ingrid stood right next to her chair, with Svetlana standing on the other side.

Along with her extended family and Ingrid and Svetlana, most of Megan's high school classmates had come to pay their respects. Ingrid felt humbled by the amount of love and compassion on display for Kathleen Avery and regretted that over the years she hadn't felt more able to show some herself.

The short service was both poignant and apt. The reverend was the same one who'd baptized Megan thirty-one years earlier. When he spoke about her in fond and glowing terms he wasn't reciting something her family had told him to say, he was actually remembering Megan's life the way it deserved to be.

When the last of Megan's family and friends had thrown a handful of soil onto her oak paneled, brass handled casket, the entourage slowly made its way back to the cars to return to Kathleen's house for the wake. As the crowd dispersed, Ingrid saw a face she hadn't laid eyes on for so many years she wasn't sure if she'd imagined it. Then the face broke into a smile. A smile she had never forgotten since junior high. Her very first unrequited crush.

It was Clark Swanson.

He gave her a subtle wave and she felt the exact same butterflies in her stomach that she had all those years ago. How was it possible he could still have this effect on her? Maybe it was because now, ironically, Clark Swanson was actually reminding her of Ralph Mills, rather than the other way around.

Clark hurried over to Kathleen and kneeled down so that his face was level with hers. "I'm so sorry, Mrs Avery. I didn't think it was possible to miss Megan more than we had, but today has proved me wrong. She was a beautiful, beautiful girl."

"Thank you, Clark. I appreciate you coming all the way back here for Megan."

"Nothing could have kept me away, ma'am." He glanced up at Ingrid as he got to his feet and nodded at her. "I thought maybe I would gather Megan's classmates together and we could reminisce a little about high school. Share a few of our memories with you, Mrs Avery.

"I'd like that. I'm sure Megan would too." She stared down at the ground, somehow managing to hold back her tears.

Ingrid dropped to her knees and took Kathleen's hand firmly in hers. Then she kissed the back of it. A feeling washed over her that she hadn't been expecting at all.

Ingrid actually felt contented to be back home.

They spent a little while longer together in silence, then Kathleen's eldest son wheeled her away toward the line of waiting cars.

When everyone else had gone, Ingrid crouched low beside the grave and asked Megan Avery to forgive her.

Would you like very special FREE short story set between the events of *Deep Hurt* and the next book in the series, *Shoot First*? *Dirty Secret* reveals what Ingrid gets up to with Clark Swanson while she's back in Minnesota and you can get your hands on it, as well as lots of other bonus material, by joining my readers' club.

Visit evahudson.com/readersclub to find out more.

In *Shoot First*, the fourth book in this rollercoaster series, Ingrid makes a decision that will change her life forever.

SHOOT FIRST

AN INGRID SKYBERG THRILLER BOOK 4

A teenage girl disappears after witnessing a gangland murder in Chicago. Nine months later, and heavily pregnant, she arrives in London only to disappear again.

Special Agent Ingrid Skyberg has just two days to find the girl and get her to testify or else a brutal killer walks free. But Ingrid isn't the only person looking for the girl, and a war that started on the streets of Chicago is about to explode in the peaceful English countryside.

Available in paperback and ebook.

THE INGRID SKYBERG THRILLERS

Run Girl - Prequel (A novella)

Secretary of State Jayne Whitticker is in the middle of delicate negotiations when her favorite grandchild disappears from Paris.

Special Agent Ingrid Skyberg is hauled out of her FBI training session at Scotland Yard to head the hunt for the eighteen-year-old girl, who the FBI believe is now in London. Will she succeed in her unexpected mission? Or will her failure lead to the collapse of the crucial peace talks?

FREE to download when you join Eva's mailing list at evahudson.com.

Fresh Doubt - Book One

A story of lies, secrets and deadly mind games.

Two hours ago, brilliant American psychology student Madison Faber found her roommate lying in a pool of blood. Now she is in police custody and suspected of murder. Madison persuades Special Agent Ingrid Skyberg to find the real killer, but the investigation soon puts Ingrid in danger. Can she unmask the murderer before she becomes a victim herself?

Kill Plan - Book Two

An American trader is poisoned in his office in the City of London. Two days later, a Latvian immigrant is discovered floating face down in the River Thames. These seemingly unrelated crimes are the work of an audacious serial killer working on both sides of the Atlantic.

When Special Agent Ingrid Skyberg starts putting the pieces together, she also puts herself in the firing line.

Deep Hurt - Book Three

In a seedy hotel in central London, the baby daughter of a US Air Force pilot lies lifeless in his wife's arms. Accused of killing the fourteen-month-old in an uncontrolled rage, Kyle Foster flees, taking his eight-year-old son with him.

Will Ingrid find Foster before he hurts anyone else? Or will she succumb to the old demons she's been trying to escape for the last eighteen years?

Shoot First - Book Four

A teenage girl disappears after witnessing a gangland murder in Chicago. Nine months later, and heavily pregnant, she arrives in London only to disappear again.

Special Agent Ingrid Skyberg has just two days to find the girl and get her to testify or else a brutal killer walks free. But Ingrid isn't the only person looking for the girl, and a war that started on the streets of Chicago is about to explode in the peaceful English countryside.

Below Zero - Book Five

Stockholm is under siege. A bomb has gone off, a series of high profile people have been kidnapped, and the city is in lockdown. Unfortunately for Special Agent Ingrid Skyberg, everything is kicking off on the same day she is in town to complete a dangerous assignment that is so secret, and so illegal, that neither the FBI or the US government can ever know about it. Her instructions are simple: no ID, no credit cards, no trace. If she ends up in jail, or floating face down in the harbor, there can be no way of identifying her.

No badge, no gun, no back-up: this time Ingrid is on her own.

Final Offer - Book Six

A shadowy UK-based group has been trying to hack the US elections. When Special Agent Ingrid Skyberg is assigned to find out who's funding the hackers, she finds herself up against an invisible enemy who is extremely powerful and utterly ruthless.

To bring them to justice, Ingrid must go undercover and infiltrate the world of super-rich Russian oligarchs. But money buys all kinds of protection and Ingrid soon realizes that by taking on this battle she's putting everything on the line – her career, her future, her life.

In a nail-biting race against time, Ingrid sets out to solve the mystery and unmask the conspirators before they can silence her. Forever.

Flight Risk - Book Seven

Ingrid is ready to walk away from her life. She wants out of London. She even wants out of the FBI. But when she attempts to board a flight at Heathrow and sneak away without telling anyone, she's arrested on suspicion of causing the death of a man she's never heard of.

Now Ingrid must stay in the country, and the Bureau, to prove her innocence. There's just one problem: she can't remember if she killed him or not

---

EVA'S OTHER BOOKS

The Loyal Servant

Winner of the Lucy Cavendish Prize for Fiction, *The Loyal Servant* is a whistleblower thriller that topped the Amazon political fiction chart. Investigative reporter Angela Tate investigates scandal and corruption in the corridors of Westminster.

The Senior Moment

Sixty-five-year-old Jean Henderson arrives in New York to find her son and his pregnant wife missing from their apartment. When she reaches out to the cops for help, Jean discovers how invisible older people really are and concocts a plan to get noticed: by robbing a series of banks.

The Deadly Silence (formerly The Third Estate)

Thirty-three years ago two little girls disappeared. Today, the man convicted of murder three decades ago is back on the streets as another girl vanishes. Angela Tate covered the first disappearances and is dragged into discovering the terrible truth behind the latest.

ABOUT THE AUTHOR

Eva was born and raised in London. She worked as a local government worker, web editor, dot com entrepreneur, portrait artist and singer. In 2011, Eva won the inaugural Lucy Cavendish Prize for Fiction for her first novel, *The Loyal Servant.* The book was also shortlisted for TV's People's Novelist Award.

In 2013, Eva published the first Ingrid Skyberg Thriller and never looked back.

To find out more about Eva or Ingrid, please visit evahudson.-com. You can get the latest on all things Skyberg at twitter.-com/eva_hudson and facebook.com/evahudsoncrimewriter.

ACKNOWLEDGMENTS

Thank you to Lucy for her tireless copyediting work. Special thanks go out to early readers: Vicki Church, Anita Hall, Karen Knox, Steve Murray and Denise Wood—your input was invaluable.

Printed in Great Britain
by Amazon